JOHN SANDFORD

NIGHT PREY

HarperCollins*Publishers*

HarperCollins*Publishers*
77–85 Fulham Palace Road,
Hammersmith, London W6 8JB

Special overseas edition 1995
This paperback edition 1997

First published in Great Britain by
HarperCollins*Publishers* 1994

First published in the USA by
G.P. Putnam's Sons 1994

Copyright © John Sandford 1994

The Author asserts the moral right to
be identified as the author of this work

ISBN 978-0-00-647896-6

For Esther Newberg

1

The night was warm, the twilight inviting: middle-aged couples in pastel shirts, holding hands, strolled the old cracked sidewalks along the Mississippi. A gaggle of college girls jogged down the bike path, wearing sweatsuits and training shoes, talking as they ran, their uniformly blond ponytails bouncing behind them. At eight, the streetlights came on, whole blocks at once, with an audible pop. Overhead, above the new green of the elms, nighthawks made their *skizzizk* cries, their wing-flashes like the silver bars on new first-lieutenants.

Spring was shading into summer. The daffodils and tulips were gone, while the petunias spread across their beds like Mennonite quilts.

Koop was on the hunt.

He rolled through the residential streets in his Chevy S-10, radio tuned to Country-Lite, his elbow out the window, a bottle of Pig's Eye beer between his thighs. The soft evening air felt like a woman's fingers, stroking his beard.

At Lexington and Grand, a woman in a scarlet jacket crossed in front of him. She had a long, graceful neck, her dark hair up in a bun, her high heels rattling on the blacktop. She was too confident, too lively, moving too quickly; she was somebody who knew where she was going. Not Koop's type. He moved on.

Koop was thirty-one years old, but at any distance, looked ten or fifteen years older. He was a short, wide man with a sharecropper's bitter face and small, suspicious gray eyes; he had a way of looking at people sideways. His

7

strawberry-blond hair was cut tight to his skull. His nose was pinched, leathery, and long, and he wore a short, furry beard, notably redder than his hair. His heavy shoulders and thick chest tapered to narrow hips. His arms were thick and powerful, ending in rocklike fists. He had once been a bar brawler, a man who could work up a hate with three beers and a mistimed glance. He still felt the hate, but controlled it now, except on special occasions, when it burned through his belly like a welding torch . . .

Koop was an athlete, of a specialized kind. He could chin himself until he got bored, he could run forty yards as fast as a professional linebacker. He could climb eleven floors of fire stairs without breathing hard.

Koop was a cat burglar. A cat burglar and a killer.

Koop knew all the streets and most of the alleys in Minneapolis and St Paul. He was learning the suburbs. He spent his days driving, wandering, looking for new places, tracking his progress through the spiderweb of roads, avenues, streets, lanes, courts, and boulevards that made up his working territory.

Now he drifted down Grand Avenue, over to Summit to the St Paul Cathedral, past a crack dealer doing business outside the offices of the archdiocese of St Paul and Minneapolis, and down the hill. He drove a couple of laps around United Hospitals, looking at the nurses on their way to their special protected lot – a joke, that. He looked in at antique stores along West Seventh, drove past the Civic Center, and then curled down Kellogg Boulevard to Robert Street, left on Robert, checking the dashboard clock. He was early. There were two or three bookstores downtown, but only one that interested him. The Saint had a reading scheduled. Some shit about Prairie Women.

The Saint was run by a graying graduate of St John's University. Books new and used, trade your paperbacks two-for-one. Coffee was twenty cents a cup, get it yourself, pay on the honor system. A genteel meat-rack, where shy people went to get laid. Koop had been inside the place only once. There'd been a poetry reading, and the store had been populated by long-haired women with disappointed faces – Koop's kind of women – and men with bald spots, potbellies, and tentative gray ponytails tied with rubber bands.

A woman had come up to ask, 'Have you read the *Rubaiyat*?'

'Uh . . . ?' What was she talking about?

'*The Rubaiyat of Omar Khayyam*? I just read it again,' she babbled. She had a thin book in her hand, with a black poetical cover. 'The Fitzgerald translation. I hadn't read it since college. It really touched me. In some ways it's analogous to the poems that James was reading tonight.'

Koop didn't give a shit about James or his poems. But the question itself, *Have you read the* Rubaiyat? had a nice ring to it. Intellectual. A man who'd ask that question, *Have you read the* Rubaiyat?, would be . . . safe. Thoughtful. Considerate.

Koop hadn't been in the market for a woman that night, but he took the book and tried to read it. It was bullshit. Bullshit of such a high, unadulterated order that Koop eventually threw it out his truck window because it made him feel stupid to have it on the seat beside him.

He threw the book away, but kept the line: *Have you read the* Rubaiyat?

Koop crossed I-94, then recrossed it, circling. He didn't want to arrive at the bookstore until the reading had begun: he wanted people looking at the reader, not at him; what he was doing tonight was out of his careful pattern. He couldn't help it – the drive was irresistible – but he would be as careful as he could.

Back across the interstate, he stopped at a red light and looked out the window at the St Paul police station. The

9

summer solstice was only two weeks away, and at eight-thirty, there was light enough to make out faces, even at a distance. A group of uniformed cops, three men, a couple of women, sat talking on the steps, laughing about something. He watched them, not a thing in his mind, just an eye . . .

The car behind him honked.

Koop glanced in the left mirror, then the right, then up at the light: it had turned green. He glanced in the rearview mirror again and started forward, turning left. In front of him, a group of people started across the street, saw him coming, stopped.

Koop, looking up, saw them and jammed on his brakes, jerking to a halt. When he realized they'd stopped, he started through the turn again; and when they saw him stop, they started forward, into the path of the truck. In the end, they scattered, and Koop swerved to miss a barrel-shaped man in coveralls who was not quite agile enough to get out of the way. One of them shouted, an odd cawing sound, and Koop gave him the finger.

He instantly regretted it. Koop was the invisible man. He didn't give people the finger, not when he was hunting or working. He checked the cops, still a half block away. A face turned toward him, then away. He looked in the rearview mirror. The people in the street were laughing now, gesturing to each other, pointing at him.

Anger jumped up in his stomach. 'Faggots,' he muttered. 'Fuckin'-A fags . . .'

He controlled it, continued to the end of the block, and took a right. A car was easing out of a parking place across the street from the bookstore. Perfect. Koop did a U-turn, waited for the other car to get out, backed in, locked the truck.

As he started across the street, he heard the cawing sound again. The group he'd almost hit was crossing the end of the block, looking toward him. One of them gestured, and they made the odd cawing sound, laughed, then passed out of sight behind a building.

'Fuckin' assholes.' People like that pissed him off, walking on the street. Ass-wipes, he oughta . . . He shook a Camel out of his pack, lit it, took a couple of angry drags, and walked hunch-shouldered down the sidewalk to the bookstore. Through the front window, he could see a cluster of people around a fat woman, who appeared to be smoking a cigar. He took a final drag on the Camel, spun it into the street, and went inside.

The place was crowded. The fat woman sat on a wooden chair on a podium, sucking on what turned out to be a stick of licorice, while two dozen people sat on folding chairs in a semicircle in front of her. Another fifteen or twenty stood behind the chairs; a few people glanced at Koop, then looked back at the fat woman. She said, 'There's a shocking moment of recognition when you start dealing with shit – and call it what it is, good Anglo-Saxon words, horseshit and pig shit and cow shit; I'll tell you, on those days when you're forkin' manure, the first thing you do is rub a little in your hair and under your arms, really rub it in. That way, you don't have to worry about getting it on yourself, you can just go ahead and work . . .'

At the back of the store, a sign said 'Photography,' and Koop drifted that way. He owned an old book called *Jungle Fever*, with pictures and drawings of naked black women. The book that still turned him on. Maybe he'd find something like that . . .

Under the 'Photography' sign, he pulled down a book and started flipping pages. Barns and fields. He looked around, taking stock. Several of the women had that 'floating' look, the look of someone reaching for connections, of not really being tuned to the author, who was saying, '. . . certain human viability from hand-hoeing beans; oh, gets hot, sometimes so hot that you can't spit . . .'

11

Koop was worried. He shouldn't be here. He shouldn't be hunting. He'd had a woman last winter, and that should have been enough, for a while. *Would* have been enough, if not for Sara Jensen.

He could close his eyes and see her . . .

Seventeen hours earlier, having never in his life seen Sara Jensen, Koop had gone into her apartment building, using a key. He'd worn a light coat and hat against the prying eyes of the video cameras in the lobby. Once past the cameras, he took the fire stairs to the top of the building. He moved quickly and silently, padding up the stairs on the rubber-soled loafers.

At three in the morning, the apartment hallways were empty, silent, smelling of rug cleaner, brass polish, and cigarettes. At the eleventh floor, he stopped a moment behind the fire door, listened, then went quietly through the door and down the hall to his left. At 1135, he stopped and pressed his eye to the peephole. Dark. He'd greased the apartment key with beeswax, which deadened metal-to-metal clicking and lubricated the lock mechanism. He held the key in his right hand, and his right hand in his left, and guided the key into the lock. It slipped in easily.

Koop had done this two hundred times, but it was a routine that clattered down his nerves like a runaway freight. What's behind door number three? A motion detector, a Doberman, a hundred thousand in cash? Koop would find out . . . He turned the key and pushed: not quickly, but firmly, smoothly, his heart in his mouth. The door opened with a light *click*. He waited, listening, then stepped into the dark apartment, closed the door behind him, and simply stood there.

And smelled her.

That was the first thing.

Koop smoked unfiltered Camels, forty or fifty a day. He used cocaine almost every day. His nose was clogged with tobacco tars and scarred by the coke, but he *was* a creature of the night, sensitive to sounds, odors, and textures – and the perfume was dark, sensual, compelling, riding the sterile apartment air like a naked woman on a horse. It caught him, slowed him down. He lifted his head, ratlike, taking it in. He was unaware that he left his own scent behind, the brown scent of old tobacco smoke.

The woman's living room curtains were open, and low-level light filtered in from the street. As his eyes began to adjust, Koop picked out the major pieces of furniture, the rectangles of paintings and prints. Still he waited, standing quietly, his vision sharpening, smelling her, listening for movement, for a word, for anything – for a little red light from an alarm console. Nothing. The apartment was asleep.

Koop slipped out of his loafers and in surefooted silence crossed the apartment, down a darker hallway past a bathroom to his left, an office to his right. There were two doors at the end of the hall, the master bedroom to the left, a guest room to the right. He knew what they were, because an ex-con with Logan Van Lines had told him so. He'd moved Jensen's furniture in, he'd taken an impression of her key, he'd drawn the map. He'd told Koop the woman's name was Sara Jensen, some rich cunt who was, 'like, in the stock market,' and had a taste for gold.

Koop reached out and touched her bedroom door. It was open an inch, perhaps two. Good. Paranoids and restless sleepers usually shut the door. He waited another moment, listening. Then, using just his fingertips, he eased the door open a foot, moved his face to the opening, and peered inside. A window opened to the left, and as in the living room, the drapes were drawn back. A half-moon hung over the roof of an adjoining building, and beyond that, he could see the park and the lake, like a beer ad.

And he could see the woman clearly in the pale moonlight.

Sara Jensen had thrown off the light spring blanket. She was lying on her back, on a dark sheet. She wore a white cotton gown that covered her from her neck to her ankles. Her jet-black hair spread around her head in a dark halo, her face tipped slightly to one side. One hand, open, was folded back, to lie beside her ear, as if she were waving to him. The other hand folded over her lower belly just where it joined the top of her pelvic bone.

Just below her hand, Koop imagined that he could see a darker triangle; and at her breasts, a shading of her brown nipples. His vision of her could not have been caught on film. The darkening, the shading, was purely a piece of his imagination. The nightgown more substantial, less diaphanous than it seemed in Koop's mind, but Koop had fallen in love.

A love like a match firing in the night.

Koop paged through the photo books, watching, waiting. He was looking at a picture of a dead movie star when his woman came around the corner, looking up at *Hobbies & Collectibles*.

He knew her immediately. She wore a loose brown jacket, a little too long, a bit out of fashion, but neat and well-tended. Her hair was short, careful, tidy. Her head was tipped back so she could look up at the top shelves, following a line of books on antiques. She was plain, without makeup, not thin or fat, not tall or short, wearing oversize glasses with tortoiseshell frames. A woman who wouldn't be noticed by the other person in an elevator. She stood looking up at the top shelf, and Koop said, 'Can I reach something for you?'

'Oh . . . I don't know.' She tried a small smile, but it seemed nervous. She had trouble adjusting it.

'Well, if I can,' he said politely.

'Thanks.' She didn't turn away. She was waiting for

something. She didn't know how to make it happen herself.

'I missed the reading,' Koop said. 'I just finished the *Rubaiyat*. I thought there might be something, you know, analogous . . .'

And a moment later, the woman was saying, '. . . it's Harriet. Harriet Wannemaker.'

Sara Jensen, spread on her bed, twitched once.

Koop, just about to step toward her dresser, froze. Sara had been a heavy smoker in college: her cigarette subconscious could smell the nicotine coming from Koop's lungs, but she was too far down to wake up. She twitched again, then relaxed. Koop, heart hammering, moved closer, reached out, and almost touched her foot.

And thought: *What am I doing?*

He backed a step away, transfixed, the moonlight playing over her body.

Gold.

He let out his breath, turned again toward the dresser. Women keep every goddamned thing in the bedroom – or the kitchen – and Jensen was no different. The apartment had a double-locked door, had monitor cameras in the hall, had a private patrol that drove past a half-dozen times a night, occasionally stopping to snoop. She was safe, she thought. Her jewelry case, of polished black walnut, sat right there on the dressing table.

Koop picked it up carefully with both hands, pulled it against his stomach like a fullback protecting a football. He stepped back through the door and padded back down the hall to the living room, where he placed the case on the rug and knelt beside it. He carried a small flashlight in his breast pocket. The lens was covered with black tape, with a pinhole through the tape. He turned it on, held it between his teeth. He had a needle of light, just enough

15

to illuminate a stone or show a color without ruining his night vision.

Sara Jensen's jewelry case held a half-dozen velvet-lined trays. He took the trays out one at a time, and found some good things. Earrings, several pair in gold, four with stones: two with diamonds, one with emeralds, one with rubies. The stones were fair – one set of diamonds were more like chips than cut stones. Total retail, maybe five thousand. He'd get two thousand, tops.

He found two brooches, one a circle of pearls, the other with diamonds, a gold wedding band, and an engagement ring. The diamond brooch was excellent, the best thing she owned. He would have come for that alone. The engagement stone was all right, but not great. There were two gold bracelets and a watch, a woman's Rolex, gold and stainless steel.

No belt.

He put everything into a small black bag, then stood, stepping carefully around the empty trays, and went back through the bedroom. Slowly, slowly, he began opening the dresser drawers. The most likely place was the upper left drawer of the chest. The next most likely was the bottom drawer, depending on whether or not she was trying to hide it. He knew this from experience.

He took the upper drawer first, easing it out, his hands kneading through the half-seen clothing. Nothing hard . . .

The belt was in the bottom left-hand drawer, at the back, under some winter woolens. So she was a bit wary. He drew it out, hefting it, and turned back toward Sara Jensen. She had a firm chin, but her mouth had gone slightly slack. Her breasts were round and prominent, her hips substantial. She'd be a big woman. Not fat, just big.

Belt in his hands, Koop started to move away, stopped. He'd seen the bottle on the dressing table, and ignored it as he always ignored them. But this time . . . He reached

16

back and picked it up. Her perfume. He started for the door again and almost stumbled: he wasn't watching the route, he was watching the woman, spread right there, an arm's length away, his breath coming hard.

Koop stopped. Fumbled for a moment, folding the belt, slipped it into his pocket. Took a step away, looked down again. White face, round cheek, dark eyebrows. Hair splayed back.

Without thinking, without even knowing what he was doing – shocking himself, recoiling inside – Koop stepped beside the bed, bent over her, and lightly, gently dragged his tongue over her forehead . . .

Harriet Wannemaker was frankly interested in a drink at McClellan's: she had color in her face, the warmth of excitement. She'd meet him there, the slightly dangerous man with the mossy red beard.

He left before she did. His nerves were up now. He hadn't made a move yet, he was still okay, nothing to worry about. Had anybody noticed them talking? He didn't think so. She was so colorless, who cared? In a few minutes . . .

The pressure was a physical thing, a heaviness in his gut, an inflated feeling in his chest, a pain in the back of his neck. He thought about heading home, ditching the woman. But he wouldn't. There was another pressure, a more demanding one. His hand trembled on the steering wheel. He parked the truck on Sixth, on the hill, opened the door. Took a nervous breath. Still time to leave . . .

He fished under the seat, found the can of ether and the plastic bag with the rag. He opened the can, poured it quickly into the bag, and capped the can. The smell of the ether was nauseating, but it dissipated in a second. In the sealed bag, it quickly soaked into the rag. Where was she?

She came a few seconds later, parked down the hill from him, behind the truck, spent a moment in the car, primping. A beer sign in McClellan's side window, flickering with a bad bulb, was the biggest light around, up at the top of the hill. He could still back out . . .

No. Do it.

Sara Jensen had tasted of perspiration and perfume . . . tasted good.

Sara moved when he licked her, and he stepped back, stepped away, toward the door . . . and stopped. She said something, a nonsense syllable, and he stepped quickly but silently out the door to his shoes: not quite running, but his heart was hammering. He slipped the shoes on, picked up his bag.

And stopped again. The key to cat burglary was simple: go slow. If it seems like you might be getting in trouble, go slower. And if things get really bad, run like hell. Koop collected himself. No point in running if she wasn't waking up, no sense in panic – but he was thinking *asshole asshole asshole.*

But she wasn't coming. She'd gone back down again, down into sleep; and though Koop couldn't see it – he was leaving the apartment, slowly closing the door behind himself – the line of saliva on her forehead glistened in the moonlight, cool on her skin as it evaporated.

Koop slipped the plastic bag in his coat pocket, stepped to the back of his truck, and popped the camper door.

Heart beating hard now . . .

'Hi,' she called. Fifteen feet away. Blushing? 'I wasn't sure you could make it.'

She was afraid he'd ditch her. He almost had. She was smiling, shy, maybe a little afraid but more afraid of loneliness . . .

Nobody around . . .

Now it had him. A darkness moved on him – literally a darkness, a kind of fog, an anger that seemed to spring up

18

on its own, like a vagrant wind. He unrolled the plastic bag, slipped his hand inside; the ether-soaked rag was cold against his skin.

With a smile on his face, he said, 'Hey, what's a drink. C'mon. And hey, look at this . . .'

He turned as if to point something out to her; that put him behind her, a little to the right, and he wrapped her up and smashed the rag over her nose and mouth, and lifted her off the ground; she kicked, like a strangling squirrel, though from a certain angle, they might have been lovers in a passionate clutch; in any case, she only struggled for a moment . . .

Sara Jensen hit the snooze button on the alarm clock, rolled over, holding her pillow. She'd been smiling when the alarm went off. The smile faded only slowly: the peculiar nightmare hovered at the back of her mind. She couldn't quite recover it, but it was there, like a footstep in an attic, threatening . . .

She took a deep breath, willing herself to get up, not quite wanting to. Just before she woke, she'd been dreaming of Evan Hart. Hart was an attorney in the bond department. He wasn't exactly a romantic hero, but he was attractive, steady, and had a nice wit – though she suspected that he suppressed it, afraid that he might put her off. He didn't know her well. Not yet.

He had nice hands. Solid, long fingers that looked both strong and sensitive. He'd touched her once, on the nose, and she could almost feel it, lying here in her bed, a little warm. Hart was a widower, with a young daughter. His wife had died in an auto accident four years earlier. Since the accident, he'd been preoccupied with grief and with raising the child. The office gossip had him in two quick, nasty affairs with the wrong women. He was ready for the right one.

And he was hanging around.

Sara Jensen was divorced; the marriage had been a one-year mistake, right after college. No kids. But the breakup had been a shock. She'd thrown herself into her work, had started moving up. But now . . .

She smiled to herself. *She* was ready, she thought. Something permanent; something for a lifetime. She dozed, just for five minutes, dreaming of Evan Hart and his hands, a little bit warm, a little bit in love . . .

And the nightmare drifted back. A man with a cigarette at the corner of his mouth, watching her from the dark. She shrank away . . . and the alarm went off again. Sara touched her forehead, frowned, sat up, looked around the room, threw back the blankets with the sense that something was wrong.

'Hello?' she called out, but she knew she was alone. She went to use the bathroom, but paused in the doorway. Something . . . what?

The dream? She'd been sweating in the dream; she remembered wiping her forehead with the back of her hand. But that didn't seem right . . .

She flushed the toilet and headed for the front room with the image still in her mind: sweating, wiping her forehead . . .

Her jewelry box sat on the floor in the middle of the front room, the drawers dumped. She said aloud, 'How'd that get there?'

For just a moment, she was confused. Had she taken it out last night, had she been sleepwalking? She took another step, saw a small mound of jewelry set to one side, all the cheap stuff.

And then she knew.

She stepped back, the shock climbing up through her chest, the adrenaline pouring into her bloodstream. Without thinking, she brought the back of her hand to her face, to her nose, and smelled the nicotine and the other . . .

The what?

Saliva.

'No.' She screamed it, her mouth open, her eyes wide. She convulsively wiped her hand on the robe, wiped it again, wiped her sleeve across her forehead, which felt as if it were crawling with ants. Then she stopped, looked up, expecting to see him – to see him materializing from the kitchen, from a closet, or even, like a golem, from the carpet or the wooden floors. She twisted this way, then that, and backed frantically toward the kitchen, groping for the telephone.

Screaming as she went.

Screaming.

2

Lucas Davenport held the badge case out the driver's-side window. The pimply-faced suburban cop lifted the yellow plastic crime-scene tape and waved him through the line. He rolled the Porsche past the fire trucks, bumped over a flattened canvas hose, and stopped on a charred patch of dirt that a few hours earlier had been a lawn. A couple of firemen, drinking coffee, turned to check out the car.

The phone beeped as he climbed out, and he bent down to pull it off the visor. When he stood up, the stink from the fire hit him: the burned plaster, insulation, paint, and old rotting wood.

'Yeah? Davenport.'

Lucas was a tall man with heavy shoulders, dark-complected, square-faced, with the beginnings of crow's feet at the corners of his eyes. His dark hair was just touched with gray; his eyes were a startling blue. A thin white scar crossed his forehead and right eye socket, and trailed down to the corner of his mouth. He looked like a veteran athlete, a catcher or a hockey defenseman, recently retired.

A newer pink scar showed just above the knot of his necktie.

'This is Sloan. Dispatch said you were at the fire.' Sloan sounded hoarse, as though he had a cold.

'Just got here,' Lucas said, looking at the burned-out Quonset.

'Wait for me. I'm coming over.'

'What's going on?'

'We've got another problem,' Sloan said. 'I'll talk to you when I get there.'

Lucas hung the phone back on the visor, slammed the door, and turned to the burned-out building. The warehouse had been a big light-green World War II Quonset hut, mostly galvanized steel. The fire had been so hot that the steel sheets had twisted, buckled, and folded back on themselves, like giant metallic tacos.

With pork.

Lucas touched his throat, the pink scar where the child had shot him just before she had been chopped to pieces by the M-16. That case had started with a fire, with the same stink, with the same charred-pork smell that he now caught drifting from the torched-out hulk. Pork-not-pork.

He touched the scar again and started toward the blackened tangle of fallen struts. A cop was dead inside the tangle, the first call had said, his hands trussed behind his back. Then Del had called in, said the cop was one of his contacts. Lucas had better come out, although the scene was outside the Minneapolis jurisdiction. The suburban cops were walking around with grim one-of-us looks on their face. Enough cops had died around Lucas that he no longer made much distinction between them and civilians, as long as they weren't friends of his.

Del was stepping gingerly through the charred interior. He was unshaven, as usual, and wore a charcoal-gray sweatshirt over jeans and cowboy boots. He saw Lucas and waved him inside. 'He was already dead,' Del said. 'Before the fire got to him.'

Lucas nodded. 'How?'

'They wired his wrists and shot him in the teeth, looks like three, four shots in the fuckin' teeth from all we can tell in that goddamned nightmare,' Del said, unconsciously dry-washing his hands. 'He saw it coming.'

'Yeah, Jesus, man, I'm sorry,' Lucas said. The dead cop was a Hennepin County deputy. Earlier in the year, he'd

23

spent a month with Del, trying to learn the streets. He and Del had almost become friends.

'I warned him about the teeth: no goddamned street people got those great big white HMO teeth,' Del said, sticking a cigarette into his face. Del's teeth were yellowed pegs. 'I told him to pick some other front. Anything would have been better. He coulda been a car-parts salesman or a bartender, or anything. He had to be a fuckin' street guy.'

'Yeah . . . so what'd you want?'

'Got a match?' Del asked.

'You wanted a match?'

Del grinned past the unlit cigarette and said, 'C'mon inside. Look at something.'

Lucas followed him through the warehouse, down a narrow pathway through holes in half-burned partitions, past stacks of charred wooden pallets. Toward the back, he could see the black plastic sheet where the body was, and the stench of burned pork grew sharper. Del took him to a fallen plaster-board interior wall, where the remnants of a narrow wooden box held three small-diameter pipes, each about five feet long.

'Are these what I think they are?' Del asked.

Lucas squatted next to the box, picked up one of the pipes, looked at the screw-threading at one end, tipped up the other end, and looked inside at the rifling. 'Yeah, they are – if you think they're fifty-cal replacement barrels.' He dropped the barrel back on the others, duckwalked a couple of feet to another flattened box, picked up a piece of machinery. 'This is a lock,' he said. 'Bolt-action single-shot fifty-cal. Broken. Looks like a stress-line crack, bad piece of steel . . . What was in this place?'

'A machine shop, supposedly.'

'Yeah, a machine shop,' Lucas said. 'They were turning out these locks, I bet. Gettin' the barrels from somewhere else – you wouldn't normally see them on single-shots, they're too heavy. We ought to have the identification

24

guys look at them, see if we can figure out where they came from, and who got them at this end.' He dropped the broken lock on the floor, stood up, and tipped his head toward the body. 'What was this guy into?'

'The Seeds, is what his friends say.'

Lucas, exasperated, shook his head. 'All we need is those assholes hanging around.'

'They're getting into politics,' Del said. 'Want to kill themselves some black folks.'

'Yeah. You want to look into this?'

'That's why I got you out here,' Del said, nodding. 'You see the guns, you smell the pork, how can you say no?'

'All right. But you check with me every fuckin' fifteen minutes,' Lucas said, tapping him on the chest. 'I want to know everything you're doing. Every name you find, every face you see. Any sign of trouble, you back away and talk to me. They're dumb motherfuckers, but they'll kill you.'

Del nodded, said, 'You're sure you don't have a match?'

'I'm serious, Del,' Lucas said. 'You fuck me around, I'll put your ass back in a uniform. You'll be directing traffic outside a parking ramp. Your old lady's knocked up and I don't wanna be raising your kid.'

'I really need a fuckin' match,' Del said.

The Seeds: the Hayseed Mafia, the Bad Seed MC. Fifty or sixty stickup men, car thieves, smugglers, truck hijackers, Harley freaks, mostly out of northwest Wisconsin, related by blood or marriage or simply shared jail cells. Straw-haired baby-faced country assholes: have guns, will travel. And they were lately infected by a virulent germ of apocalyptic anti-black weirdness, and were suspected of killing a minor black hood outside a pool hall in Minneapolis.

'Why would they have the fifty-cals?' Del asked.

'Maybe they're building a Waco up in the woods.'

'The thought crossed my mind,' Del said.

*   *   *

25

When they got back outside, a Minneapolis squad was shifting through the lines of fire trucks, local cop cars, and sheriff's vehicles. The squad stopped almost on their feet, and Sloan climbed out, bent over to the driver, a uniformed sergeant, and said, 'Keep the change.'

'Blow me,' the driver said genially, and eased away.

Sloan was a narrow man with a slatlike face. He wore a hundred-fifty-dollar tan summer suit, brown shoes a shade too yellow, and a fedora the color of beef gravy. 'How do, Lucas,' he said. His eyes shifted to Del. 'Del, you look like shit, my man.'

'Where'd you get the hat?' Lucas asked. 'Is it too late to take it back?'

'My wife bought it for me,' Sloan said, sliding his fingertips along the brim. 'She says it complements my ebullient personality.'

Del said, 'Still got her head up her ass, huh?'

'Careful,' Sloan said, offended. 'You're talking about my hat.' He looked at Lucas. 'We gotta go for a ride.'

'Where to?'

'Wisconsin.' He rocked on the toes of the too-yellow shoes. 'Hudson. Look at a body.'

'Anybody I know?' Lucas asked.

Sloan shrugged. 'You know a chick named Harriet Wannemaker?'

'I don't think so,' Lucas said.

'That's who it probably is.'

'Why would I go look at her?'

'Because I say so and you trust my judgment?' Sloan made it a question.

Lucas grinned. 'All right.'

Sloan looked down the block at Lucas's Porsche. 'Can I drive?'

'Pretty bad in there?' Sloan asked. He threw his hat in the back and downshifted as they rolled up to a stop sign at Highway 280.

'They executed him. Shot him in the teeth,' Lucas said. 'Think it might be the Seeds.'

'Miserable assholes,' Sloan said without too much heat. He accelerated onto 280.

'What happened to what's-her-name?' Lucas asked. 'Wannabe.'

'Wannemaker. She dropped out of sight three days ago. Her friends say she was going out to some bookstore on Friday night, they don't know which one, and she didn't show up to get her hair done Saturday. We put out a missing persons note, and that's the last we know until this morning, when Hudson called. We shot a Polaroid over there; it wasn't too good, but they think it's her.'

'Shot?'

'Stabbed. The basic technique is a rip – a stick in the lower belly, then an upward pull. Lots of power. That's why I'm looking into it.'

'Does this have something to do with what's-her-name, the chick from the state?'

'Meagan Connell,' Sloan said. 'Yeah.'

'I hear she's trouble.'

'Yeah. She could use a personality transplant,' Sloan said. He blew the doors off a Lexus SC, allowing himself a small smile. The guy in the Lexus wore shades and driving gloves. 'But when you actually read her files, the stuff she's put together – she's got something, Lucas. But Jesus, I hope this isn't one of his. It sounds like it, but it's too soon. If it's his, he's speeding up.'

'Most of them do,' Lucas said. 'They get addicted to it.'

Sloan paused at a stoplight, then ran the red and roared up the ramp onto Highway 36. Shifting up, he pushed the Porsche to seventy-five and kept it there, cutting through traffic like a shark. 'This guy was real regular,' he said. 'I mean, if he exists. He did one killing every year or so. Now we're talking about four months. He did the last one just about the time you were gettin' shot. Picked her up in

Duluth, dumped the body up at the Carlos Avery game reserve.'

'Any leads?' Lucas touched the pink scar on his throat.

'Damn few. Meagan's got a file.'

They took twenty minutes getting to Wisconsin, out the web of interstates through the countryside east of St Paul, the landscape green and heavy after a wet spring. 'It's better out here in the county,' Sloan said. 'Christ, the media's gonna get crazy with this cop killed.'

'Lotta shit coming down,' Lucas said. 'At least the cop's not ours.'

'Four killed in five days,' Sloan said. 'Wannemaker will make five in a week. Actually, we might have six. We're looking into an old lady who croaked in her bed. A couple of the guys think she might've been helped along. They're calling it natural, for now.'

'You cleared the domestic on Dupont,' Lucas said.

'Yeah, with the hammer and chisel.'

'Hurts to think about it.' Lucas grinned.

'Got it right between the eyes,' Sloan said, impressed. He'd never had a hammer-and-chisel job before, and novelty wasn't that common in murder. Most of it was a half-drunk guy scratching his ass and saying, *Jesus, she got me really pissed, you know?* Sloan went on: 'She waited until he was asleep, and whack. Actually, whack, whack, whack. The chisel went all the way through to the mattress. She pulled it out, put it in the dishwasher, turned the dishwasher on, and called 911. Makes me think twice about going asleep at night. You catch your old lady staring at you . . .'

'Any defense? Long-term abuse?'

'Not so far. So far, she says it was hot inside, and she got tired of him laying there snoring and farting. You know Donovan up in the prosecutor's office?'

'Yeah.'

'Says he'd of taken a plea to second if it'd been only one whack,' Sloan said. 'With whack-whack-whack, he's gotta go for first degree.'

A truck moved in front of them suddenly, and Sloan swore, braked, swung behind it to the right and passed.

'The Louis Capp thing,' Lucas said.

'We got him,' Sloan said with satisfaction. 'Two witnesses, one of them knew him. Shot the guy three times, got a hundred and fifty bucks.'

'I chased Louis for ten years, and I never touched him,' Lucas said. There was a note of regret in his voice, and Sloan glanced at him, grinned. 'He got any defense?'

'Two-dude,' Sloan said. *Some other dude done it.* 'Ain't gonna work this time.'

'He was always a dumb sonofabitch,' Lucas said, remembering Louis Capp. Huge guy, arms like logs, with a big gut. Wore his pants down under his gut, so the crotch of his pants dropped almost to his knees. 'The thing is, what he did was so simple, you had to be there to catch him. Sneak up behind a guy, hit him on the head, take his wallet. The guy must have fucked up to two hundred people in his career.'

Sloan said, 'He's as mean as he was dumb.'

'At least,' Lucas agreed. 'So that leaves what? The Hmong gang-banger and the fell-jumped-pushed waitress.'

'I don't think we'll get the Hmong; the waitress had skin under her fingernails,' Sloan said.

'Ah.' Lucas nodded. He liked it. Skin was always good.

Lucas had left the department two years earlier, under some pressure, after a fight with a pimp. He'd gone full-time with his own company, originally set up to design games. The computer kids he worked with had pushed him in a new direction, writing simulations for police dispatch computers. He'd been making a fortune when the new Minneapolis chief asked him to come back.

He couldn't return under civil service; he'd taken

political appointment as deputy chief. He'd work intelligence, as he had before, with two main objectives: put away the most dangerous and the most active criminals, and cover the department on the odd crimes likely to attract media attention.

'Try to keep us from getting ambushed by the fruitcakes out there,' the chief said. Lucas played hard to get for a little while, but he was bored with business, and he finally hired a full-time administrator to run the company, and took the chief's offer.

He'd been back on the street for a month, trying to rebuild his network, but it had been harder than he'd expected. Things had changed in just two years. Changed a lot.

'I'm surprised Louis was carrying a gun,' Lucas said. 'He usually worked with a sap, or a pipe.'

'Everybody's got guns now,' Sloan said. 'Everybody. And they don't give a shit about using them.'

The St Croix was a steel-blue strip beneath the Hudson bridge. Boats, both sail and power, littered the river's surface like pieces of white confetti.

'You oughta buy a marina,' Sloan said. 'I could run the gas dock. I mean, don't it look fuckin' wonderful?'

'Are you getting off here, or are we going to Chicago?'

Sloan quit rubbernecking and hit the brakes, cut off a station wagon, slipped down the first exit on the Wisconsin side, and headed north into Hudson. Just ahead, a half-dozen emergency vehicles gathered around a boat ramp, and uniformed Hudson patrolmen directed traffic away from the ramp. Two cops were standing by a dumpster, their thumbs hooked in their gun belts. To one side, a broad-backed blond woman in a dark suit and sunglasses was facing a third cop. They appeared to be arguing. Sloan said, 'Ah, shit,' and as they came up to the scene, ran his window down and shouted, 'Minneapolis police' at the cop directing traffic. The cop waved him into the parking area.

'What?' Lucas asked. The blonde was waving her arms.

'Trouble,' Sloan said. He popped the door. 'That's Connell.'

A bony deputy sheriff with a dark, weathered face had been talking to a city cop at the dumpster, and when the Porsche pulled into the lot, the deputy grinned briefly, called something out to the cop who was arguing with the blond woman, and started over.

'Helstrom,' said Lucas, digging for the name. 'D. T. Helstrom. Remember that professor that Carlo Druze killed?'

'Yeah?'

'Helstrom found him,' Lucas said. 'He's a good guy.'

They got out of the car as Helstrom came up to Lucas and stuck out his hand. 'Davenport. Heard you were back. Deputy chief, huh? Congratulations.'

'D. T. How are you?' Lucas said. 'Haven't seen you since you dug up the professor.'

'Yeah, well, this is sorta worse,' Helstrom said, looking back at the dumpster. He rubbed his nose.

The blond woman called past the cop, 'Hey. Sloan.'

Sloan muttered something under his breath, and then, louder, 'Hey, Meagan.'

'This lady working with you?' Helstrom asked Sloan, jerking a thumb at the blonde.

Sloan nodded, said, 'More or less,' and Lucas tipped his head toward his friend. 'This is Sloan,' he said to Helstrom. 'Minneapolis homicide.'

'Sloan,' the woman called. 'Hey, Sloan. C'mere.'

'Your friend's a pain in the ass,' Helstrom said to Sloan.

'You'd be a hundred percent right, except she's not my friend,' Sloan said, and started toward her. 'I'll be right back.'

*   *   *

31

They were standing on a blacktopped boat ramp, with striped spaces for car and trailer parking, a lockbox for fees, and a dumpster for garbage. 'What you got?' Lucas asked Helstrom as they started toward the dumpster.

'A freak . . . He did the killing on your side of the bridge, I think. There's no blood over here, except what's on her. She'd stopped bleeding before she went in the dumpster, no sign of anything on the ground. And there must've been a lot of blood . . . Jesus, look at that.'

Up on the westbound span of the bridge, a van with yellow flashing roof lights had stopped next to the rail, and a man with a television camera was shooting down at them.

'That legal?' Lucas asked.

'Damned if I know,' Helstrom said.

Sloan and the woman came up. The woman was young, large, in her late twenties or early thirties. Despite her anger, her face was as pale as a dinner candle; her blond hair was cropped so short that Lucas could see the white of her scalp. 'I don't like the way I'm being treated,' the woman said.

'You've got no jurisdiction here. You can either shut up or take yourself back across the bridge,' Helstrom snapped. 'I've had about enough of you.'

Lucas looked at her curiously. 'You're Meagan O'Connell?'

'Connell. No *O*. I'm an investigator with the BCA. Who are you?'

'Lucas Davenport.'

'Huh,' she grunted. 'I've heard about you.'

'Yeah?'

'Yeah. Some kind of macho asshole.'

Lucas half-laughed, not sure she was serious, looked at Sloan, who shrugged. She was. Connell looked at Helstrom, who had allowed himself a small grin when Connell went after Lucas. 'So can I see her, or what?'

'If you're working with Minneapolis homicide . . .' He looked at Sloan, and Sloan nodded. 'Be my guest. Just don't touch anything.'

'Christ,' she muttered, and stalked down to the dumpster. The dumpster came to her collarbone, and she had to stand on her tiptoes to look in. She stood for a moment, looking down, then walked away, down toward the river, and began vomiting.

'Be my fuckin' guest,' Helstrom muttered.

'What'd she do?' Lucas asked.

'Came over like her ass was on fire and started screaming at everyone. Like we forgot to scrape the horseshit off our shoes,' Helstrom said.

Sloan, concerned, started after Connell, then stopped, scratched his head, walked down to the dumpster, and looked inside. 'Whoa.' He turned away, and said, 'God-damnit,' and then to Lucas, 'Hold your breath.'

Lucas was breathing through his mouth when he looked in. The body was nude, and had been in a green garbage bag tied at the top. The bag had split open on impact when it hit the bottom of the dumpster, or someone had split it open.

The woman had been disemboweled, her intestines boiling out like an obscene corn smut. And Sloan's earlier description was right: she hadn't been stabbed, she'd been opened like a sardine can, a long slit running from her pelvic area to her sternum. He thought at first that maggots were already working on her, but then realized that the sprinkles of white on the body were grains of rice, apparently somebody's garbage.

The woman's head was in profile against the green garbage sack. The garbage sack had a red plastic tie, and it snuggled just above the woman's ear like a bow on a Christmas package. Flies crawled all over her, like tiny black MiGs . . . Above her breasts, two inches above the top of the slash, were two smaller cuts in what might be letters. Lucas looked at them for five seconds, then backed away, and waited until he was a half-dozen strides from the dumpster before he started breathing through his nose again.

'The guy who dumped her must be fairly strong,' Lucas said to Helstrom. 'He had to either throw her in there or carry her up pretty high, without spilling guts all over the place.'

Connell, white-faced, tottered back up the ramp.

'What'd you just say?'

Lucas repeated it, and Helstrom nodded. 'Yeah. And from the description we got, she wasn't a complete lightweight. She must've run around 135. If that's Wannemaker.'

'It is,' Sloan said. Sloan had walked around to the other side of the dumpster, and was peering into it again. From Lucas's perspective, eyes, nose, and ears over the edge of the dumpster, he looked like Kilroy. 'And I'll tell you what: I've seen a videotape of the body they found up in Carlos Avery. If the same guy didn't do this one, then they both took cuttin' lessons at the same place.'

'Exactly the same?' Lucas asked.

'Identical,' Connell said.

'Not quite,' Sloan said, backing away from the dumpster. 'The Carlos Avery didn't have the squiggles above her ti . . . breasts.'

'The squiggles?' Connell asked.

'Yeah. Take a look.'

She looked in again. After a moment, she said, 'They look like a capital *S* and a capital *J*.'

'That's what I thought,' Lucas said.

'What does that mean?' Connell demanded.

'I'm not a mind reader,' Lucas said, 'Especially with the dead.' He turned his head to Helstrom. 'No way to get anything off the edge of this thing, is there? Off the dumpster?'

'I doubt it. It's rained a couple times since Friday, people been throwing stuff in there all weekend . . . Why?'

'Better not take a chance.' Lucas went back to the Porsche, popped the trunk, took out a small emergency raincoat, a piece of plastic packed in a bag not much bigger than his hand. He stripped the coat out, carried it back to the dumpster, and said, 'Hang on to my legs so I don't tip inside, will you, D.T.?'

'Sure . . .'

Lucas draped the raincoat carefully over the edge of the dumpster and boosted himself up until he could lay his stomach over the top. His upper body hung down inside, his face not more than a foot from the dead woman's.

'She's got, uh . . .'

'What?'

'She's got something in her hand . . . Can't see it. Like maybe a cigarette.'

'Don't touch.'

'I'm not.' He hung closer. 'She's got something on her chest. I think it's tobacco . . . stuck on.'

'Garbage got tossed on her.'

Lucas dropped back onto the blacktop and started breathing again. 'Some of it's covered with blood. It's like she crumbled a cigarette on herself.'

'What're you thinking?' Helstrom asked.

'That the guy was smoking when he killed her,' Lucas said. 'That she snatched it out of his mouth. I mean, she wouldn't have been smoking, not if she was being attacked.'

'Unless it wasn't really an attack,' Sloan said. 'Maybe it was consensual, they were relaxing afterwards, and he did her.'

'Bullshit,' Connell said.

Lucas nodded at her. 'Too much violence,' he said. 'You wouldn't get that much violence after orgasm. That's sexual excitement you're looking at.'

35

Helstrom looked from Lucas to Connell to Sloan. Connell seemed oddly satisfied by Lucas's comment. 'He was smoking when he did it?'

'Get them to make the cigarette, if that's what it is. I can see the paper,' Lucas told Helstrom. 'Check the lot, see if there's anything that matches.'

'We've picked up everything in the parking lot that might mean anything – candy wrappers, cigarettes, bottle tops, all that.'

'Maybe it's marijuana,' Connell said hopefully. 'That'd be a place to start.'

'Potheads don't do this shit, not when they're smoking,' Lucas said. He looked at Helstrom. 'When was the dumpster last cleaned out?'

'Friday. They dump it every Tuesday and Friday.'

'She went missing Friday night,' Sloan said. 'Probably killed, brought here at night. You can't see into the dumpster unless you stand on your tiptoes, so he probably just tossed her in and pulled a couple of garbage bags over her and let it go at that.'

Helstrom nodded. 'That's what we think. People started complaining about the smell this morning, and a guy from the marina came over and poked around. Saw a knee and called us.'

'She's on top of that small white bag, like she landed on it. I'd see if there's anything in it to identify who threw it in,' Lucas suggested. 'If you can find the guy who dumped the garbage, you might nail down the time.'

'We'll do that,' Helstrom said.

Lucas went back for a last look, but there was nothing more to see, just the pale-gray skin, the flies, and the carefully colored hair with the streak of white frost. She'd taken care of her hair, Lucas thought; she'd liked herself for her hair, and now all that liking was gone like evaporating gasoline.

'Anything else?' Sloan asked.

36

'Nah, I'm ready.'

'We gotta talk,' Connell said to Sloan. She was squared off to him, fists on her hips.

'Sure,' Sloan said, an unhappy note in his voice.

Lucas started toward the car, then stopped so quickly that Sloan walked into him. 'Sorry,' Lucas said as he turned and looked back at the dumpster.

'What?' Sloan asked. Connell was looking at him curiously.

'Do you remember Junky Doog?' Lucas asked Sloan.

Sloan looked to one side, groping for the name, then snapped his fingers, looked back at Lucas, a kernel of excitement in his eyes. 'Junky,' he said.

'Who's that?' Connell asked.

'Sexual psychopath who fixated on knives,' Lucas said. 'He grew up in a junkyard, didn't have any folks. Guys at the junkyard took care of him. He liked to carve on women. He'd go after fashion models. He'd do grapevine designs on them, and sign them.' Lucas looked at the dumpster again. 'This is almost too crude for Junky.'

'Besides, Junky's at St Peter,' Sloan said. 'Isn't he?'

Lucas shook his head. 'We're getting older, Sloan. Junky was a long time ago, must've been ten or twelve years . . .' His voice trailed off, and his eyes wandered away to the river before he turned back to Sloan. 'By God, he was seventeen years ago. The second year I was out of uniform. What's the average time in St Peter? Five or six years? And remember a few years ago, when they came up with that new rehabilitation theory, and they swept everybody out of the state hospitals? That must've been in the mid-eighties.'

'First killing I found was in '84, in Minneapolis, and it's still open,' Connell said.

'We need to run Junky,' Sloan said.

Lucas said, 'It'd be a long shot, but he was a crazy

37

sonofabitch. Remember what he did to that model he followed out of that Dayton's fashion show?'

'Yeah,' Sloan said. He rubbed the side of his face, thinking. 'Let's get Anderson to look him up.'

'I'll look him up too,' Connell said. 'I'll see you back there, Sloan?'

Sloan was unhappy. 'Yeah. See you, Meagan.'

Back in the car, Sloan fastened his seat belt, started the engine, and said, 'Uh, the chief wants to see you.'

'Yeah? About what?' Lucas asked. 'About this?'

'I think so.' Sloan bumped the car out of the ramp and toward the bridge.

'Sloan, what did you do?' Lucas asked suspiciously.

Sloan laughed, a guilty rattle. 'Lucas, there's two people in the department who might get this guy. You and me. I got three major cases on my load right now. People are yelling at me every five minutes. The fuckin' TV is camped out in my front yard.'

'This wasn't my deal when I came back,' Lucas said.

'Don't be a prima donna,' Sloan said. 'This asshole is killing people.'

'If he exists.'

'He exists.'

There was a moment of silence, then Lucas said, 'Society of Jesus.'

'What?'

'Society of Jesus. That's what Jesuits belong to. They put the initials after their name, like, Father John Smith, SJ. Like the SJ on Wannemaker.'

'Find another theory,' Sloan said. 'The Minneapolis homicide unit ain't chasin' no fuckin' Jesuits.'

As they crossed the bridge, Lucas looked down at the dumpster and saw Connell still talking to Helstrom. Lucas asked, 'What's the story on Connell?'

'Chief'll tell you all about her,' Sloan said. 'She's a pain in the ass, but she invented the case. I haven't seen her for a month or so. Goddamn, she got here fast.'

Lucas looked back toward the ramp. 'She's got a major edge on her,' he said.

'She's in a hurry to get this guy,' Sloan said. 'She needs to get him in the next month or so.'

'Yeah? What's the rush?'

'She's dying,' Sloan said.

3

The chief's secretary was a bony woman with a small mole on her cheekbone and overgrown eyebrows. She saw Lucas coming, pushed a button on her intercom, and said, 'Chief Davenport's here.' To Lucas she said, 'Go on in.' She made her thumb and forefinger into a pistol and pointed at the chief's door.

Rose Marie Roux sat behind a broad cherrywood desk stacked with reports and memos, rolling an unlit cigarette under her nose. When Lucas walked in, she nodded, fiddled with the cigarette for a moment, then sighed, opened a desk drawer, and tossed it inside.

'Lucas,' she said. Her voice had a ragged nicotine edge to it, like a hangnail. 'Sit down.'

When Lucas had quit the force, Quentin Daniel's office had been neat, ordered, and dark. Roux's office was cluttered with books and reports, her desk a mass of loose paper, Rolodexes, calculators, and computer disks. Harsh blue light from the overhead fluorescent fixtures pried into every corner. Daniel had never bothered with computers; a late-model IBM sat on a stand next to Roux's desk, a memo button blinking at the top left corner of the screen. Roux had thrown out Daniel's leather men's-club furniture and replaced it with comfortable fabric chairs.

'I read Kupicek's report on the tomb burglaries,' she said. 'How is he, by the way?'

'Can't walk.' Lucas had two associates, Del and Danny Kupicek. Kupicek's kid had run over his foot with a Dodge Caravan. 'He's gone for a month.'

'If we get a media question on the tombs, can you handle it? Or Kupicek?'

'Sure. But I doubt that it'll ever get out.'

'I don't know – it's a good story.' A persistent series of tomb break-ins had first been attributed to scroungers looking for wedding rings and other jewelry, though the departmental conspiracy freaks had suggested a ring of satanists, getting body parts for black Masses. Whatever, the relatives were getting upset. Roux had asked Lucas to look at it. About that time, polished finger and toe bones had started showing up in art jewelry. Kupicek had found the designer/saleswoman, squeezed her, and the burglaries stopped.

'Her stuff does go well with a simple black dress,' Lucas said. ''Course, you want to match the earrings.'

Roux showed a thin smile. 'You can talk that way because you don't give a shit,' she said. 'You're rich, you're in love, you buy your suits in New York. Why should you care?'

'I care,' Lucas said mildly. 'But it's hard to get too excited when the victims are already dead . . . What'd you want?'

There was a long moment of silence. Lucas waited it out, and she sighed again and said, 'I've got a problem.'

'Connell.'

She looked up, surprised. 'You know her?'

'I met her about an hour ago, over in Wisconsin, running her mouth.'

'That's her,' Roux said. 'Running her mouth. How'd she hear about it?'

Lucas shrugged. 'I don't know.'

'Goddamnit, she's working people inside the department.' She nibbled at a fingernail, then said, 'Goddamnit,' again and heaved herself to her feet, walked to her window. She stuck two fingers between the blades of her venetian blinds, looked out at the street for a moment. She had a big butt, wide hips. She'd been a large young

41

woman, a good cop in decent shape. The shape was going now, after too many years in well-padded government chairs.

'There's no secret about how I got this job,' she said finally, turning back to him. 'I solved a lot of political problems. There was always pressure from the blacks. Then the feminists started in, after those rapes at Christmas. I'm a woman, I'm a former cop, I've got a law degree, I was a prosecutor and a liberal state senator with a good reputation on race relations . . .'

'Yeah, yeah, you were right for the job,' Lucas said impatiently. 'Cut to the chase.'

She turned back to him. 'Last winter some game wardens found a body up in the Carlos Avery reserve. You know where that's at?'

'Yeah. Lots of bodies up there.'

'This one's name was Joan Smits. You probably saw the stories in the papers.'

'Vaguely. From Duluth?'

'Right. An immigrant from South Africa. Walked out of a bookstore and that was it. Somebody stuck a blade in her just above the pelvic bone and ripped her all the way up to her neck. Dumped her in a snowdrift at Carlos Avery.'

Lucas nodded. 'Okay.'

'Connell got the case, assisting the local authorities. She freaked. I mean, something snapped. She told me that Smits comes to her at night, to see how the investigation is going. Smits told her that there'd been other killings by the same man. Connell poked around, and came up with a theory.'

'Of course,' Lucas said dryly.

Roux took a pack of Winston Lights from her desk drawer, asked, 'Do you mind?'

'No.'

'This is illegal,' she said. 'I take great pleasure in it.' She shook a cigarette out of the pack, lit it with a green plastic Bic lighter, and tossed the lighter back in the desk drawer with the cigarettes. 'Connell thinks she's found the tracks of a serial sex-killer. She thinks he lives here in Minneapolis. Or St Paul or whatever, the suburbs. Close by, anyway.'

'Is there? A serial killer?' Lucas sounded skeptical, and Roux peered across her desk at him.

'You've got a problem with the idea?' she asked.

'Give me a few facts.'

'There are several,' Roux said, exhaling smoke at the ceiling. 'But let me give you another minute of background. Connell's not just an investigator. She's big in the left-feminist wing of the state AFSCME – American Federation of State, County and Municipal Employees.'

'I know what it is.'

'That's an important piece of my constituency, Lucas. AFSCME put me in the state senate and kept me there. And maybe sixty percent of them are female.' Roux flicked a cigarette ash toward her wastebasket. 'They're my rock. Now. If I pull off this chief's job, if I go four, maybe six years, and get a little lucky, I'll go up to the US Senate as a liberal law-and-order feminist.'

'Okay,' Lucas said. Everybody hustles.

'So Connell came down to talk to me about her serial killer theory. The state doesn't have the resources for this kind of investigation, but we do. I make nice noises and say we'll get right on it. I'm thinking *Nut*, but she's got contacts all over the women's movements and she's AFSCME.'

Lucas nodded, said nothing.

'She gives me her research . . .' Roux tapped a thick file-folder on her desk. 'I carried it down to homicide and asked them to make some checks. Connell thinks there have been a half-dozen murders and maybe more. She thinks there have been two here in Minnesota, and others in Iowa, Wisconsin, South Dakota, just across the border in Canada.'

'What'd homicide say?' Lucas asked.

'I got the eye-rolling routine, and I started hearing Dickless Tracy comments again. Two of the killings had already been cleared. The Madison cops got a conviction. There're local suspects in a couple other cases.'

'Sounds like –'

He was about to say *bullshit*, but Roux tapped her desk with an index finger and rode her voice over his. 'But your old pal Sloan dug through Connell's research and he decided there's something to it.'

'He mentioned that,' Lucas admitted. He looked at the file-folder on Roux's desk. 'He didn't seem too happy with Connell, though.'

'She scares him. Anyway, what Connell had was not so much evidence as an . . .' She groped for the right word: '. . . argument.'

'Mmmm.'

The chief nodded. 'I know. She could be wrong. But it's a legitimate argument. And I keep thinking, *What if I ditch it, and it turns out that I'm wrong*? A fellow feminist, one of the constituency, comes to me with a serial killer. We blow it off and somebody else gets murdered and it all comes out.'

'I'm not sure . . .'

'Besides, I can feel myself getting in trouble here. We're gonna set a new record for murders this year, unless something strange happens. That doesn't have anything to do with me, but I'm the chief. I take the blame. You're starting to hear that "We need somebody tough up there." I'm getting it from both inside and outside the department. The union never misses a chance to kick my ass. You know they backed MacLemore for the job.'

'MacLemore's a fuckin' Nazi.'

'Yes, he is . . .' Roux took a drag on the cigarette, blew

44

smoke, coughed, laughing, and said, 'There's even more. She thinks the killer might be a cop.'

'Ah, man.'

'It's just a theory,' Roux said.

'But if you start chasing cops, the brotherhood's gonna be unhappy.'

'Exactly. And that's what makes you perfect,' Roux said. 'You're one of the most experienced serial-killer investigators in the country, outside the FBI. Inside this department, politically, you're both old-line and hard-line. *You* could chase a cop.'

'Why does she think it's a cop?'

'One of the victims, a woman in Des Moines, a real estate saleswoman, had a cellular phone in her car. She had a teenaged daughter at home, and called and said she was going out with a guy for a drink, that she might be getting home late. She said the guy was from out of town, and that he was a cop. That's all.'

'Christ.' Lucas ran his hand through his hair.

'Lucas, how long have you been back? A month?'

'Five weeks.'

'Five weeks. All right. I know you like the intelligence thing. But I've got all kinds of guys running different pieces of intelligence. We got the division, and the intelligence unit, and the gang squad in that, and vice and narcotics and licensing . . . I brought you back, gave you a nice soft political job, because I knew I'd eventually run into shit like this and I'd need somebody to handle it. You're the guy. That was the deal.'

'So you can run for the Senate.'

'There've been worse senators,' she said.

'I've got things –'

'Everybody's got things. Not everybody can stop insane killers,' Roux said impatiently. She came and stood next to him, looking out the window, took another greedy drag on her cigarette. 'I could give you some time if we hadn't had this Wannemaker thing. Now I gotta move, before the press catches on. And if we don't do something heavy, Connell might very well leak it herself.'

'I –'

'If it gets out and you're already on it, it'd go easier for all of us.'

Lucas finally nodded. 'You saved my ass from the corporate life,' he said. 'I owe you.'

'That's right,' she said. 'I did, and you do.' Roux pushed her intercom button and leaned toward it. 'Rocky? Round up the usual suspects. Get their asses in here.'

Roux took five minutes to put together a meeting: Lester, head of the Criminal Investigation Division, his deputy Swanson, and Curt Myer, the new head of intelligence. Anderson, the department's computer freak, was invited at Lucas's request.

'How're we doing?' Roux asked Lester.

'The bodies are piling up. I've honest to God never seen anything like it.' He looked at Lucas. 'Sloan tells me there's not much chance that Wannemaker got it in Hudson. She was probably transported there.'

Lucas nodded. 'Looks like.'

'So we got another one.'

Roux lit another cigarette and turned to Lucas. 'What do you need?'

Lucas looked back at Lester. 'Same deal as last time. Except I want Sloan.'

'What's the same deal?' Roux asked.

Lester looked at Roux. 'Lucas works by himself, parallel to my investigation. Everything he finds out, and everything from the up-front investigation, goes into a book on a daily basis. Anderson does the book. He essentially coordinates.'

Lester hooked a thumb at Anderson, who nodded, then turned to Lucas. 'You can't have Sloan.'

Lucas opened his mouth, but Lester shook his head. 'You can't, man. He's my best guy and we're fuckin' drowning out there.'

'I've been off the street . . .'

'Can't help it,' Lester said. To Roux: 'I'm telling you, pulling Sloan would kill us.'

Roux nodded. 'You'll have to live with it, at least for a while,' she said to Lucas. 'Can't you use Capslock?'

He shook his head. 'He's got something going with this deputy that was killed. We need to stay on it.'

'I could let you have one guy,' Lester said. 'He could run errands. Tell you the truth, you could help him out. Show him how it's done.'

Lucas's eyebrows went up. 'Greave?'

Lester nodded.

'I hear he's an idiot,' Lucas said.

'He's just new,' Lester said defensively. 'You don't like him, give him back.'

'All right,' Lucas said. He looked at Anderson. 'And I need to know where a guy is. A knife guy from years ago.'

'Who's that?'

'His name was Junky Doog . . .'

When the meeting broke up, Roux held Lucas back. 'Meagan Connell is gonna want to work it,' she said. 'I'd appreciate it if you'd take her.'

Lucas shook his head. 'Rose Marie, damnit, she's got a state badge, she can do what she wants.'

'As a favor to me,' Roux said, pressing him. 'There's no way homicide'll take her. She's really into this. She's smart. She'd help you. I'd appreciate it.'

'All right, I'll find something for her to do,' Lucas said. Then: 'You know, you never told me she was dying.'

'I figured you'd find out by yourself,' Roux said.

*   *   *

Roux's secretary had a dictation plug in her ear. When Lucas walked out of Roux's office, she pointed a finger at Lucas and held up her hand to stop, him, typed another half-sentence, then pulled the plug out of her ear.

'Detective Sloan stopped by while you were talking,' she said, her dark eyebrows arching. She took a manila file-folder from her desk and handed it to him. 'He said fingerprints confirm that it's Wannemaker. She had a piece of an unfiltered cigarette in her hand, a Camel. They sent it to the lab in Madison. He said to look at the picture.'

'Thanks.' Lucas turned away and opened the folder.

'I already looked at it,' she said. 'Gross. But interesting.'

'Umm.' Inside the folder was an eight-by-ten color photograph of a body in a snowdrift. The faceup attitude was almost the same as that of the Wannemaker woman, with the same massive abdominal wound; pieces of a plastic garbage bag were scattered around in the snow. The secretary was looking over his shoulder, and Lucas half-turned. 'There's a state investigator who's been in and out of here, name of Meagan Connell. Could you find her and ask her to call me?'

4

Lucas's office was fifteen feet square, no window, with a door that opened directly to a hallway. He had a wooden desk and chair, three visitor's chairs, two file cabinets, a bookcase, a computer, and a three-button phone. A map of the Twin Cities metro area covered most of one wall, a cork bulletin board another. He hung his jacket on a wooden hanger and the wooden hanger on a wall hook, sat down, pulled open the bottom desk drawer with his toe, put his feet on it, and picked up the telephone and dialed. A woman answered.

'Weather Harkinnen, please.' He didn't recognize all the nurses' voices yet.

'Doctor Harkinnen is in the operating room . . . Is this Lucas?'

'Yes. Could you tell her I called? I might be late getting home. I'll try her there later.'

He punched in another number, got a secretary. 'Lucas Davenport for Sister Mary Joseph.'

'Lucas, she's in Rome. I thought you knew.'

'Shit . . . Oh, jeez, excuse me.' The secretary was a novice nun.

'Lucas . . .' Feigned exasperation.

'I forgot. When is she back?'

'Two weeks yet. She's going on some kind of dig.'

'Goddamnit . . . Oh, jeez, excuse me.'

Sister Mary Joseph – Elle Kruger when they had gone to elementary school together – was an old friend and a shrink, with an interest in murder. She'd helped him out

49

on other cases. Rome. Lucas shook his head and opened the file that Connell had put together.

The first page was a list of names and dates. The next eight pages were wound photos done during autopsies. Lucas worked through them. They were not identical, but there were inescapable similarities.

The wound photos were followed by crime-scene shots. The bodies had been dumped in a variety of locations, some urban, some rural. A couple were in roadside ditches, one in a doorway, one under a bridge. One had been simply rolled under a van in a residential neighborhood. There was little effort to hide them. In the background of several, he could see shreds of plastic garbage bags.

Going back and forth from each report to the relevant photographs, Lucas picked up a thread that seemed to tie them together in his mind. The women had been . . . littered. They'd been thrown away like used Kleenex. Not with desperation, or fear, or guilt, but with some discretion, as though the killer had been afraid of being caught littering.

The autopsy reports also showed up differences.

Ripped was a subjective description, and some of the wounds looked more like frantic knife strikes than deliberate ripping. Some of the women had been beaten, some had not. Still, taken together, there was a *feel* about the killings. The feel was generated almost as much by the absence of fact as by the presence of it.

Nobody saw the women when they were picked up. Nobody saw the man who picked them up, or his car, although he must have been among them. There were no fingerprints, vaginal smears turned up no semen, although signs of semen had been found on the clothing of one of the women. Not enough for a blood or DNA type, apparently: none was listed.

When he finished the first reading, he skipped through the reports again, quickly, looking at the small stuff. He'd have to read them again, several times. There were too many details for a single reading, or even two or three. But he'd learned when he looked back from other murders that the files often pointed at the killer way before he was brought down. Truth was in the details . . .

His rummaging was interrupted by a knock. 'Yeah. Come in.'

Connell stepped through, flustered, but still pale as a ghost. 'I was in town. I thought I'd come by, instead of calling.'

'Come in. Sit down,' Lucas said.

Connell's close-cropped hair was disconcerting: it lent a punkish air to a woman who was anything but a punk. She had a serious, square face, with a short, Irish nose and a square chin. She was still wearing the blue suit she'd worn that morning, with a darker stripe of what might have been garbage juice on the front of it. An incongruous black leather hip pack was buckled around her hips, the bag itself perched just below her navel: a rip-down holster for a large gun. She could take a big gun: she had large hands, and she stuck one of them out and Lucas half-rose to shake it.

She'd opted for peace, Lucas thought; but her hand was cold. 'I read your file,' he said. 'That's nice work.'

'The possession of a vagina doesn't necessarily indicate stupidity,' Connell said. She was still standing.

'Take it easy,' Lucas said, his forehead wrinkling as he sat down again. 'That was a compliment.'

'Just want things clear,' Connell said crisply. She looked at the vacant chair, still didn't sit. 'And you think there is something?'

Lucas stared at her for another moment, but she neither flinched nor sat down. Holding her eyes, he said, 'I think so. They're all too . . . not alike, but they have the feeling of a single man.'

'There's something else,' Connell said. 'It's hard to see

it in the files, but you see it when you talk to the friends of these women.'

'Which is?'

'They're all the same woman.'

'Ah. Tell me. And sit down, for Christ's sakes.'

She sat, reluctantly, as if she were giving up the high ground. 'One here in the Cities, one in Duluth, now this one, if this latest one is his. One in Madison, one in Thunder Bay, one in Des Moines, one in Sioux Falls. They were all single, late twenties to early forties. They were all somewhat shy, somewhat lonely, somewhat intellectual, somewhat religious or at least involved in some kind of spirituality. They'd go out to bookstores or galleries or plays or concerts at night, like other people'd go out to bars. Anyway, they were all like that. And then these shy, quiet women turn up ripped . . .'

'Nasty word,' Lucas said casually. 'Ripped.'

Connell shuddered, and her naturally pale complexion went paper-white. 'I dream about the woman up at Carlos Avery. I was worse up there than I was today. I went out, took a look, started puking. I got puke all over my radio.'

'Well, first time,' Lucas said.

'No. I've seen a lot of dead people,' Connell said. She was pitched forward in her chair, hands clasped. 'This is way different. Joan Smits wants vengeance. Or justice. I can hear her calling from the other side – I know that sounds like schizophrenia, but I can hear her, and I can feel the other ones. All of them. I've been to every one of those places, where the murders happened, on my own time. Talked to witnesses, talked to cops. It's one guy, and he's the devil.'

There was a hard, crystalline conviction in her voice and eyes, the taste and bite of psychosis, that made Lucas turn his head away. 'What about the sequence you've got here?' Lucas asked, trying to escape her intensity. 'He was putting a year between most of them. But then he skipped a couple — once, twenty-one months, another time, twenty-three. You think you're missing a couple?'

'Only if he completely changed his MO,' Connell said. 'If he shot them. My data search concentrated on stabbings. Or maybe he took the time to bury them and they were never found. That wouldn't be typical of him, though. But there are so many missing people out there, it's impossible to tell for sure.'

'Maybe he went someplace else — L. A. or Miami, or the bodies were just never found.'

She shrugged. 'I don't think so. He tends to stay close to home. I think he drives to the killing scene. He picks his ground ahead of time, and goes by car. I plotted all the places where these women were taken from, and except for the one in Thunder Bay, they all disappeared within ten minutes of an interstate that runs through the Cities. And the one in Thunder Bay was off Highway 61. So maybe he went out to L. A. — but it doesn't feel right.'

'I understand that you think it could be a cop.'

She leaned forward again, the intensity returning. 'There are still a couple of things we need to look at. The cop thing is the only hard clue we have: that one woman talking to her daughter . . .'

'I read your file on it,' Lucas said.

'Okay. And you saw the thing about the PPP?'

'Mmm. No. I don't remember.'

'It's in an early police interview with a guy named Price, who was convicted of killing the Madison woman.'

'Oh, yeah, I saw the transcript. I haven't had time to read it.'

'He says he didn't do it. I believe him. I'm planning to go over and talk to him if nothing else comes up. He was in the bookstore where the victim was picked up, and he says there was a bearded man with PPP tattooed on his hand. Right on the web between his index finger and thumb.'

'So we're looking for a cop with PPP on his hand?'

'I don't know. Nobody else saw the tattoo, and they never found anybody with PPP on his hand. A computer search doesn't show PPP as an identifying mark anywhere. But the thing is, Price had been in jail, and he said the tattoo was a prison tattoo. You know, like they make with ballpoint ink and pins.'

'Well,' Lucas said. 'It's something.'

Connell was discouraged. 'But not much.'

'Not unless we find the killer – then it might help confirm the ID,' Lucas said. He picked up the file and paged through it until he found the list of murders and dates. 'Do you have any theories about why the killings are so scattered around?'

'I've been looking for patterns,' she said. 'I don't know . . .'

'Until the body you found last winter, he never had two killings in the same state. And the last one here was almost nine years ago.'

'Yes. That's right.'

Lucas closed the file and tossed it back on his desk. 'Yeah. That means different reporting jurisdictions. Iowa doesn't know what we're doing, and Wisconsin doesn't know what Iowa's doing, and nobody knows what South Dakota's doing. And Canada sure as hell is out of it.'

'You're saying he's figured on that,' Connell said. 'So it *is* a cop.'

'Maybe,' said Lucas. 'But maybe it's an ex-con. A smart guy. Maybe the reason for the two gaps is, he was inside. Some small-timer who gets slammed for drugs or burglary, and he's out of circulation.'

Connell leaned back, regarding him gravely. 'When you crawled into the dumpster this morning, you were cold. I couldn't be that cold; I never would have seen that tobacco on her.'

'I'm used to it,' Lucas said.

'No, no, it was . . . impressive,' she said. 'I need that kind of distance. When I said we only had one fact about him, the cop thing, I was wrong. You came up with a bunch of them: he was strong, he smokes –'

'Unfiltered Camels,' Lucas said.

'Yeah? Well, it's interesting. And now these ideas . . . I haven't had anybody bouncing ideas off me. Are you gonna let me work with you?'

He nodded. 'If you want.'

'Will we get along?'

'Maybe. Maybe not,' he said. 'What does that have to do with anything?'

She regarded him without humor. 'Exactly my attitude,' she said. 'So. What are we doing?'

'We're checking bookstores.'

Connell looked down at herself. 'I've got to change clothes. I've got them in my car . . .'

While Connell went to change, Lucas called Anderson for a reading on homicide's preliminary work on the Wannemaker killing. 'We just got started,' Anderson said. 'Skoorag called in a few minutes ago. He said a friend of Wannemaker's definitely thinks she was going to a bookstore. But if you look at the file when she was reported missing, somebody else said she might have been going to the galleries over on First Avenue.'

'We're hitting the bookstores. Maybe your guys could take the galleries.'

'If we've got time. Lester's got people running around like rats,' Anderson said. 'Oh – that Junky Doog guy. I got lots of hits, but the last one was three years ago. He was living in a flop on Franklin Avenue. Chances of him being there are slim and none, and slim is outa town.'

'Give me the address,' Lucas said.

*　　*　　*

When he finished with Anderson, Lucas carried his phone book down the hall, Xeroxed the Books section of the Yellow Pages, and went back to his office for his jacket. He *had* bought the jacket in New York; the thought was mildly embarrassing. He was pulling on the jacket when there was a knock at the door. 'Yeah?'

A fleshy, pink-cheeked thirties-something man in a loose green suit and moussed blond hair poked his head inside, smiled like an encyclopedia salesman, and said, 'Hey. Davenport. I'm Bob Greave. I'm supposed to report to you.'

'I remember you,' Lucas said as they shook hands.

'From my Officer Friendly stuff?' Greave was cheerful, unconsciously rumpled. But his green eyes matched his Italian-cut suit a little too perfectly, and he wore a fashionable two days' stubble on his chin.

'Yeah, there was a poster down at my kid's preschool,' Lucas said.

Greave grinned. 'Yup, that's me.'

'Nice jump, up to homicide,' Lucas said.

'Yeah, bullshit.' Greave's smile fell away, and he dropped into the chair Connell had vacated, looked up. 'I suppose you've heard about me.'

'I haven't, uh . . .'

'Greave the fuckup?'

'Haven't heard anything like that,' Lucas lied.

'Don't bullshit me, Davenport.' Greave studied him for a minute, then said, 'That's what they call me. Greave-the-fuckup, one word. The only goddamned reason I'm in homicide is that my wife is the mayor's niece. She got tired of me being Officer Friendly. Not enough drama. Didn't give her enough to gossip about.'

'Well . . .'

'So now I'm doing something I can't fuckin' do and I'm stuck between my old lady and the other guys on the job.'

'What do you want from me?'

56

'Advice.'

Lucas spread his hands and shrugged. 'If you liked being an Officer Friendly . . .'

Greave waved him off. 'Not that kind of advice. I can't go back to Officer Friendly, my old lady'd nag my ears off. She doesn't like me being a cop in the first place. Homicide just makes it a little okay. And she makes me wear these fuckin' Italian fruit suits and only lets me shave on Wednesdays and Saturdays.'

'Sounds like you gotta make a decision about her,' Lucas said.

'I love her,' Greave said.

Lucas grinned. 'Then you've got a problem.'

'Yeah.' Greave rubbed the stubble on his chin. 'Anyway, the guys in homicide don't do nothing but fuck with me. They figure I'm not pulling my load, and they're right. Whenever there's a really horseshit case, I get it. I got one right now. Everybody in homicide is laughing about it. That's what I need your advice on.'

'What happened?'

'We don't know,' Greave said. 'We've got it pegged as a homicide and we know who did it, but we can't figure out how.'

'Never heard of anything like that,' Lucas admitted.

'Sure you have,' Greave said. 'All the time.'

'What?' Lucas was puzzled.

'It's a goddamned locked-room mystery, like one of them old-lady English things. It's driving me crazy.'

Connell pushed through the door. She was wearing a navy suit with matching low heels, a white blouse with wine-colored tie, and carried a purse the size of a buffalo. She looked at Greave, then Lucas, and said, 'Ready.'

'Bob Greave, Meagan Connell,' Lucas said.

'Yeah, we sorta met,' Greave said. 'A few weeks ago.'

A little tension there. Lucas scooped Connell's file from his desk, handed it to Greave. 'Meagan and I are going out to the bookstores. Read the file. We'll talk tomorrow morning.'

'What time?'

'Not too early,' Lucas said. 'How about here, at eleven o'clock?'

'What about my case?' Greave asked.

'We'll talk tomorrow,' Lucas said.

As Lucas and Connell walked out of the building, Connell said, 'Greave's a jerk. He's got the Hollywood stubble and the *Miami Vice* suits, but he couldn't find his shoes in a goddamn clothes closet.'

Lucas shook his head, irritated. 'Cut him a little slack. You don't known him that well.'

'Some people are an open book,' Connell snorted. 'He's a fuckin' comic.'

Connell continued to irritate him: their styles were different. Lucas liked to drift into conversation, to schmooze a little, to remember common friends. Connell was an interrogator: just the facts, sir.

Not that it made much difference. Nobody in the half-dozen downtown bookstores knew Wannemaker. They picked up a taste of her at the suburban Smart Book. 'She used to come to readings,' the store owner said. He nibbled at his lip as he peered at the photograph. 'She didn't buy much, but we'd have these wine-and-cheese things for authors coming through town, and she'd show up maybe half the time. Maybe more than that.'

'Did you have a reading last Friday?'

'No, but there were some.'

'Where?'

'Hell, I don't know.' He threw up his hands. 'Goddamn authors are like cockroaches. There're hundreds of them. There's always readings somewhere. Especially at the end of the week.'

'How'd I find out where?'

'Call the *Star-Trib*. There'd be somebody who could tell you.'

Lucas called from a corner phone, another number from memory. 'I wondered if you'd call.' The woman's voice was hushed. 'Are you bringing up your net?'

'I'm doing that now. There're lots of holes.'

'I'm in.'

'Thanks, I appreciate it. How about the readings?'

'There was poetry at the Startled Crane, something called Prairie Woman at The Saint – I don't know how I missed that one – Gynostic at Wild Lily Press, and the Pillar of Manhood at Crosby's. The Pillar of Manhood was a male-only night. If you'd called last week, I probably could have gotten you in.'

'Too late,' Lucas said. 'My drum's broke.'

'Darn. You had a nice drum, too.'

'Yeah, well, thanks, Shirlene.' To Connell: 'We can scratch Crosby's off the list.'

The owner of the Startled Crane grinned at Lucas and said, 'Cheese it, the heat . . . How you been, Lucas?' They shook hands, and the store owner nodded at Connell, who stared at him like a snake at a bird.

'Not bad, Ned,' Lucas said. 'How's the old lady?'

Ned's eyebrows went up. 'Pregnant again. You just wave it at her, and she's knocked up.'

'Everybody's pregnant. I gotta friend, I just heard his wife's pregnant. How many is that for you? Six?'

'Seven . . . what's happening?'

Connell, who had been listening impatiently to the chitchat, thrust the photos at him. 'Was this woman here Friday night?'

Lucas, softer, said, 'We're trying to track down the last days of a woman who was killed last week. We thought she might've been at your poetry reading.'

Ned shuffled through the photos. 'Yeah, I know her. Harriet something, right? I don't think she was here. There were about twenty people, but I don't think she was with them.'

'But you see her around?'

'Yeah. She's a semiregular. I saw the TV stuff on *Nooner*. I thought that might be her.'

'Ask around, will you?'

'Sure.'

'What's *Nooner*?' Connell asked.

'TV3's new noon news,' Ned said. 'But I didn't see her Friday. I wouldn't be surprised if she was somewhere else, though.'

'Thanks, Ned.'

'Sure. And stop in. I've been fleshing out the poetry section.'

Back on the street, Connell said, 'You've got a lot of bookstore friends?'

'A few,' Lucas said. 'Ned used to deal a little grass. I leaned on him and he quit.'

'Huh,' she said, thinking it over. Then, 'Why'd he tell you about poetry?'

'I read poetry,' Lucas said.

'Bullshit.'

Lucas shrugged and started toward the car.

'Say a poem.'

'Fuck you, Connell,' Lucas said.

'No, c'mon,' she said, catching him, facing him. 'Say a poem.'

Lucas thought for a second then said, 'The heart asks pleasure first/And then excuse from pain/and then those little anodynes/that deaden suffering. And then to go to sleep/and then if it should be/the will of its inquisitor/the privilege to die.'

Connell, already pale, seemed to go a shade paler, and Lucas, remembering, thought, *Oh, shit.*

60

'Who wrote that?'

'Emily Dickinson.'

'Roux told you I have cancer?'

'Yes, but I wasn't thinking about that . . .'

Connell, studying him, suddenly showed a tiny smile. 'I was kind of hoping you were. I was thinking, *Jesus Christ, what a shot in the mouth.*'

'Well . . . ?'

She stepped toward the car. 'Where's next?'

'The Wild Lily Press over on the West Bank.'

She shook her head. 'I doubt it. That's a feminist store. He'd be pretty noticeable.'

'Then The Saint, over in St Paul.'

On the way to St Paul, Connell said, 'I'm in a hurry on this, Davenport. I'm gonna die in three or four months, six at the outside. Right now I'm in remission, and I don't feel too bad. I'm out of chemo for the time being, I'm getting my strength back. But it won't last. A couple weeks, three, and it'll come creeping up on me again. I want to get him before I go.'

'We can try.'

'We gotta do better than that,' she said. 'I owe some people.'

'All right.'

'I don't mean to scare you,' she said.

'You're doing it.'

The owner at The Saint recognized Wannemaker immediately. 'Yes, she was here,' he said. His voice was cool, soft. He looked at Lucas over the top of his gold-rimmed John Lennon specs. 'Killed? My God, she wasn't the kind to get killed.'

'What kind was she?' Lucas asked.

'Well, you know.' He gestured. 'Meek. A wallflower. She did ask a question when Margaret finished the reading, but I think it was because nobody was asking questions and she was embarrassed. That kind of person.'

'Did she leave with anyone?'

'Nope. She left alone. I remember, 'cause it was abrupt. Most readings, she'd hang around; she'd be the last to leave, like she had nothing else to do. But I remember, she headed out maybe fifteen minutes after we broke things up. There were still quite a few people in the store. I thought maybe she didn't like Margaret.'

'Was she in a hurry?'

The store owner scratched his head, looked out his window at the street. 'Yeah. Now that you mention it, she did sort of seem like she was going somewhere.'

Lucas looked at Connell, who was showing just the faintest color.

The store owner, frowning, said, 'You know, when I think about it, the question she asked was made up, like maybe she was dragging things out. I was sort of rolling my eyes, mentally, anyway. Then she leaves in a hurry . . .'

'Like something happened while she was in the store?' Connell prompted.

'I hate to say it, but yes.'

'That's interesting,' Lucas said. 'We'll need a list of everybody you know was here.'

The store owner looked away, embarrassed. 'Hmm. I think, uh, a lot of my clients would see that as an invasion of privacy,' he said.

'Would you like to see the pictures of Wannemaker?' Lucas asked gently. 'The guy ripped her stomach open and all her intestines came out. And we think he might be hanging around bookstores.'

The store owner looked at him for a moment, then nodded. 'I'll get a list going,' he said.

Lucas used the store phone to call Anderson, and told him about the identification. 'She left here at nine o'clock.'

'We got her car fifteen minutes ago,' Anderson said. 'It was in the impound lot, towed out of downtown St Paul. Hang on a minute . . .' Anderson spoke to somebody else, then came back. 'It was towed off a hill on Sixth. I'm told that's next to Dayton's.'

'So she must have been headed somewhere.'

'Unless she already was somewhere, and walked back to the store.'

'I don't think so. That'd be eight or ten blocks. There's a lot of parking around here. She would have driven.'

'Is there anything around Dayton's at nine? Was the store open?'

'There's a bar up there – Harp's. On the corner. Connell and I'll stop in.'

'Okay. St Paul'll process the car,' Anderson said. 'I'll pass on what you found out at this bookstore. You're getting a list of names?'

'Yeah. But it might not be much.'

'Get me the names and I'll run 'em.'

Lucas hung up and turned around. Connell was marching toward him from the back of the store, where the owner had gone to talk with one of his clerks about people at the reading.

'One of the men here was a cop,' she said fiercely. 'A St Paul patrolman named Carl Erdrich.'

'Damnit,' Lucas said. He picked up the phone and called Anderson back, gave him the name.

'What?' Connell wanted to know when he got off the phone.

'We'll check the bar,' Lucas said. 'There'll have to be some negotiations before we can get a mug of Erdrich.'

Connell spun around and planted herself in front of him. 'What the fuck is this?' she asked.

'It's called the Usual Bullshit,' he said. 'And calm down. We're talking about an hour or two, not forever.'

But she was angry, heels pounding as they walked back

63

to Lucas's Porsche. 'Why do you drive this piece of crap? You ought to buy something decent,' she snapped.

Lucas said, 'Shut the fuck up.'

'What?' She goggled at him.

'I said shut the fuck up. You don't shut the fuck up, you can take the bus back to Minneapolis.'

Connell, still angry, trailed him into Harp's and muttered, 'Oh, Lord' when she saw the bartender. The bartender was a dark-haired pixieish woman with large black eyes, two much makeup, and a bee-stung lower lip. She wore a slippery low-cut silk pullover without a bra, and a black string tie with a turquoise clasp at her throat. 'Cops?' she asked, but she was smiling.

'Yeah.' Lucas nodded, grinned, and tried to meet her eyes. 'We need to talk to somebody who was here Friday night.'

'I was,' she said, dropping her elbows on the bar and leaning toward Lucas, glancing at Connell. The bartender smelled lightly of cinnamon, like a dream; she had a soft freckled cleavage. 'What do you need?'

Lucas rolled out the photo of Wannemaker. 'Was she here?'

The bartender watched his eyes, and, satisfied with her effect, picked up the photo and studied it. 'She look like this?'

'Pretty much,' Lucas said, steadfastly holding her eyes.

'What'd she do?' the bartender asked.

'Was she here?' Lucas asked again.

'Meanie,' she said. 'You don't want to tell me.' The bartender frowned, pushed out her lower lip, studied the picture, and slowly shook her head. 'No, I don't think she was. In fact, I'm sure she wasn't, if she dressed like this. Our crowd's into black. Black shirts, black pants, black dresses, black hats, black combat boots. I'd have noticed her.'

'Big crowd?'

'In St Paul?' She picked up her bar rag and scrubbed at a spot on the bar.

'Okay . . .'

As they started out, the bartender called after them, 'What'd she do?'

'It was done to her,' Connell said, speaking for the first time. She made it sound like a punishment.

'Yeah?'

'She was killed.'

The bartender recoiled. 'Like, murdered? How?'

'Let's go,' said Lucas, touching Connell's coat sleeve.

'Stabbed,' said Connell.

'Let's go,' Lucas repeated.

' "Do not wait for the last judgment. It takes place every day," ' the bartender said solemnly, in a quotation voice.

Now Lucas stopped. 'Who was that?' he asked.

'Some dead French dude,' the bartender said.

'That was disgusting,' Connell fumed.

'What?'

'The way she was throwing it at you.'

'What?'

'You knew.'

Lucas looked back at the bar, then at Connell, a look of utter astonishment on his face. 'You think she was coming on to me?'

'Kiss my ass, Davenport,' she said, and stalked off toward the car.

Lucas called Anderson again. 'Roux's still talking to St Paul,' Anderson said. 'She wants you back here, ASAP.'

'What for?'

'I don't know. But she wants you back.'

Connell complained most of the way back. They had something, she said. They should stay with it. Lucas, tired of it, offered to drop her at the St Paul police headquarters. She declined. Roux was up to something, she said. When they walked into the chief's outer office, the bony secretary flipped a thumb toward the chief's door and they went through.

Roux was smoking furiously. She glanced at Connell, then nodded. 'I guess you better stay and hear this.'

'What's going on?' Lucas asked.

Roux shrugged. 'We're outa here, is what's going on. No crime committed in Minneapolis. You just proved it. Wannemaker goes to that bookstore in St Paul, gets dumped in Hudson. Let them fight about it.'

'Wait a minute,' said Connell.

Roux shook her head. 'Meagan, I promised to help you and I did. But we've got lots of trouble right now, and this is St Paul's killing. Your killing, up in Carlos Avery, is either Anoka County's or Duluth's. Not ours. We're putting out a press release that says our investigation concludes the murder was not committed here, that we'll cooperate with the investigating authorities, and so on.'

'WAIT A FUCKING MINUTE!' Connell shouted. 'Are you telling me we're done?'

'*We're* done,' Roux said, still friendly, but her voice sharpening. '*You've* still got some options. We'll get your research to St Paul, and I'll ask that they let you assist their investigation. Or you could continue with the Smits case. I don't know what Duluth is doing with that anymore.'

Connell turned to Lucas, her voice harsh. 'What do you think?'

Lucas stepped back. 'It's an interesting case, but she's right. It's St Paul's.'

Connell's face was like a stone. She stared at Lucas for a heartbeat, then at Roux, and then, without another word, spun and stalked out, slamming the office door behind her.

'You might have found a better way to handle that,' Lucas said.

'Probably,' Roux said, looking after Connell. 'But I didn't know she was coming, and I was so damn happy to be out from under. Christ, Davenport, you saved my ass in four hours, finding that bookstore.'

'So now what?'

Roux waved her hand expansively. 'Do what you want.' She took a drag on her cigarette, then took it out of her mouth and looked at it. 'Jesus, sometimes I wish I was a man.'

'Why?' Lucas was amused by her excitement.

''Cause then I could take out a big fuckin' Cuban cigar and smoke its ass off.'

'You could still do that.'

'Yeah, but then people who don't already think I'm a bull dyke would start thinking I'm a bull dyke. Besides, I'd barf.'

Lucas talked briefly to Anderson and Lester about wrapping up the paper on the case. 'St Paul will probably want to talk to you,' Lester said.

'That's fine. Give them my home phone number if they call. I'll be around,' Lucas said.

'Connell thinks it's a cheap shot, doesn't she? Dumping the case.'

'It *is* cheap,' Lucas said.

'Man, we're hurting,' Lester said. 'We've never hurt this bad. And if you're looking for something to do, we've still got bodies coming out of our ears. Did Greave tell you about his?'

'He mentioned something, but it didn't sound very interesting.'

Sloan wandered in, hands in his pockets. He nodded to them, yawned, stretched, and to Lester said, 'You gotta Coke or something? I'm a little dry.'

67

'Do I look like a fuckin' vending machine?' Lester asked.

'What happened, Sloan?' Lucas asked, picking up the signs.

Sloan yawned again, then said, 'A little pissant student named Lanny Bryson threw Heather Tatten off the bridge.'

'What?' A smile broke across Lester's face, like the sun coming up.

'Got him on tape,' Sloan said, ostentatiously studying his fingernails. 'She was hooking, part-time. She fucked him once, but wouldn't do it twice, not even for money. They were arguing, walking across the bridge, and he tried to smooch her but she hit him with her fist, in the nose. It hurt and he got mad and when she walked away, he hit her on the back of the head with an economics textbook – big fat motherfucker – and knocked her down. She was stunned and he just picked her up and pushed her over the railing. She tried to hang on at the last minute, scratched him all the way down his forearms.'

'Did you use the cattle prods?' Lucas asked.

'Told us the whole fuckin' thing in one long sentence,' Sloan said. 'We Miranda-ed him twice on the tape. Got Polaroids of his arms; we'll get a DNA match later. He's over in the lockup now, waiting for the public defender.'

Lucas, Anderson, and Lester looked at each other, then back at Sloan. Lester stepped close, took him by the arm, and said, 'Can I kiss you on the lips?'

'Better not,' Sloan said. 'People might think you favor me at promotion time.'

A pizza arrived, too much for somebody's lunch, so they cut it up, got Cokes from the machine in the basement, had a little party, giving Sloan a hard time.

Lucas left smiling. Sloan was a friend, maybe his best friend. But at the same time, he felt . . . He looked for a word. Disgruntled? Yes. Sloan had his victory. But somewhere out there, a monster was roaming around . . .

5

Koop was slick with sweat, eyes shut, counting: *eleven, twelve, thirteen*. His triceps were burning, his toes reaching for the floor, his mind holding them off. *Fourteen, fifteen sixteen?* No.

He was done. He dropped to the floor between the parallel bars and opened his eyes, the sweat running from his eyebrows. The burn in his arms began to even out, and he stumbled over to the toe-raise rack where he'd left the towel, mopped his face, picked up a pair of light dumbbells, and headed back to the posing room.

Two Guy's Body Shop, with a misplaced apostrophe, was the end unit of a dying shopping center on Highway 100, a shopping center marked by knee-high weeds growing out of cracked blacktop, and peeling hand-painted signs for failing tax services and obscure martial arts. Koop had parked the truck in a litter of crumbling blacktop, locked it, and gone inside.

To the right, one of the Two Guys sat behind the front desk, reading an old *Heavy Metal* magazine. To the left, a woman and two men were working around a variety of free-weight racks. The Guy looked up when Koop came in, grunted, and went back to the magazine. Koop walked past him, down a hallway where fifty musclemen stared down from curling Polaroids thumbtacked to the paneling, into the men's locker room. He changed into a jock, cutoff sweatpants, and a sleeveless T-shirt, strapped on a lifting belt, pulled on goatskin gloves stiff with dried sweat, and went back out into the main room.

Koop had a system: He divided his body into thirds, and worked a different third each day for three days. Then he took a day off, and the day after that, started over.

Shoulders and arms, first day; chest and back, second day; and then lower body. This was shoulders and arms: he worked the delts, triceps, biceps. Unlike a lot of people, he worked his forearms hard, squeezing rubber rings until the muscles screamed with acid.

And he worked his neck, both on the neck machine and with bridges. He'd never seen anyone else at Two Guy's doing bridges, but that didn't bother Koop. He'd once gone to a University of Minnesota—University of Iowa wrestling meet, and the Hawks were doing bridges. They'd kicked ass.

Koop liked bench presses. Hell, everybody liked bench presses. He did pyramids, ten reps at 350, two or three at 370, one or two at 390. He did seated behind-the-neck presses; he did curls, topping out at eighty pounds on the dumbbells, working his biceps.

At the very end, soaked with sweat, he got on a stair climber and ran up a hundred stories, then, breathing hard, he went back to the posing room.

A woman in a sweat-stained orange bikini was working in the mirrors on the west wall, moving from a frontal pose, arms over head, to a side pose, biceps flexed against her stomach. Koop dropped the dumbbells on a pad and stripped down to his jock. He picked up the dumbbells, did ten quick pumps, tossed them back on the pad, and began his routine. In the back of his mind, he could hear the woman grunting as she posed, could hear the exhaust fan overhead, but all he could see was himself . . . And sometimes, through the mist of sweat, the gossamer-wrapped body of Sara Jensen, spread-eagled on the bed, the dark pubic mound and . . .

Slam it, slam it, slam it, go, go . . .

The woman stopped, picked up her towel. He was

vaguely aware that she was standing in a corner, watching.

When he finally quit, she tossed him his towel. 'Gettin' the pecs,' she said.

'Need more work,' he mumbled, wiping himself down. 'Need more work.' He carried his workout clothes back to the locker room, soaked them under a shower, wrung them by hand, threw them into a dryer and turned the dryer on. Then he showered, toweled off, dressed, went out to the main room, bought a Coke, drank it, went back and took his clothes out of the dryer, hung them in his locker, and left.

He hadn't said a word to anyone, except, 'Need more work . . .'

John Carlson was already in summer mode, black Raiders jacket over knee-length rapper shorts and black Nikes with red laces.

'What's happening, dude?' John was black and far too heavy. Koop handed him a small roll. John didn't check it, just stuffed it in his pocket.

'Gotta date,' Koop said.

'Far out, man . . .' John rapped the car with his knuckles, as if for luck. 'Get you some latex, man, you don't want to get no fuckin' AIDS.'

'Do that,' Koop said.

John backed away, took off his cap, and scratched his head. Koop started down the block, turned the corner. Another black kid was walking down the sidewalk. He swerved across the dirt parking strip to the curb, and when Koop slowed next to him, tossed a plastic twist through the passenger window and turned away. Koop kept going. Three blocks later, with nothing in his rearview, Koop stopped for a taste. Just a taste to wake him up. Koop didn't understand his fascination with Jensen. Didn't understand why he was compelled to watch her, to get close to her. To hurry his daily rounds to meet her after work . . .

He finished liquidating the jewelry he'd taken from Jensen's apartment in a bar on the I-494 strip in Bloomington, selling the engagement ring and the wedding band to a guy who dressed and talked like an actor playing a pro athlete: a tan, a golf shirt, capped teeth, and a gold chain around his thick neck. But he knew stones, and the smile was gone from his eyes when he looked at them. He gave Koop $1,300. The total take from the apartment pushed $6,000, not counting the belt. It never occurred to Koop to feel a connection between the jewelry and the woman who'd caught his heart. The jewelry was his, not hers.

He left the Bloomington strip and idled back into Minneapolis, killing time behind the wheel, eventually turning east, to an Arby's on St Paul's east side. He'd called the moving man who'd given him the map of Jensen's apartment, and arranged to meet. Koop was both early and late for the meetings, arriving a half hour early, watching the meeting spot from a distance. When his man arrived, alone, on time, he'd watch for another ten minutes before going in. He'd never had a contact turn on him. He didn't want it to happen, either.

The moving man arrived a few minutes early, hurried straight into the Arby's. The way he moved gave Koop some confidence that everything was okay: there was no tentativeness, no looking around. He carried a notebook in his hand. Koop waited five more minutes, watching, then went in. The guy was sitting in a booth with a cup of coffee, a young guy, looked like a college kid. Koop nodded at him, stopped for a cup of coffee himself, paid the girl behind the counter, and slid into the booth.

'How're you doing?'

'It's been a while,' the guy said.

'Yeah, well . . .' Koop handed him a Holiday Inn brochure. The guy took it and looked inside.

'Thanks,' he said. 'You must've done okay.'

Koop shrugged. He wasn't much for chitchat. 'Got anything else?'

'Yeah. A good one.' The guy pushed the notebook at him. 'I was pissing my pants waiting for you to call. We was moving some stuff into this house on Upper St Dennis in St Paul, you know where that is?'

'Up the hill off West Seventh,' Koop said, pulling in the notebook. 'Some nice houses up there. A little riffraff, too.'

'This a nice house, man.' The guy's head was bobbing. '*Nice*. There was a guy from a safe company there. They'd just set a big fuckin' safe in concrete, down in the basement, in a corner of a closet. I seen it myself.'

'I don't do safes . . .' The notebook was too thick. Koop opened it and found a key impression in dried putty. He'd shown the guy how to do it. The impression was crisp, clean.

'Wait a minute, for Christ's sakes,' the guy said, holding up his hands. 'So when he was talking to the safe guy, he was walking around with this piece of paper in his hand. When they finished, he came up and asked how long we were gonna be, 'cause he wanted to take a shower and shave, 'cause he was going out. We said we'd be a while yet, and he went up and took a shower in the bathroom. The bathroom off his bedroom. We were working right down the hall, my buddy was settin' up a guest bed. So I stepped down the hall and looked into his bedroom. I could hear the shower going, and I saw this paper laying on the dresser with his billfold and watch, and I just took the chance, man. I zipped over and looked at it, and it was the fuckin' combination. How about that, huh? I wrote it down. And listen, you know what this guy does? This guy runs half the automatic car washes in the Twin Cities. And he was braggin' to us about going out to Vegas all the time. I bet that fuckin' safe is stuffed.'

'How about his family?' This sounded better; Koop would rather steal money than anything.

'He's divorced. Kids live with his old lady.'

'The key's good?'

'Yeah, but, uh . . . There's a security system on the door. I don't know nothing about that.'

Koop looked at the man for a minute, then nodded. 'I'll think about it.'

'I could use some cash, get out of this fuckin' place,' the guy said. 'My parole's up in September. Maybe go to Vegas myself.'

'I'll get back,' Koop said.

He finished his drink, picked up the notebook, nodded to the guy, and walked out. As he pulled out of the parking lot, he glanced at his watch. Sara should be getting off . . .

Koop had killed his mother.

He'd killed her with a long, slender switchblade he'd found in a pawnshop in Seoul, Korea, where he'd been with the Army. When he'd gotten back to the States, he'd spent a long weekend hitchhiking from Fort Polk to Hannibal, Missouri, for the sole purpose of ripping her.

And he'd done that. He'd banged on the door and she'd opened it, a Camel glued to her lip. She'd asked, 'What the fuck do you want?' and he'd said, 'This.' Then he'd stepped up into the trailer and she'd stepped back, and he'd stuck the knife in just about her belly button, and ripped up, right up through her breastbone. She'd opened her mouth to scream. Nothing came out but blood.

Koop had touched nothing, seen nobody. He'd grown up in Hannibal, just like Huck Finn, but he hadn't been any kind of Huck. He'd just been a dumb-shit kid who never knew his father, and whose mother gave blow jobs for money after she got off work at the bar. On a busy night she might have four or five drunks stop by, banging on the aluminum door, sucking them, spitting in the sink next to his bedroom, spitting and gargling salt-and-soda, half the night gone. She'd drag him downtown, respectable

74

eyes tearing at them, women in thigh-length skirts and tweedy jackets, pitying, disdaining. 'Bitches; bitches ain't no better'n me, you better believe it,' his mother said. But she was lying, and Koop knew *that* for sure. They *were* better than his mother, these women in their suits and hats and clack-clack high heels . . .

He'd been back at Fort Polk, sitting on his bunk reading *Black Belt* magazine, when the battalion sergeant-major came by. He'd said, 'Koop, I got some bad news. Your mother was found dead.'

And Koop had said, 'Yeah?' and turned the page.

When Koop had been in Korea, he'd learned from the hookers outside the base that he had a problem with sex. Nothing worked right. He'd get turned on thinking about it, but then the time would come . . . and nothing would happen.

Until, in his anger, he smacked one of the women. Hit her in the forehead with a fist, knocked her flat. Things started to work.

He'd killed a woman in New Orleans. He thought of the murder as an accident: he was pounding on her, getting worked up, and suddenly she wasn't fighting back, and her head was flopping a little too loosely. That'd scared him. They had the death penalty in Louisiana, and no qualms about using it. He'd run back to Fort Polk, and was astonished when nothing happened. Nothing. Not even a story in the newspaper, not that he could find.

That's when he'd gotten the idea about killing his mother. Nothing complicated. Just do it.

After the Army, he'd spent a year working on the Mississippi, a barge hand. He'd eventually gotten off in St Paul, drifted through a series of crappy jobs, finally got smart and used his veteran's preference for something a little better. A year after that, he'd picked up a woman at a

75

Minneapolis bookstore. He'd gone for a lifter's calendar and the woman had come to him. He'd recognized her immediately: she had the wool suit and the clack-clack high heels. She'd asked him something about exercise; he couldn't remember what, it'd obviously been a pickup . . .

He hadn't thought to take her off, but he had, and that had been better than pounding on hookers. There had been a quality to the woman, the nylons and the careful makeup, the well-rounded sentences. She was one of those women so distinctly better than his mother.

And they were everywhere. Some were too smart and tough to be taken. He stayed away from that kind. But there were also the tentative ones, awkward, afraid: not of death or pain or anything else so dramatic, but of simple loneliness. He found them in a Des Moines art gallery and in a Madison bookstore and a Thunder Bay record shop, a little older, drinking white wine, dressed carefully in cheerful colors, their hair done to hide the gray, their smiles constant, flitting, as though they were sparrows looking for a place to perch.

Koop gave them a place to perch. They were never so much wary as anxious to do the right thing . . .

Koop picked up Jensen when she left her office, escorted her to a Cub supermarket. Followed her inside, watching her move, her breasts shifting under her blouse, her legs, so well-muscled; the way she brushed the hair out of her eyes.

Her progress through the produce section was a sensual lesson in itself. Jensen prowled through it like a hunting cat, squeezing this, sniffing at those, poking at the others. She bought bing cherries and oranges and lemons, fat white mushrooms and celery, apples and English walnuts, grapes both green and red, and garlic. She made a brilliant salad.

Koop was in the cereals. He kept poking his head around the corner, looking at her. She never saw him, but he was so intent that he didn't see the stock kid until the kid was right on top of him.

'Can I help you?' The kid used a tone he might have used on a ten-year-old shoplifter.

Koop jumped. 'What?' He was flustered. He had a cart with a package of beef jerky and a jar of dill pickles.

'What're you looking for?' The kid had a junior-cop attitude; and he was burly, too-white, with pimples, crew cut, and small pig-eyes.

'I'm not looking. I'm thinking,' Koop said.

'Okay. Just asking,' the kid said. But when he moved away, he went only ten feet and began rearranging boxes of cornflakes, ostentatiously watching Koop.

Sara, at the very moment that the kid asked his first question, decided she'd gotten enough produce. A moment later, as the kid went to work in the cornflakes, she came around the corner. Koop turned away from her, but she glanced up at his face. Did he see the smallest of wrinkles? He turned his back and pushed his cart out of the aisle. The fact is, she might have seen him twenty times, if she'd ever scanned the third layer of people around her, if she'd noticed the guy on the bench on the next sidewalk over as she jogged. Had she remembered him? Was that why her forehead had wrinkled? The kid had seen him watching her. Would he say anything?

Koop thought about abandoning his cart, but decided that would be worse than hanging on. He pushed it to the express lane, bought a newspaper, paid, and went on to the parking lot. While he was waiting to pay, he saw the kid step out of an aisle, his fists on his hips, watching. A wave of hate washed over him. He'd get the little fucker, get him in the parking lot, rip his fucking face off ... Koop closed his eyes, controlling it, controlling himself. When he fantasized, the adrenaline started

77

rolling through his blood, and he almost *had* to break something.

But the kid just wasn't worth it. Asshole . . .

He left the supermarket parking lot, looking for the kid in his rearview mirror, but the kid had apparently gone back to work. Good enough – but he wouldn't be going back there. Out of the lot, he pulled into a street-side parking space and waited. Twenty minutes later, Jensen came by.

His true love . . .

Koop loved to watch her when she was moving. He loved her on the streets, where he could see her legs and ass, liked to see her body contorting as she leaned or bent or stooped; liked to watch her tits bobbling when she went for a run around the lake. Really liked that.

He was aflame.

Monday was a warm night, moths batting against the park lights. Jensen finished her run and disappeared inside. Koop was stricken with what might have been grief, to see her go like that. He stood outside, watching the door. Would she be back out? His eyes rolled up the building. He knew her window, had known from the first night . . . The light came on.

He sighed and turned away. Across the street, a man fumbled for keys, opened the lobby door to his apartment building, walked through, then used his key to unlock the inner door. Koop's eyes drifted upward. The top floor was just about even with Jensen's.

With a growing tingle of excitement, he counted floors. And crashed. The roof would be below her window, he thought. He wouldn't be able to see inside. But it was worth checking. He crossed the street, moving quickly, stepped into the apartment lobby. Two hundred apartments, each with a call button. He slapped a hundred of them: somebody would be expecting a visitor. The intercom scratched at him, but at the same moment the door lock buzzed, and he pushed through, leaving behind the voice on the intercom: 'Who's there? Who's there?'

This would work twice, but he couldn't count on it more often than that. He turned the corner to the elevators, rode to the top. Nobody in the hall. The Exit sign was far down to the left. He walked down to the Exit sign, opened the door, stepped through it. A flight of steps went down to the left, and two more went up to the right, to a gray metal door. A small black-and-white sign on the door said, 'Roof Access – Room Key Necessary to Unlock and to Re-enter.'

'Shit.' He pulled at the door. Nothing. Good lock.

He turned to the steps, thinking to start back down. Then thought: *Wait.* Did the window at the end of the hall look out at Jensen's building?

It did.

Koop stood in the window, looking up, and a bare two stories above, Sara Jensen came to the window in a robe and looked down. Koop stepped back, but she was looking at the street and hadn't noticed him in the semidark window. She had a drink in her hand. She took a sip and stepped away, out of sight.

Jesus. A little higher, and he'd be virtually in her living room. She never pulled the drapes. Never . . .

Koop was aflame. A match; a killer.

He needed a key. Not sometime. He needed one now.

He'd picked up his philosophy at Stillwater: power comes out of the barrel of a gun; or from a club, or a fist. Take care of number one. The tough live, the weak die. When you die, you go into a hole: end of story. No harps, no heavenly choir. No hellfire. Koop resonated with this line of thought. It fit so well with everything he'd experienced in life.

He went back to his truck for equipment, not thinking very much, not on the surface. When he needed something

– anything – that thing became his: the people who had it were keeping it from him. He had the *right* to take it.

Koop was proud of his truck. It might have belonged to anyone. But it didn't. It belonged to him, and it was special.

He didn't carry much in the back, in the topper: a toolbox, a couple of bags of Salt 'N Sand left over from winter, a spade, a set of snow tires, a tow rope that had been in the truck when he bought it. And a few lengths of rusty concrete reinforcement rod – the kind of thing you might find lying in the dirt around a construction site, which was, in fact, where he had found it. The kind of thing a workingman would have back there.

Most of the stuff was simply a disguise for the big Sears toolbox. That's where the action was. The top tray contained a few light screwdrivers, pliers, a ratchet set, a half-dozen Sucrets cans full of a variety of wood screws, and other small items. The bottom compartment held a two-pound hammer, a cold chisel, two files, a hacksaw, a short pry-bar, a pair of work gloves, and a can of glazier's putty. What looked like an ordinary toolbox was, in fact, a decent set of burglary tools.

He put the gloves in his jacket pocket, took out the glazier's putty, dumped the screws from one of the Sucrets cans into an empty compartment in the top tray, and scooped a gob of putty into the Sucrets tin. He smoothed the putty with his thumb, closed the tin, and dropped it into his pocket.

Then he selected a piece of re-rod. A nice eighteen-inch length, easy to hide and long enough to swing.

He still wasn't thinking much: the room key was his. This asshole – some asshole – was keeping it from him. *That* made him angry. Really angry. Righteously angry. Koop began to fume, thinking about – *his fuckin' key* – and headed back to the apartment building, driving the truck.

He parked half a block away, walked down to the apartment entrance, pulling on the work gloves, the re-rod up his jacket sleeve. Nobody around. He stepped into the lobby, pushed up the glass panel on the inset ceiling light, and used the re-rod to crack both fluorescent tubes. Now in the dark, he dropped the panel back in place and returned to the truck. He left the driver's-side door open an inch and waited.

And waited some more. Not much happening.

The passenger seat was what made the truck special. He'd gotten some work done in an Iowa machine shop: a steel box, slightly shallower but a bit longer and wider than a cigar box, had been welded under the seat. The original floor was the lid of the box, and from below, the bottom of the box looked like the floor of the passenger compartment. To open the box, you turned the right front seat support once to the right, and the lid popped up. There was enough room for any amount of jewelry or cash . . . Or cocaine.

Half the people in Stillwater were there because they'd been caught in a traffic stop and had the cocaine/stolen stereo/gun on the backseat. Not Koop.

He watched the door for a while longer, then popped the lid on the box, pulled out the eight-ball, pinched it, put it back. Just a little nose, just enough to sharpen him up.

Two mature arborvitae stood on either side of the apartment's concrete stoop, like sentinels. Koop liked that: the trees cut the vision lines from either side. To see into the outer lobby, you had to be standing almost straight out from the building.

A couple came down the walk, the man jingling his keys. They went inside, and Koop waited. A woman was next, alone, and Koop perked up. But she was walking straight down the sidewalk, distracted, and not until the last minute did she swerve in toward the building. She would have been perfect, but she hadn't given him time to move. She disappeared inside.

81

Two men, holding hands, came down the walk. No. Two or three minutes later, they were followed by a guy so big that Koop decided not to risk it.

Then Jim Flory turned the corner, his keys already in his hand. Flory scratched himself at his left sideburn and mumbled something, talking to himself, distracted. He was five-ten and slender. Koop pushed open the car door and slipped out, started down the sidewalk. Flory turned in at the building, took his keys out of his pocket, fumbled through them, pulled open the outer door, went inside.

Koop was angry: he could feel the heat in his bowels. *Fucker has my key. Fucker* . . .

Koop followed Flory up the walk; Koop was whistling softly, an unconscious, disguising tactic, but he was pissed. *Has my key.* . . Koop was wearing a baseball cap, jeans, a golf shirt, and large white athletic shoes, like a guy just back from a Twins game. He kept the hat bill tipped down. The steel re-rod was in his right pocket, sticking out a full foot but hidden by his naturally swinging arm.

Goddamned asshole, got my key. . . *Zip-a-dee-doo-dah,* he whistled, *Zip-a-dee-ay,* and he was getting angrier by the second. *My key* . . .

Through the glass outer door, he could see Flory fumbling in the dark at the inner lock. Key must be in his hand. Koop pulled open the outer door, and Flory, turning the key on the inner door, glanced back and said, 'Hi.'

Koop nodded and said, 'Hey,' kept the bill of his hat down. Flory turned back to the door and pulled on it, and as he did, Koop, the cocaine right there, slipped the re-rod out of his pocket.

Flory might have felt something, sensed the suddenness of the movement: he stopped with the key, his head coming up, but too late.

Motherfucker has my key/key/key . . .

Koop slashed him with the re-rod, smashed him behind

the ear. The re-rod hit, *pak!*, metal on meat, the sound of a butcher's cleaver cutting through a rib roast.

Flory's mouth opened and a single syllable came out: 'Unk.' His head bounced off the glass door and he fell, dragging his hands down the glass.

Koop, moving fast now, nothing casual now, bent, glancing ferretlike outside, then stripped Flory of his wallet: *a robbery.* He stashed the wallet in his pocket, pulled Flory's key from the lock, opened the Sucrets tin, and quickly pressed one side and then the other into the glazier's putty. The putty was just firm, and took perfect impressions. He shut the tin, wiped the key on his pants leg, and pushed it back into the lock.

Done.

He turned, still half crouching, reached for the outer door – and saw the legs.

A woman stumbled on the other side of the door, trying to backpedal, already turning.

She wore tennis shoes and a jogging suit. He'd never seen her coming. He exploded through the door, batting the glass out of his way with one hand, the other pulling the re-rod from his pocket.

'No.' She shouted it. Her face was frozen, mouth open. In the dim light, she could see the body on the floor behind him, and she was stumbling back, trying to make her legs move, to run, shocked . . .

Koop hit her like a leopard, already swinging the re-rod.

'No,' she screamed again, eyes widening, teeth flashing in fear. She put up her arm and the re-rod crashed through it, breaking it, missing her head. 'No,' she screamed again, turning, and Koop, above her and coming down, hit her on the back of the neck just where it joined her skull, a blow that would have decapitated her if he'd been swinging a sword.

Blood spattered the sidewalk and she went down to the stoop, and Koop hit her again, this time across the top of her undefended skull, a full, merciless swing, ending with a *crunch*, like a heavy man stepping on gravel.

Her head flattened, and Koop, maddened by the interference, by the trouble, by the crisis, kicked her body off the step behind the arborvitae.

'Motherfucker,' he said. 'Motherfucker.' He hadn't intended this. He had to *move*.

Less than a minute had passed since he'd hit Flory. No one else was on the walk. He looked across the street, for motion in the windows of Sara Jensen's apartment building, for a face looking down at him. Nothing that he could see.

He started away at a fast walk, sticking the re-rod in his pocket. Jesus, what was this: there was blood on his jacket. He wiped at it with a hand, smeared it. If a cop came . . .

The anger boiled up: the goddamned bitch, coming up like that.

He swallowed it, fighting it, kept moving. *Gotta keep moving.* . . He glanced back, crossed the street, almost scurrying, now with the smell of warm human blood in his nose, in his mouth. Didn't mind that, but not here, not now . . .

Maybe, he thought, he should walk out. He was tempted to walk out and return later for the company car: if somebody saw him hit the woman and followed him to the car, they'd see the badge on the side and that'd be it. On the other hand, the cops would probably be taking the license numbers of cars in the neighborhood, looking for witnesses.

No. He would take it.

He popped the driver's-side door, caught a glimpse of himself in the dark glass, face twisted under the ball cap, dark scratches across it.

He fired up the truck and wiped his face at the same time: more blood on his gloves. Christ, it was all over him. He could taste it, it was in his mouth . . .

He eased out of the parking space. Watched in the rear-view mirror for somebody running, somebody pointing. He saw nothing but empty street.

Nothing.

The stress tightened him. He could feel the muscles pumping, his body filling out. Taste the blood . . . And suddenly, there was a flush of pleasure with a rash of pain, like being hand-stroked while ants crawled across you . . .

More good than bad. Much more.

6

Weather wasn't home. Lucas suppressed a thump of worry: she should have been home an hour earlier. He picked up the phone, but there was nothing on voice mail, and he hung up.

He walked back to the bedroom, pulling off his tie. The bedroom smelled almost subliminally of her Chanel No. 5; and on top of that, very faintly of wood polish. She'd bought a new bedroom set, simple wooden furniture with an elegant line, slightly Craftsman-Mission. He grumbled. His old stuff was good enough, he'd had it for years. She didn't want to hear it.

'You've got a twenty-year-old queen-sized bed that looks like it's been pounded to death by strange women – I won't ask – and you don't have a headboard, so the bed just sits there like a launching pad. Don't you read in bed? Don't you know about headboard lights? Wouldn't you like some nice pillows?'

Maybe, if somebody else bought them.

And his old dresser, she said, looked like it had come from the Salvation Army.

He didn't tell her, but she was precisely correct.

She said nothing at all about his chair. His chair was older than the bed, bought at a rummage sale after a St Thomas professor had died and left it behind. It was massive, comfortable, and the leather was fake. She did throw out a mostly unused second chair with a stain on one arm – Lucas couldn't remember what it was, but it got there during a Vikings–Packers game – and replaced it with a comfortable love seat.

'If we're going to watch television in our old age, we should sit next to each other,' she said. 'The first goddamn thing men do when they get a television is put two E-Z Boys in front of it and a table between them for beer cans and pizzas. I swear to God I won't allow it.'

'Yeah, yeah, just don't fuck with my chair,' Lucas had said. He'd said it lightly, but he was worried.

She understood that. 'The chair's safe. Ugly, but safe.'

'Ugly? That's genuine glove . . . material.'

'Really? They make gloves out of garbage bags?'

Weather Harkinnen was a surgeon. She was a small woman in her late thirties, her blondish hair beginning to show streaks of white. She had dark-blue eyes, high cheekbones, and a wide mouth. She looked vaguely Russian, Lucas thought. She had broad shoulders for her size, and wiry muscles; she played a vicious game of squash and could sail anything. He liked to watch her move, he liked to watch her in repose, when she was working over a problem. He even liked to watch her when she slept, because she did it so thoroughly, like a kitten.

When Lucas thought of her, which he might do at any moment, the same image always popped up in his mind's eye: Weather turning to look at him over her shoulder, smiling, a simple pearl dangling just over her shoulder.

They would be married, he thought. She'd said, 'Don't ask yet.'

'Why? Would you say no?'

She'd poked him in the navel with her forefinger. 'No. I'd say yes. But don't ask yet. Wait a while.'

'Until when?'

'You'll know.'

So he hadn't asked; and somewhere, deep inside, he was afraid, he was relieved. Did he want out? He'd never experienced this closeness. It was different. It could be . . . frightening.

Lucas was down to his underpants when the phone rang in the kitchen. He picked up the silent bedroom extension and said, 'Yeah?'

'Chief Davenport?' Connell. She sounded tight.

'Meagan, you can start calling me Lucas,' he said.

'Okay. I just wanted to say, uh, don't throw away your files. On the case.' There was an odd thumping sound behind her. He'd heard it before, but he couldn't place it.

'What?'

'I said, don't throw away your files.'

'Meagan, what're you talking about?'

'I'll see you tomorrow. Okay?'

'Meagan . . . ?' But she was gone.

Lucas looked at the telephone, frowned, shook his head, and hung it up. He dug through the new dresser, got running shorts, picked up a sleeveless sweatshirt that he'd thrown on top of a hamper, pulled it on, and stopped with one arm through a sleeve. The thumping sound he'd heard behind Connell – keyboards. Wherever she was, there were three or four people keyboarding a few feet away. Could be her office, though it was late.

Could be a newspaper.

Could be a television station.

His line of thought was broken by the sound of the garage door going up. Weather. A small rock rolled off his chest. He pulled the sweatshirt over his head, picked up his socks and running shoes, and walked barefoot back through the house.

'Hey.' She'd stopped in the kitchen, was taking a Sprite out of the refrigerator. He kissed her on the cheek. 'Do anything good?'

'I watched Harrison and MacRinney do a free flap on a

kid with Bell's palsy,' she said, popping the top on the can.

'Interesting?' She put her purse on the kitchen counter and turned her face up to him: her face was a little lop-sided, as though she'd had a ring career before turning to medicine. He loved the face; he could remember reacting the first time he'd talked with her, in a horror of a burned-out murder scene in northern Wisconsin: she wasn't very pretty, he'd thought, but she was *very* attractive. And a little while later, she'd cut his throat with a jackknife . . .

Now she nodded. 'Couldn't see some of the critical stuff — mostly clearing away a lot of fat, which is pretty picky. They had a double operating microscope, so I could watch Harrison work part of the time. He put five square knots around the edge of an artery that wasn't a heck of a lot bigger than a broom straw.'

'Could you do that?'

'Maybe,' she said, her voice serious. He'd learned about surgeons and their competitive instincts. He knew how to push her buttons. 'Eventually, but . . . You're pushing my buttons.'

'Maybe.'

She stopped, stood back and looked at him, picking something up from his voice. 'Did something happen?'

He shrugged. 'I had a fairly interesting case for about fifteen minutes this afternoon. It's gone now, but . . . I don't know.'

'Interesting?' She worried.

'Yeah, there's a woman from the BCA who thinks we've got a serial killer around. She's a little crazy, but she might be right.'

Now she was worried. She stepped back toward him. 'I don't want you to get hurt again, messing with some maniac.'

'It's over, I think. We're off the case.'

'Off?'

Lucas explained, including the strange call from Connell.

Weather listened intently, finishing the Sprite. 'You think she's up to something,' she said when he finished.

'It sounded like it. I hope she doesn't get burned. C'mon. Let's run.'

'Can we go down to Grand and get ice cream afterwards?'

'We'll have to do four miles.'

'God, you're hard.'

After dark, after the run and the ice cream, Weather began reviewing notes for the next morning's operation. Lucas was amazed by how often she operated. His knowledge of surgery came from television, where every operation was a crisis, undertaken only with great study and some peril. With Weather, it was routine. She operated almost every day, and some days, two or three times. 'You've got to do it a lot, if you're going to do it at all,' she said. She'd be in bed by ten and up by five-thirty.

Lucas did business for a while, then prowled the house, finally went down the basement for a small off-duty gun, clipped it under his waistband and pulled his golf shirt over it. 'I'm going out for a while,' he said.

Weather looked up from the bed. 'I thought the case was over.'

'Ehh. I'm looking for a guy.'

'So take it easy,' she said. She had a yellow pencil clenched between her teeth, and spoke around it; she looked cute, but he picked up the tiny spark of fear in her eyes.

He grinned and said, 'No sweat. I'll tell you straight out when there might be a problem.'

'Sure.'

Lucas's house was on the east bank of the Mississippi, in a quiet neighborhood of tall dying elms and a few oaks, with the new maples and ginkgoes and ash trees replacing the disappearing elm. At night, the streets were alive with middle-class joggers working off the office flab, and couples strolling hand in hand along the dimly lit walkways. When Lucas stopped in the street to shift gears, he heard a woman laugh somewhere not too far away; he almost went back inside to Weather.

Instead, he headed to the Randolph Lake Bridge, crossed the Mississippi, and a mile farther on was deep into the Lake Street strip. He cruised the cocktail lounges, porno stores, junk shops, rental-furniture places, check-cashing joints, and low-end fast-food franchises that ran through a brutally ugly landscape of cheap lighted signs. Children wandered around at all times of day and night, mixing with the suburban coke-seekers, dealers, drunks, raggedy-hip insurance salesmen, and a few lost souls from St Paul, desperately seeking the shortcut home. A pair of cops pulled up alongside the Porsche at a stoplight and looked him over, thinking *Dope dealer.* He rolled down his window and the driver grinned and said something, and the passenger-side cop rolled down his window and said, 'Davenport?'

'Yeah.'

'Great car, man.'

The driver called across his partner, 'Hey, dude, you got a little rock? I could use a taste, mon.'

Franklin Avenue was as rugged as Lake Street, but darker. Lucas pulled a slip of paper from his pocket, turned on a reading light, checked the address he had for Junky Doog, and went looking for it. Half the buildings were missing their numbers. When he found the right place, there was a light in the window and a half-dozen people sitting on the porch outside.

Lucas parked, climbed out, and the talk on the porch stopped. He walked halfway up the broken front sidewalk and stopped. 'There a guy named Junky Doog who lives here?'

A heavyset Indian woman heaved herself out of a lawn chair. 'Not now. All my family live here now.'

'Do you know him?'

'No, I don't, Mr Police.' She was polite. 'We've been here almost four months and never heard the name.'

Lucas nodded. 'Okay.' He believed her.

Lucas started crawling bars, talking to bartenders and customers. He'd lost time on the street, and the players had changed. Here and there, somebody picked him out, said his name, held up a hand: the faces and names came back, but the information was sparse.

He started back home, saw the Blue Bull on a side street, and decided to make a last stop.

A half-dozen cars were parked at odd attitudes around the bar's tiny parking lot, as though they'd been abandoned to avoid a bombing run. The Blue Bull's windows were tinted, so that patrons could see who was coming in from the lot without being seen themselves. Lucas left the Porsche at a fire hydrant on the street, sniffed the night air – creosote and tar – and went inside.

The Blue Bull could sell cheap drinks, the owner said, because he avoided high overhead. He avoided it by never fixing anything. The pool table had grooves that would roll a ball though a thirty-degree arc into a corner pocket. The overhead fans hadn't moved since the sixties. The jukebox had broken halfway through a Guy Lombardo record, and hadn't moved since.

Nor did the decor change: red-flocked whorehouse wallpaper with a patina of beer and tobacco smoke. The obese bartender, however, was new. Lucas dropped on a stool and the bartender wiped his way over. 'Yeah?'

'Carl Stupella still work here?' Lucas asked.

The bartender coughed before answering, turning his head away, not bothering to cover his mouth. Spit flew down the bar. 'Carl's dead,' he said, recovering.

'Dead?'

'Yeah. Choked on a bratwurst at a Twins game.'

'You gotta be kidding me.'

The bartender shrugged, started a smile, thought better of it, and shrugged again. Coughed. 'His time was up,' he said piously, running his rag in a circle. 'You a friend of his?'

'Jesus Christ, no. I'm looking for another guy. Carl knew him.'

'Carl *was* an asshole,' the bartender said philosophically. He leaned one elbow on the bar. 'You a cop?'

'Yup.'

The bartender looked around. There were seven other people in the bar, five sitting alone, looking at nothing at all, the other two with their heads hunched together so they could whisper. 'Who're you looking for?'

'Randolph Leski? He used to hang out here.'

The bartender's eye shifted down the bar, then back to Lucas. He leaned forward, dropping his voice. 'Does this shit bring in money?'

'Sometimes. You get on the list . . .'

'Randy's about eight stools down,' he muttered. 'On the other side of the next two guys.'

Lucas nodded, and a moment later, leaned back a few inches and glanced to his right. Looking at the bartender again, he said quietly, 'The guy I'm looking for is big as you.'

'You mean fat,' the bartender said.

'Hefty.'

The bartender tilted his head. 'Randy had a tumor. They took out most of his gut. He can't keep the weight on no more. They say he eats a pork chop, he shits sausages. They don't digest.'

Lucas looked down the bar again, said, 'Give me a draw, whatever.'

The bartender nodded, stepped away. Lucas took a

business card out of his pocket, rolled out a twenty and the business card. 'Thanks. What's your name?'

'Earl. Stupella.'

'Carl's . . .'

'Brother.'

'Maybe you hear something serious sometime, you call me,' Lucas said. 'Keep the change.'

Lucas picked up the glass of beer and wandered down the bar. Stopped, did a double take. The thin man on the stool turned his head: loose skin hung around his face and neck like a basset hound's, but Randy Leski's mean little pig-eyes peered out of it.

'Randy,' Lucas said. 'As I live and breathe.'

Leski shook his head once, as though annoyed by a fly in a kitchen. Leski ran repair scams, specializing in the elderly. Lucas had made him a hobby. 'Go away. Please.'

'Jesus. Old friends,' Lucas said, spreading his arms. The other talk in the bar died. 'You're looking great, man. You been on a diet?'

'Kiss my ass, Davenport. Whatever you want, I don't got it.'

'I'm looking for Junky Doog.'

Leski sat a little straighter. 'Junky? He cut on somebody?'

'I just need to talk to him.'

Leski suddenly giggled. 'Christ, old Junky.' He made a gesture as if wiping a tear away from his eyes. 'I tell you, the last I heard of him, he was working out at a landfill in Dakota County.'

'Landfill?'

'Yeah. The dump. I don't know which one, I just hear this from some guys. Christ, born in a junkyard, the guy gets sent to the nuthouse. When they kick him out of there, he winds up in a dump. Some people got all the luck, huh?' Leski started laughing, great phlegm-sucking wheezes.

Lucas looked at him for a while, waiting for the wheezing to subside, then nodded.

Leski said, 'I hear you're back.'

'Yeah.'

Leski took a sip of his beer, grimaced, looked down at it, and said, 'I heard when you got shot last winter. First time I been in a Catholic church since we were kids.'

'A church?'

'I was praying my ass off that you'd fuckin' croak,' Leski said. 'After a lot of pain.'

'Thanks for thinking of me,' Lucas said. 'You still run deals on old people?'

'Go hump yourself.'

'You're a breath of fresh air, Randy . . . Hey.' Leski's old sport coat had an odd crinkle, a lump. Lucas touched his side. 'Are you carrying?'

'C'mon, leave me alone, Davenport.'

Randy Leski never carried: it was like an article of his religion. 'What the hell happened?'

Leski was a felon. Carrying could put him inside. He looked down at his beer. 'You seen my neighborhood?'

'Not lately.'

'Bad news. Bad news, Davenport. Glad my mother didn't live to see it. These kids, Davenport, they'll kill you for bumping into them,' Leski said, tilting his head sideways to look at Lucas. His eyes were the color of water. 'I swear to God, I was in Pansy's the other night, and this asshole kid starts giving some shit to this girl, and her boyfriend stands up – Bill McGuane's boy – and says to her, "C'mon, let's go." And they go. And I sees Bill, and I mention it, and he says, "I told that kid, don't fight, ever. He's no chickenshit, but it's worth your life to fight." And he's right, Davenport. You can't walk down the street without

95

worrying that somebody's gonna knock you in the head. For nothin'. For not a fuckin' thing. It used to be, if somebody was looking for you, they had a reason you could understand. Now? For nothing.'

'Well, take it easy with the piece, huh?'

'Yeah.' Leski turned back to the bar and Lucas stepped away and turned. Then Leski suddenly giggled, his flaps of facial flesh trembling with the effort, and said, 'Junky Doog.' And giggled some more.

Outside, Lucas looked around, couldn't think of anything else to do. Far away, he could hear sirens – lots of them. Something going on, but he didn't know where. He thought about calling in, finding out where the action was; but that many sirens, it was probably a fire or an auto accident. He sighed, a little tired now, and headed back to the car.

Weather was asleep. She'd be up at six, moving quietly not to wake him; by seven, she'd be in the OR; Lucas would sleep for three hours after that. Now, he undressed in the main bath down the hall from the bedroom, took a quick shower to get the bar smoke off his skin, and then slipped in beside her. He let himself roll against her, her leg smooth against his. Weather slept in an old-fashioned man's T-shirt and bikini pants, which left something – not much – to the imagination.

He lay on his back and got a quick mental snapshot of her in the shirt and underpants, bouncing around the bedroom. Sometimes, when she wasn't operating the next morning, he'd get the same snapshot, couldn't escape it, and his hand would creep up under the T-shirt . . .

Not tonight. Too late. He turned his head, kissed her goodnight. He should always do that, she'd told him: her subconscious would know.

*   *   *

What seemed like a long time later, Lucas felt her hand on him and opened his eyes. The room was dimly lit, daylight filtering around the curtains. Weather, sitting fully dressed on the bed beside him, gave him another tantalizing twitch. 'It's nice that men have handles,' she said. 'It makes them easy to wake up.'

'Huh?' He was barely conscious.

'You better come out and look at the TV,' she said, letting go of him. 'The *Openers* program is talking about you.'

'Me?' He struggled to sit up.

'What's that quaint phrase you police officers use? "The fuckin' shit has hit the fan?" I think that's it.'

7

Anderson was waiting in the corridor outside Lucas's office, reading through a handful of computer printouts. He pushed away from the wall when he saw Lucas.

'Chief wants to see us *now*.'

'I know, I got a call. I saw TV3,' Lucas said.

'Paper for you,' Anderson said, handing Lucas a manila file. 'The overnights on Wannemaker. Nothing in the galleries. The Camel's confirmed, the tobacco on her body matched the tobacco in the cigarette. There were ligature marks on her wrists, but no ties; her ankles were tied with a piece of yellow polypropylene rope. The rope was old, partially degraded by exposure to sunlight, so if we can find any more of it, they could probably make a match.'

'Anything else? Any skin, semen, anything?'

'Not so far . . . And here's the Bey file.'

'Jesus.' Lucas took the file, flipped it open. Most of the paper inside had been Xeroxed for Connell's report; a few minor things he hadn't seen before. Mercedes Bey, thirty-seven, killed in 1984, file still open. The first of Connell's list, the centerpiece of the TV3 story.

'Have you heard about the lakes?' Anderson asked, his voice pitching lower, as though he were about to tell a particularly dirty joke.

'What happened?' Lucas looked up from the Bey file.

'We've got a bad one over by the lakes. Too late to make morning TV. Guy and his girlfriend, maybe his girlfriend. Guy's in a coma, could be a veggie. The woman's dead. Her head was crushed, probably by a pipe or a steel bar. Or a rifle barrel or a long-barreled pistol, maybe a Redhawk.

Small-time robbery, looks like. Really ugly. *Really* ugly.'

'They're freaking out in homicide?'

'Everybody's freaking out,' Anderson said. 'Everybody went over there. Roux just got back. And then this TV3 thing – the chief is hot. Really hot.'

Roux was furious. She jabbed her cigarette at Lucas. 'Tell me you didn't have anything to do with it.'

Lucas shrugged, looked at the others, and sat down. 'I didn't have anything to do with it.'

Roux nodded, took a long drag on her cigarette; her office smelled like a bowling alley on league night. Lester sat in a corner with his legs crossed, unhappy. Anderson perched on a chair, peering owlishly at Roux through his thick-lensed glasses. 'I didn't think so,' Roux said. 'But we all know who did.'

'Mmm.' Lucas didn't want to say it.

'Don't want to say it?' Roux asked. 'I'll say it. That fuckin' Connell.'

'Twelve minutes,' Anderson said. 'Longest story TV3's ever run. They *must* have had Connell's file. They had every name and date nailed down. They dug up some file video on the Mercedes Bey killing. They used stuff they'd have never used back then, when they made it. And the stuff on Wannemaker, Jesus Christ, they had video of the body being hoisted out of the dumpster, no bag, no nothing, just this big fuckin' lump of guts with a face hanging off it.'

'Shot it from the bridge,' Lucas said. 'We saw them up there. I didn't know the lenses were that good, though.'

'Bey's still an open file, of course,' Lester said, recrossing his legs from one side to the other. 'No statute of limitations on murder.'

'Should have thought of that yesterday,' Roux said, getting up to pace the carpet, flicking ashes with every other step. Her hair, never particularly chic, was standing up in spots, like small horns. 'They had Bey's mother on. She's this fragile old lady in a nursing-home housecoat, a face like parchment. She said we abandoned her daughter to her killers. She looked like shit, she looked like she was dying. They must've dumped her out of bed at three in the morning to get the tape.'

'That video of Connell was pretty weird, if she's the one who tipped them,' Anderson suggested.

'Aw, they phonied it up,' Roux said, waving her cigarette hand dismissively. 'I did the same goddamned thing when I was sourcing off the appropriations committee. They take you out on the street and have you walk into some building so it looks like surveillance film or file stuff. She did it, all right.' Roux looked at Davenport. 'I've got the press ten minutes from now.'

'Good luck.' He smiled, a very thin, unpleasant smile.

'You were never taken off the case, right?' Her left eyebrow went up and down.

'Of course not,' Lucas said. 'Their source was misinformed. I spent the evening working the case and even developed a lead on a new suspect.'

'Is that right?' The eyebrow again.

'More or less,' Lucas said. 'Junky Doog may be working at a landfill out in Dakota County.'

'Huh. I'd call that a critical development,' Roux said, showing an inch of satisfaction. 'If you can bring him in today, I'll personally feed it directly and exclusively to the *Strib*. And anything else you get. Fuck TV3.'

'If Connell's their source, they'll know you're lying about not calling off the case,' Lester said.

'Yeah? So what?' Roux said. 'What're they gonna do, argue? Reveal their source? Fuck 'em.'

'Is Connell still working with me?' Lucas asked.

'We've got no choice,' Roux snapped. 'If we didn't call off the investigation, then she must still be on it, right? I'll take care of her later.'

'She's got no later,' Lucas said.

'Jesus,' Roux said, stopping in midpace. 'Jesus, I wish you hadn't said that.'

The TV3 story had been a mélange of file video, with commentary by a stunning blond reporter with a distinctly erotic overbite. The reporter, street-dressed in expensive grunge, rapped out long, intense accusations based on Connell's file; behind her, floodlit in the best Addams Family style, was the redbrick slum building where Mercedes Bey had been found slashed to death. She recounted Bey's and each of the subsequent murders, reading details from the autopsy reports. She said, 'With Chief Roux's controversial decision to sweep the investigation under the rug . . .' and 'With the Minneapolis police abandoning the murder investigation for what appear to be political reasons . . .' and 'Will Mercedes Bey's cry for justice be crushed by the Minneapolis Police Department's logrolling? Will other innocent Minneapolis-area women be forced to pay the killer's brutal toll because of this decision? We shall have to wait and see . . .'

'Nobody fucks with me like this,' Roux was shouting at her press aide when Lucas left her office with Anderson. 'Nobody fucks with me . . .'

Anderson grinned at Lucas and said, 'Connell does.'

Greave caught Lucas in the hall. 'I read the file, but it was a waste of time. I could have gotten the executive summary on TV this morning.' He was wearing a loose lavender suit with a blue silk tie.

'Yeah,' Lucas grunted. He unlocked his office door and Greave followed him inside. Lucas checked his phone for voice mail, found a message, and poked in the retrieval code. Meagan Connell's voice, humble: 'I saw the stories on TV this morning. Does this change anything?' Lucas

101

grinned at the impertinence, and scribbled down the number she left.

'What're we doing?' Greave asked.

'Gonna see if we can find a guy down in Dakota County. Former sex psycho who liked knives.' He'd been punching in Connell's number as he spoke. The phone rang once, and Connell picked up. 'This is Davenport.'

'Jeez,' Connell said, 'I've been watching TV . . .'

'Yeah, yeah. There're three guys in town don't know who the source is, and none of them are Roux. You better lay low today. She's smokin'. In the meantime, we're back on the case.'

'Back on.' She made it a statement, with an overtone of satisfaction. No denials. 'Is there anything new?'

He told her about Anderson's information from the Wisconsin forensic lab.

'Ligatures? If he tied her up, he must've taken her somewhere. That's a first. I bet he took her to his home. He lives here – he didn't at the other crime scenes, so he couldn't take them . . . Hey, and if you read the Mercedes Bey file, I think she was missing awhile, too, before they found her.'

'Could be something,' Lucas agreed. 'Greave and I are going after Junky Doog. I've got a line on him.'

'I'd like to go.'

'No. I don't want you around today,' Lucas said. 'It's best, believe me.'

'How about if I make some calls?' she asked.

'To who?'

'The people on the bookstore list.'

'St Paul should be doing that,' Lucas said.

'Not yet, they aren't. I'll get going right now.'

'Talk to Lester first,' Lucas said. 'Get them to clear it with St Paul. That part of the investigation really does belong to them.'

* * *

'Are you gonna listen to my story?' Greave asked as they walked out to the Porsche.

'Do I gotta?'

'Unless you want to listen to me whine for a couple hours.'

'Talk,' Lucas said.

A schoolteacher named Charmagne Carter had been found dead in her bed, Greave said. Her apartment was locked from the inside. The apartment was covered by a security system that used motion and infrared detectors with direct dial-out to an alarm-monitoring company.

'Completely locked?'

'Sealed tight.'

'Why do you think she was murdered?'

'Her death was very convenient for some bad people.'

'Say a name.'

'The Joyce brothers, John and George,' Greave said. 'Know them?'

Lucas smiled. 'Excellent,' he said.

'What?'

'I played hockey against them when I was a kid,' he said. 'They were assholes then, they're assholes now.'

The Joyces had almost been rich, Greave said. They'd started by leasing slum housing from the owners – mostly defense attorneys, it seemed – and renting out the apartments. When they'd accumulated enough cash, they bought a couple of flophouses. When housing the homeless became fashionable, they brought the flops up to minimum standards and unloaded them on a charitable foundation.

'The foundation director came into a large BMW shortly thereafter,' Greave said.

'Skipped his lunches and saved the money,' Lucas said.

'No doubt,' Greave said. 'So the Joyces took the money and started pyramiding apartments. I'm told they

103

controlled like five to six million bucks at one point. Then the economy fell on its ass. Especially apartments.'

'Aww.'

'Anyway, the Joyces saved what they could from the pyramid, and put every buck into this old apartment building on the Southeast Side. Forty units. Wide hallways.'

'Wide hallways?'

'Yeah. Wide. The idea was, they'd throw in some new dry-wall and a bunch of spackling compound and paint, cut down the cupboards, stick in some new low-rider stoves and refrigerators, and sell the place to the city as public housing for the handicapped. They had somebody juiced: the city council was hot to go. The Joyces figured to turn a million and a half on the deal. But there was a fly in the ointment.'

The teacher, Charmagne Carter, and a dozen other older tenants had been given long-term leases on their apartments by the last manager of the building before the Joyces bought it, Greave said. The manager knew he'd lose his job in the sale, and apparently made the leases as a quirky kind of revenge. The city wouldn't take the building with the long-term leases in effect. The Joyces bought out a few of the leases, and sued the people who wouldn't sell. The district court upheld the leases.

'The leases are $500 a month for fifteen years plus a two-percent rent increase per year, and that's that. They're great apartments for the price, and the price doesn't even keep up with inflation,' Greave said. 'That's why these people didn't want to leave. But they might've anyway, because the Joyces gave them a lot of shit. But this old lady wasn't intimidated, and she held them all together. Then she turned up dead.'

'Ah.'

'Last week, she doesn't make it to school,' Greave continued. 'The principal calls, no answer. A cop goes by for a look, can't get the door open – it's locked from the inside and there's no answer on the phone. They finally take the door down, the alarms go off, and there she is, dead in her bed. George Joyce is dabbing the tears out of his eyes and looking like the cat that ate the canary. We figured they killed her.'

'Autopsy?'

'Yup. Not a mark on her. The toxicology reports showed just enough sedative for a couple of sleeping pills, which she had a prescription for. There was a beer bottle and a glass on her nightstand, but she'd apparently metabolized the alcohol because there wasn't any in her blood. Her daughter said she had long-term insomnia, and she'd wash down a couple of sleeping pills with a beer, read until she got sleepy, and then take a leak and go to bed. And that's exactly what it looks like she did. The docs say her heart stopped. Period. End of story.'

Lucas shrugged. 'It happens.'

'No history of heart problems in her family. Cleared a physical in February, no problems except the insomnia and she's too thin – but being underweight goes against the heart thing.'

'Still, it happens,' Lucas said. 'People drop dead.'

Grave shook his head. 'When the Joyces were running the flops, they had a guy whose job it was to keep things orderly. They brought him over to run the apartments. Old friend of yours; you busted him three or four times, according to the NCIC. Remember Ray Cherry?'

'Cherry? Jesus. He *is* an asshole. Used to box Golden Gloves when he was a kid . . .' Lucas scratched the side of his jaw, thinking. 'That's a nasty bunch you got there. Jeez.'

'So what do I do? I got nothing.'

'Get a cattle prod and a dark basement. Cherry'd talk after a while.' Lucas grinned through his teeth, and Greave almost visibly shrank from him.

'You're not serious.'

'Mmm. I guess not,' Lucas said. Then, brightening: 'Maybe she was stabbed with an icicle.'

'What?'

'Let me think about it,' Lucas said.

There were two landfills in Dakota County. Adhering to Murphy's Law, they went to the wrong one first, then shifted down a series of blacktopped back roads to the correct one. For the last half-mile, they were pinched between two lumbering garbage trucks, gone overripe in the freshening summer.

'Office,' Greave said, pointing off to the left. He dabbed at the front of his lavender suit, as though he were trying to whisk away the smell of rotten fruit.

The dump office was a tiny brick building with a large plate-glass window, overlooking a set of truck scales and the lines of garbage haulers rumbling out to the edge of the raw yellow earth of the landfill. Lucas swung that way, dumped the Porsche in a corner of the lot.

Inside the building, a Formica-topped counter separated the front of the office from the back. A fat guy in a green T-shirt sat at a metal desk behind the counter, an unlit cigar in his mouth. He was complaining into a telephone and picking penny-sized flakes of dead skin off his elbows; the heartbreak of psoriasis. A door behind the fat man led to a phone booth-size room with a sink and a toilet. The door was open, and the stool was gurgling. A half-used roll of toilet paper sat on the toilet tank, and another one lay on the floor, where it had soaked full of rusty water.

'So he says it'll cost a hunnert just to come out here and look at it,' the fat guy said to the telephone, looking into the bathroom. 'I tell you, I run up to Fleet-Farm and I get the parts . . . Well, I know that, Al, but this is drivin' me fuckin' crazy.'

The fat guy put his hand over the mouthpiece and said, 'Be with you in a minute.' Then to the phone, 'Al, I gotta go, there's a couple guys here in suits. Yeah.' He looked up at Lucas and asked, 'You EPA?'

'No.'

The fat man said, 'No,' to the phone, listened, then looked up again. 'OSHA?'

'No. Minneapolis cops.'

'Minneapolis cops,' the fat man said. He listened for a minute, then looked up. 'He sent the check.'

'What?'

'He sent the check to his old lady. Put it in the mail this morning, the whole thing.'

'Terrific,' Lucas said. 'I really hope he did, or we'll have to arrest him for misfeasance to a police officer on official business, a Class Three felony.'

Greave turned away to smile, while the fat man repeated what Lucas said into the phone, then after a pause said, 'That's what the man said,' and hung up. 'He says he really mailed it.'

'Okay,' said Lucas. 'Now, we're also looking for a guy who supposedly hangs around here. Junky Doog . . .' The fat man's eyes slid away, and Lucas said, 'So he's out here?'

'Junky's, uh, kind of . . .' The fat man tapped his head.

'I know. I've dealt with him a few times.'

'Like, recently?'

'Not since he got out of St Peter.'

'I think he got Alzheimer's,' the fat man said. 'Some days, he's just not here. He forgets to eat, he shits in his pants.'

'So where is he?' Lucas asked.

'Christ, I feel bad about the guy. He's a guy who never caught a break,' the fat man said. 'Not one fuckin' day of his life.'

'Used to cut people up. You can't do that.'

'Yeah, I know. Beautiful women. And I ain't no softy on crime, but you talk to Junky, and you *know* he didn't know any better. He's like a kid. I mean, he's not like a kid, because a normal kid wouldn't do what he did . . . I mean, he just doesn't know. He's like a . . . pit bull, or something. It just ain't his fault.'

'We take that into account,' said Greave, his voice soft. 'Really, we're concerned about these things.'

The fat man sighed, struggled to his feet, walked around the counter to a window. He pointed out across the land-fill. 'See that willow tree? He's got a place in the woods over there. We ain't supposed to let him, but whatcha gonna do?'

Lucas and Greave scuffed across the yellow-dirt landfill, trying to stay clear of the contrails of dust thrown up by the garbage trucks rumbling by. The landfill looked more like a highway construction site than a dump, with big D-9 Cats laboring around the edges of the raw dirt; and only at the edges did it look like a dump: a jumble of green plastic garbage bags, throwaway diapers, cereal boxes, cardboard, scraps of sheet plastic and metal, all rolled under the yellow dirt, and all surrounded by second-growth forest. Seagulls, crows, and pigeons hung over the litter, looking for food; a bony gray dog, moving jackal-like, slipped around the edges.

The willow tree was an old one, yellow, with great weeping branches bright green with new growth. Beneath it, two blue plastic tarps had been draped tentlike over tree limbs. Under one of the tarps was a salvaged charcoal grill; under the other was a mattress. A man lay on the mattress, faceup, eyes open, unmoving.

'Jesus, he's fuckin' dead,' Greave said, his voice hushed.

Lucas stepped off the raw earth, Greave tagging reluctantly behind, followed a narrow trail around a clump of bushes, and was hit by the stink of human waste. The odor was thick, and came from no particular direction. He started breathing through his mouth, and unconsciously reached across to his hipbone and pulled his pistol a quarter inch out of the holster, loosening it, then patted it back. He moved in close before he called out, 'Hello. Hey.'

The man on the mattress twitched, then subsided again. He lay with one arm outstretched, the other over his pelvis. There was something wrong with the outstretched arm, Lucas saw, moving closer. Just off the mattress, a flat-topped stump was apparently being used as a table. A group of small brown cylinders sat on the stump, like chunks of beef jerky. Beside the stump was a one-gallon aluminum can of paint thinner, top off, lying on its side.

'Hey . . .'

The man rolled up farther, tried to sit up. Junky Doog. He was barefoot. And he had a knife, a long curved pearl-handled number, open, the blade protruding five inches from the handle. Doog held it delicately, like a straight razor, and said, 'Gothefuckaway,' one word. Doog's eyes were a hazy white, as though covered with cataracts, and his face was burned brown. He had no teeth and hadn't shaved in weeks. Graying hair fell down on his shoulders, knotted with grime. He looked worse than Lucas had ever seen him: looked worse than Lucas had ever seen a human being look.

'There's shit all over the place,' Greave said. Then: 'Watch it, watch the blade . . .'

Junky whirled the knife in his fingers with the dexterity of a cheerleader twirling a baton, the steel twinkling in the weak sunlight. 'Gothefuckaway,' he screamed. He took a step toward Lucas, fell, tried to catch himself with his free hand, the hand without the knife, screamed again, and rolled onto his back, cradling the free hand. The hand had no fingers. Lucas looked at the stump: the brown things were pieces of finger and several toes.

'Jesus Christ,' he muttered. He glanced at Greave, whose mouth was hanging open. Junky was weeping, trying to get up, still with the knife flickering in his good hand. Lucas stepped behind him, and when Junky made it to his knees, put a foot between his shoulder blades and pushed him facedown on the worn dirt just off the mattress. Pinning him, he caught the bad arm, and as Junky squirmed, crying, caught the other arm, shook the knife out of his hand. Junky was too weak to resist; weaker than a child.

'Can you walk?' Lucas asked, trying to pull Junky up. He looked at Greave. 'Give me a hand.'

Junky, caught in a crying jag, nodded, and with a boost from Lucas and Greave, got to his feet.

'We gotta go, man. We gotta go, Junky,' Lucas said. 'We're cops, you gotta come with us.'

They led him back through the shit-stink, through the weeds, Junky stumbling, still weeping; halfway up the path, something happened, and he pulled around, looked at Lucas, his eyes clearing. 'Get my blade. Get my blade, please. It'll get all rusted up.'

Lucas looked at him a minute, looked back. 'Hold him,' he said to Greave. Junky had nothing to do with the killings; no way. But Lucas should take the knife.

'Get the blade.'

Lucas jogged back to the campsite, picked up the knife, closed it, and walked back to where Greave held Junky's arm, Junky swaying in the path. Junky's mind had slipped away again, and he mutely followed Lucas and Greave across the yellow dirt, walking stiffly, as though his legs were posts. Only the big toes remained on his feet. His thumb and the lowest finger knuckles remained on his left hand; the hand was fiery with infection.

Back at the shed, the fat man came out and Lucas said, 'Call 911. Tell them a police officer needs an ambulance. My name is Lucas Davenport and I'm a deputy chief with the City of Minneapolis.'

'What happened, did you . . . ?' the fat man started, then saw first Junky's hand, and then his feet. 'Oh my sweet Blessed Virgin Mary,' he said, and he went back into the shed.

Lucas looked at Junky, dug into his pocket, handed him the knife. 'Let him go,' he said to Greave.

'What're you gonna do?' Greave asked.

'Just let him go.'

Reluctantly, Greave released him, and the knife, still closed, twinkled in his hand. Lucas stepped sideways from him, a knife fighter's move, and said, 'I'm gonna cut you, Junky,' he said, his voice low, challenging.

Junky turned toward him, a smile at the corner of his ravaged face. The knife turned in his hand, and suddenly the blade snapped out. Junky stumbled toward Lucas.

'I cut you; you not cut me,' he said.

'I cut you, man,' Lucas said, beginning to circle to his right, away from the blade.

'You not cut me.'

The fat man came out and said, 'Hey. What're you doin'?'

Lucas glanced at him. 'Take it easy. Is the ambulance coming?'

'They're on the way,' the fat man said. He took a step toward Junky. 'Junky, man, give me the knife.'

'Gonna cut him,' Junky said, stepping toward Lucas. He stumbled, and Lucas moved in, caught his bad arm, turned him, caught his shabby knife-arm sleeve from behind, turned him more, grabbed the good hand and shook the knife out.

'You're under arrest for assault on a police officer,' Lucas said. He pushed the fat man away, picked up the knife, folded it and dropped it in his pocket. 'You understand that? You're under arrest.'

Junky looked at him, then nodded.

'Sit down,' Lucas said. Junky shambled over and sat on the flat concrete stoop outside the shack. Lucas turned to the fat man. 'You saw that. Remember what you saw.'

The fat man looked at him doubtfully and said, 'I don't think he would have hurt you.'

111

'Arresting him is the best I can do for him,' Lucas said quietly. 'They'll put him inside, clean him up, take care of him.'

The fat man thought about it, nodded. The phone rang, and he went back inside. Lucas, Greave, and Junky waited in silence until Junky looked up suddenly and said, 'Davenport. What do you want?'

His voice was clear, controlled, his eyes focused.

'Somebody's cuttin' women,' Lucas said. 'I wanted to make sure it wasn't you.'

'I cut some women, long time ago,' Junky said. 'There was this one, she had beautiful . . . you know. I made a grapevine on them.'

'Yeah, I know.'

'Long time ago; they liked it,' he said.

Lucas shook his head.

'Somebody cuttin' on women?' Junky asked.

'Yeah, somebody's cuttin' on women.'

After another moment of silence, Greave asked Junky, 'Why would they do that? Why would he be cuttin' women?' In the distance, over the sound of the trucks moving toward the working edge of the fill, they could hear a siren. The fat man must have made it an emergency.

'You got to,' Junky said solemnly to Greave. 'If you don't cut them, especially the pretty ones, they get out of hand. You can't have women getting outa hand.'

'Yeah?'

'Yeah. You cut 'em, they stay put, that's for sure. They stay put.'

'So why would you go a long time and not cut any women, then start cuttin' a lot of women?'

'I didn't do that,' Junky said. He cast a defensive eye at Greave.

'No. The guy we're looking for did that.'

Lucas looked on curiously as the man in the lavender

Italian suit chatted with the man with no toes, like they were sharing a cappuccino outside a café.

'He just started up?' Junky asked.

'Yup.'

Junky thought about that, pawing his face with his good hand, then his head bobbed, as though he'd worked it out. ''Cause a woman turns you on, that's why. Maybe you see a woman and she turns you on. Gets you by the pecker. You go around with your pecker up for a few days, and you *gotta* do *something*. You know, you gotta cut some women.'

'Some woman turns you on?'

'Yup.'

'So then you cut her.'

'Well.' Junky seemed to look inside himself. 'Maybe not her, exactly. Sometimes you can't cut her. There was this one . . .' He seemed to drift away, lost in the past. Then: 'But you gotta cut somebody, see? If you don't cut somebody, your pecker stays up.'

'So what?'

'So what? You can't go around with your pecker up all the time. You can't.'

'I wish I could,' Greave cracked.

Junky got angry, intent, his face quivering. 'You can't. You can't go around like that.'

'Okay . . .'

The ambulance bumped into the landfill, followed a few seconds later by a sheriff's car.

'Come on, Junky, we're gonna put you in the hospital,' Lucas said.

Junky said to Greave, pulling at Greave's pant leg with his good hand, 'But you got to get her, sooner or later. Sooner or later, you got to get the one that put your pecker up. See, if she goes around putting your pecker up, anytime she wants, she's outa hand. She's just outa hand, and you gotta cut her.'

'Okay . . .'

Lucas filed a complaint with the sheriff's deputy who followed the ambulance in, and Junky was hauled away.

'I'm glad I came with you,' Greave said. 'Got to see a dump, and a guy cutting himself up like a provolone.'

Lucas shook his head and said, 'You did pretty good back there. You've got a nice line of bullshit.'

'Yeah?'

'Yeah. Talking to people, you know, that's half of homicide.'

'I got the bullshit. It's the other part I ain't got,' Greave said gloomily. 'Listen, you wanna stop at my mystery apartment on the way back?'

'No.'

'C'mon, man.'

'We've got too much going on,' Lucas said. 'Maybe we'll catch some time later.'

'They're wearing me out in homicide,' Greave said. 'I get these notes. They say, "Any progress?" Fuck 'em.'

Greave went on to homicide to check in, while Lucas walked down to Roux's office and stuck his head in.

'We picked up Junky Doog. He's clear, almost for sure.'

He explained, and told her how Junky had mutilated himself. Roux, nibbling her lip, said, 'What happens if I feed him to the *Strib*?'

'Depends on how you do it,' Lucas said, leaning against the door, crossing his arms. 'If you did it deep off-the-record, gave them just the bare information . . . it might take some heat off. Or at least get them running in a different direction. In either case, it'd be sorta cynical.'

'Fuck cynical. His prior arrests were here in Hennepin, right?'

'Most of them, I think. He was committed from here. If you tipped them early enough, they could get across the street and pull his files.'

'Even if it's bullshit, it's an exclusive. It's a lead story,' Roux said. She rubbed her eyes. 'Lucas, I hate to do it. But I'm taking some serious damage now. I figure I've got a couple of weeks of grace. After that, I might not be able to save myself.'

Back at his office, a message was waiting on voice mail: 'This is Connell. I got something. Beep me.'

Lucas dialed her beeper number, let it beep, and hung up. Junky had been a waste of time, although he might be a bone they could throw the media. Not much of a bone . . .

With nothing else to do, he began paging through Connell's report again, trying to absorb as much of the detail as he could.

There were several threads that tied all the killings together, but the thread that worried him most was the simplicity of them. The killer picked up a woman, killed her, dumped her. They weren't all found right away – Connell suggested he might have kept one or two of them for several hours, or even overnight – but in one case, in South Dakota, the body was found forty-five minutes after the woman had been seen alive. He wasn't pressing his luck by keeping the woman around; they wouldn't get a break that way.

He didn't leave anything behind, either. The actual death scenes might have been in his vehicle – Connell suggested that it was probably a van or a truck, although he might have used a motel if he'd been careful in his choices.

In one case, in Thunder Bay, there may have been some semen on a dress, but the stain, whatever it was, had been destroyed in a failed effort to extract a blood type. A note from a cop said that it might have been salad dressing. DNA testing had not yet been available.

Vaginal and anal examinations had come up negative, but there was oral bruising that suggested that some of the women had been orally raped. Stomach contents were negative, which meant that he didn't ejaculate, ejaculated outside their mouth, or they lived long enough for stomach fluids to destroy the evidence.

Hair was a different problem. Foreign-hair samples had been collected from several of the bodies, but in most cases where hair was collected, several varieties were found. There was no way to tell that any particular hair came from the killer – or, indeed, that any of the hair was his. Connell had tried to get the existing hair samples cross-matched, but some of it had been either destroyed or lost, or the bureaucratic tangles were so intense that nothing had yet been done. Lucas made a note to search for hair crosses on Wannemaker and Joan Smits. All were relatively recent, with autopsies done by first-rate medical examiners.

Closing the file, Lucas got out of his chair and wandered around to stare sightlessly out the window, working it through his head. The man never left anything unique. Hair, so far, was the only possibility: they needed a match, and needed it badly. They had nothing else that would tie a specific man to a specific body. Nothing at all.

The phone rang. 'This is Meagan. I've got somebody who remembers the killer . . .'

8

Late in the afternoon, sun warm on the city sidewalks. Greave didn't want to go. 'Look, I'm not gonna be much help to you. I don't know what you and Connell are into, where your heads are at – but I really want to do my own thing. And I already been to a fuckin' dump today.'

'We need somebody else current with the case,' Lucas said. 'You're the guy. I want somebody else seeing these people, talking to them.'

Greave rubbed his hair with both hands, then said, 'All right, all right, I'll go along. But – if we've got time, we stop at my apartments, right?'

Lucas shrugged. 'If we've got time.'

Connell was waiting on a street corner in Woodbury, under a Quick Wash sign, wearing Puritan black-and-white, still carrying the huge purse. An automotive diagnostic center sprawled down the block.

'Been here long?' Greave asked. He was still pouting.

'One minute,' she said. She was strung out, hard energy overlying a deep weariness. She'd been up all night, Lucas thought. Talking to the TV. Dying.

'Have you talked to St Paul?' he asked.

'They're dead in the water,' Connell said, impatience harsh in her voice. 'The cop at the bookstore was one of theirs. He drinks too much, plays around on his wife. A guy over there told me that he and his wife have gotten physical. I guess one of their brawls is pretty famous inside the department – his wife knocked out two of his teeth with an iron, and he was naked chasing her around the backyard with a mop handle, drunk, bleeding all over himself. The neighbors called the cops. They thought she'd shot him. That's what I hear.'

'So what do you think?'

'He's an asshole, but he's unlikely,' she said. 'He's an older guy, too heavy, out of shape. He used to smoke Marlboros, but quit ten years ago. The main thing is, St Paul is covering like mad. They've been called out to his house a half-dozen times, but there's never been a charge.'

Lucas shook his head, looked at the diagnosis center. 'What about this woman?'

'Mae Heinz. Told me on the phone that she'd seen a guy with a beard. Short. Strong-looking.'

Lucas led the way inside, a long office full of parts books, tires, cutaway muffler displays, and the usual odor of antifreeze and transmission fluid. Heinz was a cheerful, round-faced woman with pink skin and freckles. She sat wide-eyed behind the counter as Connell sketched in the murder. 'I was talking to that woman,' Heinz said. 'I remember her asking the question . . .'

'But you didn't see her go out with a man?'

'She didn't,' Heinz said. 'She went out alone. I remember.'

'Were there a lot of men there?'

'Yeah, there were quite a few. There was a guy with a ponytail and a beard and his name was Carl, he asked a lot of questions about pigs and he had dirty fingernails, so I wasn't too interested. Everybody seemed to know him. There was a computer guy, kind of heavyset blond, I heard him talking to somebody.'

'Meyer,' Connell said to Lucas. 'Talked to him this morning. He's out.'

'Kind of cute,' Heinz said, looking at Connell and winking. 'If you like the intellectual types.'

'What about . . . ?'

'There was a guy who was a cop,' Heinz said.

'Got him,' Lucas said.

'Then there were two guys there together, and I thought they might be gay. They stood too close to each other.'

'Know their names?'

'No idea,' she said. 'But they were very well-dressed. I think they were in architecture or landscaping or something like that, because they were talking to the author about sustainable land use.'

'And the guy with the beard,' Connell said, prompting her.

'Yeah. He came in during the talk. And he must've left right away, because I didn't see him later. I sorta looked. Jesus – I could of been dead. I mean, if I'd found him.'

'Was he tall, short, fat, skinny?'

'Big guy. Not tall, but thick. Big shoulders. Beard. I don't like beards, but I liked the shoulders.' She winked at Connell again, and Lucas covered a grin by scratching his face. 'But the thing is,' she said to Connell, 'you asked about smoking, and he snapped a cigarette into the street. I saw him do it. Snapped a cigarette and then came in the door.'

Lucas looked at Connell and nodded. Heinz caught it. 'Was that him?' she asked excitedly.

'Would you know him if we showed you a picture of him?' Lucas asked.

She cocked her head and looked to one side, as though she were running a video through her head. 'I don't know,' she said after a minute. 'Maybe, if I saw an actual picture. I can remember the beard and the shoulders. His beard looked sort of funny. Short, but really dense, like fur . . . Kind of unpleasant, I thought. Maybe fake. I can't remember much about his face. Knobby, I think.'

'Dark beard? Light?'

'Mmm . . . dark. Kind of medium, really. Pretty average hair, I think . . . brown.'

'All right,' Lucas said. 'Let's nail this down. And let's get you with an artist. Do you have time to come to Minneapolis?'

'Sure. Right now? Let me tell my boss.'

As the woman went to talk to her boss about leaving, Connell caught Lucas's sleeve. 'Gotta be him. Smokes, arrives after the talk, then leaves right away. Wannemaker is lingering after the talk, but suddenly leaves, like somebody showed up.'

'Wouldn't count on it,' Lucas said. But he was counting on it. He felt it, just a sniff of the killer, just a whiff of the track. 'We got to put her through the sex files.'

The woman came back, animated. 'How do you want to do this? Want me to follow you over?'

'Why don't I take you?' Connell offered. 'We can talk on the way over.'

Greave wanted to stop at the apartment complex so Lucas could look at the locked-room mystery. 'C'mon, man, it's twenty fuckin' minutes. We'll be back before she's done with the artist,' he said. A pleading note entered his voice. 'C'mon, man, this is killing me.'

Lucas glanced at him, hands clutched, the too-hip suit. He sighed and said, 'All right. Twenty minutes.'

They took I-94 back to Minneapolis, but turned south instead of north toward City Hall. Greave directed him through a web of streets to a fifties-era mid-rise concrete building with a hand-carved natural-wood sign on the narrow front lawn that had a loon on top and the name 'Eisenhower Docks' beneath the bird. A fat man pushed a mower down the lawn away from them, leaving behind the smell of gas and cheap cigar.

'Eisenhower Docks?' Lucas said as they got out.

'If you stand on the roof you can see the river,' Greave said. 'And they figured "Eisenhower" makes old people feel good.'

The man pushing the lawn mower made a turn at the end of the lawn and started back; Lucas recognized Ray Cherry, forty pounds heavier than he'd been when he'd fought in Golden Gloves tournaments in the sixties. Most of the weight had gone to his gut, which hung over beltless Oshkosh jeans. His face had gone from square to blocky, and a half-dozen folds of fat rolled down the back of his neck to his shoulders. His T-shirt was soaked with sweat. He saw Davenport and Greave, pushed the lawn mower up to their feet, and killed the engine.

'What're you doing, Davenport?'

'Lookin' around, Ray,' Lucas said, smiling. 'How've you been? You got fat.'

'Y'ain't a cop no more, so get the fuck off my property.'

'I'm back on the force, Ray,' Lucas said, still smiling. Seeing Ray made him happy. 'You oughta read the papers. Deputy chief in charge of finding out how you killed this old lady.'

A look crossed Cherry's face, a quick shadow, and Lucas recognized it, had seen it six or seven hundred or a thousand times: Cherry had done it. Cherry wiped the expression away, tried a look of confusion, took a soiled rag out of his pocket, and blew his nose. 'Bullshit,' he said finally.

'Gonna get you, Ray,' Lucas said; the smile stayed but his voice had gone cold. 'Gonna get the Joyces, too. Gonna put you in Stillwater Prison. You must be close to fifty, Ray. First-degree murder'll get you ... shit, they just changed the law. Tough luck. You'll be better'n eighty before you get out.'

'Fuck you, Davenport,' Cherry said. He fired up the mower.

'Come and talk to me, Ray,' Lucas said over the engine noise. 'The Joyces'll sell you out the minute they think it'll get them a break. You know that. Come and talk, and maybe we can do a deal.'

121

'Fuck you,' Cherry said, and he mowed on down the yard.

'Lovely fellow,' Greave said in a fake English accent.

'He did it,' Lucas said. He turned to Greave and Greave took a step back: Lucas's face was like a block of stone.

'Huh?'

'He killed her. Let's see her apartment.'

Lucas started for the apartment door, and Greave trotted after him. 'Hey, wait a minute, wait a minute . . .'

There were a thousand books in the apartment, along with a rolled-up Oriental carpet tied with brown twine, and fifteen cardboard cartons from U-Haul, still flat. A harried middle-aged woman sat on a piano bench, a handkerchief around her head; her face was wind- and sunburned, like a gardener's, and was touched with grief. Charmagne Carter's daughter, Emily.

'. . . Soon as they said we could take it out. If we don't, we have to keep paying rent,' she told Greave. She looked around. 'I don't know what to do with the books. I'd like to keep them, but there're so many.'

Lucas had been looking at the books: American literature, poetry, essays, history. Works on feminism, arranged in a way that suggested they were a conscious collection rather than a reading selection. 'I could take some of them off your hands,' he said. 'I mean, if you'd like to name a price. I'd take the poetry.'

'Well, what do you think?' Carter asked, as Greave watched him curiously.

'There are . . .' He counted quickly. '. . . thirty-seven volumes, mostly paper. I don't think any of them are particularly rare. How about a hundred bucks?'

'Let me look through them. I'll give you a call.'

'Sure.' He turned away from the books, more fully toward her. 'Was your mother depressed or anything?'

122

'If you're asking if she committed suicide, she didn't. She wouldn't give the Joyces the pleasure, for one thing. But basically, she liked her life,' Carter said. She became more animated as she remembered. 'We had dinner the night before and she was talking about this kid in her class, black kid, she thinks he'll be a novelist but he needs encouragement . . . No way'd she kill herself. Besides, even if she wanted to, how'd she do it?'

'Yeah. That's a question,' Lucas said.

'The only thing wrong with Mom was her thyroid. She had a little thyroid problem; it was overactive and she had trouble keeping her weight up,' Carter said. 'And her insomnia. That might have been part of the thyroid problem.'

'She was actually ill, then?' Lucas glanced sideways at Greave.

'No. No, she really wasn't. Not even bad enough to take pills. She was just way too thin. She weighed ninety-nine pounds and she was five-six. That's below her ideal weight, but it's not emaciated or anything.'

'Okay.'

'Now that kid isn't gonna get help, the novelist,' Emily said, and a tear started down her cheek.

Greave patted her on the shoulder – Officer Friendly – and Lucas turned away, hands in pockets, stepping toward the door. Nothing here.

'You ought to talk to Bob, next apartment down the hall,' Emily said. She picked up a roll of packaging tape and a box, punched it into a cube. She stripped off a length of tape, and it sounded as if she were tearing a sheet. 'He came in just before you got here.'

'Bob was a friend of Charmagne's,' Greave explained to Lucas. 'He was here the night she died.'

Lucas nodded. 'All right. I'm sorry about your mother.'

'Thanks. I hope you get those . . . those fuckers,' Emily said, her voice dropping into a hiss.

'You think she was murdered?'

'Something happened,' she said.

Bob Wood was another teacher, general science at Central in St Paul. He was thin, balding, worried.

'We'll all go, now that Charmagne's gone. The city's going to give us some moving money, but I don't know. Prices are terrible.'

'Did you hear anything that night? Anything?'

'Nope. I saw her about ten o'clock; we were taking our aluminum cans down for recycling and we came up in the elevator together. She was going off to bed right then.'

'Wasn't depressed . . .'

'No, no, she was pretty upbeat,' Wood said. 'I'll tell you something I told the other policemen: when she closed the door, I heard the lock snap shut. You could only throw the bolt from inside, and you had to do it with a key. I know, because when she got it, she was worried about being trapped inside by a fire. But then Cherry scared her one day – just looked at her, I guess, and scared her – and she started locking the door. I was here when they beat it down. They had to take a piece of the wall with it. They painted, but you can kind of see the outline there.'

The wall showed the faint dishing of a plaster patch. Lucas touched it and shook his head.

'If anything had happened in there, I would have heard it,' Wood said. 'We share a bedroom wall, and the air-conditioning had been out for a couple of days. There was no noise. It was hot and spooky-quiet. I didn't hear a thing.'

'So you think she just died?'

Wood swallowed twice, his Adam's apple bobbing. 'Jeez. I don't know. If you know Cherry, you gotta think . . . Jeez.'

In the street, Lucas and Greave watched a small girl ride down the sidewalk on a tiny bicycle, fall down, pick it up, start over, and fall down again. 'She needs somebody to run behind her,' Greave said.

Lucas grunted. 'Doesn't everybody?'

'Big philosopher, huh?

Lucas said, 'Wood and Carter shared a wall.'

'Yes.'

'Have you looked at Wood?'

'Yeah. He thinks newspaper comics are too violent.'

'But there might be something there. What can you do with a shared wall? Stick a needle through it, pump in some gas or something?'

'Hey. Davenport. There's no toxicology,' Greave said with asperity. '*There's no fuckin' toxicology.* You look up *toxicology* in the dictionary, and there's a picture of the old lady and it says, "Not Her." '

'Yeah, yeah . . .'

'She wasn't poisoned, gassed, stabbed, shot, strangled, beaten to death . . . what else is there?'

'How about electrocuted?' Lucas suggested.

'Hmph. How'd they do it?'

'I don't know. Hook some wires up to her bed, lead them out under a door, and when she gets in bed, zap, and then they pull the wires out.'

'Pardon me while I snicker,' Greave said.

Lucas looked back at the apartment building. 'Let me think about it some more.'

'But Cherry did it?'

'Yup.' They looked down the lawn. Cherry was at the other end, kneeling over a quiet lawn mower, fiddling, watching them. 'You can take it to the bank.'

Lucas glanced at his watch as they got back to the car: they'd been at the apartments for almost an hour. 'Connell's gonna tear me up,' he said.

'Ah, she's a bite in the ass,' Greave said.

They bumped into Mae Heinz in the parking ramp,

getting into her car. Lucas beeped the horn, called out, 'How'd it go?'

Heinz came over. 'That woman, Officer Connell . . . she's pretty intense.'

'Yes. She is.'

'We got one of those drawings, but . . .'

'What?'

Heinz shook her head. 'I don't know whether it's my drawing or hers. The thing is, it's too specific. I can mostly remember the guy with the beard, but now we've got this whole picture, and I don't know if it's right or not. I mean, it seems right, but I'm not sure I'm really remembering it, or if it's just because we tried out so many different pictures.'

'Did you look at our picture files, the mugs . . . ?'

'No, not yet. I've got to get my kid at day care. But I'm coming back tonight. Officer Connell is going to meet me.'

Connell was waiting in Lucas's office. 'God, where've you been?'

'Detour,' Lucas said. 'Different case.'

Connell's eyes narrowed. 'Greave, huh? Told you.' She gave Lucas a sheet of paper. 'This is him. This is the guy.'

Lucas unfolded the paper and looked at it. The face that looked back was generally square, with a dark, tight beard, small eyes, and hard, triangular nose. The hair was medium length and dark.

'We gotta feed it to the TV. We don't have to say we're looking for a serial killer, just that we're looking for this guy on the Wannemaker case,' Connell said.

'Let's hold off on that for a bit,' Lucas said. 'Why don't we take this around to the other people who were in the store and get it confirmed. Maybe ship it out to Madison, and anywhere else the guy might have been seen.'

'We gotta get it out,' Connell objected. 'People gotta be warned.'

'Take it easy,' Lucas said. 'Make the checks first.'

'Give me one good reason.'

'Because we haven't gotten anything unique to this guy,' Lucas said. 'If we wind up in court with a long circumstantial case, I don't want the defense to pull out this picture, hold it up by our guy, and say, "See – he doesn't look anything like this." That's why.'

Connell pulled at her lip, then nodded. 'I'll check with people tonight. I'll get every one of them.'

9

Koop was at Two Guy's, working his quads. The only other patron was a woman who'd worked herself to exhaustion, and now sat, legs apart, on a bent-up folding chair by the Coke machine, drinking Gatorade, head down, her sweat-soaked hair dangling almost to the floor.

Muscle chicks didn't interest Koop: they just weren't right. He left them alone, and after a couple of tentative feelers, they left him alone.

Koop said to himself, *Five*, and felt the muscle failing.

A TV was screwed to the wall in front of the empty stair climbers, tuned to the midday news program, *Nooner*. A stunning auburn-haired anchorwoman said through a suggestive overbite that Cheryl Young was dead of massive head wounds.

Koop strained, got the last inch, and dropped his feet again, came back up, the muscle trembling with fatigue. He closed his eyes, willed his legs up; they came up a half inch, another quarter inch, to the top. *Six*. He dropped them, started up again. The burn was massive, as though somebody had poured alcohol on his legs and lit it off. He shook with the burn, eyes clenched, sweat popping. He needed an inch, one inch . . . and failed. He always worked to failure. Satisfied, he let the bar drop and pivoted on the bench to look at the television.

'. . . believed to be the work of young drug addicts.' And a cop saying, '. . . the attack was incredibly violent for so little gain. We believe Mr Flory had less than thirty dollars in his wallet – that we believe it was probably the work of younger gang members who build their status with this kind of meaningless killing . . .'

Good. They put it on the gangs. Little motherfuckers deserved anything they got. And Koop couldn't wait any longer. He knew he should wait. The people in the building would be in an uproar. If he was seen, and recognized as an outsider, there could be trouble.

But he just couldn't wait. He picked up his towel and headed for the locker room.

Koop went into the lakes neighborhood on foot, a few minutes before nine, in the dying twilight. There were other walkers in the neighborhood, but nothing in particular around the building where he'd killed the woman: the blood had been washed away, the medical garbage picked up. Just another door in another apartment building.

'Stupid,' he said aloud. He looked around to see if anyone had heard. Nobody close enough. Stupid, but the pressure was terrific. And different. When he went after a woman, that was sex. The impulse came from his testicles; he could literally feel it.

This impulse seemed to come from somewhere else; well, not entirely, but it was different. It drove him, like a child looking for candy . . .

Koop carried his newly minted key and a briefcase. Inside the briefcase was a Kowa TSN-2 spotting scope with a lightweight aluminum tripod, a setup recommended for professional birders and voyeurs. He swung the briefcase casually, letting it dangle, keeping himself loose, as he started up the apartment walk. Feelers out: nothing. Up close, the arborvitae beside the apartment door looked beaten, ragged; there were footprints in the mud around the shrubs.

Inside, the lobby light was brighter, harsher. The management's response to murder: put in a brighter bulb.

Maybe they'd changed locks? Koop slipped the key into the door, turned it, and it worked just fine.

He took the stairs to the top, no problem. At the top, he checked the hallway, nervous, but not nearly as tense as he was during an entry. He really shouldn't be here . . . Nobody in the hall. He walked down it, to the Exit sign, and up the stairs to the roof access. He used the new key again, pushed through the door, climbed another short flight to the roof, and pushed through the roof door.

He was alone on the roof. The night was pleasant, but the roof was not a particularly inviting place, asphalt and pea-rock, and the lingering odor of sun-warmed tar. He walked as quietly as he could to the edge of the roof, and looked across the street. Damn. He was just below Sara Jensen's window. Not much, but enough that he wouldn't be able to see her unless she came and stood near the window.

An air-conditioner housing squatted on the rooftop, a large gray-metal cube, projecting up another eight feet. Koop walked around to the back of it, reached up, pushed the briefcase onto the edge of it, then grabbed the edge, chinned and pressed himself up on top, never breaking a sweat or even holding his breath. A three-foot-wide venting stack poked up above the housing. Koop squatted behind the stack and looked across the street.

Jensen's apartment was a fishbowl. To the right, there was a balcony with a wrought-iron railing in front of sliding glass doors, and through the doors, the living room. To the left, he looked through the knee-high windows into her bedroom. He was now a few feet higher than her floor, he thought, giving him just a small down-angle. Perfect.

And Jensen was home.

Ten seconds after Koop boosted himself onto the air-conditioner housing, she walked through the living room wearing a slip, carrying a cup of coffee and a paper. She was as clear as a goldfish in an illuminated aquarium.

'Goddamn,' Koop said, happy. This was better than anything he'd hoped for. He fumbled with the briefcase, pulled out the spotting scope. 'Come on, Sara,' he said. 'Let's see some puss.'

Koop had two eyepieces for the Kowa, a twenty-power and a sixty. The sixty-power put him virtually inside her room, but was sensitive to the slightest touch, and the field of view was tiny: with the sixty, her face filled the field. He switched to the twenty-power, fumbling the eyepiece in his haste, cursing, screwing it down. Jensen walked back through the living room and in and out of the kitchen, which he couldn't see. He settled down to wait: he'd begun carrying a kerchief with him, with just a dab of her Opium. As he watched her windows, he held the kerchief beside his nose so he could smell her.

While she was out of sight, he scanned the living room. Huh. New lock. Something really tough. He'd expected that. She also had a new door. It was flat gray, as though awaiting a coat of paint. Metal, probably. Jensen had bought herself a steel-sheathed door after his visit.

Jensen showed up again in the bedroom and pulled the slip over her head, then stripped off her panty hose. She disappeared into the bathroom, came back out without her bra. Koop sucked air like a teenager at a carnival strip show.

Jensen had large, rounded breasts, the left one a bit larger than the right, he thought. She went back to the bathroom, came back a moment later without underpants. Koop was sweating, watched her digging something out of a dresser drawer – a towel? He couldn't quite tell. She disappeared again.

This time she didn't come back right away. Koop, feverish, heart pounding, kept his eye to the scope so long that his neck began to hurt, while running through his mind the sight of her body. She was solid, and jiggled a little when she walked, not quite a roll at her waist, but a certain

131

fullness; she had an excellent ass, again the way he liked them, solid, sizable. With a little jiggle.

He took his face away from the eyepiece, dropped well below the level of the vent, lit a Camel in his carefully cupped hand, and looked down at the metal surface under his arm. He was not introspective, but now he thought: *What's going on?* He was breathing hard, as though he'd been on the stair climber. He was beginning to feel some kind of burn ... Goddamn. He squeezed his eyes shut, imagined catching her on the street, getting her in the truck.

But then he'd have to do her. He frowned at the thought. And then he wouldn't have this. He peered over the top of the vent; she was still out of sight, and he dropped back on his elbow. He liked this. He needed this time with her. Eventually, he'd have to get with her. He could see that. But for now ...

He peeked back over the edge. She was still out of sight, and he took two more hurried drags on the cigarette and ground it out. Another peek, and he lit another Camel.

When Sara Jensen finally emerged from the bathroom, she was nude except for a white terry-cloth towel wrapped around her head; she looked like a dark angel. She wasn't hurried, but she was moving with deliberation. Going somewhere, Koop thought, his heart pounding, his mouth dry. She was bouncing, her nipples large and dark, pubic hair black as coal. She took something from the same dressing table where he'd found the jewelry box – the box wasn't there anymore, and he wondered briefly where she'd put it – then sat on the bed and began trimming her toenails.

He groped in his pocket for the sixty-power eyepiece, made the switch. The new lens put him within a foot of her face: she was trimming her nails with a fierce concentration, wrinkles in her forehead and in the flesh along her sides, foot pulled within a few inches of her nose. She

132

carefully put each clipping aside, on the bedspread. He let the scope drop to her legs; she was sitting sideways to him, her far leg pulled up; her navel was an 'innie'; her pubic hair seemed artificially low. She probably wore a bikini in the summer. She had a small white scar on her near knee. On her hip, a tattoo? What? No, a birthmark, he thought. Or a bruise.

She finished with the far foot, and lifted the near one. From his angle on the roof, he could see just the curve of her vulva, with a bit of hair. He closed his eyes and swallowed, opened them again. He went back to her hip: definitely a birthmark. To her breasts, back to the pubic hair, to her face: she was so close, he could almost feel the heat from her.

When she finished with her foot, she gathered the trimmed nails in the palm of her hand and carried them out of sight into the bathroom. Again she was gone for a while, and when she came back, the towel was no longer wrapped around her head and her hair fell on her shoulders, frizzy, coiled, still damp.

She took her time finding a nightgown; walked around nude for a while, apparently enjoying it. When she finally pulled a nightgown out of her dresser, Koop *willed* her naked for just another second. But she pulled the nightgown over her head, facing him, and her body disappeared in a slow white erotic tumble of cotton. He closed his eyes: he simply couldn't take it. When he opened them, she was buttoning the gown at the neck; so virginal now, when just a moment before . . .

'No . . .' A single dry word, almost a moan. Go back, start over . . . Koop needed something. He needed a woman, was what he needed.

Koop put Sara Jensen to bed before he left, developing the same sense of loss he always felt when he left her; but this time he closed his eyes, saw her again. He waited a half hour, looking at nothing but darkness; when he finally dropped off the air conditioner and took the stairs, he could barely remember doing it. He just suddenly found himself in the street, walking toward the truck.

And the pressure was intense. The pressure was always there, but sometimes it was irresistible, even though it put his life in jeopardy.

Koop climbed into the truck, took Hennepin Avenue back toward the loop, then slid into the side streets, wandering aimlessly around downtown. He ran Sara Jensen behind his eyes like a movie. The curve of her leg, the little pink there ... Thought about buying a bottle. He could use a drink. He could use several. Maybe find John, pick up another eight-ball. Get an eight-ball and a bottle of Canadian Club and a six-pack of 7-Up, have a party ...

Maybe he should go back. Maybe she'd get up and he could see her again. Maybe he could call her number on a cellular phone, get her up ... but he didn't have a cellular phone. Could he get one? Maybe she'd undress again ... He shook himself. Stupid. She was asleep.

Koop saw the girl as he passed the bus station. She had a red nylon duffel bag by her feet and she was peering down the street. Waiting for a bus? Koop went by, looked her over. She was dark-haired, a little heavy, with a round, smooth, unblemished face. If you squinted, she might be Jensen; and she had the look he always sought in the bookstores, the passivity ...

Impulsively, he did a quick around-the-block, dumped the truck behind the station, started into the station, turned, ran back to the truck, opened the back, pulled out the toolbox, closed up the truck, and went through the station.

The girl was still standing at the corner, looking down Hennepin. She turned when she sensed him coming, gave him the half-smile and the shifting eyes that he saw from women at night, the smile that said, 'I'm nice, don't hurt me,' the eyes that said, 'I'm not really looking at you . . .'

He toted the heavy toolbox past her, and she looked away. A few feet farther down, he stopped, put a frown on his face, turned and looked at her.

'Are you waiting for a bus?'

'Yes.' She bobbed her head and smiled. 'I'm going to a friend's in Upper Town.'

'Uptown,' he said. She wasn't from Minneapolis. 'Uh, there aren't many buses at this time of night. I don't even know if they run to Uptown . . . Can your friend come and get you?'

'He doesn't have a phone. I've only got his address.'

Koop started away. 'You oughta catch a cab,' he said. 'This is kind of a tough street. There're hookers around here, you don't want the cops thinking . . .'

'Oh, no . . .' Her mouth was an *O*, eyes large.

Koop hesitated. 'Are you from Minnesota?'

She really wasn't sure about talking to him. 'I'm from Worthington.'

'Sure, I've been there,' Koop said, trying a smile. 'Stayed at a Holiday Inn on the way to Sioux Falls.'

'I go to Sioux all the time,' she said. Something in common. She'd held her arms crossed over her stomach as they talked; now she dropped them to her sides. Opening up.

Koop put the toolbox on the sidewalk. 'Look, I'm a maintenance guy with Greyhound. You don't know me, but I'm an okay guy, really. I'm on my way to South Minneapolis, I could drop you in Uptown . . .'

She looked at him closely now, afraid but tempted. He didn't look that bad: tall, strong. Older. Had to be thirty.

'I was told that the bus . . .'

'Sure.' He grinned again. 'Don't take rides from strangers. That's a good policy. If you stick close to the bus stop and the station, you should be okay,' he said. 'I wouldn't go down that way, you can see the porno stores. There're weirdos going in and out.'

'Porno stores?' She looked down the street. A black guy was looking in the window of a camera store.

'Anyway, I gotta go,' Koop said, picking up his toolbox. 'Take it easy . . .'

'Wait,' she said, her face open, fearful but hoping. She picked up the duffel. 'I'll take the ride, if it's okay.'

'Sure. I'm parked right behind the station,' Koop said. 'Let me get my tools stowed away . . . You'll be there in five minutes.'

'This is my first time in Minneapolis,' the girl said, now chatty. 'But I used to go up to Sioux every weekend, just about.'

'What's your name?' Koop asked.

'Marcy Lane,' she said. 'What's yours?'

'Ben,' he said. 'Ben Cooper.'

Ben was a nice name. Like Gentle Ben, the bear, on television. 'Nice to meet you, Ben,' she said, and tried a smile, a kind of bohemian, woman-of-the-road smile.

She looked like a child.

A pie-faced kid from the country.

10

Weather heard the phone at the far end of the house, woke up, poked him.

'Phone,' she mumbled. 'It must be for you.'

Lucas fumbled around in the dark, found the bedroom phone, picked it up. Dispatch patched him through to North Minneapolis. Another one.

'. . . recovered her purse and a duffel bag with some clothes. We got a license, says she's Marcy Lane with an address in Worthington,' Carrigan said. His voice sounded like a file being run over sheet metal. 'We're trying to run her folks down now. You better get your ass over here.'

'Did you call Lester?' Lucas was sitting on the bed, hunched in the light from the bedside lamp, bare feet on the floor. Weather was still awake, unmoving, listening to the conversation over her shoulder.

'Not yet. Should I?'

'I'll call him,' Lucas said. 'Freeze every fuckin' thing. Freeze it. The shit's gonna hit the fan, and you don't want any mistakes. And don't talk to the uniforms, for Christ's sakes.'

'It's froze hard,' Carrigan said.

'Keep it that way.' Lucas poked the phone's Cancel button, then redialed.

'Who's dead?' Weather asked, rolling onto her back.

'Some kid. Looks like our asshole did it,' Lucas said. The dispatcher came on and he said, 'This is Davenport. I need a number for a Meagan Connell. And I need to talk to Frank Lester. Now.'

They found a number for Connell and he scribbled it

down. As they put him through to Lester, he grinned at Weather, sleepy-eyed, looking up at him. 'How often do they call you in the middle of the night?' she asked. 'When you're working?'

'Maybe twenty times in twenty years,' he said.

She rolled toward her nightstand, looked at the clock. 'I get up in three hours.'

'Sorry,' he said.

She propped herself up on one elbow and said, 'I never thought of it until now, but you've got very little hair on your ass.'

'Hair?' The phone was ringing at the other end, and he looked down at his ass, confused. A sleepy Lester grunted, 'Hello?'

'This is Davenport,' Lucas said, going back to the phone, trying to get his mind off hair. 'Carrigan just called. A young girl from Worthington got gutted and dumped in a vacant lot up on the north side. If it ain't the one that did Wannemaker, it's his twin brother.'

After a moment of silence, Lester said, 'Shit.'

'Yeah. So now we got a new one. You better get with Roux and figure out what you're gonna do, publicity-wise.'

'I'll call her. Are you going up there? Wherever?'

'I'm on my way,' Lucas said.

Lucas hung up, then dialed the number for Connell. She picked it up, her voice a weak croak: 'Hello?'

'This is Davenport,' he said. 'A girl from out in the country just got killed and dumped up on the north side. It looks like it's our guy.'

'Where?' Wide-awake now. Lucas gave her the address. 'I'll see you there.'

Lucas hung up, hopped out of bed, and headed for the bathroom. 'You were going to observe tomorrow,' Weather said.

Lucas stopped, turned back. 'Oh, jeez, that's right. Listen.

138

If I finish up out there, I'll come over to the hospital. You're starting at seven-thirty?'

'Yes. That's when the kid's coming in.'

'I can make that,' he said. 'Where do I go?'

'Ask at the front desk. Tell them the operating suite, and when you get up there, ask for me. They'll be expecting you.'

'I'll try,' he said. 'Seven-thirty.'

Carrigan's second claim to fame was that he had small, fine feet, with which he danced. He had once appeared on stage at the Guthrie, in a modern interpretation of *Othello*, wearing nothing but a gold lamé jock and a headband.

His third claim to fame was that when a rookie had referred to him as a fag dancer, he'd held the rookie's head in a locker-room toilet for so long that homicide submitted the kid's name to the *Guinness Book of Records* for the longest free dive. The claim was noted, but rejected.

Carrigan's first claim to fame was that a decade earlier, he'd twice won the NCAA wrestling title at 198 pounds. Nobody fucked with him.

'Couldn't have been too long ago,' he told Lucas, looking back at the crowd gathering on the corner. Carrigan was black, as was most of the crowd gathered across the street. 'There was some people up here playing ball until dark, and there was no body then. Some kids cuttin' across the park found her a little after one o'clock.'

'Anybody see any vehicles?'

'We've got people going door to door across the park there, but I don't think we'll get much. There's an interstate entrance just down the block and it's easy to miss it: people come in here to turn around and go back, so there's cars in and out all the time. Nobody pays any attention. Come on, take a look.'

The body was still uncovered, lying on bare ground between a couple of large bushes. The bushes lined a bank that ran parallel to the third-base line on a softball field. Whoever had killed her didn't care if she was found; he must have realized that she'd be found almost immediately. Portable lights illuminated the area around the body, and a crime-scene crew was working it over. 'Look for cigarettes,' Lucas told Carrigan. 'Unfiltered Camels.'

'Okay . . .'

Lucas squatted next to the dead girl. She was lying on her side, twisted, her head and shoulders facing down, her hips half-turned toward the sky. Lucas could see enough of the wound to tell that it was identical to Wannemaker's: a stab and a disemboweling rip. He could smell the body cavity . . . 'Nasty,' Lucas said.

'Yeah,' Carrigan said sourly.

'Can I move her?'

'What for?'

'I want to roll her back and look at her chest,' Lucas said.

'If you want to – we got photos and all,' Carrigan said. 'But there's blood all over her, you better use gloves. Hang on . . .' He came back a moment later with a pair of thin yellow plastic gloves and handed them to Lucas. Lucas pulled them on, took the woman by the arm, and rolled her back.

'Look at this,' Lucas said. He pointed at two bloody squiggles on her breast. 'What do they look like?'

'Letters. An S and J,' Carrigan said, shining a penlight on the girl's body. 'Kiss my rosy red rectum. What is this shit, Davenport?'

'Insanity,' Lucas said as he studied the body.

A moment later, Carrigan said, 'Who's this?'

Lucas looked over his shoulder and saw Connell striding toward them, wrapped in a raincoat. 'My aide,' he said.

'Your fuckin' what?'

'Is it him?' Connell asked, coming up. Lucas stood up and stripped off the gloves.

'Yeah. Cut the *SJ* into her,' Lucas said. He crooked his head back and looked up at the night sky, the faint stars behind the city lights. The guy had pissed him off. Somehow, Wannemaker didn't reach him so personally; this kid did. Maybe because he could still feel the life in her. She hadn't been dead long.

'He's out of his pattern,' Connell said.

'Fuck pattern. We know he did Wannemaker,' Lucas said. 'The girl up north didn't have the letters cut into her.'

'But she was on schedule,' Connell said. 'Wannemaker and this one, these are two that are out of order. I hope we don't have two guys.'

'Nah.' Lucas shook his head. 'The knife in the stomach, man, it's a signature. More than the letters, even.'

'I better look at her,' Connell said. She crept under the bushes for a better look, squatted next to the body, turned the light on it. She studied it for a minute, then two, then walked away to spit. Came back. 'I'm getting used to it,' she said.

'God help you,' said Carrigan.

A patrolman and a tall black kid were walking fast up the block, the kid a half-step ahead of the patrolman. The kid wore knee shorts, an oversize shirt, Sox hat, and an expression of eye-rolling exasperation.

Carrigan took a step toward them. 'What you got, Bill?'

'Kid saw the guy,' the patrolman said. 'Sure enough.'

Lucas, Connell, and Carrigan gathered around the kid. 'You see him?'

'Man . . .' The kid looked up the block, where more people were wandering in, attracted by word of a murder.

'What's your name?' Connell asked.

'Dex?' The answer sounded like a question, and the kid's eyes rolled up to the sky.

'How long ago?' Lucas asked.

The kid shrugged. 'Do I look like a large fuckin' clock?'

'You're gonna look like a large fuckin' scab if you don't watch your mouth,' Carrigan said.

Lucas held up a hand, got close to the kid. 'This is a farm girl, Dex. Just came up to the city, somebody let the air out of her.'

'Ain't got nothin' to do with me,' Dex said, looking at the crowd again.

'Come over here,' Lucas said, his voice friendly. He took the kid's arm. 'Look at the body.'

'What?'

'Come on . . .' He waved the kid over, then said to the patrolman, 'Loan me your flashlight, will you, pal?'

Lucas took Dex around the bush, then duckwalked with him toward the woman on the wound side. He went willingly enough; hell, he'd seen six thousand bodies on TV, and once had walked by a place where some ambulance guys were taking a body out of a house. This'd be cool.

A foot from the body, Lucas turned the light on the stomach wound.

'Fuck,' said Dex. He stood up, straight through the bush, and started thrashing his way out.

Lucas caught his web pocket, hauled him back down, rough. 'Come on, man, you can tell people about this. How the cops let you check her out.' He put the flashlight on the girl's face. 'Look at her eyes, man, they're still open, they look like eggs. You can smell her guts if you get closer, kind of soapy smelling.'

Dex's eyes moved toward the corpse's, and he shuddered and stood and tried to run. Lucas let him go: Carrigan was waiting when the kid fought free of the bush.

'Never saw nothin' like that before,' Dex said. A line of saliva dribbled from one edge of his mouth, and he wiped it with his hand.

'So who was it?' Carrigan asked.

'White dude. Driving a pickup.'

'What kind of pickup?'

'White with dark on it, maybe red, I don't know; I know the white part for sure,' Dex said. He kept moving away from the body, around the bushes back toward the curb. Carrigan held one arm and Dex babbled on. 'There was a camper on the back. People come up here to throw garbage sometimes. I thought that's what he was doin', throwing garbage.'

'How close were you?' Connell asked.

'Down to the corner,' Dex said, pointing. A hundred yards.

'What'd he look like, far as you could tell?' Connell pressed. 'Big guy? Small guy? Skinny?'

'Pretty big. Big as me. And I think maybe he plays basketball, the way he got in the truck. He like hopped up there, you know. Just real quick, like he's got some speed. Quick.'

Connell fumbled in her purse and took out a folded square of paper. She started to unfold it when Lucas realized what it was, reached out and caught her hand, shook his head. 'Don't do that,' he said. He looked at Dex and asked, 'How long ago?'

'Hour? I don't know. 'Bout an hour.' That meant nothing. For most witnesses, an hour was more than fifteen minutes and less than three hours.

'What else?'

'Man, I don't think there's anything else. I mean, let me think about it . . .' He looked past Lucas. 'Here comes my mom.'

A woman rolled right through the police line, and when a cop reached out toward her, she turned around and snapped something that stopped him short, and she came on.

'What're you doing here?' she demanded.

'Talking to your son,' Carrigan said, facing her. 'He's a witness to a crime.'

143

'He's never been in no trouble,' the woman said.

'He's not in any trouble now,' Connell said. 'He might've seen a killer – a white man. He's just trying to remember what else he might've seen.'

'He's not in no trouble?' She was suspicious.

Connell shook her head. 'He's helping out.'

'Momma, you oughta see that girl,' Dex said, swallowing. He looked back toward the bush. The girl's hip was just visible from where they were standing. He looked back at Carrigan. 'The truck had those steps on the sides, you know, what do they call them?'

'Running boards?' Lucas suggested.

Dex nodded. 'That's it. Silver running boards.'

'Chevy, Ford?'

'Shoot, man, they all look the same to me. Wouldn't have one, myself . . .'

'What color was the camper?'

The kid had to think about it. 'Dark,' he said finally.

'What else?'

He scratched behind one ear, looked at his mother, then shook his head. 'Just some white dude dumping garbage, is what I thought.'

'Were you alone when you saw him?' Lucas asked.

He swallowed again and glanced at his mother. His mother saw it and slapped his back, hard. 'You tell.'

'I saw a guy named Lawrence, was up here,' he said.

His mother put her hands on her hips. 'You with Lawrence?'

'I wasn't with Lawrence, Momma. I just saw him up here, is all. I wasn't with him.'

'You goddamn better not be with him or I throw your butt outa the house. You know what I told you,' his mother said, angry. She looked at Carrigan and said, 'Lawrence a pusher.'

'Lawrence his first name or his last name?' Carrigan asked.

144

'Lawrence Wright.'

'Lawrence Wright? I know him,' Carrigan said. ''Bout twenty-two or -three, tall skinny guy, used to wear a sailor hat all the time?'

'That's him,' the woman said. 'Trash. He comes from a long line of trash. Got a trashy mother and all his brothers are trash,' she said. She smacked the kid on the back again. 'You hanging around with that trash?'

'Where'd he go?' Lucas asked. 'Lawrence?'

'He was around here until they found the body,' Dex said, looking around as if he might see the missing man. 'Then he left.'

'Did he see the white guy?' Connell asked.

Dex shrugged. 'I wasn't with him. But he was closer than me. He was walking up this way when the white dude went out of the park. I saw the white dude lookin' at him.'

Lucas looked at Carrigan. 'We need to get to this Lawrence right now.'

'Does he smoke?' Carrigan asked Dex.

Dex shrugged, but his mother said, 'He smokes. He's all the time walking around with his head up in the sky with that crack shit.'

'We gotta get him,' Lucas said again.

'I don't know where he hangs out, I just knew him from the neighborhood when I was working dope five years ago,' Carrigan said uncertainly. 'I could call a guy, Alex Drucker, works dope up here.'

'Get him,' Lucas said.

Carrigan glanced at his watch and chuckled. 'Four-thirty. Drucker's been in bed about two hours now. He'll like this.'

As Carrigan went back to his car, one of the crime-scene crew came over and said, 'No cigarettes from tonight, just old bits and pieces.'

'Forget it,' Lucas said. 'We're told she was dumped an

hour ago. Might check the street from here back to . . .
Nah, fuck it. We know who did it.'

'We'll check,' the crime-scene guy said. 'Camels . . .'

'Unfiltered,' Lucas said. He turned to the mother. 'We
need to send Dex downtown with an officer to make a
statement, and maybe get him to describe this guy for an
artist. We'll bring him back. Or, if you want, you can ride
along.'

'Ride along?'

'If you want.'

'I better do that,' she said. 'He's not in trouble?'

'He's not in trouble.'

Carrigan came back. 'Nobody at Drucker's place. No
answer.'

'The guy's known around here – why don't we walk
down to the corner and ask?'

Carrigan looked down to the corner, then back to Lucas
and Connell. 'You two are pretty white to be askin' favors
from them.'

Lucas shrugged. 'I'm not going to sweat them; I'm just
gonna ask. Come on.'

They walked down toward the corner, and Connell
asked, 'Why can't I show him the picture? He could give
us a confirmation.'

'I don't want to contaminate his memory. If we get a
sketch out of him, I'd rather have it be what he remembers,
not what he saw when you showed him a picture.'

'Oh.' She thought about it for a minute, then nodded.

As they reached the corner, the crowd went quiet, and
Carrigan pushed right up to it. 'Some white dude just cut
open a little girl and dumped her body in the bushes back
there,' Carrigan said conversationally, without preamble.
'A guy named Lawrence Wright saw him. We don't want
to hassle Lawrence, we just want a statement: if anybody's
seen him, or if he's here?'

'That girl, black or white?' a woman asked.

'White,' Lucas said.

'Why you need to talk to Lawrence? Maybe he didn't see nothin'.'

'He saw something,' Carrigan said. 'He was right next to this white dude.'

'The guy is nuts,' Lucas said. 'He's like that guy over in Milwaukee, killed all those boys. This has got nothing to do with nothing, he's just killing people.'

A ripple of talk ran through the crowd, and then a woman's voice said, 'Lawrence went to Porter's.' Somebody else said, 'Shush,' and the woman's voice said, 'Shush, your ass, he's killing little girls, somebody is.'

'White girls . . . that don't make no difference . . . still white . . . What'd Lawrence do . . . ?'

'We better get going,' Carrigan said quietly. 'Before somebody runs down to Porter's and tells Lawrence we're coming.'

Lucas and Connell rode with Carrigan. 'Porter's is an after-hours place down on Twenty-ninth,' Carrigan said. 'We oughta get a squad to do some blocking for us.'

'Wouldn't hurt,' Lucas said. 'The place'd still be open?'

'Another fifteen minutes or so. He usually closes about five in the summertime.'

They met the squad four minutes later at a Perkins restaurant parking lot. One patrolman was black, the other white, and Lucas talked to them through the car windows, told them who they were looking for. 'Just hold anybody coming out . . . You guys know where it is?'

'Yeah. We'll slide right down the alley. As soon as you see us going in, though, you better get in the front.'

'Let's do it,' Carrigan said.

'How bad might this get?' Connell asked.

Carrigan glanced at her. 'Shouldn't be bad at all. Porter's

147

is an okay place; Porter goes along. But you know . . .'

'Yeah. Lucas and I are white.'

'Better let me go first. Don't yell at anybody.'

They hesitated at the corner, just long enough for the squad to cut behind them, go halfway down the block, then duck into the mouth of the alley. Carrigan rolled up to the front of a 1920s-style four-square house with a wide porch. The porch was empty, but when they climbed out of the car, Lucas could hear a Charles Brown tune floating out through an open window.

Carrigan led the way up the walk, across the porch. When he went through the door, Lucas and Connell paused a moment, making just a little space, then followed him through.

The living room of the old house had been turned into a bar; the old parlor had a half-dozen chairs in it, three of them filled. Two men and two women sat around a table in the living room to the left. Everything stopped when Lucas and Connell walked in. The air was layered with tobacco smoke and the smell of whiskey.

'Mr Porter,' Carrigan was saying to a bald man behind the bar.

'What can I do for you gentlemen?' Porter asked, both hands poised on the bar. Porter didn't have a license, but it wasn't usually a problem. One of the men at the table moved his chair back an inch, and Lucas looked at him. He stopped moving.

'One of your patrons saw a suspect in a murder – a white man who killed a white girl and dumped her body up in the park,' Carrigan said, his voice formal, polite. 'Guy's a maniac, and we need to talk to Lawrence Wright about it. Have you seen Lawrence?'

'I really can't recall. The name's not familiar,' Porter said, but his eyes drifted deliberately toward the hall. A door had a hand-lettered sign that said Men.

'Well, we'll get out of your way, then,' Carrigan said. 'I'll just take a leak, if you don't mind.'

Lucas had moved until his back was to a Grain Belt clock and where he could still block the door. His pistol was clipped to his back belt line, and he put one hand on his hip, as if impatient about waiting for Carrigan. A voice said, 'Cops out back,' and another voice asked, 'What's that mean?'

Carrigan stepped down the hall, went past the door, then stepped back and pulled it open.

And smiled. 'Hey,' he called to Lucas, smiling, surprised. 'Guess what? Lawrence is right here. Sittin' on the potty.'

A whine came out of the room: 'Shut that door, man. I'm doing my business. Please?'

The voice sounded like something from a bad sitcom. After a moment of silence, somebody in the living room laughed, a single, throaty, feminine laugh, and suddenly the entire bar fell out, the patrons roaring. Even Porter put his forehead down on his bar, laughing. Lucas laughed a little, not too much, and relaxed.

Lawrence was thin, almost emaciated. At twenty, he'd lost his front teeth, both upper and lower, and he made wet slurping sounds when he spoke: '. . . I don't know, *slurp*, it was dark. Blue and white, I think, *slurp*. And he had a beard. Shitkicker wheels on the truck.'

'Real big?'

'Yeah, real big. Somebody say he had running boards? *Slurp*. I don't think he had running boards. Maybe he did, but I didn't see any. He was a white guy, but he had a beard. Dark beard.'

'Beard,' Connell said.

'How come you're sure he was a white guy?'

Lawrence frowned, as if working out a puzzle, then brightened. 'Because I saw his hands. He was takin' a pinch, man. He was tootin', that's why I looked at him.'

'Coke?'

'Gotta be,' Lawrence said. 'Ain't nothing else looks like that, you know, when you're trying to toot while you're walkin' or doin' something else. *Slurp*. You just get a pinch and you put it up there. That's what he was doin'. And I saw his hands.'

'Long hair, short?' Connell asked.

'Couldn't tell.'

'Bumper stickers, license plates, anything?' asked Lucas.

Lawrence cocked his head, lips pursed. 'Nooo, didn't notice anything like that, *slurp*.'

'Didn't see much, did you?' said Carrigan.

'I told you he was tootin',' Lawrence said defensively. 'I told you he was white.'

'Big fuckin' deal. That's Minneapolis outside, if you ain't noticed,' Carrigan said. 'There are approximately two point five million white people walking around.'

'Ain't my fault,' Lawrence said.

Red-and-white truck, or maybe blue-and-white, maybe with silver running boards, but then again, maybe not. Cokehead. White. A beard.

'Let's send him downtown and take him through the whole thing,' Lucas said to Carrigan. 'Get him on tape.'

They went back to the scene, but nothing had changed except that the sun had come up and the world had a pale, frosted look. Crime scene was videotaping the area, and trucks from TV3 and Channel 8 hung down the block.

'Your pals from TV3,' Lucas said, poking Connell with an elbow.

'Cockroaches,' she said.

'C'mon.' He looked back at the truck. A dark-haired woman waved. He waved back.

'They make entertainment out of murder, rape, pornography, pain, disease,' Connell said. 'There's nothing

150

bad that happens to humans that they can't make a cartoon out of.'

'You didn't hesitate to go to them.'

'Of course not,' she said calmly. 'They're cockroaches, but they're a fact of life, and they *do* have their uses.'

11

Connell wanted to hear the interview with Lawrence, and to press the medical examiner on the Marcy Lane autopsy. Lucas let her go, looked at his watch. Weather would be leaving home in fifteen minutes; he couldn't make it before she left. He drove back to the Perkins where they'd met the squad, bought a paper, and ordered pancakes and coffee.

Junky Doog dominated the *Strib*'s front page: two stories, a feature and a harder piece. The hard story began, 'A leading suspect in a series of midwestern sex slayings was arrested in Dakota County yesterday . . .' The feature said, 'Junky Doog lived under a tree at a Dakota County landfill, and one by one cut off the fingers of his left hand, and the toes . . .'

'Good story.' A pair of legs – nice legs – stopped by the table. Lucas looked up. A celebrity smiled down at him. He recognized her but couldn't immediately place her. 'Jan Reed,' she said. 'With TV3? Could I join you for a cup?'

'Sure . . .' He waved at the seat opposite. 'I can't tell you much.'

'The camera guys said you were pretty good about us,' Reed said.

Reed was older than most TV reporters, probably in her middle thirties, Lucas thought. Like all of the latest crop of on-camera newswomen, she was strikingly attractive, with large dark eyes, auburn hair falling to her shoulders, and just a hint of the fashionable overbite. Lucas had suggested to Weather that a surgeon was making a fortune somewhere, turning out TV anchors with bee-stung lips and overbites. Weather told him that would be unethical; the next day, though, she said she'd been watching, and there were far too many overbites on local television to be accounted for by simple jaw problems.

'Why is that?' she'd asked. She seemed really interested.

Lucas said, 'You don't know?'

'No. I don't,' she said. She looked at him skeptically. 'You're gonna tell me it's something dirty?'

'It's because it makes guys think about blow jobs,' Lucas said.

'You're lying to me,' Weather said, one hand on her hip.

'Honest to God,' Lucas said. 'That's what it is.'

'This society is out of luck,' Weather said. 'I'm sorry, but we're going down the tubes. Blow jobs.'

Jan Reed sipped her coffee and said, 'One of our sources says it's the serial killer. We saw Officer Connell there, of course, so it's a reasonable presumption. Will you confirm it?'

Lucas thought about it, then said, 'Listen, I hate talking on the record. It gets me in trouble. I'll give you a little information, if you just lay it off on an unnamed source.'

'Done,' she said, and she stuck her hand out. Lucas shook it: her hand was soft, warm. She smiled, and that made him feel even warmer. She *was* attractive.

Lucas gave her two pieces of information: that the victim was female and white, and that investigators believed it was the work of the same man who killed Wannemaker.

'We already had most of that,' she said gently. She was working him, trying to make him show off.

He didn't bite. 'Well, what can I tell you,' he said. 'Another day in the life of a TV reporter, fruitlessly chasing down every possible scrap.'

She laughed, a nice laugh, musical, and she said, 'I understand you used to date a reporter.'

'Yes. We have a daughter,' Lucas said.

'That's serious.'

'Well. It was,' Lucas said. He took a sip of coffee. 'Some time ago.'

'I'm divorced myself,' she said. 'I never thought it would happen.' She looked at her hands.

Lucas thought he ought to mention Weather, but he didn't. 'You know, I recognized you right away – I thought you were anchoring.'

'Yes – I will be. I've done a little already, but I only got here three months ago. They're rotating me through the shifts so I can see how things work, while I anchor on a fill-in basis. In another month, I'll start getting more anchor time.'

'Smart. Get to know the place.'

They chatted for a few more minutes, then Lucas glanced at his watch and said, 'Damn. I've got to go,' and slid out of the booth.

'Got a date?' She looked up at him, and he almost fell into her eyes.

'Sort of,' Lucas said, trying to look somewhere else. 'Listen, uh . . . see you around, huh?'

'No doubt,' she said, sending him off with a bee-stung smile.

Weather had seen Lucas working at close range, as he broke a murder case in her small northern Wisconsin town. Lucas had seen Weather working as a coroner – doctors were scarce up north, and they took turns at the county coroner's job – but the only time he'd been around when she was working on a live patient, he'd been unconscious: he'd been the patient.

He had promised her he'd come and watch what she did, not thinking about it much. She'd become insistent, and they'd set the visit up a week earlier, before the Wannemaker killing. He could just squeeze it in, he thought.

He touched the scar on his throat, thinking about

Weather. Most of the scar had been caused by a Swiss Army knife that she'd used to open him up; the rest came from a .22 slug, fired by a little girl . . .

Lucas left his car in a parking ramp three blocks from University Hospitals and walked down through the cool morning, among the medical students in their short white coats, the staff doctors in their longer coats. A nurse named Jim showed Lucas the men's locker room, gave him a lock and key for a locker, and told him how to dress: 'There're scrub suits in the bins, three different sizes. The shoe covers are down there in the bottom bin. The caps and masks are in those boxes. Take one of the shower cap types, and take a mask, but don't put it on yet. We'll show you how to tie it when you're ready . . . Take your billfold and watch and any valuables with you. Dr Harkinnen'll be out in a minute.'

Weather's eyes smiled at him when he stepped out of the locker room. He felt like an idiot in the scrub suit, like an impostor.

'How does it feel?' Weather asked.

'Strange. Cool,' Lucas said.

'The girl who was killed . . . was it him?'

'Yes. Didn't get much out of it. A kid saw him, though. He's white, he probably snorts coke, he drives a truck.'

'That's something.'

'Not much,' he said. He looked down the hall toward the double doors that led to the operating rooms. 'Is your patient already doped up?'

'She's right there,' Weather said, nodding.

Lucas looked to his left. A thin, carefully groomed blond woman and a tiny redheaded girl sat in a waiting area, the little girl looking up at the woman, talking intently. The girl's arms were bandaged to the shoulder. The woman's head was nodding, as if she were explaining something; the little girl's legs twisted and retwisted as they dangled off the chair. 'I need to talk to them for a minute,' Weather said.

Weather went down the hall. Lucas, still self-conscious about the scrub suit, hung back, drifting along behind her. He saw the girl when she spotted Weather; her face contorted with fear. Lucas, even more uncomfortable, slowed even more. Weather said something to the mother, then squatted and started talking to the girl. Lucas stepped closer, and the little girl looked up at him. He realized that she was weeping, soundlessly, but almost without control. She looked back at Weather. 'You're going to hurt me again,' she wailed.

'It'll be fine,' Weather said quickly.

'Hurts bad,' the girl said, tears running down. 'I don't want to get fixed anymore.'

'Well, you've got to get better,' Weather said, and as she reached out a finger to touch the girl's cheek, the dam burst, and the girl began to cry, clutching at her mother's dress with her bandaged arms like tree stumps.

'This won't hurt so bad today. Just a little pinch for the IV and that's all,' Weather said, patting her. 'And when you wake up, we'll give you a pill, and you'll be sleepy for a while.'

'That's what you said last time,' the girl wailed.

'You've got to get better, and we're almost done,' Weather said. 'Today, and one more day, and we should be finished.' Weather stood and looked at the mother. 'She hasn't eaten anything?'

'Not since nine o'clock,' the woman said. Tears were running down her cheeks. 'I've got to get out of here,' she said desperately. 'I can't stand this. Can we get going?'

'Sure,' Weather said. 'Come on, Lucy, take my hand.'

Lucy slipped slowly out of the chair, took one of Weather's fingers. 'Don't hurt me.'

'We're gonna try really hard,' Weather said. 'You'll see.'

*   *   *

156

Weather left the girl with the nurses and took Lucas along to an office where she started going through an inch-high stack of papers, checking them and signing. 'Preop stuff,' she said. 'Who was the girl last night?'

'A teenager from out of state. From Worthington.'

Weather looked up. 'Pretty bad?'

'You'd have to see it to believe it.'

'You sound a little pissed,' she said.

'On this one, I am,' he said. 'This girl looked like . . . she looked like somebody who did her first communion last week.'

The routine of the operation caught him: precise, but informal. Everybody in the room except Lucas and the anesthesiologist was female, and the anesthesiologist left for another operation as soon as the girl was down, leaving the job in the hands of a female anesthetist. The surgical team put him in a rectangular area along a wall and suggested that he stay there.

Weather and the surgical assistant worked well together, the assistant ready with the instruments almost before Weather asked for them. There was less blood than Lucas expected, but the smell of the cautery bothered him; burning blood . . .

Weather explained quickly what she was doing, expanding and spreading skin to cover the burns on the girl's arms. Weather ran the show with quick, tight directions, and there were no questions.

And she spoke to Lucas from time to time, distractedly, focusing on the work. 'Her father was running a power line from a 220 outlet to a pump down by the lake using an extension cord. The connection where the two cords came together . . . started to pull apart. That's what they think. Lucy grabbed them to put them back together. They don't know exactly what she was doing, but there was a flash and she'd gotten hit on both arms, and around her

157

back on her shoulder blades ... We'll show you. We're doing skin grafts where we can, and in some places we're expanding the skin to cover.'

After a while, talk around the table turned to a book about a love affair that was dominating the best-seller lists. About whether the lovers should have gone off together, destroying a marriage and a family.

'She was living a lie afterwards; she was hurting everyone,' one of the nurses declared. 'She should have gone.'

'Right. And the family is wrecked and just because she has a fling doesn't mean she still doesn't love them.'

'This was not exactly a fling.'

In the background, music oozed from a portable radio turned to an easy-listening station; on the table, under Weather's gloved hands and knife, Lucy bled.

They harvested skin from Lucy's thigh to cover a part of the wound. The skin harvester looked like a cross between an electric sander and a sod cutter.

'This looks like it's going to hurt,' Lucas said finally. 'Hurt a lot.'

'Can't help it,' Weather grunted, not looking up. 'These are the worst, burns are. Skin won't regenerate, but you've got to cover the wounds to prevent infection. That means grafts and expansions ... We put the temporary skin on because we couldn't get enough off her the first couple of times, but you can't leave the temporary stuff, she'll reject it.'

'Maybe you should have told her it was going to hurt,' Lucas said. 'When you were talking to her outside.'

Weather glanced up briefly, as though considering it, but shook her head as she continued to tack down the advanced skin on one of the expansions. 'I didn't tell her it wouldn't hurt. The idea was to get her in here, quiet, with a minimum of resistance. Next time, I can tell her it's the last time.'

'Will it be?'

'I hope so,' Weather said. 'We might need a touch-up if we get some rough scar development. Might have to release scar tissue. But the next one should be the last one for a while.'

'Huh.'

She looked at him, grave, quiet, over the top of her mask, her pink-stained fingers held in front of her, away from the girl's open wounds; the nurses were looking at him as well. 'I don't do therapy,' she said. 'I do surgery. Sometimes you can't get around the pain. All you can do is fix them, and eventually the pain stops. That's the best I can do.'

And later, when she was finished, they sat together in the surgeon's lounge for a few minutes and she asked, 'What do you think?'

'Interesting. Impressive.'

'Is that all?' There was a tone in her voice.

'I've never seen you before as the commander in chief,' he said. 'You do it pretty well.'

'Any objections?'

'Of course not.'

She stood up. 'You seemed disturbed. When you were watching me.'

He looked down, shook his head. 'It's pretty strong stuff. And it wasn't what I'd expected, the blood and the smell of the cautery and that skin harvester thing . . . It's kind of brutal.'

'Sometimes it is,' she said. 'But you were most bothered about my *attitude* toward Lucy.'

'I don't know . . .'

'I can't get involved,' she said. 'I have to turn off that part of me. I can like patients, and I like Lucy, but I can't afford to go into the operating room worrying that I'll hurt them, or wondering if I'm doing the right thing. I've worked that out in advance. If I didn't, I'd screw up in there.'

'It did seem a little cold,' he admitted.

'I wanted you to see that,' she said. 'Lucas, as part of my . . . surgeon persona, I guess you'd call it, I'm different. I have to make brutal decisions, and I do. And I run things. I run them very well.'

'Well . . .'

'Let me finish. Since I moved down here, we've had some very good times in bed. We've had nice runs at night, and some fun going out and fooling around. *But this is what I am, right here.* What you saw.'

Lucas sighed, and nodded. 'I know that. And I admire you for it. Honest to God.'

She smiled then, just a little. 'Really?'

'Really. It's just that what you do . . . is so much harder than I thought.'

Much harder, he thought again as he left the hospital.

In his world, or in Jan Reed's world, for that matter, very few thing were perfectly clear: the best players were always figuring odds. Mistakes, stupidity, oversights, lies, and accidents were part of the routine. In Weather's world, those things were not routine; they were, in fact, virtually unforgivable.

The surgery was another thing. The blood hadn't bothered him, but he *was* bothered by that moment where the knife hovered above the uncut skin, as Weather made her last-minute decisions on how she would proceed. Cutting in hot blood was one thing; doing it in cold blood – doing it on a child, even for the child's own good – was something else. It took an intellectual toughness of an order that Lucas hadn't encountered on the street. Not outside a psychopath.

That was what she'd wanted him to see.

Was she trying to tell him something?

12

Lucas's head felt large and fuzzy as he walked through the doors of City Hall and up to the chief's office. Lack of sleep. Getting older. Roux's secretary thumbed him through the door, but Lucas stopped for a second. 'Check around and see if Meagan Connell's in the building, will you? Tell her where I am.'

'Sure. Do you want me to send her in?'

'Yeah, why not?'

'Because she and the chief might get in a fistfight?'

Lester and Anderson were in visitor's chairs. Lonnie Shantz, Roux's press aide, leaned on the windowsill, arms crossed, an accusation on his jowly ward heeler's face. Roux nodded when Lucas arrived. 'They're pissed over at the *Strib*,' she said. 'Have you seen the paper?'

'Yeah. The big thing on Junky.'

'With this killing last night, they think we sandbagged them,' Shantz said.

Lucas sat down. 'What can you do? The guy's flipped out. Any other time, it might've held them for a few days.'

'We're not looking good, Lucas,' Roux said.

'What about the St Paul cop?' Shantz asked. 'Anything there?'

'I'm told that St Paul had a shrink talk to him,' Lester said. 'They don't think he's capable of it.'

'Beat up his wife,' Shantz suggested.

'The charges were dropped. More like a brawl. His old lady got her licks in,' Anderson said. 'Hit him in the face with a Mr Coffee.'

'I heard it was an iron,' Lucas said. 'Where was he last night, by the way?'

'Bad news,' Lester said. 'His old lady moved out after the last big fight, and he was home. Alone. Watching TV.'

'Shit,' Lucas said.

'St Paul's talking to him again, pinning down the shows he saw.'

'Yeah, yeah, but with VCR time delays, he could have been anywhere,' Shantz said.

'Bullshit,' said Anderson.

Shantz was talking to Roux. 'All we'd have to do is leak a name and the spousal-abuse charge. We could do it a long way from here – I could have one of my pals at the DFL do it for me. Hell, they like doing favors for media, for the paybacks. TV3'd pee their pants with that kind of tip. And it really *does* smell like a cover-up.'

'They'd crucify him,' Lester said. 'They'd make it look like the charges were dropped because he's a cop.'

'Who's to say they weren't?' Shantz asked. 'And it would take some of the heat off us. Christ, this killing over at the lakes, that's a goddamn disaster. The woman's dead and the guy's a cabbage. Now we get this serial asshole again, knocking off some country milkmaid, we're talking firestorm.'

'If you feed the St Paul guy to the press, you'll regret it. It'd kill the Senate for you,' Lucas said to Roux.

'Why is that?' Shantz demanded. 'I don't see how . . .'

Lucas ignored him, spoke to Roux. 'Word would get out. When everybody figured out what happened – that you threw an innocent cop to the wolves to turn the attention away from you – they'd never forget and never forgive you.'

Roux looked at him for a moment, then shifted her gaze to Shantz. 'Forget it.'

'Chief . . .'

'Forget it,' she snapped. 'Davenport is right. The risk is

too big.' Her eyes moved to her left, past Lucas, hardened. Lucas turned and saw Connell standing in the doorway.

'Come on in, Meagan,' he said. 'Do you have the picture?'

'Yeah.' Connell dug in her purse, took out the folded paper, and handed it to Lucas. Lucas unfolded it, smoothed it, and passed it to Roux.

'This is not bullshit; this could be our man. More or less. I'm not sure you should release it.'

Roux looked at the picture for a moment, then at Connell, then at Lucas. 'Where'd you get this?' she asked.

'Meagan found a woman yesterday who remembers a guy at the St Paul store who was there the same time Wannemaker was there. He's not on our list of names and this fits some of the other descriptions we've had. A guy last night who definitely saw him says he has a beard.'

'And drives a truck,' said Connell.

'Everybody who drives a truck has a beard,' Lester said.

'Not quite,' Lucas said. 'This is actually . . . something. A taste of the guy.'

'Why wouldn't I release it?' Roux asked.

'Because we're not getting enough hard evidence. Nothing that can tie him directly to a killing – a hair or a fingerprint. If this isn't a good picture of him, and we do finally track him down, and we're scraping little bits and pieces together to make a case . . . a defense attorney will take this and stick it up our ass. You know: *Here's the guy they were looking for – until they decided to pin it on my client.*'

'Is there anything working today? Anything that'd give us a break?'

'Not unless it comes out of the autopsy on Lane. That'll be a while yet.'

'Um, Bob Greave got a call from TV3 – a tip on a suspect,' Connell said. 'It's nothing.'

'What do you mean, nothing? What is this, Lucas?' Roux asked.

'Beats me. First I heard of it,' he said.

'Get his ass down here,' Roux said.

Greave came down carrying a slip of yellow paper, leaned in the doorway.

'Well?' Roux said.

He looked at the paper. 'A woman out in Edina says she knows who the killer is.'

Lucas: 'And the bad news is . . .'

'She called TV3 first. They're the ones who called us. They want to know if we're going to make an arrest based on their information.'

'You should have come and told us,' Roux said. 'We've been sitting here beating our heads against the wall.'

Greave held up a hand. 'You have to understand, the woman doesn't have any actual proof.'

Roux said, 'Keep talking.'

'She remembers the killer coming back from each of the murders, washing the blood off the knife and his clothes, and then raping her. She repressed all this until yesterday, when the memories were liberated with the help of her therapist.'

'Oh, no,' Lucas groaned.

'It could be,' Shantz said, looking around.

'Did I mention that the killer is her father?' Greave asked. 'Sixty-six years old, the former owner of a drive-in theater? A guy with arteriosclerosis so bad that he can't walk up a flight of stairs?'

'We gotta check it,' Shantz said. 'Especially with the TV all over it.'

'It's bullshit,' Lucas said.

'We gotta check,' Roux said.

'We'll check,' Lucas said, 'But we really need to catch this guy, and talking to old heart-attack victims isn't gonna do it.'

'This one time, Lucas, goddamnit,' Roux said, adamant.

'I want you out there interviewing the guy, and I want you giving the statement to TV3.'

'When the fuck did the TV start running our investigations?' Lucas asked.

'Jesus, Lucas – we're entertainment now. We're cheap film footage. We sell deodorant and get votes. Or lose votes. It's all a big loop; I've been told you were the first guy to realize that.'

'Christ, it wasn't like this,' Lucas said. 'It was more like one hand washing the other. Now it's . . .'

'Entertainment for the unwashed.'

As Lucas walked out the door, Roux called, 'Lucas. Hey – don't kill this old guy, huh? When you talk to him?'

They took a company car, all three of them, Greave sprawled in the back.

'Let me do the TV interview,' he suggested to Lucas. 'I did them all the time when I was Officer Friendly. I'm good at that shit. I got the right suits.'

'*You* were Officer Friendly?' Connell snorted, looking over the seat at him. Then, 'You know, it fits.'

She said it as an insult. Lucas glanced at her and almost said something, but Greave was rambling on. 'Really? I thought so. Go into all those classrooms, tell all the little boys that they'd grow up to be firemen and policemen, all the little girls that they'd be housewives and hookers.'

Lucas, moderately surprised, shut his mouth and looked straight out over the wheel, and Connell said, 'Fuck you, Greave.'

Greave, still cheerful, said, 'Say, did I tell you about the deaf people?'

'Huh?'

'Some deaf people went into the St Paul cops. They saw the thing on TV, you know, that Connell fed them? They think they saw the guy at the bookstore the night

Wannemaker was taken off. Bearded guy with a truck. They even got part of his license tag.'

Connell turned to look over the seat. 'Why didn't you say something?'

'Unfortunately, they didn't get any numbers. Only the letters.'

'Well, that'd get it down to a thousand –'

'Uh-uh,' Greave said. 'The letters they got were *ASS*.'

'*ASS?*'

'Yeah.'

'Damnit,' Connell said, turning back front. The state banned license plates with potentially offensive letter combinations: there were no *FUK*, *SUK*, *LIK*, or *DIK*. No *CNT* or *TWT*. There was no *ASS*.

'Did we check?'

'Yup,' Greave said. 'There's nary a one. I personally think this old guy did it, then comes home and gives the daughter a little tickle.'

'Kiss my ass,' Connell said.

'Any time, any place,' said Greave.

A TV3 truck was parked on the street in front of the Weston house, a reporter combing her strawberry-blond hair in the wing mirror, a cameraman in a travel vest sitting on the curb, eating an egg-salad sandwich. The cameraman said something to the reporter as Lucas stopped at the house, and the reporter turned, saw him, and started across the street. She had long smooth legs on top of black high heels. Her dress clung to her like a new paint job on a '55 Chevy.

'I think she's in my *Playboy*,' Greave said, his face pressed to the window. 'Her name is Pamela Stern. She's a piranha.'

Lucas got out and Stern came up, thrust out her hand, and said, 'I think we've got him bottled up inside.'

'Yeah, well . . .' Lucas looked up at the house. The

curtains twitched in an old-fashioned picture window. The reporter reached out and turned over his necktie. Lucas looked down and found her reading the orange label.

'Hermes,' she said. 'I thought so. Very nice.'

'His shoes are from Payless,' Connell said from across the car.

'His shorts are from Fruit of the Loom,' said Greave, chipping in. 'He's one of the fruits.'

'I *love* your sunglasses,' Stern said, ignoring them, her perfect white teeth catching her lower lip for just an instant. 'They make you look mean. Mean is *so* sexy.'

'Jesus,' Lucas said. He started up the walk with Greave and Connell, and found the woman right at his elbow. Behind her, the cameraman had the camera on his shoulder, and rolling. Lucas said, 'When we get to the steps, I'm going to ask the guy if he wants me to arrest you for trespassing. If he does, I will. And I suspect he does.'

She stopped in her tracks, eyes like chips of flint. 'It's not nice to fuck with Mother Nature,' she said. And then, 'I don't know what Jan Reed sees in you.'

Connell said, 'Who? Jan Reed?' and Greave said, 'Whoa,' and Lucas, irritated, said, 'Bullshit,' and rang the doorbell. Ray Weston opened the door and peeked out like a mouse. 'I'm Lucas Davenport, deputy chief of police, City of Minneapolis. I'd like to speak to you.'

'My daughter's nuts,' Weston said, opening the door another inch.

'We need to talk,' Lucas said. He took off the sunglasses.

'Let them in, Ray,' a woman's voice said. The voice was shaky with fear. Weston opened the door and let them in.

Neither Ray nor Myrna Weston knew anything about the killings; Lucas, Connell, and Greave agreed on that in the first five minutes. They spent another half-hour pinning down times on the Wannemaker and Lane killings. The Westons were in bed when Lane was taken, and were

167

watching *The Wild Ones* with friends when Wannemaker was picked up.

'Do you think you can get these bums off our back?' Ray Weston asked when they were ready to leave.

'I don't know,' he said honestly. 'That stuff your daughter's giving them – it's pretty heavy.'

'She's nuts,' Weston said again. 'How can they believe that stuff?'

'They don't,' Lucas said.

Outside, Stern was waiting, microphone in hand, the camera rolling, when Lucas, Connell, and Greave left the house. 'Chief Davenport,' she said. 'What have you learned? Will you arrest Ray Weston, father of Elaine Louise Weston-Brown?'

Lucas shook his head. 'Nope. Your whole irresponsible story is a crock of shit and a disgrace to journalism.'

Greave was laughing about Stern's reaction on the way back, and even Connell seemed a little looser. 'I liked the double take she did. She was already rolling with the next question,' Greave said.

'It won't seem so funny if they put it on the air,' Connell said.

'They won't do that,' Lucas said.

'The whole thing is like some weird feminist joke,' Greave said. 'If there was such a thing as a feminist joke.'

'There are lots of feminist jokes,' Connell said.

'Oh. Okay, I'm sorry. You're right,' Grave admitted. 'What I meant to say is, there are no *funny* feminist jokes.'

Connell turned to him, a tiny light in her eye. 'You know why women are no good at math?' she asked.

'No. Why?'

She held her thumb and forefinger two inches apart. 'Because all their lives they're told this is eight inches.'

Lucas grinned, and Greave let a smile slip. 'One fuckin' funny joke after thirty years of feminism.'

'You know why men give names to their penises?'

'I'm holding my breath,' Greave said.

'"Cause they don't want a complete stranger making all their important decisions for them.'

Greave looked into his lap. 'You hear that, Godzilla? She's making fun of you.'

Just before they got back, Connell asked, 'Now what?'

'I don't know,' Lucas said. 'Think about it. Read your files some more. Dredge something up. Wait.'

'Wait for him to kill somebody else?'

'Something,' Lucas said.

'I think we ought to push him. I think we ought to publish the artist's drawing. I couldn't find anybody to confirm it, but I'd bet there's some resemblance.'

Lucas sighed. 'Yeah, maybe we should. I'll talk to Roux.'

Roux agreed. 'It'll give us a bone to throw them,' she said. 'If they believe us.'

Lucas went back to his office, stared at the phone, nibbling at his lower lip, trying to find a hold on the case. The easy possibilities, like Junky, were fading.

The door opened without a knock, and Jan Reed stuck her head in. 'Whoops. Was I supposed to knock? I thought this was an outer office.'

'I'm not a big enough deal to have an outer office,' Lucas said. 'Come on in. You guys are killing us.'

'Not me,' she said, sitting down, her legs crossed to one side. She'd changed since he saw her in the morning, and must've gotten some sleep. She looked fresh and wide awake, in a simple skirt with a white silk blouse.

'I wanted to apologize for Pam Stern. She's been out there a little too long.'

'Who turned up the original story?'

'I really don't know – it was phoned in,' she said. 'The therapist.'

'I really don't know,' she said, smiling. 'And I wouldn't tell you if I did.'

'Ah. Ethics raise their ugly head.'

'Is there anything new?' she asked. She took a short reporter's notebook out of her purse.

'No.'

'What should I look for next?'

'The autopsy. Evidence of the killer's semen or blood. If we get that, we've got something. There's a good chance that he's a prior sexual offender, and the state's got a DNA bank on prior offenders. That's next.'

'All right,' she said. She made a few notes. 'I'll look for that. Anything else?'

Lucas shrugged. 'That's about it.'

'Okay. Well, that's it, then.' And she left, leaving behind her scent. There'd been just the tiniest, microscopic pause after she'd said 'Okay.' An opportunity to get personal? He wasn't sure.

Connell came by late in the afternoon. 'Nothing from the autopsy yet. There's a bruise on her face where it looks like somebody pinched her, and they're bringing in a specialist to see if they can lift a fingerprint. No great hopes.'

'Nothing else?'

'Not yet. And I'm drawing blanks,' she said.

'How about the PPP guy, the convict who saw the tattoo? What was his name – Price? If nothing comes up, why don't we drive over to Waupun tomorrow and talk to him?'

'Okay. What about Greave?'

'I'll tell him to work his own case for the day. That's all he wants to do anyway.'

'Good. How far is Waupun?'

'Five or six hours.'

'Why don't we fly?'

'Ah . . .'

'I can get a state patrol plane, I think.'

Weather's head was snuggled in under Lucas's jaw, and she said, 'You should have driven. You don't need the stress.'

'Yeah, but I sound like such a chicken.'

'Lots of people don't like to fly.'

'But they do,' he said.

She patted his stomach. 'You'll be okay. I could get you something that'd mellow you out a little, if you want.'

'That'd mess up my head. I'll fly.' He sighed and said 'My main problem is, I'm not running this investigation. Connell's done everything, and I can't see beyond what she's done. I'm not thinking: the gears aren't moving like they used to.'

'What's wrong?'

'I don't know, exactly – I can't get anything to start with. If I could get the smallest bite of personal information on the guy, I'd have something – we just can't get it. All I have to work with is paper.'

'You said he might do cocaine . . .'

'Maybe fifty thousand people in the Twin Cities do cocaine on a more or less regular basis,' Lucas said. 'I could jump a few dealers, but the chances of getting anywhere are nil.'

'It's something.'

'I need something else, and soon. He's gone crazy – less than a week between kills. He'll be doing another one. He'll be thinking about it already.'

13

Lucas hated airplanes, feared them. Helicopters, for reasons he didn't understand, were not so bad. They flew to Waupun in a small four-seater fixed-wing plane, Lucas in the back.

'I've never seen anything like that,' Connell said, an undercurrent of satisfaction in her voice.

'You're exaggerating it,' Lucas said, his face grim. The airport was open, windy, a patch on the countryside. A brown state car waited by the Waupun sign, and they walked that way.

'I thought you were going to throw the pilot out the window when we hit those bumps. I thought you were gonna explode. It was like your head was blowing up, like one of those Zodiac boats where the pressure builds up.'

'Yeah, yeah.'

'I hope you and the pilot can kiss and make up before we fly back,' Connell said. 'I don't want him flying scared.'

Lucas turned to her and she stepped away, half smiling, half frightened. With the fish-white stone face behind the black glasses, he looked like a maniac; Lucas did not like airplanes.

A Waupun guard tossed a newspaper in the backseat of the state car and got out as they came up. 'Ms Connell?'

'Yes.'

'Tom Davis.' He was a mild-looking, fleshy man with rosy cheeks and vague blue eyes under a smooth, baby-clear forehead. He had a small graying mustache, just a bit wider than Hitler's. He smiled and shook her hand, then to Lucas, 'And you're her assistant?'

'That was a joke,' Connell said hastily. 'This is, uh, Deputy Chief Lucas Davenport from Minneapolis.'

'Whoops, sorry, Chief,' Davis said. He winked at Connell. 'Well, hop in. We got a little ride.'

Davis knew D. Wayne Price. 'He's not a bad fella,' he said. He drove with one foot on the gas and the other on the brake. The constant surging and slowing reminded Lucas of the airplane's motion.

'He was convicted of murdering a woman by slicing her open with a knife,' Connell said. 'They had to remove her intestines from the street with a bucket.' Her voice was conversational.

'That wouldn't put him in the top ten percent of his class,' the guard said, just as conversationally. 'We got guys in here who raped and killed little boys before they ate them.'

'*That's* bad,' Lucas said.

'That *is* bad,' said Davis.

'Is there any talk about Price?' Lucas asked. 'He says he's innocent.'

'So do fifty percent of the others, though most of them don't actually claim to be innocent. They say the law wasn't followed, or the trial wasn't fair. I mean, they did it, whatever it was, but they say the state didn't dot every single *i* and cross every single *t* before puttin' them away – and they say that's just not fair. There's nobody finickier about the law than a con,' Davis said.

'How about Price?'

'I don't know D. Wayne that good, but some of the guys believe him,' Davis said. 'He's been pretty noisy about it, filing all kinds of appeals. He's never stopped; he's still doing it.'

'Don't like prisons,' Connell said. The interview room had the feel of a dungeon.

'Like the doors might not open again after you're inside,' Lucas said.

'That's exactly it. I could stand it for about a week, and then they'd come to put me back in the cell, and I'd freak. I don't think I'd make a full month. I'd kill myself,' Connell said.

'People do,' Lucas said. 'The saddest ones are the people they put on a suicide watch. They can't get out, and they can't get it over with. They just sit and suffer.'

'Some of them deserve it.'

Lucas disagreed. 'I don't know if anybody deserves that.'

D. Wayne Price was a large man in his early forties; his face looked as if it had been slowly and incompetently formed with a ballpeen hammer. His forehead was shiny and pitted, with scars running up into his hairline. He had rough poreless skin under his eyes, scar tissue from being punched. His small round ears seem to be fitted into slots in his head. When the escort brought him to the interview room, he smiled a convict's obsequious smile, and his teeth were small and chipped. He was wearing jeans and a white T-shirt with 'Harley-Davidson' on the front.

Lucas and Connell were sitting on a couple of slightly damaged green office chairs, facing a couch whose only notable quality was its brownness. The escort was a horse-faced older man with a buzz cut; he was carrying a yellow-backed book, said, 'Sit,' to Price, as though he were a Labrador retriever, said, 'How do' to Lucas and Connell, then dropped onto the other end of the couch with his book.

'You smoke?' Connell asked Price.

'Sure.' She fished in a pocket, handed him an open pack of Marlboros and a butane lighter. Price knocked a cigarette out of the pack, lit it, and Connell said, voice soft, 'So, this woman in Madison. You kill her?'

'Never touched the bitch,' Price said, testing, his eyes lingering on her.

'But you knew her,' Connell said.

'I knew who she was,' Price said.

'Sleep with her?' Lucas asked.

'Nope. Never got that close,' Price said, looking at Lucas. 'Had a nice ass on her, though.'

'Where were you when she was killed?' asked Connell.

'Drunk. My buddies dropped me off at my house, but I knew if I went inside I'd start barfin', so I walked down to this convenience store for coffee. That's what got me.'

'Tell me,' said Connell.

Price looked up at the ceiling, stuck the cigarette in his mouth, looked down at it long enough to light it, blew some smoke and closed his eyes, remembering. 'I was out drinking with some buddies. Shit, we were drinking all afternoon and shootin' pool. And so about eight o'clock my buddies brought me home 'cause I was too fuckin' drunk to drink.'

'That's pretty drunk,' Lucas said.

'Yeah, pretty,' Price said. 'Anyway, they dumped me off on my porch, and I sat there for a while, and when I could get going, I decided to go up to the corner and get some coffee. There was a 7-Eleven in one of them side-street shopping centers. There was like a drugstore and a cleaners and this bookstore. I was in the 7-Eleven, and she came down from the bookstore to get something. I was drunker'n shit, but I remembered her from some welding I done for her.'

'Welding?'

'Yeah.' Price laughed, the laugh trailing off into a cough. 'She had this piece-of-shit '79 Cadillac, cream over key-lime green, and the bumper fell off. Just fuckin' fell off one day. The Cadillac place wanted like four hundred bucks to fix it, so she brought it over to my place and asked me what I could do. I welded the sonofabitch back on for

175

twenty-two dollars. If that bumper hadn't fell off, I'd be a free man today.'

'So you remembered her,' Connell prompted. 'In the store.'

'Yeah. I said hello and come on to her a little bit, but she wasn't having it, and she left. I sort of followed along.' Price's voice was slow and dreamy, pulling details out of his memory. 'She went down to this bookstore. I was so fuckin' drunk, I kept thinking, *Hell, I'm gonna get lucky with this chick*. There was no chance. Even if she'd said, "Hell, yes," I was in no shape to . . . you know. Anyway, I went into the bookstore.'

'How long did you stay?'

'About five minutes. There was a crowd in there, and I didn't fit so good. For one thing, I smelled like a Budweiser truck had peed on me.'

'So?' Connell prompted.

'So I left.' His voice hardened, and he sat up. 'There was this pimply-faced asshole kid in there, a clerk. He said I stayed, and that later, when this book thing was over, I followed her out of the store. That's what he said. The lawyer asked him on the witness stand, he said, "Can you point to the man who followed her out?" And this kid said, "Yessir. That's the man right there." He pointed to me. I was a gone motherfucker.'

'But it wasn't you.'

'Hell no. The kid remembered me because I bumped into him. Sorta pushed him.'

'What's this tattoo business?' Lucas asked.

Price's eyes slid toward the escort, back to Lucas, back to the escort, back to Lucas, and his chin moved quickly right and left, no more than a quarter inch. 'Tattoo? Kid didn't have no tattoo.'

Connell, jotting down notes, missed it. She looked up. 'According to my notes,' she said, but Lucas rode over her.

176

'We gotta talk,' he said to her. 'I'd rather Mr Price didn't hear this . . . C'mon.'

The escort had been browsing *The Encyclopedia of Pop, Rock and Soul*. He looked up and said, 'I could take him . . .'

'The corner is fine,' Lucas said, pulling Connell along.

'What?' she asked, low-voiced.

Lucas got his back to Price and the escort. 'D. Wayne doesn't want to talk about tattoos in front of the guard,' Lucas said. 'Talk to him for another five minutes, then ask the guard where the ladies' room is. Get him to take you – it's back through one set of doors.'

'I can do that,' she said.

The escort was back in his book when they sat down again. 'So where'd you go when you left the store?' Lucas asked.

'Home.'

'You didn't stay with her? You didn't try again?'

'Fuck, no. I was too drunk to follow her anywhere. I went back to the convenience store and got a couple more beers – never even got my coffee. I barely made it back home. I sat on my steps for a while, drank the beers, then I went inside and passed out. I didn't wake up until the cops came to get me.'

'Must've been more to it than that,' Lucas said.

Price shrugged. 'There wasn't. The guy across the street even saw me sittin' on the steps, and said so. They found the fuckin' beer cans next to the step. Said it didn't prove nothing.'

'Must've had a horseshit attorney,' Lucas said.

'Public defender. He was all right. But you know . . .'

'Yeah?'

Price leaned back and looked at the ceiling again, as though weary of the story. 'The cops wanted me. I was stealing stuff. I admit that. Tools. I specialized in tools. Most people steal, like, stereos. Shit, you can't get nothing for a stereo compared to what you can get for a good set of

177

mechanic's tools, you know? Anyway, the cops were trying to get me forever, but they never could. I'd steal something, and before anybody knew it was gone, there was
three niggers down in Chicago with a new welding rig, or
something. I go into a shop, take out the tools, drive two
hours and a half down to Chicago, unload them, drive
back, and be drunk on my butt with the money in my
pocket before anybody knows anything happened. I
thought I was pretty smart. The cops *knew*, and I knew
that they knew, but I never thought they'd just *get* me.
But that's what they did.'

'I read a file that said you might have done a couple of
liquor stores, that some people got hurt. Old man got beat
with a pistol,' Connell said.

'Not me,' Price said, but his eyes slid away.

'Took some booze with the cash,' Connell said. 'You *are*
a booze hound.'

'Look, I admitted the stealing,' Price said. He licked his
lips. 'But I didn't kill the bitch.'

'When you were in the store, did you see anybody else
that might have been with her?'

'Man, I was *drunk*,' Price said. 'When the cops come for
me, I couldn't even remember seeing this gal, until they
reminded me a lot.'

'So you don't know shit about shit,' Lucas said.

A little coal sparked in Price's eye that said he'd like to
be alone with Lucas. 'That's about it,' Price said. Lucas held
his eyes, and the coal died. 'There were people down in
the bookstore that night that nobody ever found. They
were reading poems down there, and there was a whole
bunch of people. It could have been any of them,
more'n me.'

Connell sighed, then looked at the escort. 'Excuse me —
is there a ladies' room back there?'

'Noooo . . .' He had to think about it. 'Closest one is
out.'

'I wonder, do you mind? Could you?'

'Sure.' The escort looked at Price. 'You sit still, okay?'

Price spread his hands. 'Hey, these guys are trying to help me out.'

'Sure,' the guard said. And to Connell: 'Come along, girl.'

Lucas winced, but Connell went. As soon as the door closed, Price leaned forward, voice low. 'You think they're listening in?'

'I doubt it,' Lucas said, shaking his head. 'This is a defendant's interview room. If they got caught, they'd be in deep shit.'

Price looked around at the pale walls, as though trying to spot a microphone. 'I gotta take the chance,' he said.

'On what?' Lucas asked, letting the skepticism ride in his voice.

Price leaned toward him again, talking in a harsh whisper.

'At my trial I said I saw another con in the bookstore. A guy with a beard and PPP on his hand. Prison tattoo, ballpoint ink and straight pin. Nobody ever found him.'

'That's why we're here,' Lucas said. 'We're trying to track the guy.'

'Yeah, well, it wasn't PPP,' Price said. He looked around at the walls again, then back to Lucas. He was literally sweating, his hammered forehead glistening in the lights. 'Jesus Christ. You can't tell anybody.'

'What?'

'I've seen the tattoo again. It wasn't PPP. I was looking at it upside down, and got it backwards. It was 666.'

'Yeah? What is it – some kind of cult?'

'No, no,' Price whispered. 'It's the goddamn Seeds.'

Now Lucas dropped his voice. 'You sure?'

'Sure I'm sure. There are four or five of them in here right now. That's what's got me nervous. If they knew I was talking about them, I'd be a dead motherfucker. The

179

666 comes from Bad Seeds; that used to be the bikers.'

'Can you describe him?'

'I can do better than that. His name is Joe Hillerod.'

'How'd you get that?' They were both talking in whispers now, and Lucas had picked up Price's habit of scanning the walls.

'They brought me up here, and after I got through orientation and went into the population, one of the first guys I see, shit, *I thought it was him*. They looked just fuckin' exactly alike. The guy even had the same tattoo.'

'This is the Joe guy?'

'No, no, this is Bob. The guy in here was Bob Hillerod, Joe's brother.'

'What?'

'See, I started lifting weights, just to get close to this guy. Bob. I find out he's been in for a while – from way before this chick gets killed. And I see he's older than the guy in the store. I couldn't figure it out. But then I hear, Bob's got a brother, six or seven years younger. It's got to be him. Got to be.'

Lucas leaned back, his voice rising. 'Sounds like bullshit.'

'No, no, I swear to Christ. It's him. Joe Hillerod. And this Joe – he's been inside. For sex.' Price reached out and touched Lucas's hand. His eyes were wide, frightened.

'Sex?'

'Rape.'

'Did you ask Bob . . . is it Bob in here?'

'Yeah, Bob was here, Joe was out. Joe is the guy. Bob is out now, but Joe is the guy.'

'Did you ask Bob if Joe has the tattoo?'

Price leaned back. 'Fuck no. One thing you learn in here is, you don't ask about those fuckin' tattoos. You just pretend they're not there,' he said. 'But Joe was inside. He was one of the Seeds. He's got it, I bet. I bet anything.'

*　　*　　*

When Connell and the escort returned, Lucas was taking notes. 'Harry Roy Wayne and Gerry Gay Wayne,' Price was saying, 'They're brothers and they work at the Caterpillar place down there. They'll tell you.'

'But that's all you got?' Lucas asked.

'You got everything else.' D. Wayne slumped on the couch, smoking a second cigarette. He picked up the pack and put them in his pocket.

'I won't bullshit you,' Lucas said. 'I don't think that's enough.'

'It will be if you catch the right guy,' Price said.

'Yeah. If there is one,' Lucas said. He stood up and said to Connell, 'Unless you've got some more questions, we're outta here.'

14

'What do we have?' Connell asked as they waited for the car. She was digging into a pack of chive-flavored potato chips, sixty cents from a machine.

'A hell of a coincidence,' Lucas said. He told her briefly about Price's nervous statement, and about Del's investigation at the fire, the dead deputy, and the .50-caliber tubes. 'So the Seeds are in the Cities.'

'And this Joe Hillerod was convicted of rape?'

'Price said sex, so I don't know exactly what it was. If our guy is a member of the Seeds, it'd explain a lot,' Lucas said. 'Gimme a couple of chips.'

She passed the pack. 'What does it explain?'

Lucas crunched: starch and fat. Excellent. 'They've had years of hassles with the law, they've even got a lawyer on retainer. They know how we operate. They move around all the time, but mostly in the Midwest, the states we're talking about. The gaps in the killings – this Joe guy might have been inside.'

'Huh.' Connell took the chips back, finished them. 'That sounds *very* good. God knows, they're crazy enough.'

Connell made a long phone call from the airport, talked to a woman at her office, took some notes. Lucas stood around, looking at nothing, while the pilot avoided him.

'Hillerod lives up near Superior,' Connell said when she got off the phone. 'He was convicted of aggravated assault in Chippewa County in March of '86 and served thirteen months. He got out in April of '87. There was a killing in August of '87.'

'That's neat. He didn't do any other time?'

'Yeah. A couple of short jail terms, and then in January of '90, he was convicted for sexual assault and served twenty-three months, and got out a month before Gina Hoff was assaulted in Thunder Bay.'

'But wasn't the South Dakota case –'

'Yeah,' she said. 'It was in '91, while he was inside. But that was the weirdest of all the cases I found. That's where the woman was stabbed as much as ripped. Maybe that *was* somebody else.'

'What's he done since he got out?' Lucas asked.

Connell flipped through her notes. 'He was charged with a DWI in '92, but he beat it. And a speeding ticket this year. His last known address was somewhere up around Superior, a town called Two Horse. Current driver's license shows an address in a town called Stedman. My friend couldn't find it on a map, but she called the Carren County sheriff's department, and they say Stedman is a crossroads a couple of miles out of Two Horse.'

'Did your friend ask them about the Hillerods?'

'No. I thought we ought to do that in person.'

'Good. Let's get our ass back to the Cities. I want to talk to Del before we start messing with the Seeds,' Lucas said. He looked across the lounge at the pilot, who was sipping a cup of coffee. 'Assuming that we make it back.'

Halfway back, Lucas, with his eyes closed and one hand tight around an overhead grip, said, 'Twenty-three months. Couldn't have been much of a rape.'

'A rape is a rape,' Connell said, an edge in her voice.

'You know what I mean,' Lucas said, opening his eyes.

'I know what *men* mean when they say that,' Connell said.

'Kiss my ass,' Lucas said. The pilot winced – almost ducked – and Lucas closed his eyes again.

'I'm not interested in putting up with certain kinds of

183

bullshit,' Connell said levelly. 'A male commentary on rape is one of them. I don't care if the guy back at Waupun calls me a girl, because he's stupid and out of touch. But you're not stupid, and when you imply –'

'I didn't imply jackshit,' Lucas said. 'But I've known women who were raped who had to think about it before they realized what happened. On the other hand, you get some woman who's been beaten with a bat, her teeth are broken out, her nose is smashed, her ribs are broken, she's gotta have surgery because her vagina is ripped open. She doesn't have to think about it. If it's gonna happen, which way would you want it?'

'I don't want it at all,' Connell said.

'You don't want death and taxes, either,' Lucas said.

'Rape isn't death and taxes.'

'All of the big ones are death and taxes,' Lucas said. 'Murder, rape, robbery, assault. Death and taxes.'

'I don't want to argue,' Connell said. 'We have to work together.'

'No, we don't.'

'What, you're gonna dump me because I argue with you?'

Lucas shook his head. 'Meagan, I just don't like getting jumped when I say something like, "It must not have been much of a rape," and you know what I'm talking about. I mean, there must not have been a lot of obvious violence with the rape, or they would have given him more time. Our killer is ripping these women. He might be smoking a cigarette while he's doing it. He's a fuckin' monster. If he rapes somebody, he's not gonna be subtle about it. I don't know the details of this rape, but twenty-three months doesn't sound like our man.'

'You just don't want it to be that easy,' Connell said.

'Bullshit.'

'I'm serious. I keep getting the feeling you're playing some kind of weird game, looking for this guy. I'm not. I

the old biker gang the Bad Seeds. They're dope and women. A couple of them supply women to the massage parlors over in Milwaukee and here in the Cities. One of them has a porno store in Milwaukee.'

Lucas scratched his head and looked at Connell, who'd been peering over Del's shoulder. 'I guess the only way we're gonna find out is go up there and roust them.'

'Be a little careful,' Del said.

'When?' Connell asked.

'Tomorrow,' Lucas said. 'I'll call the sheriff tonight, and we'll go first thing in the morning.'

'Driving?'

Lucas showed a sickly grin. 'Driving.'

Lucas and Connell agreed to meet at eight o'clock for the drive up north. 'I'll check the medical examiner on Marcy Lane and see if anything's come up,' she said. 'I'll get everything I can on the Hillerods. The whole file.'

Lucas stopped at homicide to check with Greave, but was told he was out. Another cop said, 'He's down with that thing at Eisenhower Docks. He should be back by now.'

From his office, Lucas called Lincoln County Sheriff Sheldon Carr at Grant, Wisconsin; touched the scar on his neck as Carr picked up the phone. Carr had been there when Lucas was shot by the child.

'Lucas, how are things?' Carr was hardy and country and smart. 'You comin' up to fish? Is Weather pregnant yet?'

'Not yet, Shelly. We'll let you know . . . Listen, I gotta talk to George Beneteau over in Carren County. Do you know him?'

'George? Sure. He's okay. Should I give him a call?'

'If you would. I'll call him later on and talk. I'm going up there tomorrow to look at a guy involved with the Seeds.'

'Ah, those assholes,' Carr said with disgust. 'They used to be around here, you know. We ran them off.'

'Yeah, well, we're bumping into them down here now. I would appreciate an introduction, though.'

'I'll call him right now. I'll tell him to expect to hear from you,' Carr said. 'You take it easy with those bad boys.'

Greave came in with a kid. The kid was wearing a black-and-white-striped French fisherman's T-shirt, dirty jeans, and stepped-on white sneakers. He had a pound of dirty-blond hair stuck up under a long-billed red Woody Woodpecker cap.

'This is Greg,' Greave said, throwing a thumb at the kid. 'He does handyman work around the apartments.'

Lucas nodded.

'Don't tell nobody you talked to me or they'll fire my ass,' Greg said to Lucas. 'I need the job.'

'Greg says that the day before the old lady died, the air-conditioning went out and it got really hot in the apartments. He and Cherry spent the whole day down the basement, taking things apart. He says it was so hot, almost everybody left their windows and even their doors open.'

'Yeah?'

'Yeah.' Greave prodded the kid. 'Tell him.'

'They did,' the kid said. 'It was the first real hot day of the year.'

'So maybe they could have gotten in the old lady's apartment,' Greave said. 'Come in with a ladder and figured out some way to drop the window, locked. We know it couldn't be the door.'

'What'd they do to her after they came in the window?'

'They smothered her.'

'The medical examiner could determine that. And how do you drop a window, locked? Did you try it?'

'I haven't got it figured out yet,' Greave said.

'We tried it a lot,' the kid said to Lucas; Greave looked at him in exasperation. 'Ain't no way.'

'Maybe there's some way,' Greave said defensively. 'Remember, Cherry's the maintenance man, he'd know tricks.'

'Woodworking tricks? Listen, Cherry's no smarter than you are,' Lucas said. 'If he could figure out a way to do it, you could. Whatever it was, must've been quiet. The neighbor didn't hear a thing. He said it was spooky-quiet.'

'I thought maybe you could come down and take a look,' Greave said. 'Figure something out.'

'I don't have the time,' Lucas said, shaking his head. 'But if you can figure a way to get them in and out . . . but even then, you'd have to figure out what killed her. It wasn't smothering.'

'They must've poisoned her,' Greave said. 'You know how jockeys dope up horses and still pass the drug tests? That must be what they did – they went out and got some undetectable poison, put it in her booze, and she croaked.'

'No toxicology,' Lucas said.

'I *know* that. That's the whole *point*. It's undetectable, see?'

'No,' said Lucas.

'That's gotta be it,' Greave said.

Lucas grinned at him. 'If they did, then you should lie down, put a cold rag on your forehead, and relax, 'cause you're never gonna convict anybody on the vanishing-drug theory.'

'Maybe,' Greave said. 'But I'll tell you something else I figured out: it's gotta have something to do with the booze. The old lady takes booze and a couple of sleeping pills. That's the most noticeable thing she did, far as we know. Then she's murdered. That shit *had* to be poisoned. Somehow.'

'Maybe she masturbated at night, and it put a heavy strain on her heart and she croaked,' Lucas said.

'I thought of that,' Greave said.

'You did?' Lucas started to laugh.

'But how does that explain the fact that Cherry did it?'

Lucas stopped laughing. Cherry *had* done it. 'You got me there,' he said. He looked at the kid. 'Do you think Cherry did it?'

'He *could* do it,' the kid said. 'He's a mean sonofabitch. There was a little dog from across the street, belonged to this old couple, and he'd come over and poop on the lawn, and Ray caught it with a rope and strangled it. I seen him do it.'

Greave said, 'See?'

'I know he's mean,' Lucas said. Then, to Greave: 'Connell and I are headed up north tomorrow, checking on a guy.'

'Hey, I'm sorry, man,' Greave said. 'I know I'm not helping you much. I'll do whatever you want.'

'Anderson's doing a computer run: known sex offenders against trucks. Why don't you start pulling records, looking for any similarities in old charges, anything that refers to the motorcycle gang called the Bad Seeds. Or any motorcycle gang, for that matter. Flag anything that's even a remote possibility.'

The phone was ringing when Lucas got home: Weather. 'I'll be a while,' she said.

'What happened?' He was annoyed. No. He was jealous.

'A kid chopped his thumb off in a paper cutter at school. We're trying to stick it back on.' She was both excited and tired, the words stumbling over each other.

'A tough one?'

'Lucas, we took two hours trying to find a decent artery and get it hooked up, and George is dissecting out a vein right now. Christ, they're so small, they're like tissue paper, but if we get it back on, we'll give the kid his hand back . . . I gotta go.'

'You'll be really late?'

'I'm here for another two hours, if the vein works,' she said. 'If it doesn't, we'll have to go for another one. That'd be late.'

'See you then,' he said.

Lucas had been in love before, but with Weather, it was different. Everything was tilted, a little out of control. He might be overcommitting himself, he thought. On the other hand, there was a passion that he hadn't experienced before . . .

And she made him happy.

Lucas sometimes found himself laughing aloud just at the thought of her. That hadn't happened before. And the house in the evening felt empty without her.

He sat at his desk, writing checks for household bills. When he finished, he dropped the stamped envelopes in a basket on an antique table by the front door. The antique was the first thing they'd bought together.

'Jesus.' He rubbed his nose. He was in deep. But the idea of one single woman, for the rest of time . . .

15

Sara Jensen worked at Raider-Garrote, a stockbrokerage in the Exchange Building. The office entry was glass, and on the other side of the glass was a seating area where investors could sit and watch the numbers from the New York Stock Exchange and NASDAQ scroll across a scoreboard. Few people actually went inside. Most of them – thin white guys with glasses, briefcases, gray suits, and thinning hair – stood mouth-open in the skyway until their number came up, then scurried away, muttering.

Koop loitered with them, hands in pockets, his look changing daily. One day it was jeans, white T-shirt, sneakers, and a ball cap; the next day it was long-sleeved shirt, khakis, and loafers.

Through the window, over the heads of the few people in the display area, past the rows of white-shirted men and well-dressed women who sat peering at computer terminals and talking on telephones, in a separate large office, Jensen worked alone.

Her office door was usually open, but few people went in. She wore a telephone headset most of the day. She often talked and read a newspaper at the same time. A half-dozen different computer terminals lined a shelf behind her desk, and every once in a while she'd poke one, watch the screen; occasionally, she'd rip paper out of a computer printer, look at it, or stuff it in her briefcase.

Koop had no idea what she was doing. At first, he thought she might be some kind of super secretary. But she never fetched anything, nobody ever gave her what appeared to be an order. Then he noticed that when one of the white shirts wanted to talk to her, the shirt was distinctly deferential. Not a secretary.

As he watched, he began to suspect that she was involved in something very complicated, something that wore her down. By the end of the day, she was haggard. When the white shirts and conservative dresses were standing up, stretching, laughing, talking, she was still working her headset. When she finally left, her leather briefcase was always stuffed with paper.

On this day, she left a bit earlier than usual. He followed her through the skyway to the parking ramp, walked past her, face averted, in a crowd. At the elevator, he joined the short queue, feeling the tension in the back of his neck. He'd not done this before. He'd never been this close . . .

He felt her arrive behind him, kept his back to her, his face turned away. She'd ride up to the sixth floor, if she remembered where she left her car. Sometimes she forgot, and wandered through the ramp, lugging the briefcase, looking for it. He'd seen her do it. Today her car was on six, just across from the doors.

The elevator arrived and he stepped inside, turned left, pushed seven, stepped to the back. A half-dozen other people got on with her, and he maneuvered until he was directly behind her, not eight inches away. The smell of her perfume staggered him. A small tuft of hair hung down on the back of her neck; she had a mole behind her ear — but he'd seen that before.

The smell was the thing. The Opium . . .

The elevator started up and a guy at the front lost his balance, took a half-step back into her. She tried to back up, her butt bumping Koop in the groin. He stood his ground and the guy in front muttered 'Sorry,' and she half-turned to Koop at the same time, not looking at him, and said, 'Sorry,' and then they were at six.

Koop's eyes were closed, holding on. He could still feel her. She'd *pressed*, he thought.

She'd apparently noticed him, noticed his body under the chameleon's shirt, and had been attracted. She'd *pressed*. He could still feel her ass.

Koop got off at seven, stunned, realized he was sweating, had a ferocious hard-on. She'd done it on purpose. *She knew. . .* Or did she?

Koop hurried to his truck. If he came up beside her, maybe she'd give him a signal. She was a high-class woman, she wouldn't just come on to him. She'd do something different, none of this 'Wanna fuck?' stuff. Koop fired up the truck, rolled down the ramp, around and around, making himself dizzy, the truck's wheels screeching down the spiral. Had to stay with her.

At the exit, there were three cars ahead of him. Jensen hadn't come down yet . . . The first and second cars went quickly. The third was driven by an older woman, who said something to the ticket taker. The ticket taker stuck his head out the window and pointed left, then right. The woman said something else.

A car came up from behind Koop, stopped. Not her. Then another car, lights on, down the last ramp, breaking left into the monthly-parker exit line. Jensen had an exit card. He caught a glimpse of her face as she punched the card into the automatic gate. The gate rose and she rolled past him on the left.

'Motherfucker, what's wrong? What're you doing?' Koop poked his horn.

The woman in the car ahead of him took ten seconds to turn and look behind her, then shrugged and started digging into her purse. She took forever, then finally passed a bill to the ticket taker. The ticket taker said something, and she dug into the purse again, finally producing the parking ticket. He took the ticket, gave her change, and then she said something else . . .

Koop beeped again, and the woman looked into her rearview mirror, finally started forward, stopped at the curb, took a slow left. Koop thrust his money and ticket at the ticket taker.

'Keep the change,' he said.

'Can't do that.' The ticket taker was an idiot, some kind of goddamned faggot. Koop felt the anger crawling up his neck. In another minute . . .

'I'm in a fuckin' hurry,' Koop said.

'Only take a second,' the ticket man said. He screwed around with the cash register and held out two quarters. 'Here you go, in-a-fuckin'-hurry.'

The gate went up and Koop, cursing, pushed into the street. Jensen usually took the same route home. He started after her, pushing hard, making lights.

'C'mon, Sara,' he said to his steering wheel. 'C'mon, where are you?' He caught her a mile out. Fell in behind.

Should he pull up beside her? Would she give him a signal?

She might.

He was thinking about it when she slowed, took a right into a drugstore parking lot. Koop followed, parked at the edge of the lot. She sat inside her car for a minute, then two, looking for something in her purse. Then she swung her legs out, disappeared into the store. He thought about following, but the last time, he'd run into that kid. It was hard to watch somebody in a store unobtrusively, with all the anti-shoplifting mirrors around.

So he waited. She was ten minutes, came out with a small bag. At her car, she fumbled in her purse, fumbled some more. Koop sat up. What?

She couldn't find her keys. She started back toward the store, stopped, turned and looked thoughtfully at the car, and walked slowly back. She stooped, looked inside, then straightened, angry, talking to herself.

Keys. She'd locked her keys in the car.

He could talk to her: 'What's the problem, little lady?'

But as he watched, she looked quickly around, walked

195

to the rear of the car, bent, and ran her hand under the bumper. After a moment of groping, she came up with a black box. Spare key.

Koop stiffened. When people put spare keys on their car, they usually put in a spare house key, just in case. And if she had — and if she'd changed them since she changed her locks . . .

He'd have to look.

Koop went to the roof as soon as it was dark. Jensen had changed to a robe, and he watched as she read, listened to a stereo, and checked the cable movies. He was becoming familiar with her personal patterns: she never watched talk shows, never watched sitcoms. She sometimes watched game shows. She watched the news rerun on public television, late at night.

She liked ice cream, and ate it slowly, with a lot of tongue-on-the-spoon action. When she was puzzled about something, trying to make up her mind, she'd reach back and scratch the top of her ass. Sometimes she'd lie in bed with her feet straight up in the air, apparently looking past them for no reason. She'd do the same thing when she put on panty hose — she'd drop onto her back in bed, get her toes into the feet of the hose, then lift her legs over her head and pull them on. Sometimes she'd wander around the apartment while she was flossing.

Once, she apparently caught sight of her reflection in the glass of her balcony's sliding doors, and dropped into a series of poses, as though she were posing for the cover of *Cosmo*. She was so close, so clear, that Koop felt she was posing for him.

She went to bed at midnight, every working night. Two women friends had come around, and once, before Koop began following her home, she hadn't shown up at all until midnight. A date? The idea pissed him off, and he pushed it away.

When she went to bed – a minute of near nakedness, large breasts bobbling in the fishbowl – Koop left her, bought a bottle of Jim Beam at a liquor store, and drove home.

He barely lived in his house, a suburban ranch-style nonentity he'd rented furnished. A garden service mowed the lawn. Koop didn't cook, didn't clean, didn't do much except sleep there, watch some television, and wash his clothes. The place smelled like dust with a little bourbon on top of it. Oh, yes, he'd brought in Wannemaker. But only for an hour or two, in the basement; you could hardly smell that anymore . . .

The next morning, Koop was downtown before ten o'clock. He didn't like the daylight hours, but this was important. He called her at her office.

'This is Sara Jensen . . . Hello? Hello?'

Her voice was pitched higher than he'd expected, with an edge to it. When he didn't answer her second hello, she promptly hung up, and he was left listening to a dial tone. So she was working.

He headed for the parking ramp, spiraled up through the floors. She was usually on five, six, or seven, depending on how early she got in. Today, it was six again. He had to go to eight to find a parking place. He walked back down, checked under the bumper of her car, found the key box. He opened it as he walked away. Inside was a car key and a newly minted door key.

Shazam.

He felt like victory, going back in. Like a conqueror. Like he was home, with his woman.

Koop spent half the day at her apartment.

As soon as he got in, he opened a tool chest in front of the television. If somebody showed up, a cleaning woman, he could say he'd just finished fixing it . . . but nobody showed up.

He ate cereal from one of her bowls, washed the bowl, and put it back. He lounged in her front room with his shoes off, watching television. He stripped off his clothes, pulled back the bedcovers, and rolled in her slick cool sheets. Masturbated into her Kleenex.

Sat on her toilet. Took a shower with her soap. Dabbed some of her perfume on his chest, where he could smell it. Posed in her mirror, his blond, nearly hairless body corded with muscle.

This, he thought, she'd love: he threw the mirror a quarter-profile, arms flexed, butt tight, chin down.

He went through her chest of drawers, found some letters from a man. He read them, but the content was disappointing: had a good time, hope you had a good time. He checked a file cabinet in a small second bedroom-office, found a file labeled 'Divorce.' Nothing much in it. Jensen was her married name – her maiden name was Rose.

He went back to the bedroom, lay down, rubbed his body with the sheets, turned himself on again . . .

By five, he was exhausted and exhilarated. He saw the time on her dresser clock, and got up to dress and make the bed: she'd just about be leaving her office.

Sara Jensen got home a few minutes before six, carrying a sack full of vegetables under one arm, a bottle of wine and her purse in the opposite hand. The wet smell of radishes and carrots covered Koop's scent for the first few steps inside the door, to the kitchen counter, but when she'd dropped her sacks and stepped back to shut the door, she stopped, frowned, looked around.

Something wasn't right. She could smell him, but only faintly, subconsciously. A finger of fear poked into her heart.

'Hello?' she called.

198

Not a peep. *Paranoid.*

She tilted her head back, sniffing. There was something . . . She shook her head. Nothing identifiable. Nervous, she left the hallway door open, walked quickly to the bedroom door, and poked her head inside. Called out: 'Hello?' Silence.

Still leaving the door open, she checked the second bedroom-office, then ventured into the bathroom, even jerking open the door to the shower stall. The apartment was empty except for her.

She went to the outer door and closed it, still spooked. Nothing she could put her finger on. She started unpacking her grocery sacks, stowing the vegetables in the refrigerator.

And stopped again. She tiptoed back to the bedroom. Looked to her right. A closet door was open just a crack. A closet she didn't use. She turned away, hurried to the hall door, opened it, stopped. Turned back. 'Hello?'

The silence spoke of emptiness. She edged toward the bedroom, looked in. The closet door was just as it had been. She took a breath, walked to the closet. 'Hello?' Her voice quieter. She took the knob in her hand, and feeling the fright of a child opening the basement door for the first time, jerked the closet door open.

Nobody there, Sara.

'You're nuttier'n a fruitcake,' she said aloud. Her voice sounded good, broke the tension. She smiled and pushed the closet door shut with her foot, and started back to the living room. Stopped and looked at the bed.

There was just the vaguest body-shape there, as though somebody had dropped back on the bedspread. Had she done that? She sometimes did that in the morning when she was putting on her panty hose.

But had she gotten dressed first that morning, or made the bed first?

Had her head hit the pillow like that?

Spooked again, she patted the bed. The thought crossed her mind that she should look under it.

But if there were a monster under there . . .

'I'm going out to dinner,' she said aloud. 'If there's a monster under the bed, you better get out while I'm gone.'

Silence and more silence.

'I'm going,' she said, leaving the room, looking back. Did the bed tremble?

She went.

16

The Carren County courthouse was a turn-of-the-century sandstone building, set in the middle of the town square. A decaying bandstand stood on the east side of the building, facing a street of weary clapboard buildings. A bronze statue of a Union soldier, covered with pigeon droppings, guarded the west side with a trapdoor rifle. On the front lawn, three old men, all wearing jackets and hats, sat alone on separate wooden benches.

A squirrel ignored them, and Lucas and Connell walked past them, the old men as unmoving, unblinking as the Union soldier.

George Beneteau's office was in the back, off a parking lot sheltered by tall, spreading oaks. Lucas and Connell were passed through a steel security door and led by a secretary through a warren of fabric partitions to Beneteau's corner office.

Beneteau was a lanky man in his middle thirties, wearing a gray suit with a string tie under a large Adam's apple, and a pair of steel-rimmed aviator sunglasses. He had a prominent nose and small hairline scars under his eyes: old sparring cuts. A tan Stetson sat on his desk in-basket. He showed even, white teeth in a formal smile.

'Miz Connell, Chief Davenport,' he said. He stood to shake hands with Lucas. 'That was a mess over in Lincoln County last winter.'

The observation sounded like a question. 'We're not looking for trouble,' Lucas said. He touched the scar on his throat. 'We just want to talk to Joe Hillerod.'

Beneteau sat down and steepled his fingers. Connell was

wearing sunglasses that matched his. 'We know that Joe Hillerod crossed paths with our killer. *At least* crossed paths.'

Beneteau peered at her from behind the steeple. 'You're saying that he might be the guy?'

'That's a possibility.'

'Huh.' He sat forward, picked up a pencil, tapped the pointed end on his desk pad. 'He's a mean sonofagun, Joe is. He might kill a woman if he thought he had reason . . . but he might need a reason.'

Lucas said, 'You don't think he's nuts.'

'Oh, he's nuts all right,' Beneteau said, tapping the pencil. 'Maybe not nuts like your man is. But who knows? There might be something in him that likes to do it.'

'You're sure he's around?' Lucas asked.

'Yes. But we're not sure exactly where,' Beneteau said. His eyes drifted up to a county road map pinned to one wall. 'His truck's been sitting in the same slot since you called yesterday, down at his brother's place. We've been doing some drive-bys.'

Lucas groaned inwardly. If they'd been seen . . .

Beneteau picked up his thought and shook his head, did his thin dry smile. 'The boys did it in their private cars, only two of them, a couple of hours apart. Their handsets are scrambled. We're okay.'

Lucas nodded, relieved. 'Good.'

'On the phone last night, you mentioned those .50-caliber barrels you found in that fire. The Hillerods have some machine tools down in that junkyard,' Beneteau said.

'Yeah?'

'Yeah.' Beneteau stood up, looked at a poster for a missing girl, then turned back to Lucas. 'I thought we oughta take along a little artillery. Just in case.'

* * *

202

They went in a caravan, two sheriff's cars and an unmarked panel truck, snaking along a series of blacktop and gravel roads, past rough backwoods farms. Mangy cud-chewing cows, standing in patchy pastures marked by weather-bleached tree stumps, turned their white faces to watch the caravan pass.

'They call it a salvage yard, but the local rednecks say it's really a distribution center for stolen Harley-Davidson parts,' Beneteau said. He was driving, his wrist draped casually over the top of the steering wheel. 'Supposedly, a guy rips off a good clean bike down in the Cities or over in Milwaukee or even Chicago, rides it up here overnight. They strip it down in an hour or so, get rid of anything identifiable, and drop the biker up at the Duluth bus station. Proving that would be a lot of trouble. But you hear about midnight bikers coming through here, and the bikes never going back out.'

'Where do they sell the parts?' Connell asked from the backseat.

'Biker rallies, I guess,' Beneteau said, looking at her in the rearview mirror. 'Specialty shops. There's a strong market in old Harleys, and the older parts go for heavy cash, if they're clean.' They topped a rise and looked down at a series of rambling sheds facing the road, with a pile of junk behind a gray board fence. Three cars, two bikes, and two trucks faced the line of buildings. None of the vehicles were new. 'That's it,' Beneteau said, leaning on the accelerator. 'Let's try to get inside quick.'

Lucas glanced back at Connell. She had one hand in her purse. Gun. He slipped a hand under his jacket and touched the butt of his .45. 'Let's take it easy in there,' he said casually. 'They're not really suspects.'

'Yet,' said Connell.

Beneteau's eyes flicked up to the rearview mirror again. 'Got your game face on,' he said to Connell in his casual drawl.

They clattered across a small board bridge over a drainage ditch and Lucas hooked the door handle with the fingers of his right hand as Beneteau drove them into the junkyard's parking lot. The other car went a hundred feet down the road, to the end of the lot, while the panel truck hooked in short. There were four deputies in the van, armed with M-16s. If somebody starting pecking at them with a fifty, the M-16s would hose them down.

The gravel parking lot was stained with oil and they slid the last few feet, raising a cloud of dust. 'Go,' Beneteau grunted.

Lucas was out a half second before Connell, headed toward the front door. He went straight through, not quite running, his hand on his belt buckle. Two men were standing at the counter, one in front of it, one in back, looking at a fat, greasy parts catalog. Startled, the man behind the counter backed up, said, 'Hey,' and Lucas pushed through the swinging counter gate and flashed his badge with his left hand and said, 'Police.'

'Cops,' the counterman shouted. He wore a white T-shirt covered with oil stains, and jeans with a heavy leather wallet sticking out of his back pocket, attached to his belt with a brass chain. The man at the front of the counter, bearded, wearing a railway engineer's hat, backed away, hands in front of him. Connell was behind him.

'You Joe?' Lucas asked, crowding the counterman. The counterman stood his ground, and Lucas shoved his chest, backing him up. An open doorway led away to Lucas's right, into the bowels of the buildings.

'That's Bob,' Beneteau said, coming in. 'How you doing, Bob?'

'What the fuck do you want, George?' Bob asked.

A cop out front yelled, 'We got runners . . .' and Beneteau ran back out the door.

'Where's Joe?' Lucas asked, pushing Bob.

'Who the fuck are you?'

'Keep them,' Lucas said to Connell.

Connell pulled her pistol from her purse, a big stainless-steel Ruger wheelgun, held with both hands, the muzzle up.

'And for Christ's sake, don't shoot anybody this time, unless you absolutely have to,' Lucas said hastily.

'You're no fun,' Connell said. She dropped the muzzle of the gun toward Bob, who had taken a step back toward Lucas, and said, 'Stand still or I'll punch a fuckin' hole right through your nose.' Her voice was as cold as sleet, and Bob stopped.

Lucas freed his gun and went through the door into the back, pausing a second to let his eyes adjust to the gloom. The walls were lined with shelves, and a dozen free-standing metal parts racks stood between the door and the back wall. The racks were loaded with bike parts, fenders and tanks, wheels, stacks of Quaker State oil cans, coffee cans full of rusty nails, screws, and bolts. Two open cans of grease sat on the floor, and two open-topped fifty-five-gallon drums full of trash were at his elbow. A metal extrusion that might have been a go-cart chassis was propped against them. The only light came from small dirty windows on the back wall, and through a door at the back right. The whole place smelled of dust and oil.

Lucas started toward the door, gun barrel up, finger off the trigger. Then to the left, between a row of metal racks, he saw a scattering of white. Beyond it, an open door led into a phone booth-size bathroom, the brown-stained toilet directly in front of the door. He stepped toward the smear of white, which had broken out of a small plastic bag. Powder. Cocaine? He bent down, touched it, lifted his finger to his nose, sniffed it. Not coke. He thought about tasting it: for all he knew it was some kind of powdered bike cleaner, something like Drāno. Put a tiny taste on his tongue anyway, got the instant acrid cut: speed.

'Shit.' The word was spoken almost next to his ear, and

Lucas jumped. The rack beside him lurched and toppled toward him, boxes of odd metal parts sliding off the shelf. Something heavy and sharp sliced into his scalp as he put an arm out to brace the rack. He pushed the rack back, staggering, and a man bolted out from behind the next row, ran down to the right toward the door, and out.

Lucas, struggling with the rack, aware of a dampness in his hair, fought free and went after him. As he burst through the door into the light, he heard somebody yell and looked right, saw Beneteau standing in an open field, pointing. Lucas looked left, saw the man cutting toward the junkyard, and ran after him.

Lost him in the piles of trash. Old cars, mostly from the sixties; he spotted the front end of a '66 bottle-green Pontiac LeMans, just like the one he'd owned when he'd first been in uniform. Lucas stalked through the piles, taking his time: the guy couldn't have gone over the fence, he'd have made some noise. He moved farther in: wrecks with hand-painted numbers on their doors, victims of forgotten county-fair enduro races.

Heard a clank to his left, felt a wetness in his eyebrow. Reached up and touched it: blood. Whatever had fallen off the shelf had cut him, and he was bleeding fairly heavily. Didn't hurt much, he thought. He moved farther left, around a pile, around another pile . . .

A thin biker in jeans, a smudged black T-shirt, and heavy boots looked up at the board fence around the yard. He was dark-complected, with a tan on top of that.

The man goggled at Lucas's bloody head. 'Jesus, what happened to you?'

'You knocked some shit on me,' Lucas said.

The man showed a pleased smile, then looked at the top of the fence. 'I'd never make it,' he said finally. He stepped back toward Lucas. 'You gonna shoot me?'

'No, we just want to talk.' Lucas slipped the pistol back in its holster.

'Yeah, right,' the man said, showing his yellow teeth. Suddenly he was moving fast. 'But I'm gonna kick your ass first.'

Lucas touched the butt of his pistol as the man's long wild swing came in. He lifted his left hand, batted the fist over his shoulder, hooked a short punch into the biker's gut. The man had a stomach like an oak board. He grunted, took a step back, circled. 'You can hit me all day in the fuckin' gut,' he said. He'd made no attempt at Lucas's pistol.

Lucas shook his head, circling to his right. 'No point. I'm gonna hit you in the fuckin' head.'

'Good luck.' The biker came in again, quick but inept, three fast roundhouse swings. Lucas stepped back once, twice, took the third shot on his left shoulder, then hooked a fast right to the man's nose, felt the septum snap under the impact. The man dropped, one hand to his face, rolled onto his stomach, got shakily back to his feet, blood running out from under his hands. Lucas touched his own forehead.

'You broke my nose,' the man said, looking at the blood on his fingers.

'What'd you expect?' Lucas asked, probing his scalp with his fingertips. 'You cut my head open.'

'Not on purpose. You broke my fuckin' nose on purpose,' he complained. Beneteau ran into the junkyard, looked at them. The man said, 'I give up.'

Beneteau stood in the parking lot and said quietly, 'Earl says Joe is down at the house.' Earl was the man who'd fought Lucas. 'He's scared to death Bob'll find out he told us.'

'Okay,' Lucas said. He held a first-aid pad against his scalp. He'd already soaked one of them through, and was on his second.

'We're gonna head down there,' Beneteau said. 'Do you

207

want to come? Or do you want to go into town and get that cut fixed up?'

'I'm coming,' Lucas said. 'How about the search warrants?'

'We got them, both for this place and Joe's and Bob's. That's a fine amount of speed back there, if that's what it is,' Beneteau said.

'That's what it is,' Lucas said. 'There's probably six or eight ounces there on the floor.'

'Biggest drug bust we've ever had,' Beneteau said with satisfaction. He looked at the porch, where Bob Hillerod and Earl sat on a bench, in handcuffs. They'd cut the customer loose; Beneteau was satisfied that he'd been there for cycle parts. 'I'm kind of surprised Earl was involved with it.'

'It'd be hard to prove that he was,' Lucas said. 'I didn't see him with the stuff. He says he was back there getting an alternator when everybody started running. He said one of the guys who went into the woods panicked, and threw the bag toward the toilet as they ran out the back. He might be telling the truth.'

Beneteau looked at the woods and laughed a little. 'We got those guys pinned in the marsh over there. Can't see them, but I give them about fifteen minutes after the bugs come out tonight. If they last that long – they were wearing short-sleeved shirts.'

'So let's get Joe,' Lucas said.

Beneteau turned the junkyard over to a half-dozen arriving deputies, including his crime-scene specialists. They took the same two sheriff's cars and the panel truck to Hillerod's house.

Joe Hillerod lived ten miles from the junkyard, in a rambling place built of three or four old lake cabins shoved together into one big tar-paper shack. A dozen cords of firewood were dumped in the overgrown back, in a tepee-shaped pile. Three cars were parked in the front.

'I love this backwoods shit,' Lucas said to Beneteau as they closed on the house. 'In the city, we'd call in the Emergency Response Unit . . .'

'That's a Minnesota liberal's euphemism for SWAT team,' Connell said to Beneteau, who nodded and showed his teeth.

'. . . and we'd stage up, and everybody'd get a job, and we'd put on vests and radios, and we'd sneak down to the area, and clear it,' Lucas continued. 'Then we'd sneak up to the house and the entry team'd go in . . . Up here, it's jump in the fuckin' cars, arrive in a cloud of hayseed, and arrest everybody in sight. Fuckin' wonderful.'

'The biggest difference is, we arrive in a cloud of hayseed. Down in the Cities, you arrive in a cloud of bullshit,' Beneteau said. 'You ready?'

They hit Hillerod's house just before noon. A yellow dog with a red collar was sitting on the blacktop in front of the place, and got up and walked off the road into a cattail ditch when he saw the traffic coming.

A young man with a large belly and a Civil War beard sat on the porch steps, drinking a beer and smoking a cigarette, looking as though he'd just got up. A Harley was parked next to the porch, and a scarred white helmet lay on the grass beside it like a fiberglass Easter egg produced by a condor.

When they slowed, he stood, and when they stopped, he ran in through the door. 'That's trouble,' Beneteau yelled.

'Go,' Connell said, and she jumped out and headed for the door.

Lucas said, 'Wait, wait,' but she kept going, and he was two steps behind her.

Connell went through the screen door like a cornerback through a wide receiver, in time to see the fat man running up a flight of stairs in the back of the house. Connell ran that way, Lucas yelling, 'Wait a minute.'

In a back room, a naked couple was crawling off a fold-out couch. Connell pointed the pistol at the man and yelled, 'Freeze,' and Lucas went by her and took the stairs. As he went, he heard Connell say to someone else, 'Take 'em, I'm going up.'

The fat man was in the bathroom, door locked, working the toilet. Lucas kicked the door in, and the fat man looked at him and went straight out a window, through the glass, onto the roof beyond. He heard cops yelling outside and ran on down the hall, Connell now a step behind him.

The door at the end of the hall was closed and Lucas kicked it just below the lock, and it exploded inward. Behind it, another couple were crawling around in their underpants, looking for clothes. The man had something in his hand and Lucas yelled, 'Police, drop it,' and tracked his body with the front sight of the pistol. The man, looking up, dazed with sleep, dropped a gun. The woman sat back on the bed and pulled a bedspread over her breasts.

Beneteau and two deputies came up behind them, pistols drawn. 'Got 'em?' He looked past Lucas. 'That's Joe.'

'What the fuck are you doing, George?' Joe asked.

Beneteau didn't answer. Instead, he looked at the woman and said, 'Ellie Rae, does Tom know about this?'

'No,' she said, hanging her head.

'Aw, God,' Beneteau said, shaking his head. 'Let's get everybody downstairs.'

A deputy was waiting for them on the stairs. 'Did you look in the dining room, Sheriff?'

'No, what'd we get?'

'C'mon, take a look,' the deputy said. He led the way back through a small kitchen, then through a side arch to the dining room. Two hundred semiautomatic rifles were stacked against the walls. A hundred and fifty handguns, glistening with WD-40, were slotted into cardboard boxes on the floor.

Lucas whistled. 'The gun-store burglaries. Out in the 'burbs around the cities.'

'This is good stuff,' Beneteau said, squatting to look at the long guns. 'This is gun-store stuff all the way.' Springfield M-1s, Ruger Mini-14s and Mini-30s, three odd-looking Navy Arms, a bunch of Marlins, a couple of elegant Brownings, an exotic Heckler and Koch SR9.

Beneteau picked up the H&K and looked at it. 'This is a fifteen-hundred-dollar gun, I bet,' he said, aiming it out the window at a Folger's coffee can in the side yard.

'What's the story on the woman up there?' Connell asked.

'Ellie Rae? She and her husband run the best diner in town. Rather, she runs it and he cooks. Great cook, but when he gets depressed, he drinks. If they break up, he'll get steady drunk, and she'll quit, and that'll be the end of the diner.'

'Oh,' Connell said. She looked at him to see if he was joking.

'Hey, that's a big deal,' Beneteau said defensively. 'There are only two of them, and the other one's a grease pit.'

Joe Hillerod looked a lot like his brother, with the same blunt, tough German features. 'I got fifteen hundred bucks in my wallet, cash, and I want witnesses to that. I don't want the money going away,' he said sullenly.

Ellie Rae said, 'I'm a witness.'

'You shut up, Ellie Rae,' Beneteau said. 'What the hell are you doing here, anyway?'

'I love him,' she said. 'I can't help myself.'

A deputy helped the fat man into the room. He was bleeding all over his head, shoulders, and arms from the window, and was dragging one leg.

'Dumb bunny jumped off the roof,' the deputy said. 'After he crashed through the window.'

211

'He was flushing shit upstairs,' Lucas said. *Dumb bunny? The guy looks like a mastodon.* 'He got some of it on the toilet seat, though.'

'Check that,' Beneteau said to one of the deputies.

Connell had put away her gun, and now she stepped up behind Hillerod and pulled at his hand, immobilized by the cuffs.

'What the fuck?' Hillerod said, trying to turn to see what she was doing.

'See?'

Lucas looked. Hillerod had the 666 on the web between his thumb and forefinger. 'Yeah.'

The woman who'd been on the fold-out couch had been watching Connell, taking in Connell's inch-long hair. 'I was sexually abused,' she said finally. 'By the cops.'

Connell said, 'Yeah?'

Lucas was climbing the stairs, and Connell hurried after him. In the bedroom, a decrepit water bed was pushed against one wall, with a bedstand and light to one side and a chest of drawers against the wall at the foot of the bed. Magazines and newspapers were scattered around the room. An ironing board sat in a corner, buried in wrinkled clothing, the iron lying on its side at the pointed end of the board.

A long stag-handled folding knife sat in a jumble of junk on the chest of drawers. Connell bent over next to it, carefully not touching it, looked at it, and said, 'Goddamn, Davenport. The autopsies say it's a knife like this. The blade's just right.'

She picked up a matchbook and used it to rotate the knife. The excitement rose in her voice. 'There's some gunky stuff in the hinge or whatever you call it, where it folds; it could be blood.'

'But look at the cigarettes,' Lucas said.

A pack of Marlboros sat on the nightstand. There wasn't a Camel in the house.

17

The Hillerods called a Duluth lawyer named Aaron Capella. The lawyer arrived at midafternoon in a dusty Ford Escort, talked to the county attorney, then to his clients. Lucas went to the local emergency room, had four stitches taken in his scalp, then met Connell for a late lunch. Afterward, they hung out in Beneteau's office or wandered around the courthouse, waiting for Capella to finish with the Hillerods.

The crime-scene crew called from the junkyard to say they'd found three half-kilo bags of cocaine behind a false panel in the junkyard bathroom. Beneteau was more than pleased: he was on television with each of the Duluth-Superior stations.

'Gonna get my ass reelected, Davenport,' he said to Lucas.

'I'll send you a bill,' Lucas said.

They were talking in his office, and they saw Connell coming up the walk outside. She'd been down at a coffee shop, and carried a china cup with her.

'That's a fine-looking woman,' Beneteau said, his eyes lingering on her. 'I like the way she sticks her face into trouble. If you don't mind my asking, have you two . . . got something going?'

Lucas shook his head. 'No.'

'Huh. Is she with anybody else?'

'Not as far as I know,' Lucas said. He started to say something about her being sick, hesitated.

'I mean, she's not a lesbian or anything,' Beneteau said.

'No, she's not. Look, George . . .' He still couldn't think

of exactly what he wanted to say. What he said was, 'Look, do you want her phone number, or what?'

Beneteau's eyebrows went up. 'Well, I get down to the Cities every now and then. You got it?'

Aaron Capella was a pro. Beneteau knew him, and they shook hands when Capella walked into the sheriff's office. Beneteau introduced Lucas and Connell.

'I've spoken to my clients. Another unconscionable violation of their civil rights,' Capella said mildly to Beneteau.

'I know, it's a shame,' Beneteau said, tongue in cheek. 'The right of felons to bear stolen assault weapons while distributing cocaine and speed.'

'That's what I keep telling people, and you're the only guy who understands,' Capella said. 'C'mon, Bich is waiting.'

They walked through the courthouse, Beneteau and Capella talking about Capella's sailboat, which he kept on Lake Superior. '. . . guy from Maryland was telling me, "A lake just isn't the ocean." So I say, "Where do you sail?" and he says, "The Chesapeake." And I say, "You could put six Chesapeakes in Superior, and still have a Long Island Sound around the edges." '

Bich was the county attorney, a serious, red-faced man in a charcoal suit. 'They're bringing your client up now, Aaron,' he said to Capella. They all followed the prosecutor into his office, settling into chairs, Bich joining the sailing talk until a deputy brought Joe Hillerod down from the lockup.

Hillerod's lip lifted in an uncontrollable sneer when he saw Beneteau. He dropped into a chair next to Capella and said, 'How're we doing?'

Bich spoke to Capella as if Hillerod weren't there, but everything he said was aimed at Hillerod: Capella and Bich had already been over the ground.

'Tell you what, Aaron, your client's in bad shape,' Bich said professorially. 'He's got two years left on his parole. Possession of a gun'll put him back inside. There won't be any trial, none of that bullshit. All it takes is a hearing.'

'We'd contest.'

Bich rolled past him. 'We found him with a house full of stolen guns. We could try him for possessing firearms as a felon and possession of stolen firearms. Then we could send him to Minnesota, to be tried for burglary. He'd go back to Waupun, serve out the rest of his parole, start his new Wisconsin time after that, and then go to Minnesota to serve out his time over there. That's a lot of time.'

The lawyer spread his hands. 'Joe had nothing to do with the guns. He thought they were legit. A friend left them there, the same guy you grabbed up in the bathroom.'

'Right.' Bich rolled his eyes.

'But we're not discussing the guns; that's another issue,' Capella said. 'We can talk, right? That's why Lucas and Ms Connell are here, right? A little friendly extortion?'

'If he'll ride along with us,' Bich said, poking a finger at Hillerod's chest, 'we might be inclined to forget the parole violation, the possession of a gun. That we got him on already.'

'So what are we talking about?' Capella asked.

Bich looked at Lucas. 'Do you want to explain to Mr Hillerod?'

Lucas looked at him and said, 'I won't bullshit you. There are some good reasons to think that you've been slicing up women. Ripping their guts out. Six or more times now. We need to ask you some questions and get some answers.'

Hillerod had known what was coming, having spoken to Capella. He started shaking his head before Lucas was finished talking. 'Nah, nah, never did it, that's bullshit, man.'

'We're running your knife through the crime lab,'

215

Connell said. 'It looks like it might have some blood gummed up in the hinges.'

'Well, shit,' Hillerod said, and he looked uncomfortable for a moment as he thought about what she'd said. 'If there's blood, it's animal blood. That's a hunting knife.'

'This ain't exactly deer season,' Lucas said.

'If there's any goddamned blood on that knife, it's deer blood – or you put it there just to get me,' Hillerod said heatedly. 'You fuckin' cops think you can get away with anything.'

Capella's voice rode over his client's. 'My client remembers the bookstore in Madison.'

'That's a long time to remember,' Bich marveled. 'Several years, if I've got it right.'

'I remember 'cause it's the only bookstore I ever been in,' Hillerod snarled.

Capella kept talking. '. . . and he's got a witness of good reputation who spent that whole night with him down in Madison, and he's sure she'll remember it independently of anything we talk about here. Without any prompting from me or Joe. I will state that we have not been in touch with her, and that Joe's confident that she'll remember.'

'You've got a name?' Lucas asked.

'You can have the name and the circumstances in which they met,' the lawyer said. 'The fact is, he picked her up at the bookstore.'

'I didn't have nothing to do with the guns,' Hillerod said sullenly.

'We're not talking about that,' his lawyer said quickly. He patted Hillerod on the knee. 'That's not part of the deal.'

'We know the killer smokes Marlboros,' Lucas said, leaning toward Hillerod. 'You smoke Marlboros, right?'

'No, no, I usually smoke Merits, I'm trying to quit,' Hillerod said. 'I just got the Marlboros that once.'

'Your man is lying to us,' Lucas said to Capella. 'We know he's smoked Marlboros for years.'

Capella said, 'He says Merits . . . I gotta believe him.'

'Merits taste like shit,' Bich said. 'Why'd you smoke Merits? Is that all you smoke?'

'Well, I'm trying to quit,' Hillerod said, not meeting their eyes. 'I smoke some Marlboros, but I didn't kill anybody. I smoke some Ventures, too.'

The Marlboro bluff hadn't worked. 'We want to know about the bookstore,' Connell said.

'In Madison?' Hillerod's eyes defocused for a moment, and then he said, 'How'd you know about that, anyway?'

'We've got a witness,' Connell said. 'You left with a woman.'

'That's right,' Hillerod said. Then he said, 'She's gotta be the one who told you.'

'She's not,' Lucas said. 'Our witness . . . well, it's a woman, but it's not your friend. If you've *got* a friend. But we want to know about the other woman. The one who turned up dead the next day.'

'Wasn't me,' Hillerod said. 'The woman I left with, she's still alive. And she must've told you that I couldn't have done it, 'cause I was with her.'

'What's her name?' asked Connell.

Hillerod scratched his face, glaring at her, but Connell looked levelly back, as though she were an entomologist examining a not-particularly-interesting beetle. 'Abby Weed,' he said finally.

'Where does she live?'

Hillerod shrugged. 'I don't know the address, just how to get there. But you can get her at the university.'

'She works at the university?' Lucas asked.

'She's a professor,' he said. 'In fine art. She's a painter.'

Lucas looked at Connell, who rolled her eyes. 'Who were you there with? At the bookstore?'

'Wasn't there with nobody,' Hillerod said. 'I went in

217

to get a book on my bike, if they had one, which they didn't.'

'How long were you in there?'

Hillerod shrugged. 'Hour.'

'That's a long time to look for a book that they didn't have,' Lucas said.

'I only spent five minutes looking for the book. Then I saw Abby giving me the eye, and I hung around to bullshit her a little bit. She had the big . . .' He glanced at Connell. 'Headlights.'

'She went home with you?' Connell said.

'We went to her place.'

'You spent the night?'

'Shit, I spent about four nights,' Hillerod said with a small smile, talking to Connell. 'Every time I tried to get out of bed, I'd find her hanging on to my dick . . .' The smile went flat, and he looked at Lucas. 'The fuckin' cop,' he said. 'That fuckin' cop picked me out, didn't he?'

'What cop?'

'The cop at the store.'

Lucas looked at him for a long beat, then said, 'You have a 666 on your hand.'

Hillerod looked at the tattoo, shook his head. 'Goddamnit, I knew that was stupid, the fuckin' 666. Everybody was getting them. I told people, the cops'll use them against us.'

'Did you see anybody in the store that looked like this?' Connell asked. She handed him the composite.

Hillerod looked it over, then looked curiously from Connell to Lucas to Bich to Capella. 'Well. Not anyone else. Not that I remember.'

'What? What'd you mean, anyone else?' Lucas asked.

He shrugged. 'You should know. It looks like your cop.'

'The cop?' Connell looked at Lucas again. 'How did you know he was a cop?'

'The way he looked at me. He was a cop, all right. He looked at my hand, then at me, and then my hand. He knew what it was.'

'Could have been a con,' Lucas said.

Hillerod thought about it, then said, 'Yeah. Could have been, I guess. But I felt like he was a cop.'

'And he looked like this picture,' Connell said.

'Yeah. It's not quite right, I don't think. I can't remember that well, but his beard's wrong,' he said, studying the drawing. 'And there's something wrong about the mouth. And the guy's hair was flatter . . . But that's who it mostly looks like.'

'The cop,' Lucas said.

'Yeah. The cop.'

'Sonofagun,' Connell said bitterly. They stood next to a water fountain, the office lawyers and secretaries flowing around them. 'The cop shows up again. Davenport — I believe him.' She gestured down the hall at Bich's office, where Hillerod waited. 'I can't believe he just pulled that out of his ass. He's not smart enough.'

'Don't panic yet,' Lucas said. 'We've still got some lab work to do. We've got the knife.'

'You know as well as I do . . . Are we sure the St Paul cop is out of it?'

'St Paul says he is.'

'There's no way they'd cover for a guy on something like this,' she said, not quite making it a question.

'No way,' Lucas agreed. 'I talked to one of their guys, and they worked him over pretty good.'

'Goddamnit,' Connell said. She shook her head. 'We're going back to the beginning.'

Connell drove: she wanted to handle the Porsche. On the way out to the interstate, the sun dropping toward the horizon, windshield greased by a million bugs from the roadside ditches, she said, 'George Beneteau was surprisingly professional. I mean, for a county sheriff.'

Lucas rode along for a minute, then said, 'He asked about you. Marital status, that kind of thing.'

'What?'

Lucas grinned at her and she flushed. 'He said . . .' Lucas dropped into a cornball accent, which Beneteau didn't have, 'that's a fine-lookin' woman.'

'You are lying to me, Davenport.'

'Honest to God,' Lucas said. After a minute, he said, 'He wanted your phone number.'

'Did you give it to him?'

Lucas said, 'I didn't know what to do, Meagan. I didn't know whether to tell him you were sick, or what. So I . . . yeah, I gave it to him.'

'You didn't tell him I was sick?'

'No. I didn't.'

They drove on for another minute, in silence, and then Connell began to weep. Eyes open, head up, big hands square on the wheel, she began sobbing, breath tearing from her chest, tears streaming down her face. Lucas started to say something, looking for words, but she just shook her head and drove on.

18

Evan Hart stood with one hand in his pocket, his voice low, concerned. His back was to the balcony, so he was framed in the dark square; he wore a blue suit with a conservative striped shirt, and carried a square Scotch glass in his left hand. He'd taken his necktie off and thrust it in his pocket. Sara could see just the point of it sticking out from under the flap of his coat pocket. 'Have you talked to the police?'

She shook her head. 'I don't know what I'd tell them.' She crossed her arms over her chest, rubbed her triceps with her hands, as though she were cold. 'It's like having a ghost,' she said. 'I *feel* somebody, but I've never *seen* anything. I had the burglary, and since then . . . nothing. They'd say it's paranoia — paranoia brought on by the burglary. And I hate being patronized.'

'They'd be right about the paranoia. You can't be a good trader if you're not paranoid,' Hart said. He sipped the Johnnie Walker Black.

''Cause somebody *is* out to get you,' she said, finishing the old Wall Street joke. She drifted across the front room toward him. She also had a glass, vodka martini, three olives. She looked out across the balcony, over the building across the street, toward the park. 'To tell the truth, I am a little scared. A woman was killed just across the street, and the guy with her is still in a coma. This was just a few days ago, a couple of days after my burglary. They haven't caught anybody yet — they say it was gang kids. I've never seen any gang kids here. It was supposed to be safe. I used to walk around the lake in the evenings, but I've stopped.'

Hart's face was serious again. He reached out and brushed her arm with two fingertips, just a light touch. 'Maybe you should think about moving out of here.'

'I've got a lease,' Sara said, away from the balcony, toward him. 'And the apartment is really handy to work. And it should be safe. It *is* safe. I've changed the locks, I've got a steel door. I don't know . . .'

Hart stepped over to the balcony, looked out, his back toward her. She wondered if she made him nervous. 'It's a pretty neighborhood. And I guess no place is really perfectly safe. Not anymore.'

There was a moment of silence, and then she asked, 'Do I make you nervous?'

He turned, a weak, slowly dying smile on his face. 'Yeah, a little.'

'Why?'

He shrugged. 'I like you too much. You're very attractive . . . I don't know, I'm just not very good at this.'

'It is awkward,' she said. 'Look, why don't you come over and sit down, and I'll put my head on your shoulder, and we'll go from there.'

He shrugged again. 'All right.' He put down his glass, crossed the room, sat quickly, put his arm around her shoulder, and she let her head sink onto his chest.

'Now, is this bad?' she asked, and suddenly broke into a giggle.

'No, this isn't bad at all,' Evan said. He sounded nervous, but he felt committed, and when she lifted her head to smile at him, he kissed her.

She felt good. She made a hundred and thirty thousand dollars a year, took vacations in Paris and Mexico and Monaco; she was the toughest woman she knew.

But a chest felt . . . excellent. She snuggled into it.

Koop grabbed the edge of the air-conditioner housing, pulled himself up, and saw Jensen on the couch with a man, saw her turn her face up and the man kiss her.

'Oh, fuck me,' he said aloud. 'Oh, fuck me,' and he felt his world shake.

The guy across the street put his hand on Jensen's waist, then moved it up a few inches, under her breast. Koop thought he recognized the guy, then realized he'd seen somebody like him on television, an old movie. Henry Fonda, that was it; Henry Fonda, when he was young. 'Motherfucker . . .'

Koop stood up without thinking, hand holding the scope, the living room couch jumping toward him. Their faces were locked together and the guy was definitely copping a feel. Remembering himself, Koop dropped to a crouch, felt the heat climbing into his face. He looked down and hammered his fist into the steel housing; and for the first time since – when? never? – felt something that might have been emotional pain. How could she do this? This wasn't right, she was *his* . . .

He looked back toward Sara's apartment. They were talking now, backed off a little. Then she tipped her head onto his shoulder, and that was almost worse than the kiss. Koop put the scope on them, and watched so hard that his head began to hurt. Christ, he hoped they didn't fuck. Please, don't do it. Please.

They kissed again, and this time the guy's hand cupped Jensen's breast, held it. Koop, in agony, rolled over on his shoulder and looked away, decided not to look back until he counted to a hundred. Maybe it would go away. He counted one, two, three, four, five and got to thirty-eight before he couldn't stand it, and flipped over.

The guy was standing.

She'd said something to him; a pulse of elation streaked through his soul. She must've. She was getting ready to throw him out, by God. Why else would he have stopped; Christ, he had her on the couch. He had her in hand, for Christ's sake. Then the guy picked up a glass and looked at her, said something, and she threw back her head and laughed.

No. That didn't look good.

Then she was on her feet, walking toward him. Slipped two fingers between the buttons of his shirt, said something – Koop would have mortgaged his life for the ability to lip-read – then stood on tiptoe and kissed him again, quickly this time, and walked away, picked up a newspaper, and waved it at him, said something else.

They talked for another five minutes, both standing now, circling each other. Sara Jensen kept touching him. Her touch was like fire to Koop. When she touched the guy, Koop could feel it on his arm, in his chest.

Then the guy moved toward the door. He was leaving. Both still smiling.

At the door she stepped into him, her face up, and Koop rolled over again, refusing to watch, counting: one, two, three, four, five. Only got to fifteen, counting fast, before he turned back.

She was still in his arms, and he'd pressed her to the door. Jesus.

Gotta take him. Gotta take him now.

The impulse was like a hammer. He'd gut the cocksucker right in the driveway. He was messing with Koop's woman . . .

But Koop lingered, unwilling to leave until the guy was out the door. They finally broke apart, and Koop, in a half-crouch, waited for him to go. Jensen was holding his hand. Didn't want him to go. Tugged at him.

'Cocksucker . . .' he thought, and realized he'd spoken aloud. Said it again: 'Cocksucker, cut your fuckin' heart out, man, cut your fuckin' . . .'

And the roof access door opened. A shaft of light, shocking, blinding, snapped across the roof and climbed the air-conditioner housing. Koop went flat, tense, ready to fight, ready to run.

Voices crossed each other, ten feet away. There was a sharp rattle and a bang as the door was pushed open, then closed of its own weight.

Cops.

'Gotta be quick.' Not cops. A woman's voice.

Man's voice. 'It's gonna be quick, I can promise that, you got me so hot I can't hold it.'

Woman's voice: 'What if Kari looks for the pad?'

'She won't, she's got no interest in camping . . . c'mon, let's go behind the air-conditioner thing. C'mon.'

The woman giggled and Koop heard them rattling across the graveled roof, and the sound of a plastic mat being unrolled on the gravel. Koop looked sideways, past the duct toward Jensen's building. She was kissing the guy good-bye again, standing on her tiptoes in the open door, his hand below her waist, almost on her ass.

Below him, eight feet away, the man was saying, 'Let me get these, let me get these . . . Oh, Jesus, these look great . . .'

And the woman: 'Boy, what if Kari and Bob could see us now . . . Oh, God . . .'

Across the street, Jensen was pushing the door shut. She leaned back against it, her head cocked back, an odd, loose look on her face, not quite a smile.

The woman: 'Don't rip it, don't rip it . . .'

The man: 'God, you're wet, you're a hot little bitch . . .'

Koop, blind with fury, his heart pounding like a trip-hammer, lay quiet as a mouse, but getting angrier and angrier. He thought about jumping down, of taking the two of them.

He rejected the idea as quickly as it had come. A woman had already died at this building, and a man was in a coma. If another two died, the cops would know *something* was happening here. He'd never get back up.

Besides, all he had was his knife. He might not get them both – and he couldn't see the guy. If the guy was big, tough, it might take a while, make a lot of noise.

Koop bit his lip, listening to the lovemaking. The woman tended to screech, but the screeching sounded fake. The guy said, 'Don't scratch,' and she said, 'I can't help myself,' and Koop thought, *Jesus* . . .

And Sara Jensen's lover was getting away. Better to let him go . . . goddamnit.

He turned his head back to Jensen's apartment. Jensen went into the bathroom and shut the door. He knew from watching her that when she did that, she'd be inside for a while. Koop eased himself over onto his back and looked up at the stars, listened to the couple on the roof below him. Goddamnit.

Man's voice: 'Let me do it this way, c'mon . . .'

The woman: 'God, if Bob knew what I was doing . . .'

19

Greave had his feet up on his desk, talking on the phone, when Lucas arrived in the morning. Anderson drifted over and said, 'A homicide guy in Madison interviewed somebody named Abby Weed. He says she confirmed that she met Joe Hillerod in a bookstore. She doesn't remember the date, but she remembered the discussion, and it was the right one. She said she spent the night with him, and she was unhappy about being questioned.'

'Damnit,' Lucas said. He said it without heat. Hillerod hadn't felt right, and he hadn't expected much. 'Have you seen Meagan Connell?'

Anderson shook his head, but Greave, still on the phone, held up a finger, said a few more words, then covered the mouthpiece with his palm. 'She called in, said she was sick. She'll be in later,' he said. He went back to the phone.

Sick. Connell had been plummeting into depression when Lucas left her the night before. He hadn't wanted to leave – he'd suggested that she come home with him, spend the night in a guest room, but she'd said she was fine.

'I shouldn't have mentioned Beneteau asking about you,' Lucas said.

She caught his arm. 'Lucas, you did right. It's one of the nicer things that's happened to me in the last year.' But her eyes had been ineffably sad, and he'd had to turn away.

Greave dropped the receiver on the hook and sighed. 'How far did you get on the sex histories?' Lucas asked.

'Not very far.' Greave looked away. 'To tell you the

truth, I hardly got started. I thought I might have something on my apartment.'

'Goddamnit, Bob, forget the fuckin' apartment,' Lucas said, his voice harsh. 'We need these histories – and we need as many people thinking about the case as we can get.'

Greave stood up, shook himself like a dog. He was a little shorter than Lucas, his features a little finer. 'Lucas, I can't. I try, but I just can't. It's like a nightmare. I swear to God, I was eating an ice cream cone last night and I started wondering if they poisoned her ice cream.' Lucas just looked at him, and Greave shook his head after a minute and said, 'They didn't, of course.'

And they both said, simultaneously, 'No toxicology.'

Jan Reed found Lucas in his office. She had great eyes, he thought. Italian eyes. You could fall into them, no problem. He had a quick male mini-vision: Reed on the bed, pillow under her shoulders, head back, a half inch from orgasm. She looks up at the final instant, eyes opening, her awareness of him the sexiest thing in the universe . . .

'Nothing,' he said, flustered. 'Not a thing.'

'But what about the people you grabbed in that raid over in Wisconsin?' There was a pinprick of amusement in her eyes. She knew the effect she had on him.

And she knew about the raid. 'An unrelated case, but a good story,' Lucas lied. He babbled: 'It's a group of people called the Seeds – there used to be a motorcycle gang called the Bad Seeds, from up in northwest Wisconsin, and they evolved into a criminal organization. Cops call it the Hayseed Mafia. Anyway, these are the guys who were hitting the suburban gun stores. We got a lot of the guns back.'

'That *is* interesting,' she said. She made a note in her notebook, then put the eraser end of her pencil against her teeth, pensively, erotically. He was starting to fixate on the idea of television anchorwomen and oral sex, Lucas thought. 'The gun issue's so hot . . . right now.' She would pause every so often, leaving a gap in the conversation, almost as though she were inviting him to fill it in.

She paused now, and Lucas said, 'Reed's an English name, right?'

'Yes. I'd be English on my father's side,' she said. 'Why?'

'I was thinking,' Lucas said. 'You've got great Italian eyes, you know?'

She smiled and caught her bottom lip with an upper tooth, and said, 'Well, thank you . . .'

When she left, Lucas went to the door with her. She moved along a little more slowly than he did, and he found himself almost on top of her, ushering her out. She smelled fine, he thought. He watched her down the hall. She wouldn't be an athlete. She was soft, smooth. She turned at the corner to see if he was watching, and just at that moment, when she turned, and though they resembled each other not at all, she reminded him of Weather.

The rest of the day was a wasteland of paper, old reports, and conjectures. Connell wandered in after two, even paler than usual, said she'd been working on the computers. Lucas told her about the interview with Abby Weed. Connell nodded: 'I'd already written them off. Hitting the Hillerods was just our good deed for the day.'

'How're you feeling?'

'Sick,' she said. Then quickly: 'Not from last night. From . . . the big thing. It's coming back.'

'Jesus, Meagan . . .'

'I knew it would,' she said. 'Listen, I'm going to talk to Anderson, and start helping Greave on those histories. I can't think of anything else.'

She left, but came back ten seconds later. 'We've got to get him, Lucas. This week or next.'

'I don't know . . .'

'That's all the time I've got this round . . . and the next round will be even shorter.'

Lucas got home early, found Weather on the couch reading *The Robber Bride*, her legs curled beneath her.

'A dead end?'

'Looks like it,' Lucas said. 'The woman in Madison confirmed Joe Hillerod's story. We're back to looking at paper.'

'Too bad. He sounds like a major jerk.'

'We've got him on the guns, anyway,' Lucas said. 'He handled most of the rifles, and their ID guys got good prints. And they found bolt cutters and a crowbar in his truck, and the tool-marks guy matched them to the marks on a gun-shop door out in Wayzata.'

'So what's left? On the murder case?'

'God, I don't know. But I feel like things are moving.'

Lucas spent the late evening in the study, going through Anderson's book on the case – all the paper that anybody had brought in, with the histories that Greave had completed. Weather came to the door in her cotton nightgown and said, 'Be extra quiet when you come to bed. I've got a heavy one tomorrow.'

'Yeah.' He looked up from the paper, his hair in disarray, discouraged. 'Christ, you know, there's so much stuff in here, and so much of it's bullshit. The stuff in this file, you could spend four years investigating and never learn a fuckin' thing.'

She smiled and came over and patted his hair back into place, and he wrapped an arm around her back and pulled her close, so he could lean his head between her breasts. There was something animal about this: it felt so good, and so natural. Like momma. 'You'll get him,' she said.

An hour later, he was puzzling over Anderson's note on the deaf people. Everything sounded right: a guy with a beard, going to the bookstore, in a truck. How in the hell did they screw up the license so bad? He glanced at his watch: one o'clock, too late to call anybody at St Paul. He leaned back in his chair and closed his eyes. Maybe something would bubble to the surface of his mind . . .

20

Koop brought a sack of Taco Bell soft tacos to the rooftop, tossed the sack on top of the air-conditioner housing, and pulled himself up after them. There was still enough light that Sara Jensen might see him if she looked out her window, so he duckwalked across the housing until he was behind the exhaust vent.

Putting the tacos aside, he shook the Kowa scope out of its canvas case and surveyed the apartment. Where was the blond guy? Had he come back? His heart was chilly with the fear . . .

The drapes from both rooms were open, as usual. Sara Jensen was nowhere in sight. The bathroom door was closed.

Satisfied for the moment, Koop settled in behind the vent, opening the tacos, gulping them down. He dripped sour cream on his jacket: Shit. He brushed the sour cream with a napkin, but there would be a grease stain. He tossed the napkin off the edge off the housing, then thought, *I shouldn't do that*, and made a mental note to pick it up before he left.

Ten minutes after he arrived, Sara Jensen walked – hurried – out of the bathroom. She was nude, and the thrill of her body ran through him like an electric current, like a hit of speed. He put the scope on her as she sat at her dressing table and began to work on her makeup. He enjoyed seeing this, the careful work under the eyes, the touch-up of the lashes, the sensuous painting of her full lips. He dreamed about her lips . . .

And he loved to watch her naked back. She had

smoothly molded shoulders, the ripple of her spine from the top of her round ass straight to the nape of her neck. Her skin was fine, clear – one small dark mole on her left shoulder blade, the long, pale neck . . .

She stood, turned toward him, face intent, her breasts bobbing, the gorgeous pubic patch . . . She dug through her dresser, looking at what? Underwear? She pulled on a pair of underpants, took them off, threw them back, pulled on a much briefer pair, looked at herself in the mirror. Looked again, backed away, pulled the bottom elastic of her pants away from her thighs, let it snap back, turned to look at her butt.

And Koop began to worry.

She found a bra to go with the pants, an underwired bra, perhaps: it seemed to push her up. She didn't really need it, he thought, but it did look good. She turned again, looking at her self, snapped the elastic on her pants leg again.

Posed.

She was pleased with herself.

'What are you doing, Sara?' Koop asked. He tracked her with the scope. 'What the fuck are you doing?'

She disappeared into a closet and came back out with a simple dark dress, either very dark blue or black. She held it to her breasts, looked into the mirror, shook her head at herself, and went back into the closet. She came back out with blue jeans and a white blouse, held them up, put them on, tucked in the shirt. Looked at herself, made a face in the mirror, shook her head, went back into the closet, emerged with the dress. She took off the jeans, stripping for him again, exciting him. She picked up the dress, pulled it over her head, smoothed it down.

'Are you going out, Sara?'

She looked in the mirror again, one hand on her ass, then took the dress off, tossed it on the bed, and looked thoughtfully at her chest of drawers. Walked to the chest, opened the bottom drawer, and took out a pale-blue cotton sweat suit. She pulled it on, pushed up the sleeves on the sweatshirt, went back to the mirror. Pulled off the sweatshirt, took off the bra, pulled the sweatshirt back on.

Koop frowned. Sweat suit?

The dress had been simple but elegant. The jeans casual but passable at most places in the Cities. But the sweat suit? Maybe she'd just been trying on stuff. But if so, why all the time in the bathroom? Why the sense of urgency?

Koop turned away, dropped behind the duct, lit a Camel, then rolled onto his knees and looked back through her window. She was standing in front of her mirror, flipping her hair with her hands. Brushing it back: breaking down its daytime structure.

Huh.

She stopped suddenly, then ducked back at the mirror, gave her hair a last flip, then hurried – skipped once – going out of the bedroom, into the front room, to the door. Said something, a smile on her face, then opened the door.

Goddamn it.

The blond guy was there. He had a chin on him, a butt-chin, with a dimple in it. He was wearing jeans and a canvas shirt, looking as tousled as she did. She stepped back from him, pulled a piece of her sweat suit out from her leg, almost as if she were about to curtsy.

Butt-chin laughed and stepped inside and leaned forward as if he were about to peck her on the cheek, and then the peck ignited and they stood there in each other's arms, the hallway door still open behind them. Koop rose to a half-stoop, looking across the fifty feet of air at his true love in another man's arms. He groaned aloud and hurled his cigarette toward them, at the window. They never saw it. They were too busy.

'Motherfuckers . . .'

They didn't go out. Koop watched in pain as they moved to the couch. He realized, suddenly, why she had rejected the jeans and vacillated between the dress and the sweat suit: access.

A guy can't get his hands in a tight pair of jeans, boyo. Not without a lot of preliminaries. With a sweatsuit, there were no barriers. No problems getting your hands in. And that's where Blondy's were – in Sara's loose sweatpants, under her loose sweatshirt, Sara writhing beneath his touch – before they went to the bedroom.

Blondy stayed the night.

So did Koop, huddled behind the vent on the air-conditioner housing, fading from consciousness to unconsciousness – not exactly sleep, but something else, something like a coma. Toward dawn, with just the light jacket, he got very cold. When he moved, he hurt. About four-thirty, the stars began to fade. The sun rose into a flawless blue sky and shone down on Koop, whose heart had turned to stone.

He felt it: a rock in his chest. And no mercy at all.

He had to wait more than an hour in the light before there was any movement in Sara Jensen's apartment. She woke first, rolled over, said something to the lump on the other side. Then he said something – Koop thought he did, anyway – and she moved up behind him, both of them on their sides, talking.

Two or three minutes later, Blondy got up, yawning, stretching. He sat naked on the bed, his back to Koop, then suddenly snatched the blankets down. Sara was there, as naked as he was, and he flopped on top of her, his head between her breasts. Koop turned away, squeezed his eyes shut. He just couldn't watch.

And he just couldn't *not* watch. He turned back. Blondy was nibbling on one of Sara Jensen's nipples, and Sara, back arched, her hands in his hair, was enjoying every second of it. The stone in Koop's heart began to fragment, to be replaced by a cold, unquenchable anger. The fucking whore was taking on another man. The fucking whore . . .

But he loved her anyway.

He couldn't help himself.

And couldn't help watching when she pushed him flat on the bed, and trailed her tongue from his chest down across his navel . . .

The blond guy finally left at seven o'clock.

Koop had stopped thinking long before that. For an hour, he'd simply been waiting, his knife in his hand. He occasionally ran it down his face, over his beard, as if he were shaving. He was actually getting in tune with it, the steel in the blade . . .

When the door closed behind Blondy, Koop barely gave Sara Jensen a thought. There'd be time for her later. She turned away, hurrying back to the bedroom to get ready for work.

Koop, wearing his glasses and snap-brimmed hat, flew off the air-conditioner housing. He had just enough control to check the apartment hallway before bursting into it from the roof access; a man stood in it, facing the elevator. Koop cursed, but the man suddenly stepped forward and was gone. Koop ran the length of the hall and took the stairs.

Took the stairs as though he were falling, a long circular dash, with no awareness of steps or landings, just a continuous drop, his legs flashing, shoes slapping like a machine gun on the concrete.

At the bottom, he checked the lobby through the window in the stairway door. Three or four people, and the elevator bell dinged: more coming. Frustrated, he looked around, then went down another flight, into the basement. And found a fire exit, leading out through the back. Just before he hit the back door, he saw a sign and read the first words, DO NOT, and then he was through.

Somewhere behind him, an alarm went off, a shrill ringing like King Kong's telephone.

Were there pictures? The possibility flashed through his brain and then disappeared. He'd worry about that later. That he hadn't been seen in the building – that was important. That he catch Blondy in the street – that was even more important.

Koop ran down the alley at the back of the building, around the building. There were a dozen people up and down the street, in business clothes, some coming toward him, some walking away, briefcases, purses. A cane.

He groped in his pocket, wrapping his fist around the knife again. Checked faces, checked again. Blondy was not among them. Where in the hell . . . ?

Koop pulled the hat farther down on his head, looked both ways, then started walking toward the entrance of Sara Jensen's apartment. Had he already gotten down? Or was he slow getting down? Or maybe she'd given him a parking card and he'd left his car in her ramp. He swerved toward the ramp exit, although if the guy was in a Mercedes or a Lexus what was he gonna do, stab it? He thought he might.

A car came out of the ramp, with a woman driver. Koop looked back at the door – and saw him.

Blondy had just come out. His hair was wet, his face soft, sated. His necktie, a conservative swath of silk, was looped untied around his shirt collar. He carried a raincoat.

Koop charged him. Started way back at the entrance to the parking ramp and hurtled down the sidewalk. He wasn't thinking, wasn't hearing, wasn't anything: wasn't aware of anyone other than Blondy.

Wasn't aware of the noise that came out of his mouth, not quite a scream, more of a screech, the sound of bad brakes . . .

Wasn't aware of other people turning . . .

Blondy saw him coming.

237

The soft look fell off his face, to be replaced by a puzzled frown, then alarm as Koop closed.

Koop screamed, 'Motherfucker,' and went in, the blade flicking out of his fist, his long arm arcing in a powerful, upward rip. But quicker than Koop could believe, Blondy stepped right, swung his arm and raincoat, caught Koop in the wrist, and Koop's hand went past Blondy's left side. They collided and they both staggered: the guy was heavier than he looked, and in better shape. Koop's mind began working again, touched by a sudden spark of fear. Here he was, on the street, circling a guy he didn't know . . .

Koop screamed again, and went in. He could hear the guy screaming 'Wait, wait,' but it sounded distant, as though it came from the opposite shore of a lake. The knife seemed to work on its own, and this time he caught the blond, caught his hand, and blood spattered across Koop's face. He went in again, and then staggered: he'd been hit. He was astonished. The man had hit him.

He went in again, and Blondy kept backing, swinging. Koop was ready this time, blocked him.

And got him.

Really got him.

Felt the knife point go in, felt it coming up . . .

Then he was hit again, this time on the back of the head. He spun, and another man was there, and a third one coming, swinging a briefcase like a club. Koop felt Blondy go down behind him, with a long ripping groan; almost tripped over his body, avoiding the briefcase, swung the blade at the new attacker, missed, slashed at the second one, the one who'd hit him in the head, missed again.

His attackers both had dark hair. One had glasses, both had bared teeth, and that was all he saw: hair, glasses, teeth. And the briefcase.

Blondy was down and Koop stumbled and looked down at him, saw the scarlet blood on his shirt and a fourth man yelled at him, and Koop ran.

He could hear them screaming, 'Stop him, stop him . . .'
He ran sideways across the street, between parked cars. A
woman on the sidewalk jumped out of the way. Her face
was white, frightened; she had a red necktie and matching
hat and large horsy teeth, and then he was past her.

One of the men chased him for two hundred feet, alone.
Koop suddenly stopped and started back at him, and the
man turned and started to run away. Koop ran back
toward the park, into it, down the grassy tree-shaded
walks.

Ran, blood gushing from his nose, the knife folding in
his hand, as if by magic, disappearing into his pocket. He
wiped his face, pulled off the hat and glasses, slowed to a
walk.

And was gone.

21

The curb outside City Hall was lined with TV vans. Something had happened.

Lucas dumped the Porsche in a ramp and hurried back. A *Star-Tribune* reporter, a young guy with a buzz cut, carrying a notebook, was coming up from the opposite direction. He nodded at Lucas and held the door. 'Anything happening with your case?' he asked.

'Nothing serious,' Lucas said. 'What's going on?'

'You haven't heard?' Buzz Cut did a mock double take.

'I'm just coming in,' Lucas said.

'You remember that couple that was jumped up by the lakes, the woman was killed?'

'Yeah?'

'Somebody else got hit, right across the street. Four hours ago. Thirty feet away from the first scene,' Buzz Cut said. 'I ain't bullshitting you, Lucas: I been out there. Thirty feet. This guy came out of nowhere like a maniac, broad daylight. Big fucking switchblade. He sounded like somebody from a horror movie, had a hat over his face, he was screaming. But it wasn't any gang. It was white-on-white. The guy who got stabbed is a lawyer.'

'Dead?' Lucas asked. He'd relaxed a notch: not his case.

'Not yet. He's cut to shit. Got a knife in the guts. He's still in the operating room. He spent the night with his girlfriend, and the next morning, he walks out the door and this asshole jumps him.'

'Has she got a husband or ex-husband?'

'I don't know,' the reporter said.

'If I were you, I'd ask,' Lucas said.

The reporter held up his notebook, which was turned over to a page with a list of indecipherable scrawls. 'First question on the list,' he said. Then he said, 'Whoa.'

Jan Reed was lounging in the hall, apparently waiting for the press conference to start. She saw Lucas and lifted her chin and smiled and started toward them, and the reporter, without moving his lips, said, 'You dog.'

'Not me,' Lucas muttered.

'Lucas,' she said, walking up. Big eyes. Pools. She touched him on the back of his hand and said, 'Are you in on this?'

Lucas despised himself for it, but he could feel the pleasure of her company unwinding in his chest. 'Hi. No, but it sounds like a good one.' He bounced on his toes, like a basketball player about to be sent into a game.

She looked back toward the briefing room. 'Pretty spectacular right now. It could wind up as a domestic.'

'It's right across the street from that other one.'

She nodded. 'That's the angle. That's what makes it good. Besides which, the people are white.'

'Is that a requirement now?' Buzz Cut asked.

'Of course not,' she said, laughing. Then her voice dropped to the confidential level, including him in the conspiracy. 'But you know how it goes.'

The reporter's scalp flushed pink and he said, 'I better get inside.'

'What's wrong with him?' she asked, watching him go. Lucas shrugged, and she said, 'So, do you have time for a cup of coffee? After the press conference?'

'Uhhmm,' Lucas said, peering down at her. She definitely wound his clock. 'Why don't you stop by my office,' he said.

'Okay ... but, your tie, your collar's messed up. Here ...'

She fixed his collar and tie, and though he was fairly

certain that there'd been nothing wrong with them, he liked it, and carried her touch down the hall.

Connell was the perfect contrast to Jan Reed: a big solid blonde who carried a gun the size of a toaster and considered lipstick a manifestation of Original Sin. She was waiting for him, dark circles under her eyes.

'How're you feeling?'

'Better. Still a little morning sickness,' she said dismissively, brushing the illness away. 'Did you read the histories?'

'Yeah. Not much.'

She looked angry: not at Lucas or Greave, but maybe at herself, or the world. 'We're not gonna get him this time, are we? He's gonna have to kill somebody else before we get him.'

'Unless we get a big fuckin' break,' Lucas said. 'And I don't see a break coming.'

Jan Reed came by Lucas's office after the press conference, and they ambled through the Skyways to a restaurant in the Pillsbury Building. Since she was new to Minnesota, they chatted about the weather, about the lakes, about the Guthrie Theater, and about the other places she'd worked: Detroit, Miami, Cleveland. They found a table not too close to anyone else, Reed with her back to the door – 'I get pestered sometimes' – and ordered coffee and croissants.

'How was the press conference?' Lucas asked, peeling open one of the croissants.

Reed opened her notebook and looked at it. 'Maybe not domestic,' she said. 'The guy's name is Evan Hart. His girlfriend's been divorced for seven years. Her ex lives out on the West Coast and he was there this morning. Besides, she says he's a nice guy. That they broke up because he was too mellow. No alimony or anything. No kids. Sort of a hippie mistake. And she hasn't gone out with anybody else, seriously, for a couple of years.'

'How about this Hart?' Lucas asked. 'Has he got an ex? Is he bisexual? What does he do?'

'He's a widower,' Reed said. She put the yellow pencil in her mouth and turned pages. A little clump of hair fell over her eyes and she brushed it back; Weather did that. 'His wife was killed in a traffic accident. He's a lawyer for a stockbrokerage company, he has something to do with municipal bonds. He doesn't sell anything, so it's not that. He didn't ruin anybody.'

'Doesn't sound like a fruitcake, though,' Lucas said. 'It sounds like the guy was mad about something.'

'That's what it sounds like,' she said. 'But Jensen's really freaked out. That other attack happened right down below her apartment window.'

'That's what I heard. Jensen's his girlfriend? She was actually there at the press conference?'

'Yeah. She was. Sara Jensen. Sharp. Good-looking, runs her own mutual fund, probably makes two hundred thousand a year,' Reed said. 'Dresses like it. She has just gorgeous clothes – she must go to New York. She was really angry. She wants the guy caught. Actually, it sounded like she wants the guy killed, like she was there to ask the cops to find him and kill him.'

'Very strange,' Lucas said. 'The guys in homicide are having a hard time right now . . .'

The conversation rambled along, through new subjects, Lucas enjoying it, laughing. Reed was nice-looking, amusing, and had spent a little time on the streets. They had that in common. Then she said something about gangs. Gangs was a code word for blacks, and as she talked, the code word pecked away at the back of Lucas's mind. Reed, he thought after a bit, might have a fine ass and great eyes, but she was also a bit of a racist. Racism was becoming fashionable in the smart set, if done in a suitably subtle way. Was it immoral to jump a racist? How about if she didn't have a good time, but you did?

He was smiling and nodding and Reed was rambling on about something sexual but safe, the rumored affair between an anchorwoman and a cameraman, carried out in what she said was a TV van with bad springs.

'. . . So there they were on Summit Avenue outside the governor's mansion, and everybody's going in for the ball and this giant van with TV3 on the side is practically jumping up and down, and her husband is out on the sidewalk, pacing back and forth, looking for her.' Reed was playing with her butter knife as she talked, and she twirled it in her fingers, a cheerleader's baton twirl.

Like Junky Doog, Lucas thought. What had Junky said when Greave had asked him why a man might start cutting on women? *'Cause a woman turns you on, that's why. Maybe you see a woman and she turns you on. Gets you by the pecker . . .*

The Society of Jesus, SJ.

Or . . .

Lucas said, suddenly, sitting up, 'What was the guy's wound like?'

'What?' She'd been in midsentence.

'This guy who was attacked this morning,' Lucas said impatiently.

'Uh . . . well, he was stabbed in the stomach,' Reed said, startled by the sudden roughness in his voice. 'Two or three times. He was really messed up. I guess they're still trying to put him together in the operating room.'

'With a switchblade. The kid from the *Strib* said it was a switchblade.'

'A witness said that,' Reed said. 'Why?'

'I gotta go,' Lucas said, looking at his watch. He threw a handful of dollars on the table. 'I'm sorry, but I really got to run. I'm sorry . . .'

Now she looked distinctly startled, but he did run, once

244

he was out of sight. His office was locked, nobody around. He went down the hall to homicide and found Anderson eating an egg-salad sandwich at his desk. 'Have you seen Connell?'

'Uh, yeah, she just went into the women's can.' He had a fleck of egg white on his lip.

Lucas went down to the women's can and pushed the door open. 'Connell?' he shouted. 'Meagan?'

After a moment, a reluctant, hollow, tile-walled 'Yeah?'

'Come out here.'

'Christ . . .' She took two minutes, Lucas walking up and down the hall, cooling off. Very unlikely, he thought. But the wound sounded right . . .

Connell came out, tucking her shirt into her skirt. 'What?'

'The guy that was attacked this morning,' Lucas said. 'He was ripped in the stomach by a guy with a switchbladelike knife.'

'Lucas, it was a guy, it was daylight, he doesn't fit anything . . .' She was puzzled.

'He'd spent the night with his girlfriend, Sara Jensen.'

Still she looked puzzled.

Lucas said, '*SJ.*'

22

They found Sara Jensen at Hennepin General, distraught, pacing the surgical waiting room. A uniformed cop sat in a plastic chair reading *Road & Track*. They took Jensen to an examination room, shut the door, and sat her down.

'It's about goddamn time somebody started taking this seriously,' Jensen said. 'You had to wait until Evan got stabbed . . .' Her voice was contained, but with a thread of fear that suggested she was at the edge of her self-control. 'It's the goddamn burglar. If you'd find him . . .'

'What burglar?' Lucas asked. The place smelled like medical alcohol and skin and adhesive tape.

'What burglar?' Her voice rose in anger, until she was nearly shouting. 'What burglar? What burglar? The burglar at my place.'

'We don't know anything about that,' Connell said quickly. 'We work homicide. We're looking for a man who has been killing women for years. The last two he's marked with the initials *S J* – your initials. We're not sure it's you, but it might be. The attack on Mr Hart resembles the technique he has used to kill the women. The weapon appears to be similar. He fits the descriptions we've had . . .'

'Oh, God,' Jensen said, her hand going to her mouth. 'I saw it on TV3, the man with the beard. The man who attacked Evan had a beard.'

Lucas nodded. 'That's him. Do you know anybody who looks like that? Somebody you've dated, somebody you have a relationship with? Maybe with some frustration?

Or maybe somebody who just watches you, somebody you can feel in your office?'

'No.' She thought about it again. 'No. I know a couple of guys with beards, but I haven't dated them. And they seem to be ordinary enough . . . Besides, it's not them. It's the goddamn burglar. I think he's been coming back to my apartment.'

'Tell us about the burglar,' Lucas said.

She told them: the initial burglary, the loss of her jewelry and belt, the smell of saliva on her forehead. And she told them about the sense she had, that somebody had been in and out of her apartment since the burglary – and the feeling that it was the same man. 'But I'm not sure,' she said. 'I thought I was going crazy. My friends thought it was stress from the burglary, that I was imagining it. But I don't think so: the place just didn't feel right, like there was something in the air. I think he sleeps in my bed.' Then she laughed, a short, barely amused bark. 'I sound like the Three Bears. Somebody's been eating my porridge. Somebody's been sleeping in my bed.'

'So you say that when he came in the first time, he must've touched you – kissed you on the forehead.'

'More like a lick,' she said, shuddering. 'I can remember it, like a dream.'

'What about the actual entry?' Lucas asked. 'Did he break the door?'

There hadn't been a sound, she said, and the door had been untouched, so he must have had a key. But she was the only one with a key – and the building manager, of course.

'What's he like? The manager?'

'Older man . . .'

They went through the list: who had the key, who could get it, who could copy it. More people than she'd realized. Building employees, a cleaning woman. How about valet-parking places? A few valets – 'But I changed the locks again after the burglary. He'd have to get my key twice.'

'Gotta be somebody in the building,' Connell said to Lucas. She'd grabbed his wrist to get his attention. She was sick, but she was a strong woman, and her grip had the strength of desperation.

'If somebody's actually coming back,' Lucas said. 'But whoever it was is a pro. He knew what he wanted and where it was. He didn't rip the place apart. A cat burglar.'

'A cat burglar?' Jensen said doubtfully.

'I'll tell you something: movies romanticize cat burglars, but real cat burglars are cracked,' Lucas said. 'They get off on creeping around apartments while the residents are home. Most burglars, the last thing they want is to run into a home owner. Cat burglars get off on the thrill. Every one of them does dope, cocaine, speed, PCP. Quite a few of them have rape records. A lot of them eventually kill somebody. I'm not trying to scare you, but that's the truth.'

'Oh, God . . .'

'The way the attack happened would suggest that the guy knows about you and Mr Hart,' Connell said. 'Do you talk to anybody in your building about him?'

'No, I really don't have any close friends in the building, other than just to say hello to,' Jensen said. Then, 'Last night was the first time Evan stayed over. It was actually the first time we'd slept together. Ever. It's like whoever it is, knew about us.'

'Did you tell anybody at work that he was coming over?'

'I have a couple of friends who knew we were getting close . . .'

'We'll need their names,' Lucas said. And to Connell: 'Somebody at the office might have occasional access to her purse; they could get the keys that way. We should check all the apartments that adjoin hers, too. People in her hallway.' To Jensen: 'Do you feel any attention from anybody in your apartment? Just a little creepy feeling?

248

Somebody who seems sort of anxious to meet you, or talk to you, or just looks you over?'

'No, no, I don't. The manager is a heck of a nice guy. Really straight. I don't mean, you know, repressed, or weird, or a Boy Scout leader or anything. He's like my dad. God, it gives me the shakes, thinking about somebody watching me,' she said.

'How about an outsider?' Lucas asked. 'Is there a building across the street where you could be watched from? A Peeping Tom?'

She shook her head. 'No. There's a building across the street – that's the building where that woman was killed last week – but I'm on the top floor, which is higher even than their roof,' Jensen said. 'I look right across their roof into the park, and the other side of the park is residential. There's nothing as high as me on the other side of the park. Besides, that's a mile away.'

'Okay . . .' Lucas studied her for a moment. She was very different than the other victims. Watching her, Lucas felt a small chord of doubt. She was fashionable, she was smart, she was tough. There was no hint of deference, no air of wistfulness, no feeling of time and years slipping away.

'I've got to get out of the apartment,' Jensen said. 'Could a policeman come with me while I get some things?'

'You can have a cop with you until we get the guy,' Lucas said. He reached forward to touch her arm. 'But I hope you won't leave. We could move you to another apartment inside the building, and give you escorts: armed policewomen in plain clothes. We'd like to trap the guy, not scare him off.'

Connell joined in: 'We don't really have any leads, Ms Jensen. We're almost reduced to waiting until he kills somebody else, and hoping we find something then. This is the first break we've had.'

Jensen stood up and turned away, shivered, looked

down at Lucas, and said, 'How much chance is there that he'd . . . get to me?'

Lucas said, 'I won't lie to you: there's always a chance. But it's small. And if we don't get him, he might outwait our ability to escort you and then come after you. We had a case a few years ago where a guy in his middle twenties went after a woman who'd been his ninth-grade teacher. He'd brooded about her all that time.'

'Oh, Jesus . . .' Then, suddenly: 'All right. Let's do it. Let's get him.'

The uniformed cop who'd been in the waiting room rapped on the door, stuck his head inside, and said to Jensen, 'Dr Ramihat is looking for you.'

Jensen took Lucas's forearm, her fingers digging in, as they went back down the hall to the waiting area. They found the surgeon greedily sucking on a cigarette and eating a Twinkie. 'There's an awful lot of damage,' he said, in light Indian accents. 'There aren't any guarantees, but we've got him more or less stable and we've stopped the bleeding. Unless we get something unexpected, his chances are good. There'll be an infection problem, but he's in good physical shape and we should be able to handle it.'

Jensen collapsed in a chair, face in her hands, began to blubber. Ramihat patted her on the shoulder with one hand, ate the second Twinkie with his cigarette hand, and winked at Lucas. Connell pulled Lucas aside and said quietly, 'If we can keep her in line, we got him.'

They spent the rest of the morning setting it up: Sloan came in to work with Lucas, Connell, and Greave in checking people with access to Jensen's keys. Five women from intelligence, narcotics, and homicide would rotate as close escorts.

After some discussion, Jensen decided that she could stay in the apartment as long as an escort was always with her. That way, she wouldn't have to move anything out, and open the possibility that if the killer was in the building, she'd be seen doing it.

Hart came out of surgery at three o'clock in the afternoon, hanging on.

23

Koop was still in a rage as he fled the lakes. He couldn't think of the guy in bed with Jensen without hyperventilating, without choking the truck's steering wheel, gripping it, screaming at the windshield . . .

In calmer moments, he could still close his eyes and see her as she was that first night, lying on the sheets, her body pressing up through the nightgown . . .

Then he'd see her on Hart again, and he'd begin screaming, strangling the steering wheel. Crazy. But not entirely gone. He was sane enough to know that the cops might be coming for him. Somebody might have seen him getting in the truck, might have his license number.

Koop had done his research in his years at Stillwater: he knew how men were caught and convicted. Most of them talked to the cops when they shouldn't. Many of them kept scraps and pieces of past crimes around them — television sets, stereos, watches, guns, things with serial numbers.

Some of them kept clothing with blood on it. Some of them left blood behind, or semen.

Koop had thought about it. If he was taken, he swore to himself that he would say nothing at all. Nothing. And he would get rid of everything he wore or used in any crime: he would not give the cops a scrap to hang on to. He would try to build an alibi — anything that a defense attorney could use.

He was still in psychological flight from the attack on Hart when he dumped the coat and hat. The coat was smeared with Hart's blood, a great liverish-black stain. He wrapped it, with the hat, in a garbage bag and dumped it with a pile of garbage bags on a residential street in Edina. The garbage truck was three blocks away. The bag would be at the landfill before noon. He threw the plain-pane glasses out the car window into the high grass of a roadside ditch.

Turned on the radio, found an all-news station. Bullshit, bullshit, and more bullshit. Nothing about him.

In his T-shirt, he stopped at a convenience store, bought a six-pack of springwater, a bar of soap, a laundry bucket, and a pack of Bic razors. He continued south to Braemar Park, climbed into the back of the truck, and shaved in the bucket. His face felt raw afterward; when he looked in the truck mirror, he barely recognized himself. He'd picked up a few wrinkles since he'd last been bare-faced, and his upper lip seemed to have disappeared into a thin, stern line.

He couldn't bring himself to throw away the knife or the apartment keys. He washed the knife as well as he could, using the last of the springwater, sprayed both the knife and the keys with WD-40, wrapped them in another garbage bag, knotted the mouth of the bag, walked up a hill near the park entrance, and buried the bag near a prominent oak. He felt almost lonely when he walked away from it. He'd recover it in a week or so . . . if he was still free.

Cleansed of the immediate evidence of the crime, Koop headed east out of St Paul.

As he passed White Bear Avenue:

Police are on the scene of a brutal murder attempt in south Minneapolis that took place about an hour and fifteen minutes ago. The site is less than a block from the building where a woman was murdered and a man was badly beaten last week; the man is still in a coma from that attack, and may not recover. In this latest attack, witnesses say a tall, bearded man wearing steel-rimmed glasses and a brown snap-brimmed hat attacked attorney Evan Hart as he left a friend's apartment this morning. Hart is currently in surgery at Hennepin General, where his condition is listed as critical. The attacker fled and may be driving a mint-green late-model Taurus sedan. Witnesses say that the attacker repeatedly slashed Hart with a knife . . .

Green Taurus sedan? What was that? Tall? He was five-eight.

Was either white or a light-skinned black man . . .

What? They thought he was black. Koop stared at the radio in amazement. Maybe he didn't have to run at all.

Still: He drove for an hour and a half, losing the Twin Cities radio stations sixty miles out. He stopped at a big sporting goods outlet off I-94, bought a shirt, a sleeping bag, a cheap spinning rod with a reel, a tackle box, and some lures. He stripped them of bags and receipts, threw the paper in a trash can, and turned north, plotting the roads in his head. At Cornell, he bought some bread, lunch meat, and a six-pack of Miller's, and carefully kept the receipt with its hour-and-day stamp, crumbled in the grocery sack, thrust under the seat. Before he left the store parking lot, he looked carefully around the lot for any discarded receipts, but didn't see any.

North of Cornell, he turned into the Brunet Island State Park and parked at a vacant campsite away from the boat launching ramp. Two boat trailers were parked at the ramp, hooked onto pickups. When he had the ramp to himself, he dug around in a trash can for a moment. There were two grocery bags crumpled inside; he opened the first, found it empty, but in the second, he found another grocery receipt. There was no time on it, but the date and the store name were, and the date was from the day before.

He carried it back to the truck and threw it in the back.

He could see only one boat on the water, so far away that he could barely make out the occupants. Koop was not much of a fisherman, but he got the rod and reel, tied on a spinner bait, and walked back toward the ramp.

Nobody around. Ducking through the brush, he moved up to one of the trailers, unscrewed a tire cap, and pushed the valve stem with his fingernails. When the tire was flat, he carefully backed away and tossed the cap into weeds.

After that, he waited; wandered down the shoreline, casting. Thinking about Jensen's treachery. How could a woman do that? It wasn't right . . .

Deep in thought, he was annoyed, five minutes later, when he got a hit. He ripped a small northern off the hook and tossed the fish back up in the weeds. Fuck it.

An hour after he'd let the air out of the trailer tire, an aluminum fishing boat cut in toward the ramp. Two men in farm coveralls climbed out of the boat and walked back to the trailer with the flat. The older of the two backed the trailer into the water while the other stood on the side opposite the flat and helped the boat up to the ramp. After the boat was loaded and pulled out, the man on the ramp yelled something, and after some talk back and forth, the man in the car got out to look at the trailer tire. Koop drifted toward them, casting.

'Got a problem?' he called.

'Flat tire.'

'Huh.' Koop reeled in his last cast and walked over toward them. The driver was talking to his friend about taking the boat off, pulling the wheel, and driving it into town to get it fixed.

'I got a pump up in my truck,' Koop said. 'Maybe it'd hold long enough to get you into town.'

'Well.' The farmers looked at each other, and the driver said, 'Where's your truck?'

'Right over there, you can see it . . .'

'We could give 'er a try,' the driver said.

Koop retrieved the pump. 'Hell of a nice boat,' he said as they pumped up the tire. 'Always wanted a Lund. Had it long?'

'Two years,' the driver said. 'Saved for that sucker for

ten years; got it set up perfect.' When the tire was up, they watched it for a moment, then the driver said, 'Seems to hold.'

'Could be a real slow leak,' Koop said. 'Check it this morning before you went out?'

'Can't say as I did,' the driver said, scratching his head. 'Listen, thank you very much, and I think I'll get our butts into town before it goes flat again.'

So he had receipts and he'd been seen fishing on the ramp; and he took the boat registration number. He'd have to think about that: maybe he shouldn't be able to remember all of it, just that it was a red Lund and the last two registration letters were *LS*. . . Or maybe that the first number on it was 7. He'd have to think about it.

On his way through town, he stopped at the store that issued the register receipt he'd found in the trash can, bought a Slim Jim and a can of beer, and stuffed the receipt and the sack under the seat. Maybe they'd remember his face in the store, maybe not – but he'd been there, he could describe the place, and he could even describe the young woman who'd waited on him. Too heavy. Wore dark-green fashion overalls.

A little before five, he started back to the Cities. He wanted to be within radio range, to pick up the news. To see if they were looking for him . . .

They were not, as far as he could tell. One of the evening talk shows was devoted to the attack, and the attack the week before, but it was all a bunch of crazies calling in.

Huh.

They were looking for the wrong guy . . .

He went back to the park, got the knife and keys. Felt better for it.

At one o'clock in the morning, Koop wasn't quite drunk, but he was close. Driving around, driving around, up and down the Cities, Jensen was more and more on his mind.

At one, he drove past her apartment. A light shone behind her window. A man was walking down the street, walking a small silvery dog. At one-fifteen, Koop cruised it again. Still the light. She was up late; couldn't sleep, after the fight – Koop thought about it as a fight. Blondy'd asked for it, fucking Koop's woman; what was a guy supposed to do?

Koop's mind was like a brick, not working right. He knew it wasn't working right. He could not pull it away from Jensen. He had other things to think about – he'd been cruising his next target, he was ready to make an entry. He couldn't think about it.

At one-thirty, the light was still on in Jensen's apartment, and Koop decided to go up to his spy roost. He knew he shouldn't risk it; but he would. He could feel himself being pulled in, like a nail to a magnet.

At one thirty-five, he went into the apartment across the street from Jensen's and climbed the stairs. Physically, he was fine, moving as smoothly and quietly as ever. It was his mind that was troubling . . .

He checked the hall. Empty. Had to be quiet: everybody would be spooked. He went to the roof entry, climbed the last flight, pushed through the door, and quickly closed it behind himself. He stood there for a moment, the door-knob still in his hand, listening. Nothing. He stepped to the edge of the door hutch and looked up at Jensen's window. The light was on, but at the angle, he couldn't see anything.

He crossed to the air-conditioner housing, grabbed the edge, and pulled himself up. He crawled to the vent and looked around the corner. Nobody in sight. He leaned back behind the vent, put his back to it. Looked up at the stars.

He thought about what he'd become, caught by this passion. He would have to stop. He knew he would have to stop, or he was doomed. He could think of only one way to stop it – and that way touched him. But he would like to have her first, if he could.

Before he killed her.

Koop looked around the corner past the vent, and, shocked, almost snatched his head back. Almost, but not quite. He had the reflexes and training of a cat burglar, and had taught himself not to move too quickly. Across the street, in Jensen's window, a man was looking out. He was six feet back from the glass, as though he were taking care not to be seen from the street. He wore dark slacks and a white dress shirt, without a jacket.

He wore a shoulder holster.

A cop. They knew. They were waiting for him.

24

Weather curled up on the couch. The television was tuned to CNN, and Lucas watched it without seeing it, brooding. 'Nothing at all?' she asked.

'Not a thing,' he said. He didn't look at her, just pulled at his lip and stared at the tube. He was tired, his face gray. 'Three days. The media's killing us.'

'I wouldn't worry so much about the media, if I were you.'

Now he turned his head. 'That's because you don't have to worry. You guys bury your mistakes,' Lucas said. He grinned when he said it, but it wasn't a pleasant smile.

'I'm serious. I don't understand . . .'

'The media's like a fever,' Lucas explained. 'Heat starts to build up. The people out in the neighborhoods get scared, and they start calling their city councilmen. The councilmen panic – that's what politicians, do, basically, is panic – and they start calling the mayor. The mayor calls the chief. The chief is a politician who is appointed by the mayor, so she panics. And the shit flows downhill.'

'I don't understand all the panic. You're doing everything you can.'

'You have to look at Davenport's first rule of how the world really works,' Lucas said.

'I don't think I've heard that one,' Weather said.

'It's simple,' he said. '*A politician will never, ever, get a better job when he's out of office.*'

'That's it?'

'That's it. That explains everything. They're desperate to

hang on to their jobs. That's why they panic. They lose the election, it's back to the car wash.'

After a moment of silence, Weather asked, 'How's Connell?'

'Not good,' Lucas said.

Connell's facial skin was stretched, taut; dark smudges hung under her eyes, her hair was perpetually disarranged, as though she'd been sticking her fingers into an electric outlet.

'Something's wrong,' she said. 'Maybe the guy knows we're here. Maybe Jensen was imagining it.'

'Maybe,' Lucas said. They waited in Jensen's living room, stacks of newspapers and magazines by their feet. A Walkman sat on a coffee table. A television was set up in the second bedroom, but they couldn't listen to the stereo for fear that it would be heard in the hallway. 'It sure felt good, though.'

'I know . . . but you know what maybe it could be?' Connell had a foot-high stack of paper next to her hand, profiles and interviews with apartment employees, residents of Jensen's floor, and everyone else in the building with a criminal record. She had been pawing through it compulsively. 'It could be, like, a relative of somebody who works here. And whoever works here goes home and lets it slip that we're in here.'

Lucas said, 'The keys are a big question. There are any number of ways that a cat burglar could get one key, but two keys – that's a problem.'

'Gotta be an employee.'

'Could be a valet service at a restaurant,' he said. 'I've known valets who worked with cat burglars. You see the car come in, you get the plate number, and from that, you can get an address and you've got the key.'

'She said she hadn't used a valet since she got the new key,' Connell said.

'Maybe she forgot. Maybe it's something so routine that she doesn't remember it.'

'I bet it's somebody at her office – somebody with access to her purse. You know, like one of the messenger kids, somebody who can go in and out of her office without being noticed. Grab the key, copy it . . .'

'But that's another problem,' Lucas said. 'You've got to have some knowledge to copy it, and a source of blanks.'

'So it's a guy working with a cat burglar. The burglar supplies the knowledge, the kid supplies the access.'

'That's one way that it works,' Lucas admitted. 'But nobody in her office seems like a good bet.'

'A boyfriend of somebody in the office; a secretary picks up the key, lays it off . . .'

Lucas stood up, yawned, wandered around the apartment, stopped to look at a framed black-and-white photograph. It wasn't much, a flower in a roundish pot, a stairway in the background. Lucas didn't know much about art, but this felt like it. A tiny penciled signature said Andre something, something with a *K*. He yawned again and rubbed the back of his neck and looked at Connell going through the paper.

'How'd you feel this morning?'

She looked up. 'Hollow. Empty.'

'I don't understand how it works, the whole chemotherapy thing,' Lucas said.

She put down the paper. 'Basically, the kind of chemo I get is poisonous. It knocks down the cancer, but it also knocks down my body,' she said. Her voice was neutral, informed, like a medical commentator on public television. 'They can only use it so long before the chemotherapy starts doing too much damage. Then they take me off it, and my body starts recovering from the chemo, but so does the cancer. The cancer gains a little every time. I've been on it for two years. I'm down to seven weeks between treatments. I've been five. I'm feeling it again.'

'Lots of pain?'

She shook her head. 'Not yet. I can't really describe it. It's a hollow feeling, and a weakness, and then a sickness, like the worst flu in the world. I understand, toward the end, it'll get painful, when it gets into my bone marrow . . . I expect to opt for other measures before then.'

'Jesus,' he said. Then: 'What are the chances that the chemo will knock it down completely?'

'It happens,' she said with a brief, ghostly smile. 'But not for me.'

'I don't think I could handle it,' Lucas said.

The balcony door was closed, and Lucas moved over toward it, staying six feet back from the glass, and looked out at the park. Nice day. The rain had quit, and the light-blue sky was dappled with fair-weather clouds, cloud shadows skipping across the lake. A woman dying.

'But the other problem,' Connell said, almost to herself, 'besides the key, I mean, is why he hasn't come up here. Four days. Nothing.'

Lucas was still thinking about cancer, had to wrench himself back. 'You're talking to yourself,' Lucas said.

'That's because I'm going crazy.'

'You want a pizza?' Lucas asked.

'I don't eat pizza. It clogs up your arteries and makes you fat.'

'What kind don't you eat?'

'Pepperoni and mushroom,' Connell said.

'I'll get one delivered to the manager. I can run down and get it when it comes in,' he said, yawning again. 'This is driving me nuts.'

'Why doesn't he come?' Connell asked rhetorically. 'Because he knows we're here.'

'Maybe we just haven't waited long enough,' Lucas said.

Connell continued: 'How does he know we're here? One: he sees us. Two: he hears about us. Okay, if he sees us, how does he know we're cops? He doesn't – unless he's a cop, and he recognizes people coming and going. If he hears about us, how does he hear about us? We've been over that.'

'Pepperoni and mushroom?'

'No fuckin' anchovies.'

'No way.' Lucas picked up the phone, frowned, hung it up, and walked back to the glass door. 'Did somebody check the roof on the other side of the street?'

Connell looked up. 'Yeah, but Jensen was right. It's below the level of her window. She doesn't even bother to pull the drapes.'

'It's not below the level of the air-conditioner housing,' Lucas said. 'C'mere. Look at this.'

Connell stood up and looked. 'There's no way to get up on it.'

'He's a cat burglar,' Lucas said. 'And if he got up on it, he'd be looking right into the apartment. Who went over the roof?'

'Skoorag — but he just strolled around the roof. I saw him do it. Said there wasn't anything up there.'

'We ought to take a look,' Lucas said.

Connell looked at her watch. 'Greave and O'Brien'll be here in an hour. We could go over then.'

O'Brien carried a brown paper sack with a magazine inside, and tried to hide it from Connell. Greave said, 'I've been thinking: how about if we picked up all three of them, the brothers and Cherry, separate them, tell them we've got a break, and tell them the first one who talks gets immunity.'

Lucas grinned but shook his head. 'You're thinking right, but you've got to have *something*. If you don't, they'll either tell you to go fuck yourself, or, which is worse, the guy who actually did the killing is the one who talks. He walks, and Roux hangs you out the window by your nuts. So, you gotta get something.'

'I've gotten something,' Greave said.

'What?'

'I've gotten desperate.'

'O'Brien had a *Penthouse*,' Connell said.

'It's a very boring job,' Lucas said mildly.

'Think about this,' Connell said. 'What if women brought porno magazines to work, pictures of men with huge penises? And the women sat there and looked at the pictures, then looked at you, then looked at the picture. Wouldn't you find that just a little demeaning?'

'Not me, personally,' Lucas said, face straight. 'I'd just see it as another career opportunity.'

'Goddamn you, Davenport, you always weasel away.'

'Not always,' Lucas said. 'But I do have a well-developed sense of *when* to weasel.' Then, as they crossed the street, 'This is where the woman was killed and the guy fucked up.'

They climbed the steps and buzzed the manager. A moment later, a door opened in the lobby and a middle-aged woman looked out. Her hair was not quite blue. Lucas held up his badge, and she let him in.

'I'll get somebody to let you up on the roof,' the woman said when Lucas explained what they wanted. 'That was awful, that poor guy stabbed.'

'Were you here when those two people were attacked outside?'

'No, nobody was here. Except tenants, I mean,' she said.

'I understand the guy was between the inner and outer doors when he was attacked.'

The woman nodded. 'One more second and he would have been inside. His key was in the lock.'

'Sonofabitch,' Lucas said. To Connell: 'If somebody wanted to get a key and cover what they were doing . . . The whole attack didn't make sense, so they said gang kids did it. Trouble is, the gang unit hasn't heard a thing from the gangs. And they should have heard.'

*　　*　　*

The janitor's name was Clark, and he opened the door to the roof and blocked it with an empty Liquid Plumber bottle. Lucas walked across the gravel-and-tar-paper roof. Greave and O'Brien were standing in Jensen's apartment, visible from the shoulders up.

'Can't see much from here,' Lucas said. He turned to the air-conditioner housing.

'It looks high enough,' Connell said. They walked around it: it was a gray cube, with three featureless metal faces. A locked steel service hatch, and a warranty sticker with a service number, were the only items on the fourth side. There was no access to the top of the cube.

'I can get a stepladder,' Clark offered.

'Why don't you just give me a boost,' Lucas said. He slipped out of his shoes and jacket, and Clark webbed his fingers together. Lucas put his foot in the other man's hands and stepped up. When his shoulders were over the edge of the housing, he pushed himself up with his hands.

The first thing he saw were the cigarette butts, forty or fifty of them, water-stained, filterless. 'Oh, Christ.' One butt was fresh, and he duckwalked over to it, peered at it.

'What?' Connell called.

'About a million cigarette butts.'

'Are you serious? What kind?'

Lucas duckwalked back to the edge, peered down, and said, 'Unfiltered Camels, each and every one.'

Connell looked across the street. 'Can you see in the apartment?'

'I can see O'Brien's shoes,' Lucas said.

'The sonofabitch *knew*,' Connell cried. 'He was up here, he looked in, he saw us. *We were this fuckin' close.*'

The crime-scene tech lifted the single fresh Camel with a pair of tweezers, put it in a bag, and passed it down. 'We can try,' he said to Lucas, 'but I wouldn't count on much. Sometimes you get a little skin stuck to the butts, sometimes enough to do a DNA or at least get a blood type, but these have been out here a while.' He shrugged. 'We'll try, but I wouldn't hold my breath.'

'What're the chances of DNA?' Connell demanded.

He shrugged. 'Like I said, we'll try.'

Connell looked at Lucas. 'We've had cold matches on DNA.'

'Yeah – two,' Lucas said.

'We gotta make a run at it,' she said.

'Sure.' He looked across the street. Sloan waved. 'We'll put a night-vision scope over there, in case he comes back. Goddamnit. I hope we haven't scared him completely.'

'If we haven't, he's nuts,' Connell said.

'We *know* he's nuts,' Lucas answered. 'But I'm afraid that if he has seen us, we're frustrating the hell out of him. I hope he doesn't go for another. I hope he comes in first . . .'

25

John Posey's house was a three-level affair, like a white-brick-and-cedar layer cake, overlooking a backyard duck pond rimmed by weeping willows. From a street that ran at a ninety-degree angle to Posey's street, Koop could see the back of the house. Two separate balconies overlooked the pond, one above the other, slightly offset.

A security-system warning sign was stuck in the front yard, by the door. Koop knew the system: typically magneto-offset doors, usually with motion detectors sweeping the first floor.

If the detectors were tripped, they'd automatically dial out to an alarm service after a delay of a minute to two minutes. The alarm service would make a phone check, and if not satisfied, would call the cops. If the phone wires were cut, an alarm would go off at the monitoring service. If other phones in the neighborhood weren't out, the cops would be on their way.

Which didn't make the place impossible. Not at all. For one thing, Posey had a dog, an old Irish setter. The setter was often in the front window, even when Posey wasn't home. If there was a motion detector, it was either turned off or it only guarded the parts of the house that the dog couldn't get to.

He would wait until Posey left and then go straight in, Koop decided. No hiding, nothing subtle. Smash and grab.

Koop was in no condition for subtlety. He thought about Sara Jensen all the time. Reran his mental tapes. He would see her in another woman – with a gesture or a certain step, a turn of the head.

Jensen was a sliver under the skin. He could try to ignore her, but she wouldn't go away. Sooner or later, he'd have to deal with her. Bodyguards or no bodyguards.

But Koop knew something about the ways of cops. They'd watch her for a while, and then, when nothing happened, they'd be off chasing something else.

The only question was, could he wait?

At eight-thirty, Koop stopped at a downtown parking garage. He followed a Nissan Maxima up the ramp, parked a few slots away from it, got slowly out of the truck. The Maxima's owners took the elevator; Koop took the plates off the Maxima.

He carried them back to the truck, stepped out of sight for a moment when another car came up the ramp, then clipped the stolen plates on top of his own with steel snap-fasteners. A matter of two minutes.

Posey had an active social life and went out almost every night, mostly to sports bars. Koop checked by calling, calling again, calling a third time, never getting an answer, before heading back to the house.

The night was warm, humid, and smelled like cut grass. The whole neighborhood hummed with the air conditioners tucked in at the sides of the houses. Windows and doors would be closed, and he could get away with a little more noise, if he had to.

Four blocks from Posey's, a group of teenagers, three girls, two boys, stood on a street corner smoking, long hair, long shirts hung out over their jeans, looking at him with narrowed eyes as he passed in the truck.

A few porch lights were still on, yellow and white, and the sound of easy-listening music seeped from an open, lit garage. There were cars – not many – parked on the street; the neighborhood was too affluent for that.

He cruised the house. It looked right – Posey usually left two lights on when he was out. Koop had an eight-ball with him: he did a hit, then another, got his tools from under the passenger seat, and drove back to the house. Pulled into the driveway. Waited a second, watching the curtains, checking the street, picked up his tools and got out, walked up to the front door, and rang the doorbell.

The dog barked; the bark was loud, audible in the street. Nobody came to the door. The dog kept barking. Koop walked back down the front of the house, checked the neighborhood one last time, then walked down the side of the garage.

The side of the garage was windowless, and faced the windowless garage next door. Between them, he couldn't be seen. The backyard, though, was different, potentially dangerous. He stopped at the corner of the garage and scanned the houses on the next street, facing Posey's. There were lights, and a man reading a newspaper behind a picture window two houses down. Okay . . .

Koop wore a jogging suit, the jacket open over a white T-shirt. In the hand-warmer pocket he carried a pair of driving gloves. A sailing compass, called a 'hockey puck,' was stuffed in one glove, a small plastic flashlight in the other. He carried an eighteen-inch crowbar down his pants' leg, the hook over the waistline of the pants.

He waited two minutes, three, his heartbeat holding up, then zipped the jacket and pulled on the gloves. Nearly invisible, he edged around the corner of the house until he was standing behind a dwarf spruce, looking up at the first balcony.

The bottom of the balcony was eight feet overhead. He bent the spruce, found a branch two feet above the ground that would bear his weight. He stepped up, feeling the spruce sag, but hooked the lower bar of the railing with one hand, then the other. He swarmed up like a monkey, scuffing his kneecap on the concrete edge of the balcony. He waited a few seconds, ignoring the pain in his knee, listening, hearing nothing, then tested the balcony railing for rigidity.

Solid. He stood on it, balancing carefully, reached around the edge of the upper balcony, grabbed the railing, and let himself swing free. When his swinging motion slowed, he pulled himself up and clambered over the railing onto the higher balcony.

Again he stopped to listen. The dog had stopped barking. Good. He was now on the third floor, outside a room he believed was unused. He'd spotted Posey's bedroom in a second-floor corner. This should be a guest room, if the moving man's map was correct. And it wouldn't be rigged for an alarm, unless Posey was truly paranoid.

Hearing nothing, he stood up and looked at the sliding glass doors. The track was not blocked: that made things easier. He tried the door itself, on the chance that it was unlocked. It was not. He took the crowbar out of his pants, pressed the point of it against the glass, and slowly, carefully put his weight against it. The glass cracked, almost silently. He started again, just above the first point, bearing down . . . and got another crack.

The third time, the glass suddenly collapsed, leaving a hole the size of his palm. He hadn't made a sound louder than a careful cough. He reached through the hole, flipped up the lock and pulled the latch, and slid the door back. Stopped. Listened. Inside, he turned on the flashlight. Yes. A bedroom, with a feel of disuse.

He crossed the room to the bedroom door, which was closed, took out the compass, waited until the needle settled, then ran it along the edge of the door. The needle remained steady, except at the handle, where it deflected. The door was not protected; he hadn't expected it to be, but it took only a moment to check.

He opened the door, half expecting the dog to be there, but found an empty hall, dimly lit from the lights downstairs.

Down the stairs, slowly, listening. Nothing. Through the hall.

Then: the dog's nails on the kitchen's vinyl floor, with a tentative *woof*. A few woofs were okay, but if the dog got out of hand . . . He reversed his grip on the crowbar, holding it by the flat end.

The dog came around the corner of the kitchen, saw him standing there, barked. Old dog, his legs stiff, his muzzle hair going white . . .

'Here, boy, c'mere,' Koop said, his voice soft. 'C'mere, boy . . .' He walked toward the dog, his left hand out, cupped, right hand behind him. The dog backed away, upright, barking, but let Koop get closer . . .

'Here, boy.' One more step, one more.

'Woof.' Sensing danger, trying to back away . . .

Koop swatted the dog like a fly. The crowbar caught it in the center of the skull, and the dog went down without a whimper, just a final *woof*. Dead when it hit the floor, its legs jerked, running spasmodically on the vinyl.

Koop turned away. No need to be quiet anymore. He checked the front door. There was a keypad next to it showing an alarm light: the system was armed, but he wasn't sure what that meant. At the basement door, he again checked with the compass. Again, nothing. Must only be the outer doors.

He eased the door open, took a step. Okay. Walked down to the bottom of the stairs, into the basement – and the moment he stepped into the basement, heard the rapid *beep-beep-beep* of the alarm system's warning, a bit louder than an alarm clock.

'Shit,' he said.

One minute. He started a running count at the back of his head. *Sixty, fifty-nine* . . .

The safe was there, just as the moving man said. He worked the combination the first time and looked inside. Two sacks, two jewelry boxes. He took them out. One sack

271

was cash. The other was as heavy as a car battery. Gold, probably. No time to think.

Thirty. Twenty-nine, twenty-eight . . .

He ran back up the stairs, to the front door, the alarm making its urgent *beep-beep-beep* warning. He hit it with the crowbar, silencing it. The call would be made anyway, but if someone was passing in the street, he wouldn't hear the beeping.

Koop walked out the front door, back to the truck. Tossed the tools and the money bags on the front seat, started the truck, backed into the street.

Thinking: *Fourteen, thirteen, twelve . . .*

At *zero*, he'd turned the corner and was heading down the hill to West Seventh Street. Fifteen seconds later, he was in heavy traffic. He never did see a cop.

Koop checked the bags in a Burger King parking lot. The first contained forty-five hundred dollars in cash: twenties, fifties, and hundreds. The second bag held fifty gold coins, Krugerrands. Already, one of the best scores he'd ever had. The first box held a gold chain with a ten-diamond cross. The diamonds were small but not tiny. He had no idea what they were worth. A lot, he thought, if they were real. In the second box, earrings to go with the necklace.

A wave of pleasure ran through him. The best score; the best he'd ever done. Then he thought of Jensen, and the pleasure began to fade.

Shit. He looked at the gold in his lap. He really didn't want this. He could get money anytime.

He knew what he wanted.

He saw her every time he closed his eyes.

Koop cruised Jensen's apartment. The apartment was lit up. He slowed, and thought he might have seen a shadow on the window. Was she naked? Or was the place full of cops?

He couldn't loiter. The cops might be watching.

He thought about the dog, the feet scratching on the vinyl floor. He wondered why they did that . . .

The night had pushed him into a frenzy: exhilaration over the take at Posey's, frustration over the lights at Jensen's. He drove down to Lake Street, locked up the truck, and started drinking. He hit Flower's Bar, Lippy's Lounge, the Bank Shot, and Skeeter's. Shot some pool with a biker at Skeeter's. Scored another eight-ball at Lippy's and snorted most of it sitting on the toilet in the Lippy's men's room.

The coke gave him a ferocious headache after a while, tightening up his neck muscles until they felt like a suspension spring. He bought a pint of bourbon, went out to his truck and drank it, and started doing exercises: bridges, marine push-ups.

At one o'clock, Koop started back downtown, drunk. At five after one, drunk, he saw the woman walking back toward the hotel off Lyndale. A little tentative, a little scared. Her high heels going clackety-clack on the street . . .

'Fuck her,' he said aloud. He didn't have his ether, but had muscle and his knife. He passed the woman, going in the same direction, pulled the truck to the curb, put it in neutral. He popped the passenger seat, groped beneath it until he found the bag, stripped out the knife, and threw the keys back in the box. Did a quick pinch of cocaine, then another. Groped behind the seat until he found his baseball hat, put it on.

'Fuck her,' he said. She was walking up to the back of the truck, on the sidewalk. The night was warm for Minnesota, but she wore a light three-quarters trench coat. Koop wore a T-shirt that said 'Coors.'

Out of the truck, around the nose, a gorilla, running.

The woman saw him coming. Screamed, 'Don't!'

Dropped her purse.

273

Everything cocaine sharp, cocaine powerful.

Plenty of fuel, plenty of hate: 'FUCK YOU.'

Koop screamed it, and the knife blade snicked out, and she backed frantically away. He grabbed her, got the shoulder of her coat. 'Get in the fuckin' truck.'

He could see the whites of her eyes, turning up in terror, pulled at her. The coat came away, the woman thrashing, slipping out of it, trying to run. She went through a sidewalk flower garden, crushing pink petunias, lost one of her shoes, backed against the building and began to scream; the odor of urine rode out on the night air.

And she screamed. A high, piercing, loud scream, a scream that seemed to echo down the sidewalks.

Koop, drunk, stoned, teeth as large as tombstones, on top of her: 'Shut the fuck up.' He hit her backhanded, knocked her off her feet. The woman sobbing, trying to crawl.

Koop caught her by the foot, dragged her out of the flower garden, the woman trying to hold on to petunias. Petunias . . .

She began screaming again; no more words, screaming, and Koop, angrier and angrier, dragged her toward the truck.

Then, from above:

'You stop that.' A woman's voice, shrill, as angry as Koop was. 'You stop that, you asshole, I'm calling the police.'

Then a man's voice: 'Get away from her . . .'

From the apartment across the street, two people yelling down at him, one two or three floors up, the other five or six. Koop looked up, and the woman began to sob.

'Fuck you!' Koop screamed back.

Then a flash: the woman had taken a picture of him. Koop panicked, turned to run. The woman on the sidewalk looked at him, still screaming, pulling away.

Christ: she'd seen him close, from two inches.

Another flash.

Man's voice: 'Get away from that woman, police are coming, get away.'

And another light, steady this time: somebody was making movies.

The rage roared out of him, like fire; the knife with a mind of its own.

Koop grabbed the woman by the throat, lifted her off the sidewalk, the woman kicking like a chicken.

And the knife took her. She slipped away from him, onto the sidewalk, almost as though she had fainted.

Koop looked down. His hands were covered with blood; blood ran down the sidewalk, black in the streetlight . . .

'Get away from that woman, get away . . .'

No need to be told. Panic was on him, and he ran to the truck, climbed in, gunned it.

Around the corner, around another.

Two minutes, up the interstate ramp. Cop cars everywhere, down below lights flashing, sirens screeching. Koop took the truck off the interstate, back into the neighborhoods, and pushed south. Side streets and alleys all the way.

He stayed inside for ten minutes, then jumped on the Crosstown Expressway for a quick dash to the airport. Took a ticket, went up the ramp, parked. Crawled in the back.

'Motherfucker,' he breathed. Safe for the moment. He laughed, drank the last mouthful from the pint bottle.

He got out of the truck, hitched his pants, walked around behind, and climbed in.

Safe, for the time being.

He rolled up his jogging jacket to use as a pillow, lay down, and went to sleep.

Eloise Miller was dead in a pool of black blood before the cops got there.

In St Paul, a patrol cop looked at Ivanhoe the dog and wondered who in the fuck would do that . . .

26

'We got pictures of him,' Connell said. Lucas found her on the sixth floor, in the doorway of a small apartment, walking away from a gray-haired woman. Connell was as cranked as Lucas had ever seen her, a cassette of thirty-five-millimeter film in her fist. 'Pictures of him and his truck.'

'I heard we got movies,' Lucas said.

'Aw, man, come on . . .' Connell led him down the stairs. 'You gotta see this.'

On four, two cops were talking to a thin man in a bathrobe. 'Could you run the tape?' Connell asked.

One of the cops glanced at Lucas and shrugged. 'How's it going, chief?'

'Okay. What've we got?'

'Mr Hanes here took a videotape of the attack,' the older of the two cops said, pointing a pencil at the man in the bathrobe.

'I didn't think,' the man said. 'There wasn't any time.'

The younger cop pushed the button on the VCR. The picture came up, clear and steady: a picture of a bright light shining into a window. At the bottom of it, what appeared to be two sets of legs doing a dance.

They all stood and watched silently as the tape rolled on: they could see nothing on the other side of the window except the legs. They saw the legs only for a few seconds.

'If we get that downtown, we should be able to get a height estimate on the guy,' Lucas said.

The bathrobe man said, mournful as a bloodhound, 'I'm sorry.'

The older cop tried to explain. 'See, the light reflected almost exactly back at the lens, so whatever he pointed it at is behind the light.'

'I was so freaked out . . .'

In the hallway, Lucas said, 'How do we know we don't have the same thing on the film?'

''Cause she went out on her terrace and shot it,' Connell said. 'There was no window to reflect back at her . . . There's a one-hour development place at Midway, open all night.'

'Isn't there a better –'

She was shaking her head. 'No. I've been told that the automated processes are the most reliable for this Kodak stuff. One is about as good as another.'

'Did you see enough of the woman on the street?' Lucas asked.

'I saw too much,' Connell said. She looked up at Lucas. 'He's flipped out. He started out as this sneaky, creepy killer, really careful. Now he's Jack the Ripper.'

'How about you?'

'I flipped out a long time ago,' she said.

'I mean . . . are you hanging in there?'

'I'm hanging in,' she said.

The Quick-Shot operator was by himself, processing film. He could stop everything else, he said, and have prints in fifteen minutes, no charge.

'There's no way they can get messed up?' Lucas asked.

The operator, a bony college kid in a Stone Temple Pilots T-shirt, shrugged. 'One in a thousand – maybe less than that. The best odds you're going to get.'

Lucas handed him the cassette. 'Do it.'

Seventeen minutes later, the kid said, 'The problem is, she was trying to take a picture from a hundred and fifty or two hundred feet away, at night, with this little teeny flash.

The flash is supposed to light up somebody's face at ten feet.'

'There's nothing fuckin' there,' Connell shouted at him, spit flying.

'Yeah, there is – you can see it,' the kid said, indignant, peering at one of the almost-black prints. That particular print had a yellow smudge in the middle of it, what might have been a streetlight, above what might have been the roof of a truck. 'That's exactly what you get when you take pictures in the dark with one of those little fuckin' cameras.'

There was something going on in the prints, but they couldn't tell what. Just a lot of smudges that might have been a woman being stabbed to death.

'I don't believe it,' Connell said. She slumped in the car seat, sick.

'I don't believe in eyewitnesses or cameras,' Lucas said.

Another three blocks and Connell said suddenly, urgently, 'Pull over, will you? Right there, at the corner.'

'What?' Lucas pulled over.

Connell got out and vomited. Lucas climbed out, walked around to her. She looked up weakly, tried to smile. 'Getting worse,' she said. 'We gotta hurry, Lucas.'

'We're talking firestorm,' Roux said. She had two cigarettes lit at the same time, the one on the window ledge burning futilely by itself.

'We'll get him,' Lucas said. 'We've still got the surveillance at Sara Jensen's. There's a good chance he'll come in.'

'This week,' Roux said. 'Gotta be this week.'

'Very soon,' Lucas said.

'Promise?'

'No.'

*　　*　　*

Lucas spent the day following the Eloise Miller routine, reading histories, calling cops. Connell did the same, and so did Greave. Results from the street investigation began coming in. The guy was big and powerful, batted the woman like a rag doll.

There were three eyewitnesses: one said the killer had a beard, the other two said he did not. Two said he wore a hat, the other said he had black hair. All three said he drove a truck, but they didn't know what color. Something and white. There wasn't much dirt in the street to pick up tire tracks, even if two cop cars and an ambulance hadn't driven over them.

The autopsy came in. Nothing good. No DNA source. No prints. Still checking for hair.

At four o'clock, he gave up. He went home, took a nap. Weather got home at six.

At seven, they lay on top of the bedsheet, sweat cooling on their skin. Outside the window, which was cracked just an inch or two, they could hear the cars passing in the street a hundred feet away, and sometimes, quietly, the muttering of voices.

Weather rolled up on her elbow. 'I'm amazed at the way you can separate yourself from what you're doing,' she said. She traced a circle on his chest. 'If I was as stuck on a problem as you are, I couldn't think of anything else. I couldn't do this.'

'Waiting is part of the deal,' Lucas said. 'It has always been that way. You can't eat until the cake is baked.'

'People get killed while you're waiting,' she said.

'People die for bad reasons all the time,' Lucas said. 'When we were running around in the woods last winter, I begged you to stay away. You refused to stay away, so I'm alive. If you hadn't been out there . . .' He touched the scar on his throat.

'Not the same thing,' she objected. She touched the scar.

Most of it, she'd made herself. 'People die all the time because of happenstance. Two cars run into each other, and somebody dies. If the driver of one of them had hesitated five seconds at the last stoplight, they wouldn't have collided, and nobody would die. That's just life. Chance. But what you do ... somebody might die because you can't solve a problem that's solvable. Or like last winter, you seemed to reach out and solve a problem that was unsolvable, and so people who probably would have died, lived.'

He opened his mouth to reply, but she patted him on the chest to stop him. 'This isn't criticism. Just observation. What you do is really ... bizarre. It's more like magic, or palm reading, than science. I do science. Everybody I work with does science. That's routine. What you do ... it's fascinating.'

Lucas giggled, a startling sound, high-pitched, unlike anything she'd ever heard from him. Not a chuckle. A giggle. She peered down at him.

'Goddamn, I'm glad you moved in with me, Harkinnen,' he said. 'Conversations like this could keep me awake for weeks at time. You're better than speed.'

'I'm sorry ...'

'No, no.' He pushed up on his elbow to face her. 'I need this. Nobody ever looked into me before. I think a guy could get old and rusty if nobody ever looked into him.'

When Weather went into the bathroom, Lucas got up and wandered around, naked, hunting from room to room, not knowing exactly what. A picture of the dead Eloise Miller hung in his mind's eye: a woman on the way to feed a friend's dog while the friend was out of town. She'd made that walk, late at night, just once in her life. Once too often.

Lucas could hear Weather running water in the

bathroom, and thought guiltily about the attractions of Jan Reed. He sighed, and pushed the reporter out of his mind. That's not what he was supposed to be thinking about.

They knew so much about the killer, he thought. Generally what he looked like, his size, his strength, what he did, the kinds of vehicles he drove, if indeed he drove that Taurus sedan in addition to the truck. Anderson was now cross-indexing joint ownerships, green Taurus sedans against pickups.

But so much of what they knew was conflicting, and conflicts were devastating in a trial.

Depending on who you believed, the killer was a white, short or tall police officer (or maybe a convict), a cocaine user who drove either a blue-and-white or red-and-white pickup truck, or a green Taurus sedan, and he either wore glasses or he didn't, and while he probably wore a beard at one time, he might have shaved it off by now. Or maybe not.

Terrific.

And even if that could be sorted out, they had not a single convicting fact. Maybe the lab would come through, he thought. Maybe they'd pull some DNA out of a cigarette, and maybe they'd find the matching DNA signature in the state's DNA bank. It had been done.

And maybe pigs would fly.

Lucas wandered into the dining room, tinkled a few keys on the piano. Weather had offered to teach him how to play – she'd taught piano in college, as an undergraduate – but he said he was too old.

'You're never too old,' she'd said. 'Here, have some more wine.'

'I am too old. I can't learn that kind of stuff anymore. My brain doesn't absorb it,' Lucas said, taking the wine. 'But I can sing.'

'You can sing?' She was amazed. 'Like what?'

'I sang "I Love Paris" in the senior concert in high school,' he said, somewhat defensively.

'Do I believe you?' she asked.

'Well, I did.' He sipped.

And she sipped, then put the glass on a side table and rummaged, somewhat tipsily, through the piano bench and finally said, 'Ah-ha, she calls his bluff. I have here the music to "I Love Paris."'

She played and he sang; remarkably well, she said. 'You have a really nice baritone.'

'I know. My music teacher said I had a large, vibrant instrument.'

'Ah. Was she attractive?'

'It was a he,' Lucas said. 'Here. Have some more wine.'

Lucas struck a few more notes, then wandered back toward the bedroom, thinking again about his eyewitnesses. They had more than a dozen of them now. Several had been too far away to see much; a couple of them had been so scared that they were more confusing than helpful; two men had seen the killer's face during the attack on Evan Hart. One said he was white, the other said he was a light-skinned black.

And some had seen the killer too long ago, and remembered nothing about him at all . . .

Weather was naked, bent over the sink, her hair full of shampoo. 'If you touch my butt, I'll wait until you're asleep and I'll disfigure you,' she said.

'Cut off your nose to spite your face, huh?'

'We're not talking noses,' Weather said, scrubbing.

He leaned in the doorway. 'There's something women don't understand about good asses,' he said. 'A really good ass is an object of such sublime beauty, that it's almost *impossible* to keep your hands off.'

'Try to think of a way,' she said.

Lucas watched for a moment, then said, 'Speaking of asses, some deaf people thought they saw the killer's truck. They were sure of it. But they gave us an impossible license plate number. A number that's not issued – ass, as in *A-S-S*.' He touched her ass.

'I swear to God, Lucas, just 'cause you've got me helpless . . .'

'Why would they be so sure, and then have such a bad number?'

Weather stopped scrubbing for a moment and said, 'A lot of deaf people don't read English.'

'What?'

She looked at him from under her armpit, her head still in the sink. 'They don't read English. It's very difficult to learn English if you're nonhearing. A lot of them don't bother. Or they learn just enough to read menus and bus signs.'

'Then what do they do? To communicate?'

'They sign,' she said.

'I mean, communicate with the rest of us.'

'A lot of them aren't interested in communicating with the rest of us. Deaf people have a complete culture: they don't need us.'

'They can't read or write?' Lucas was astonished.

'Not English. A lot of them can't, anyway. Is that important?'

'I don't know,' Lucas said. 'But I'll find out.'

'Tonight?'

'Did you have other plans?' He touched her ass again.

She said, 'Not really. I've got to get to bed.'

'Maybe I'll make a call,' he said. 'It's not even ten o'clock.'

Annalise Jones was a sergeant with the St Paul Police Department. Lucas got her at home.

'We had an intern do the translating. A student at

St Thomas. He seemed to know what he was doing,' she said.

'Don't you have a regular guy?' Lucas asked.

'Yeah, but he was out.'

'How do I get the names of these people? The deaf people?'

'Jeez, at this time of night? I'd have to call around,' Jones said.

'Could you?'

At eleven o'clock he had a name and address off St Paul Avenue. Maybe two miles away. He got his jacket. Weather, in bed, called sleepily, 'Are you going out?'

'Just for a while. I gotta nail this down.'

'Be careful . . .'

The houses along St Paul Avenue were modest postwar cottages, added-to, modified, with small, well-kept yards and garages out back. Lucas ran down the house numbers until he found the right one. There were lights in the window. He walked up the sidewalk and rang the bell. After a moment, he heard voices and then a shadow crossed the picture-window drapes, and the front door opened a foot, a chain across the gap. A small, elderly man peered out. 'Yes?'

'I'm Lucas Davenport of the Minneapolis Police Department.' Lucas showed his ID card and the door opened wider. 'Does Paul Johnston live here?'

'Yes. Is he all right?'

'There's no problem,' Lucas said. 'But he went in and talked to the St Paul police about a case we're working on, and I need to talk to him about it.'

'At this time of night?'

'I'm sorry, but it's pretty urgent,' Lucas said.

'Well, I suppose he's down at the Warrens'.' He turned and called back into the house, 'Shirley? Is Paul at the Warrens'?'

'I think so.' A woman in a pink housecoat walked into the front room, clutching the housecoat closed. 'What happened?'

'This is a policeman, he's looking for Paul . . .'

The Warrens were a family of deaf people in Minneapolis, and their home was an informal gathering spot for the deaf. Lucas parked two houses away, at the end of a line of cars centered on the Warrens' house. A man and a woman were sitting on the front stoop, drinking beer, watching him. He walked up the sidewalk and said, 'I'm looking for Paul Johnston?'

The two looked at each other, and then the man signed at him, but Lucas shook his head. The man shrugged and made a croaking sound, and Lucas took out his ID, showed them, pointed toward the house and said, louder, 'Paul Johnston?'

The woman sighed, held up a finger, and disappeared inside. A moment later she came back, followed by a stringy blond teenage girl with a narrow face and small gray eyes. The first woman sat down again, while the blonde said, 'Can I help you?'

'I'm a Minneapolis police officer and I'm looking for a Paul Johnston who contacted the St Paul police about a case we're working on.'

'The killings,' the girl said. 'We've been talking about that. Nothing ever happened.'

'I understand St Paul took a statement.'

'Yeah, but we never heard any more . . . Wait, I'll get Paul.'

She went back inside and Lucas waited, avoiding eye contact with the two people on the porch. They knew it, and seemed to think he was amusing. Every once in a while he'd accidentally make eye contact and either nod or lift his eyebrows, which made him feel stupid.

A moment later, the stringy teenager came back with a

stocky dark-haired man, who looked closely at Lucas and then croaked once, querulously. Heavy oversize glasses with thick lenses made his eyes seem moonlike. He stood under the porch light, and the light made a halo of his long hair.

'I don't sign,' Lucas said.

The blonde said, 'No shit. So what do you want to know?'

'Just what he saw. We got a report with a license number, but the number was an impossible one. The state doesn't allow vulgarities or anything that might be a vulgarity, so there is no plate that says *ASS* on it.'

The girl opened her mouth to say something, then turned to Johnston, her hands flying. A second later, Johnston shook his head in exasperation and began signing back.

'He says the guy at the police station is a jerk,' the blonde said.

'I don't know him,' Lucas said.

The blonde signed something, and Johnston signed back. 'He was afraid that they might have messed up, but that jerk they had at the police station just couldn't sign,' she said, watching his hands.

'It wasn't *ASS*?'

'Oh, yeah. That's why they remembered it. This guy almost ran over them, and Paul saw the plate, and started laughing, because it said *ASS*, and the guy was an ass.'

'There aren't any plates that say *ASS*.'

'How about ass backwards?'

'Backwards?'

She nodded. 'To Paul, it doesn't make much difference, frontwards or backwards. He just recognizes a few words, and this *ASS* popped right out at him. That's why he remembered it. He knew it was backwards. He tried to explain all this, but I guess not everything got through.

286

Paul said the guy at the police station was an illiterate jerk.'

'Jesus. So the plate was *SSA*?'

'That's what Paul says.'

Lucas looked at Paul, and the deaf man nodded.

27

Lucas, on the phone, heard Connell running down the hall and smiled. She literally skidded into the office. Her face was ashen, bare of any makeup; tired, drawn.

'What happened?'

Lucas put his hand over the receiver. 'We maybe got a break. Remember those deaf people? St Paul got the license number wrong.'

'Wrong? How could they be wrong?' she demanded, fist on her hips. 'That's stupid.'

'Just a minute,' Lucas said, and into the phone, 'Can you shoot that over? Fax it? Yeah. I've got a number. And listen, I appreciate your coming in. I'll talk to your boss in the morning, and I'll tell him that.'

'What?' Connell demanded when he hung up.

Lucas turned in the chair to face her. 'The deaf guy who saw the plate – the translation got screwed up. The translator couldn't sign, or something. I looked at that report a half-dozen times, and I kept thinking, how could they screw that up? And I never went back and asked until tonight. The plate was *SSA* – ass backwards.'

'I don't believe it.'

'Believe it.'

'It can't be that simple.'

'Maybe not. But there are a thousand *SSA* plates out there, and two hundred and seventy-two of them are pickups. And what I got from the deaf guy sounded pretty good.'

Anderson came in with two Styrofoam cups full of

coffee. He sat down and started drinking alternately from the two cups. 'You get the stuff?'

'They're faxing it to you.'

'There oughta be a better way to do this,' Anderson said. 'Tie everything together. You oughta get your company to write some software.'

'Yeah, yeah, let's go get it.'

Greave, wearing jeans and T-shirt, caught up with them as they walked through the darkened hallways to Anderson's cubicle in homicide. Lucas explained to him as they walked along the hall. 'So we'll look at everything Anderson can pump out of his databases. Looking for a cop, or anybody with a prison record, particularly for sex crimes or anything that resembles cat burglary.'

At four o'clock in the morning, having found nothing at all, Lucas and Connell walked down to the coffee machine together.

'How're you feeling?'

'A little better today. Yesterday wasn't so good.'

'Huh.' They watched the coffee dribble into a cup, and Lucas didn't know quite what to say. So he said, 'There's a lot more paper than I thought there'd be. I hope we can get through it.'

'We will,' Connell said. She sipped her coffee and watched Lucas's dribble into the second cup. 'I can't believe you figured that out. I can't see how it occurred to you to check.'

Lucas thought of Weather's ass, grinned, and said, 'It sorta came to me.'

'You know, when I first saw you, I thought you were a suit. You know, a *suit*,' she said. 'Big guy, kind of neat-looking in a jockstrap way, buys good suits, gets along with the ladies, backslaps the good old boys, and he cruises to the top.'

'Change your mind?'

'Partially,' she said. She said it pensively, as though it were an academic question. 'I still think there might be some of that — but now I think that, in some ways, you're smarter than I am. Not a suit.'

Lucas was embarrassed. 'I don't think I'm smarter than you are,' he mumbled.

'Don't take the compliment too seriously,' Connell said dryly. 'I said *in some ways*. In other ways, you're still a suit.'

At six o'clock in the morning, with the flat early light cutting sharp through the window like summer icicles, Greave looked up from a stack of paper, rubbed his reddened eyes, and said, 'Here's something pretty interesting.'

'Yeah?' Lucas looked up. They had seven possibilities, none particularly inspiring. One cop, one security guard.

'Guy named Robert Koop. He was a prison guard until six years ago. Drives a '92 Chevy S-10, red over white, no security agreement, net purchase price of $17,340.'

'Sounds like a possibility,' Connell said.

'If he was a prison guard, he probably doesn't have the big bucks,' Greave said, as though he were thinking aloud. 'He says he works at a gym called Two Guy's . . .'

'I know the place,' Lucas said.

'And he declares income of fifteen thousand a year since he left the prison. Where does he get off driving a new seventeen-thousand-dollar truck? And he paid cash, over a seven-thousand-dollar trade-in.'

'Huh.' Lucas came over to look at the printout, and Connell heaved herself out of her chair. 'Lives in Apple Valley. Houses out there probably average what, one-fifty?'

'One-fifty for a house and a twenty-three-thousand-dollar truck is pretty good, on fifteen thousand a year.'

'Probably skips lunch,' Greave said.

'Several times a day,' Lucas said. 'Where's his license information?'

'Right here . . .' Greave folded over several sheets, found it.

'Five-ten, one-ninety,' Lucas said. 'Short and heavy.'

'Maybe short and strong,' Connell said. 'Like our guy.'

'What's his plate number?' Anderson called. His hands were playing across his keyboard. They had limited access to intelligence division's raw data files. Lucas read it off the title application, and Anderson punched it into the computer.

A second later he said, surprise in his voice, 'Jesus, we got a hit.'

'What?' This was the first they'd had. Lucas and Connell drifted over to Anderson to look over his shoulder. When the file came up, they found a long list of license plates picked up outside Steve's Fireside City. Intelligence believed that the stove and fireplace store was a front for a fence, but never got enough to make an arrest.

'High-level fence,' Lucas said, reading between the lines of the intelligence report. 'Somebody who would be moving jewelry, Rolexes, that kind of thing. No stereos or VCRs.'

'Maybe he was buying a fireplace,' Greave said.

'Couldn't afford one, after the truck,' Lucas said. He took his phone book out of his coat pocket, thumbed through it. 'Tommy Smythe, Tommy . . .' He picked up a telephone and dialed, and a moment later said, 'Mrs Smythe? This is Lucas Davenport, Minneapolis Police. Sorry to bother you, but I need to talk to Tommy . . . Oh, jeez, I'm sorry . . . Yeah, thanks.' He scribbled a new number in the notebook.

'Divorced,' he said to Connell.

'Who is he?'

'Deputy warden at Stillwater. We went to school together . . . He's another suit.' He dialed again, waited. 'Tommy? Lucas Davenport. Yeah, I know what time it is, I've been up all night. Do you remember a guard out at Stillwater, six years ago, named Robert Koop? Resigned?'

Smythe, his voice rusty with sleep, remembered. '. . . never caught him, but there wasn't any doubt. He was snitched out by two different guys who didn't know each other. We told him we were ready to bring him up on charges; either that, or get out. He got. Our case wasn't strong enough to just go ahead.'

'Okay. Any rumors about sex problems?'

'Nothing that I know of.'

'Any connection with burglars?'

'Jeez, I can't remember all the details, but yeah. I think the main guy he was dealing to was Art McClatchey, who was a big-time burglar years ago. He fucked up and killed an old lady in one of his burglaries, got caught. That was down in Afton.'

'Cat burglar?' Lucas asked.

'Yeah. Why?'

'Look, anything you can get from records, connecting the two of them, we'd appreciate. Don't go out in the population, though. Don't ask any questions. We're trying to keep all this tight.'

'Do I want to know why you're asking?' Smythe asked.

'Not yet.'

'We're not gonna get burned, are we?'

'I don't see how,' Lucas said. 'If there's any chance, I'll give you a ring.'

Lucas hung up and said to the others, 'He was selling dope to the inmates. Cocaine and speed. One of his main contacts was an old cat burglar named McClatchey.'

'Better and better,' Connell said. 'Now what?'

'We finish the records, just in case we find another candidate. Then we talk to Roux. We want to take a close look at this Koop. But do it real easy.'

*   *   *

292

They finished with eleven possibilities, but Robert Koop was the good one. They put together a file of information from the various state licensing bureaus – car registration, driver's license, an old Washington County carry permit – with what they could get from Department of Revenue and the personnel section of the Department of Revenue.

When he'd worked at Stillwater, Koop had lived in Lakeland. A check with the property tax department in Washington County showed the house where Koop lived was owned by a Lakeland couple; Koop was apparently a renter. A check on the Apple Valley house, through the Dakota County tax collector, suggested that the Apple Valley house was also rented. The current owner showed an address in California, and tax stamps showed a 1980 mortgage of $115,000.

'If the owner's carrying a mortgage of $115,000 . . . let's see, I'm carrying $80,000. Jeez, I can't see that he could be renting it for less than fifteen hundred a month,' Greave said. 'Koop's income is coming up short.'

'Nothing much from the NCIC,' Anderson said. 'He shows prints from Stillwater, and another set from the Army. I'm working on getting his Army records.'

The phone rang and Lucas picked it up, listened, said, 'Thanks,' and put it back down.

'Roux,' he said to Connell. 'She's in. Let's go talk.'

They got Sloan and Del to help out, and a panel truck with one-way windows, equipped with a set of scrambled radios from intelligence. Lucas and Connell rode together in her car; Sloan and Del took their own cars. Greave and O'Brien drove the truck. They met at a Target store parking lot and picked out a restaurant where they could wait.

'Connell and I'll take the first shift,' Lucas said. 'We can rotate out every couple of hours; somebody can cruise it while we're moving the truck to make the change . . . Let's give him a call now, see if he's around.'

Connell called, got an answer, and asked for Mr Clark in the paint department. 'He's home,' she said when she'd rung off the cellular phone. 'He sounded sleepy.'

'Let's go,' Lucas said.

They cruised past Koop's house, a notably unexceptional place in a subdivision of carefully differentiated houses. They parked two blocks away and slightly above it. The lawn was neat but not perfect, with an artificially green look that suggested a lawn service. There was a single-door, two-car garage. The windows were covered with wooden blinds. There was no newspaper, either on the lawn or porch.

Lucas parked the truck and crawled between seats into the back, where there were two captain's chairs, an empty cooler, and a radio they wouldn't use. Connell was examining the house with binoculars.

'It looks awful normal,' she said.

'He's not gonna have a billboard out front,' Lucas said. 'I had a guy, a few years ago, lived in a quadruplex. Everybody said he was a great neighbor. He probably was, except when he was out killing women.'

'I remember that,' Connell said. 'The mad dog. You killed him.'

'He needed it,' Lucas said.

'How do you think you would've done in court? I mean, if he hadn't gotten shot?'

Lucas grinned slightly. 'You mean, if I hadn't shot him to death . . . Actually, we had him cold. It was his second attack on the woman.'

'Was he obsessed by her?'

'No, I think he was just pissed off. At me, actually. We were watching him, and somehow he figured it out, slipped the surveillance and went after her. It was almost . . . sarcastic. He was crazier than a shithouse mouse.'

'We don't have that good a case on Koop.'

'That's an understatement,' Lucas said. 'I've been worried about it.'

They talked for a while, slowly ran down. Nothing happened. After two hours, they drove around the block, traded vehicles with Sloan and O'Brien, and walked up to the restaurant and sat with Del and Greave.

'We're talking about going to the movies,' Del said. 'We all got beepers.'

'I think we should stay put,' Connell said anxiously.

'Say that after you've had fifteen cups of coffee,' Greave said. 'I'm getting tired of peeing.'

Del and Greave took the next shift, then Lucas and Connell again. O'Brien had brought his *Penthouse* with him again, forgot it in the truck. Halfway through the shift, Connell fell to reading it and looking at the pictures, occasionally laughing. Lucas nervously looked elsewhere.

Del and Greave were back on when Koop started to move. Their beepers went off simultaneously, and everybody in the restaurant looked at them. 'Doctors' convention,' Sloan said to an openmouthed suburbanite as they left.

'What do you got, Del?' Lucas called.

'We got the garage door up,' Del said. 'Okay, we got the truck, a red-and-white Chevy . . .'

They first saw Koop when he got out of his truck at a Denny's restaurant.

'No beard,' Connell said, examining him with the binoculars.

'There's been a lot of publicity since Hart,' Lucas said. 'He would've shaved. Two of the Miller witnesses said he was clean-shaven.'

Koop parked in the lot behind the restaurant and walked inside. He walked with a spring, as though he were coiled.

He was wearing jeans and T-shirt. He had a body like a rock.

'He's a lifter,' Lucas said. 'He's a goddamned gorilla.'

'I can see him, he's in a front booth,' Sloan said. 'You want me inside?'

'Let me go in,' Connell said.

'Hang on a minute,' Lucas said. He called back to Sloan. 'Is he by himself?'

'Yeah.'

'Don't go in unless somebody hooks up with him. Otherwise, stand off.' To Connell: 'You better stay out of sight. If this drags out and we need to keep you close to Jensen, you gotta be a fresh face.'

'Okay.' She nodded.

Lucas went back to the radio. 'Sloan, can he see his truck from where he's at?'

'No.'

'We're gonna take a look,' Lucas said. They'd pulled into a car wash. 'Let's go,' he said to Connell.

Connell crossed the street, pulled in next to Koop's truck. Lucas got out, looked across the roof of the car toward the truck, then got back inside.

'Jesus,' he said.

'What?' She was puzzled. 'Aren't you gonna look?'

'There's a pack of Camels on the dashboard.'

'What?' Like she didn't understand.

'Unfiltered Camels,' he said.

Connell looked at Lucas, eyes wide. 'Oh my God,' she breathed. 'It's him.'

Lucas went to the radio. 'Sloan, everybody, listen up. We sorta have a confirmation on this guy. Stay cool but stay back. We're gonna need some technical support . . .'

28

They tracked Koop while they talked at police head-quarters, laying out the case. Thomas Troy, of the county attorney's criminal division, declared that there wasn't enough, yet, to pick him up.

He and Connell, sitting in Roux's office with Roux and Lucas and Mickey Green, another assistant county attorney, ran down the evidence:

— The woman killed in Iowa told a friend that her date was a cop. But Koop never was, said Troy.

— Hillerod saw him in Madison, said Koop recognized his prison tattoo, Connell said. Sounds like ESP, Troy said, and ESP doesn't work on the witness stand. Besides, Hillerod can't remember what he looked like, Green said, and Hillerod's just been arrested for a whole series of heavy felonies, along with a parole violation, and has a long criminal record. The defense will claim he'll tell us anything we want to get a deal. And, in fact, we've already negotiated a deal.

— He was seen dumping a body by two witnesses, Connell said, who described both him and his truck. The witnesses' descriptions conflict, even on the matter of the truck, Troy said. They saw the guy at night at a distance. One of them is an admitted crack dealer, and the other guy hangs around with a crack dealer.

— Camels, said Connell. There are probably fifty thousand Camel smokers in the Cities. And probably most of them drive trucks, Troy said.

— Shape was right for the man who attacked Evan Hart — big and muscular. *Tall*, big, and muscular, is what the witnesses said, Troy replied. Koop is distinctly short. Besides, the attack on Hart isn't necessarily related to the attacks on the women. The man who attacked Hart had a beard and wore glasses. Koop is clean-shaven, shows no glasses requirement on his driver's license, and wasn't wearing glasses that morning. The witnesses hadn't been able to pick his photo out of a display.

'You're working against us,' Connell fumed.

'Bullshit,' said Troy. 'I'm just outlining an elementary defense. A good defense attorney will tear up everything you've got. We need one hard thing. Just one. Just get me one, and we'll take him down.'

Koop spent the first day of surveillance in his truck, driving long complicated routes around the Cities, apparently aimlessly. He stopped at Two Guy's gym, was inside for two hours, then moved on, stopping only to eat at fast-food joints, and once to get gas.

'I think he must've made us,' Del called on one of the scrambled radios as they sat stalled in traffic on I-94 between Minneapolis and St Paul. 'Unless he's nuts.'

'We know he's nuts,' Connell said. 'The question is, what's he doing?'

'He's not scouting,' Lucas said from a third car. 'He's moving too fast to be scouting. And he never goes back. He just drives. He doesn't seem to know where he's going – he's always getting caught in those circles and dead ends.'

'Well, we gotta do something,' Del said. ''Cause if he hasn't made us yet, he will. He'll get us up in some of those suburban switchbacks and we'll bump into him one too many times. Where in the hell is tech support?'

'We're here,' the tech-support guy said on the radio. 'You stop the sonofabitch, and we'll tag him.'

At three o'clock, Koop stopped at a Perkins restaurant and took a booth. While Lucas and Connell watched from outside, Henry Ramirez from intelligence slipped under

Koop's truck and hooked up a remote-controlled battery-powered transmitter, and placed a flat, battery-powered infrared flasher in the center of the topper. If Koop climbed on top of the truck, he'd see it. Otherwise, it was invisible, and the truck could be unmistakably tracked at night, from the air.

At nine o'clock, in the last dying light of the day, Koop wandered out of the web of roads around Lake Minnetonka and headed east toward Minneapolis. They no longer had a lead car. Leading had proven impossible. The trailing cars were all well back. The radio truck followed silently, with the tracking plane doing all the work. From the air, the spotter, using infrared glasses, said Koop was clear all the way, and tracked him street by street into the Cities.

'He's going for Jensen,' Lucas said to Connell as he followed the track on a map.

'I don't know where I am anymore.'

'We're coming up on the lakes.' Lucas called out to the others: 'We're breaking off, we'll be at Jensen's.'

He called ahead to Jensen's, but there was no answer at her phone. He called dispatch and got the number for the resident manager: 'We've got a problem and we need a little help . . .'

The manager was waiting by the open door of the parking garage, the door open. Lucas pulled inside and dumped the car in a handicapped space.

'What do you want me to do?' the manager asked, handing him a key to Jensen's apartment.

'Nothing,' Lucas said. 'Go on back to your apartment. We'd like you near a telephone. Just wait. Please don't go out in the hallway.'

To Connell: 'If he comes up, we've got him. If we get him inside Jensen's place, that ties him to the stalking and the Camels on the air conditioner across the street. And the knife attack ties him to the other killings and the Camel we found on Wannemaker.'

'You think he'll come up?' She asked as they hurried to the elevators.

'I hope so. Jesus, I hope so. That'd be it.' At Jensen's apartment, they let themselves in, and Lucas turned on one light, slipped his .45 out of his shoulder holster and checked it.

'What's he doing?' Lucas asked.

'Moving very slowly, but he's moving,' the spotter called. 'Now, now, we've lost him, he's under some trees or some shit, wait, I got a flash, I see him again, now he's gone . . .'

'I see him,' Del called. 'I'm parked in the bike shop lot, and he's coming this way. He's moving faster, but he's under trees, he'll be out in a sec . . .'

'Got him,' the spotter said. 'He's going around the block again. Slowing down . . .'

'Real slow,' Del called. 'I'm on the street, walking, he's right in front of the apartment, real slow, almost stopped. No, there he goes . . .'

'He's outa here,' the spotter called a minute later. 'He's heading into the loop.'

'Did he see you, Del?'

'No way.'

Connell said, 'Well, shit . . .'

'Yeah.' Lucas felt like a deflated balloon. He walked twice around the room. 'Goddamnit,' he said. 'Goddamnit. What's wrong with the guy? Why didn't he come up?'

Koop continued through downtown to a bar near the airport, where he drank three solitary beers, paid, bought a bottle at the liquor store down the street, and drove back to his house. The last light went off a few minutes after two o'clock.

Lucas went home. Weather was asleep. He patted her affectionately on the ass before he went down himself.

Koop resumed the driving the next day, trailing through the suburbs east and south of St Paul. They tracked him until one o'clock in the afternoon, when he stopped at a Wendy's. Lucas went on down the block to a McDonald's. Feeling dried out, older, bored, he got a double cheeseburger, a sack of fries, and a malt, and ambled back to the car, where Connell was eating carrot sticks out of a Tupperware box.

'George Beneteau called yesterday, while we were out,' Connell said when they'd run out of everything else to talk about.

'Oh, yeah?' She had a talent for leaving him short of words.

'He left a message on my machine. He wants to go out and get a steak, or something.'

'What'd you do?'

'Nothing.' She said it flatly. 'I can't deal with it. I guess tomorrow I'll give him a call and explain.'

Lucas shook his head and pushed fries into his face, hoping that she wouldn't start crying again.

She didn't. But a while later, as they escorted Koop across the Lake Street bridge, Connell said, 'That TV person, Jan Reed. You guys seem pretty friendly.'

'I'm friendly with a lot of media,' Lucas said uncomfortably.

'I mean friendly-friendly,' she said.

'Oh, not really.'

'Mmm,' she said.

'Mmm, what?' Lucas asked.

'I'd think a very long time. This is one of those things where, you know – I suspect you're just a suit.'

'Not quite bright,' he said.

'Took the words out of my mouth,' Connell said.

*   *   *

Koop stopped at a Firestone store but just sat in the truck. The surveillance van, watching him from a Best Buy store parking lot, said he seemed to be looking at a Denny's restaurant across the street.

'He ate less than an hour ago,' Lucas said. They were a block away, parked in front of a used-car lot, a bit conspicuous. 'Let's go look at some cars.'

They got out and walked into the lot, where they could watch Koop through the windows of a used Buick. After ten minutes in the Firestone lot, Koop started the truck, rolled it across the street to the Denny's and went inside.

'He's looking for surveillance,' Lucas said. On the radio: 'Del, could you get in there?'

'On my way . . .' Then, a few seconds later, 'Shit, he's coming back out. I'm turning around.'

Koop walked out with a cup of coffee. Lucas caught Connell's arm as she started toward the car, and brought the radio to his face. 'We're gonna stay here a minute; you guys tag him. Hey, Harvey?'

Harvey ran the surveillance van. 'Yeah?'

'Could you put a video on the front of that Denny's see who else comes out?'

'You got it.'

'He wasn't in there long enough,' Lucas said to Connell. 'He talked to somebody. Not long enough for a friend, so it must have been business.'

'Unless his friend wasn't there,' Connell said.

'He was *too* long for that . . .' A moment later he said, 'Here we go. Oh, shit, Harvey, cover that guy, you remember him?'

'I don't . . .'

'Just Plain Schultz,' Lucas said.

Del, on the radio, from tracking Koop: '*Our* Just Plain Schultz?'

'Absolutely,' Lucas said.

Schultz got in a red Camaro and carefully backed out of his parking slot. 'C'mon,' Lucas said to Connell, hustling her down to the car.

'Who is he?'

'Fence. Very careful.'

In the car, Lucas tagged a half-block behind Schultz and called in a squad. 'Just pull him over to the curb,' he told the squad. 'And stand by.'

The squad picked Schultz up at the corner, stopped him halfway down the block, under a bright-green maple. Lucas and Connell passed them, pulled to the curb. A kid on a tricycle watched from the sidewalk, the flashing lights, the cop standing inside his open door. Schultz was watching the cop in his rearview mirror and didn't see Lucas coming from the front, until Lucas was right on top of him.

'Schultzie,' Lucas said, leaning over the window, his hands on the roof. 'How you been, my man?'

'Aw, fuck, what do you want, Davenport?' Schultz, shocked, tried to cover.

'Whatever you just bought from Koop,' Lucas said.

Schultz was a small man with a round, blemished face. He had dark whiskers a razor couldn't quite control. His eyes were slightly protuberant, and when Lucas said 'Koop,' they seemed to bug out a bit farther.

'I can't believe *that* crazy motherfucker belongs to you,' Schultz said after a moment, popping the door to get out of the car.

'He doesn't, actually,' Lucas said. Connell was standing on the other side of the car, her hand in her purse.

'Who's the puss?' Schultz asked, tipping his head toward her.

'State cop,' Lucas said. 'And is that any way to talk about the government?'

'Fuck you, Davenport,' Schultz said, leaning back against the car's front fender. 'So what're we doing? Do I call a lawyer, or what?'

'Schultzie . . .' Lucas said, spreading his arms wide.

'That's just plain Schultz,' Schultz said.

Thomas Troy wore a blue military sweater over jeans. He looked neat but tough, like a lieutenant colonel in the paratroops. He was shaking his head.

'We don't have enough on the killings, by themselves, even with him cruising Jensen's place. We could fake it, though, and put him away.'

'Like how?' Roux asked. 'What do you suggest?'

'We take him on the burglary charges. We've got enough from Schultz to get a conviction on those. And we've got enough on the burglary charges to get search warrants for the truck and the house. If we don't find anything on the murders or his stalking Jensen, well – we got him on the burglaries, and in the presentencing report, we let the judge know we think he's tied in to the murders. If we get the right judge, we can get an upward departure on the sentence and keep him inside for five or six years.'

'Five or six years?' Connell came up out of her chair.

'Sit down,' Troy snapped. She sat down. 'If you get anything in the search, then there're more possibilities. If we find evidence of more burglaries, we'll get a couple of more years. If we get evidence that he's stalking Jensen, then we get another trial and go for a few more. And if there's anything that would suggest the murders – any tiny little thing more than what you've got – we could set up the murder trials to go at the end of the sequence, and maybe the publicity from the first two will put him away on the others.'

'We're really betting on the come,' Lucas said.

'All you need is a few hairs from Wannemaker or Marcy Lane, and with the circumstantial stuff you've got, that'd be enough,' Troy said. 'If you can give me *anything* – a weapon, a hair, a couple drops of blood, a print – we'd go with it.'

Connell looked at Lucas, then Roux. 'If we stay with him, we might see him approach somebody.'

'What if he kills her the second they're in the truck?' Roux asked.

Lucas shook his head. 'He doesn't always do that. Wannemaker had ligature marks on her wrists. He kept her a while, maybe a day, and messed with her.'

'Didn't mess with Marcy Lane. He couldn't have had her more than an hour,' Connell said grimly.

'We can't take that chance,' Roux said. 'We'd be crazy to take that chance.'

'I don't know,' Troy said. 'If he even showed a knife — that'd be the ballgame.'

'So we should wait?'

Lucas looked at Connell, then shook his head. 'I think we should take him.'

'Why?' Connell asked. 'Getting him for five or six years, if we're lucky?'

'We've only been watching him for two days and a night. What if he's got somebody down his basement right now? What if he goes in the house and kills her while we're sitting outside? We know that he kept at least one of them for a while.'

Connell swallowed, and Roux straightened and said, 'If that's a possibility . . .'

'It's a very remote possibility,' Lucas said.

'I don't care how remote,' Roux said. 'Take him now.'

29

Koop was in Modigliani's Wine & Spirits off Lyndale Avenue when the cops got him. His arm was actually in the cold box, pulling out a six-pack of Budweiser, when a red-faced man in a cheap gray suit said, 'Mr Koop?' Koop realized a large black man had stepped to his elbow, and a uniformed cop was standing by the door. They'd appeared as if by magic; as if they had a talent for it, popping out of nowhere.

Koop said, 'Yeah?' And straightened up. His heart beat a little faster.

'Mr Koop, we're Minneapolis police officers,' the red-faced man said. 'We're placing you under arrest.'

'What for?'

Koop stood flat-footed, hands in front of him, forcing himself to be still. But his back and arm muscles were twitching, ready to go. He'd thought about this possibility, at night, when he was waiting to go to sleep, or watching television. He'd thought about it a lot, a favorite nightmare.

Resisting a cop could bring a heavier charge than anything else they might have on you. In the joint, they warned you that if the cops really wanted you, and you gave them a chance, they just might blow you away. Of course, it was mostly the spooks that said that. White guys didn't see it the same way. But everybody agreed on one thing: your best shot was a decent defense attorney.

The red-faced cop said, 'I think you know.'

'I don't know,' Koop protested. 'You're making a mistake. You've got the wrong guy.' He glanced toward the door. Maybe he *should* make a run for it. The red-faced guy didn't look like that much. The black guy he could outrun, and he'd take the guy at the door like a bowling pin. He had the power . . . but he didn't know what was outside. And these guys were armed. He sensed the cops were waiting for something, were looking at him for a decision. Everything in the store was needle-sharp, the rows of brown liquor bottles and green plastic jugs of mix, stacks of beer cans, the tops of potato chip bags, the black-and-white checkered tiles on the floor. Koop tensed, felt the cops pull into themselves. They were ready for him, and not particularly scared.

'Turn around, please, and place your hands on the top of the cooler,' Red-face said. Koop heard him as though from a distance. But there was a hardness in the guy's voice. Maybe he couldn't take them. Maybe they'd beat the shit out of him. And he didn't know yet what he was being arrested for. If it wasn't too serious, if it was buying cocaine, then resisting would bring him more trouble than the charge.

'Turn around . . .' Peremptory this time. Koop gave the door a last look, then let out a breath and turned.

The cop patted him down, quickly but thoroughly. Koop had done it often enough at Stillwater to appreciate the professionalism.

'Drop your hands behind you, please. We're going to put handcuffs on, Mr Koop, just as a precaution.' The red-faced man was crisp and polite, the prefight tension gone now.

The black cop said, 'You have the right to see an attorney . . .'

'I want a lawyer,' Koop said, interrupting the Miranda. The cuffs closed over his wrists and he instinctively flexed against them, pushing down a spasm of what felt like claustrophobia, not being able to move. The red-faced cop took him by the elbow and pivoted him, while the other finished the Miranda.

'I want a lawyer,' Koop said. 'Right now. You're making a mistake, and I'm gonna sue your butts.'

'Sure. Step over this way, we'll go out to the car,' the red-faced cop said.

They walked down a row of potato chips and bean dip and the black cop said, 'Jesus, you sound like some kind of parrot. Polly want a lawyer?' but he grinned, friendly. His hand was hard on Koop's triceps.

'I want a lawyer.' In the joint they said that after they warn you, the cops'll get friendly, try to get you talking about anything. After they get you rolling, when you're trying to make them happy – because you're a little scared, you don't want to get whacked around – then you'll start talking. Don't talk, they said in the joint. Don't say shit except 'I want a lawyer.'

They went out the door, a customer and the counterman gawking at them, and the red-faced man said, 'My name is Detective Kershaw and the man behind you is Detective Carrigan, the famous Irish dancer. We'll need your keys to tow your truck, or we could just pop the tranny and tow it.'

Two squad cars were nosed into the parking lot, one blocking the truck, four more cops standing by. Too many for a routine coke bust, Koop thought. 'Keys are in my right side pocket,' Koop said. He desperately wanted to know why he'd been arrested. Burglary? Murder? Something to do with Jensen?

'Hey, he can talk,' the black cop said.

He slapped Koop on the shoulder in a comradely way, and they stopped while the red-faced cop took his keys out and tossed them to a patrolman and said, 'Tow truck is on its way.' To Koop, Kershaw said, 'That black car over there.'

While they opened the back door of the car, Koop said, 'I don't know why I'm arrested.' He couldn't help it, couldn't keep his mouth shut. The open back door of the car looked like a hungry mouth. 'Why?'

308

Carrigan said, 'Watch your head,' and he put a hand on top of Koop's head and eased him into the car, and then said, 'Why do you think?' and shut the door.

The two detectives spent a few minutes talking to the uniformed cops, letting Koop stew in the backseat of the car. The back doors had no inside handles, no way to get out. With his hands pinned behind him, he couldn't sit easily, had to sit upright on the too-soft seats. And the backseat smelled faintly of disinfectant and urine. Koop felt another spasm of claustrophobic panic, something he hadn't expected. The damn cuffs: he twisted against them, hard, gritting his teeth; no chance. The cops outside were still not looking at him. He was an insect. Why in the hell . . .

And then Koop thought, *Softening me up.*

He'd done the same thing when there was a prison squabble that they had to look into. When the cops got back into the car, one of them would look at him, friendly-like, and ask, 'Well, what do you think?'

The plainclothes cops spent another minute talking to the uniforms, then drifted back to the car, talking to each other, as if Koop were the last thing on their minds. A screen divided the front seat from the back. The black guy drove, and after he started the engine he looked at his partner in the passenger seat and said, 'Let's stop at a Taco Bell.'

'Oooh, good call.' When they got going, the red-faced guy turned and grinned and said, 'Well, what do you think?'

'I want a lawyer,' Koop said. The red-faced guy pulled back a quarter inch on the other side of the screen, his eyes going dark. He couldn't help it, and Koop almost smiled. He could play this game, he thought.

30

Lucas and Connell watched the arrest from a Super America station across the street, leaning on Connell's car, eating ice cream sandwiches. Koop came out, Kershaw a step behind, with one hand on Koop's right elbow. 'I wanted to take him,' Connell said between bites.

'Not for burglary,' Lucas said.

'No.' She looked at her watch. 'The search warrants should be ready.'

Carrigan and Kershaw were pushing Koop into the car. Koop's arms were flexed, and his muscles stood out like ropes. Lucas balled up the ice cream sandwich wrapper and fired it at a trash can; it bounced off onto the pavement.

'I want to get down to the house,' Connell said. 'See you there?'

'Yeah. I'll wait until they open the truck – I'll let you know if there's anything good.'

Lucas wanted crime-scene people to open the truck. 'We might be talking about a couple of hairs,' he told the patrolman with the keys. 'Let's wait.'

'Okay. Who was that guy?' the patrolman asked.

'Cat burglar,' Lucas said. 'He sure went nice and easy.'

'He scared the shit out of me,' the patrolman confessed, his eyes drifting back toward the store. 'I was in the door and he looked over toward me, like he was gonna run. He had crazy eyes, man. He was right on the edge of flipping out. Did you see his arms? I wouldn't have wanted to fight the sonofabitch.'

Crime scene arrived five minutes later. A half-carton of

unfiltered Camels sat on the front seat. A bag of mixed salt and sand, jumper cables, a toolbox, and other junk occupied the back.

Lucas poked carefully through it but found nothing. He pulled the keys Koop had produced. There were two truck keys, what looked like two house keys, and a fifth one. Jensen's maybe. But it didn't look new enough. They'd have to check.

'Got a nice set of burglary tools back here,' one of the crime-scene guys said. Lucas walked around to the back of the truck, where they'd carefully opened the toolbox. Unfortunately, burglary tools were nothing more than a slightly unusual selection of ordinary tools. You had to prove the burglary first. The crime-scene guy picked up a small metal-file and looked at it with a magnifying glass, just like Sherlock Holmes.

'Got some brass,' he said.

'That'll help,' Lucas said. Koop was cutting his own keys, by hand. 'Anything like a knife? Any rope?'

'No.'

'Goddamnit. Well, close it up and take it down,' Lucas said, disappointed. 'We want everything – prints, hair, skin, fluid. Everything.'

Lucas dropped the Porsche at the curb and started up the driveway to Koop's house. The front and side doors were open, and two unmarked vans sat in the driveway, along with Connell's anonymous gray Chevy. Lucas was almost to the front steps when he saw two neighborhood women walking down the street, one of them pushing a baby buggy. Lucas walked back toward them.

'Hello,' he said.

The woman pushing the buggy had her hair in curlers, covered with a rayon scarf. The other one had dishwater-blond hair with streaks of copper through it. They stopped. 'Are you police?' Neighbors always knew.

'Yes. Have you seen Mr Koop recently?'

'What'd he do?' asked the copper-streaked one. The kid in the buggy was sucking on a blue pacifier, looking fixedly at Lucas with pale-blue eyes.

'He's been arrested in connection with a burglary,' Lucas said.

'Told you,' Copper Streak said to Hair Curler. To Lucas, she said, 'We always knew he was a criminal.'

'Why? What'd he do?'

'Never got up in the morning,' she said. 'You'd hardly ever see him at all. Sometimes, when he put his garbage out. That was it. He was never in his yard. His garage door would go up, always in the afternoon, and he'd drive away. Then he'd come back in the middle of the night, like three o'clock in the morning, and the garage door would go up, and he'd be inside. You *never* saw him. The only time I ever saw him, except for garbage, was that Halloween snowstorm a couple of years ago. He came out and shoveled his driveway. After that, he always had a service do it.'

'Did he have a beard?'

Copper Streak looked at Hair Curler, and they both looked back at Lucas. 'Sure. He's always had one.'

One more thing, Lucas thought. They talked for another minute, then Lucas broke away and went inside.

Connell was in the kitchen, scribbling notes on a yellow pad.

'Anything?' Lucas asked.

'Not much. How about the truck?'

'Nothing so far. No weapon?'

'Kitchen knives. But this guy isn't using a kitchen knife. I'd be willing to bet on it.'

'I just talked to a couple of neighbors,' Lucas said. 'They say he's always had a beard.'

'Huh.' Connell pursed her lips. 'That's interesting . . . C'mere, down the basement.' Lucas followed her down a short flight of stairs off the kitchen. The basement was finished. To the left, through an open door, Lucas could see a washer, dryer, laundry sink, and a water heater, sitting on a tiled floor. The furnace would be back here too, out of sight. The larger end of the basement was carpeted with a seventies-era two-tone shag. A couch, a chair, and a coffee table with a lamp pressed against the walls. The center of the rug was dominated by a plastic painter's drop cloth, ten feet by about thirteen or fourteen, laid flat on the rug. A technician was vacuuming around the edges of the drop cloth.

'Was that plastic sheet like that?' Lucas asked.

'No. I put it there,' Connell said. 'C'mere and look at the windows.'

The windows were blacked out with sheets of quarter-inch plywood. 'I went outside and looked,' Connell said. 'He's painted the outside of them black, so unless you get down on your knees and look into the window wells, it just looks like the basement is dark. He went to a lot of trouble with it: the edges are caulked.'

'Yeah?'

'Yeah.' She looked down the sheet. 'I think this is where he killed Wannemaker. On a piece of plastic. There're a couple of three-packs of drop cloths in the utility room. One of them is unopened. The other one only had one cloth in it. I was walking around down here, and it looked to me like the rug was matted in a rectangle. Then I noticed the furniture: it's set up to look at something in the middle of the rug. When I saw the drop cloths . . .' She shrugged. 'I laid it out, and it fit perfectly.'

'Jesus . . .' Lucas looked at the tech. 'Anything?'

The tech nodded and said, 'A ton of shit: I don't think the rug's ever been cleaned, and it must've been installed fifteen years ago. It's gonna be a goddamned nightmare, sorting everything out.'

'Well, it's something, anyway,' Lucas said.

'There's one other thing,' Connell said. 'Up in the bedroom.'

Lucas followed her back up the stairs. Koop's bedroom was spare, almost military, though the bed was unmade and smelled of sweat. Lucas saw it right away: on the chest of drawers, a bottle of Opium.

Lucas: 'You didn't touch it?'

'Not yet. But it wouldn't make any difference.'

'Jensen said he took it from her place. If her fingerprints are on it . . .'

'I called her. Her bottle was a half-ounce. She always gets herself a half-ounce at Christmas because it lasts almost exactly a year.'

Lucas peered at the perfume bottle: a quarter-ounce. 'She's sure?'

'She's sure. Damnit, I thought we had him.'

'We should check it anyway,' Lucas said. 'Maybe she's wrong.'

'Yeah, we'll check – but she was sure. Which brings up the question, why Opium? Does he obsess on the perfume? Does the perfume attract him somehow? Or did he go out and buy some of his own, to remind him of Jensen?'

'Huh,' Lucas said.

'Well? Is it the perfume or the woman?' She looked at him, expecting to pull a rabbit out of a hat. Maybe he could. Lucas closed his eyes. After a moment, he said, 'It's because Jensen uses it. He's creeping into her apartment in the dark, goes into her bedroom, and something sets him off. The perfume. Or maybe seeing her there. But the perfume really brings it back to him. It's possible, if he's really freaked out, that he used everything in the bottle he stole from her.'

'Do you think it's enough? The beard being shaved, and the perfume bottle?'

He shook his head. 'No. We've got to find something. One thing.'

Connell moved around until she was looking straight into Lucas's eyes from no more than two feet. Her face was waxy, pale, like a dinner candle. 'I was sick again this morning. In two weeks, I won't be able to walk. I'll be back in chemo, I'll start shedding hair. I won't be able to think straight.'

'Jesus, Meagan . . .'

'I want the sonofabitch, Lucas,' she said. 'I don't want to be dead in a hole and have him walking around laughing. You know he's the one, I know he's the one.'

'So?'

'So we gotta talk. We gotta figure something out.'

31

Koop got out of jail a few minutes after noon, blinking in the bright sunshine, his lawyer walking behind, a sport coat over his shoulder, talking.

Koop was very close to the edge. He felt as though he had a large crack in his head, that it was about to split in half, that a wet gray worm would spill out, a worm the size of a vacuum-cleaner hose.

He didn't like jail. He didn't like it at all.

'Remember, not a thing to anybody, okay?' the lawyer said, shaking his finger into the air. He'd learned not to shake it at his clients: one had almost pulled it off. He was repeating the warning for at least the twentieth time, and Koop nodded for the twentieth time, not hearing him. He was looking around at the outdoors, feeling the tension falling away, as though he were coming unwrapped, like a mummy getting its sheet pulled.

Jesus. His head was really out of control. 'Okay.'

'There's nothing you can say to the cops that would help you. Nothing. If you want to talk to somebody, talk to me, and if it's important, I'll talk to them. Okay?'

'No deals,' Koop said. 'I don't want to hear about no fuckin' deals.'

'Is there any chance you can find the guy who sold you the stuff?' The lawyer looked like a mailman on PCP. Ordinary enough, but everything in his face too tight, too stretched. And though each of his words was enunciated clearly, there were far too many of them, spoken too quickly, a torrent of 'I thinks' and 'Maybe we'd bests.' Koop couldn't keep up with them all, and had begun ignoring them. 'What do you think, huh? Any chance you could find him? Any chance?'

Koop finally heard him, and shrugged, and said, 'Maybe. But what should I do if I find him? Call the cops?'

'No-no. Nuh-nuh-no. No. No. You call me. You don't talk to the cops.' The lawyer's eyes were absolutely flat, like old pasteboard poker chips. Koop suspected he didn't believe a word of his story.

Koop had told him that he bought the diamond cross and the matching earrings from a white boy – literally a boy, a teenager – wearing a Minnesota National Guard fatigue shirt, who hung around the Duck Inn, in Hopkins. The kid had a big bunch of dark hair and an earring, Koop had said. He said he bought the brooch and earrings for $200. The kid knew he was getting ripped off, but didn't know what else to do with them.

'How do we explain that you sold them to Schultz?' the attorney had asked.

Koop had said, 'Hell, everybody knows Schultz. The cops call him Just Plain Schultz. If you've got something you want to sell, and you're not quite sure where it came from, you talk to Schultz. If I was really a smart burglar like the cops said, I sure as shit would never have gone to him. He's practically on their payroll.'

The attorney had looked at him for a long time, and then said, 'Okay. Okay. Okay. So you've been out of steady work since the recession started, except for this gig at the gym, and you saw a chance to pick up a few bucks, took it, and now you're sorry. Okay?'

That had been fine with Koop.

Now, with the lawyer following him out of the jail, babbling, Koop put his hands over his ears, pushed his head together. The lawyer stepped back, asked, 'Are you all right?'

'Don't like that place,' Koop said, looking back over his shoulder.

*   *   *

Koop hurt. Almost every muscle in his body hurt. He could handle the first part of the detention. He could handle the bend-over-and-spread-'em. But he could feel his blood draining away the closer he got to a cell. They'd had to urge him inside the cell, prod him, and once inside, the door locked, he'd sat for a moment, the fear climbing up into his throat.

'Motherfucker,' he'd said aloud, looking at the corners of the cells. Everything was so close. And pushing in.

He could have gone over the edge at that moment. Instead, he started doing sit-ups, push-ups, bridges, deep knee bends, toe-raises, push-offs, leg lifts. He did step-ups onto the bunk until his legs quit. He'd never worked so hard in his life; he didn't stop until his muscles simply quit on him. Then he slept; he dreamed of boxes with hands and holes with teeth. He dreamed of bars. When he woke up, he started working again.

Halfway through the next morning, they'd taken him down to his lawyer. The lawyer'd said the cops had his truck, had searched his house. 'Is this charge the only thing you see coming? The only thing, the only thing?' he'd asked. He seemed a bit puzzled. 'The cops are all over you. All over you. This charge – this is minor shit. Minor shit.'

'Nothing else I know of,' Koop said. But he thought, *Shit*. Maybe they knew something else.

The lawyer met him again at the courthouse, for the arraignment. He waived a preliminary hearing at the advice of the lawyer. The arraignment was quick, routine: five thousand dollars bail, the bail bondsman right there to take the assignment of his truck.

'Don't fuck with the truck,' Koop said to the bail bondsman. 'I'll be coming to you with the cash, as soon as I get it.'

'Yeah, sure,' the bondsman said. He said it negligently. He'd heard all this too many times.

'Don't fuck with it,' Koop snarled.

The bondsman didn't like Koop's tone, and opened his mouth to say something smart, but then he saw Koop's eyes and understood that he was a very short distance from death. He said, 'We won't touch it,' and he meant it. Koop turned away, and the bondsman swallowed and wondered why they'd let an animal like that out of jail once they had him in.

Koop had not decided what to do. Not exactly. But he knew for sure that he wouldn't be going back to jail. He couldn't handle that. Jail was death. There would be no deals, nothing that would put him inside.

There was an excellent chance he'd be acquitted, his attorney said: the state's case seemed to be based entirely on Schultz's testimony. 'In fact, I'm surprised they bothered to arrest you. Surprised,' the attorney said.

If he was convicted, though, Koop'd have to do some small amount of time – certainly not a year, although technically he could get six years. After the conviction, the state would continue bail through a presentencing investigation. He'd be free for at least another month . . .

But if he was convicted, Koop knew, he'd be gone. Mexico. Canada. Alaska. Somewhere. No more jail . . .

The attorney had told him where he could get the truck. 'I checked, and they're finished with it.' He needed the truck. The truck was *his*, gave him security. But what if the cops had him on some kind of watch list? What if they tagged him to the bank, where he had his stash? He needed to get at the stash, for the money to pay the bondsman.

Wait, wait, wait . . .

The trial wasn't even going to be for a month. He didn't have to do anything in the next fifteen minutes. If they were watching him, he'd spot it. Unless they'd bugged the truck. Koop put his hands to his head and pushed: holding it together.

He got the truck back – it was all routine, clerical, the bureaucrats didn't give a shit, as long as you had the paper – and drove to his house. Two of the neighborhood cunts were walking on the street and stepped up on a lawn when they saw him coming, wrenching a baby buggy up on the grass with them.

Bitches, he mouthed at them.

He pushed the button on the garage-door opener when he was still a half-block away, and rolled straight into the garage stall, the door dropping behind him. He took ten minutes to walk around the house. The cops had been all over the place. Things were moved, and hadn't been put back quite right. Nothing was trashed. Nothing was missing, as far as he could tell. The basement looked untouched.

He walked through the front room. An armchair sat facing the television. 'Cocksucker,' he screamed. He kicked the side of it, and the fabric caved in. Koop, breathing hard, looked around the room, at the long wall reaching down toward the bedrooms. Sheetrock. A slightly dirty, inoffensive beige. 'Cocksucker,' he screamed at it. He hit the wall with his fist; the sheetrock caved in, a hole like a crater on the moon. 'Cocksucker.' Struck again, another hole. 'Cocksucker . . .'

Screaming, punching, he moved sideways down the hall, stopped only when he was at the end of it, looked back. Nine holes, fist-size, shoulder height. And pain. Dazed, he looked at his hand: the knuckles were a pulp of blood. He put the knuckles to his mouth, licked them off, sucked on them. Tasted good, the blood.

Breathing hard, blowing like a horse, Koop staggered back to the bedroom, sucking his knuckles as he went.

In the bedroom, the first thing he saw was the bottle of

Opium, sitting on the chest. He unscrewed the top, sniffed it, closed his eyes, saw her.

White nightgown, black triangle, full lips . . .

Koop put some Opium on his fingertips, dabbed it under his nose, stood swaying with his eyes closed, just visiting . . .

Finally, with the dreamlike odor of Sara Jensen playing with his mind, and the pain in his hand helping to reorder it, he got a flashlight and went back out to the garage. He began working through the truck, inch by inch, bolt by bolt, sucking his knuckles when the blood got too thick . . .

32

Lucas hovered in the men's accessories, next to the cologne, behind a rotating rack of wallets, keeping the top of Koop's head in sight. He carried a fat leather briefcase. Koop loitered in the men's sportswear, his hands in his pockets, touching nothing, not really looking.

Connell beeped. 'What's he doing?'

'Killing time,' Lucas said. A short elderly lady stopped to look at him, and he turned away. 'Can you see him?'

'He's two aisles over.'

'Careful. You're too close. Sloan?'

'Yeah, I got him. I'm going over to the north exit. That's the closest way out now. I'll go on through the skyway if he moves that way.'

'Good. Del?'

'Just coming up to sportswear. I can't see him, but I'm right across from Connell. I can see Connell.'

'You're real close to him. He's behind the shirt rack,' Connell chirped.

'Excuse me, could you tell me where men's bathrobes are?' Lucas turned around, and looked down at the short elderly lady. She had ear curls like a lamb, and small thick glasses.

'Down by that post where you see the Exit sign,' Lucas said.

'Thank you,' she said, and tottered away.

Lucas angled through Ralph Lauren into Guess. A blond woman in a black dress stepped up to him and said, 'Escape?'

'What?' He stepped toward her, and she stepped back

and held up a cylindrical bottle as though she were defending herself.

'Just a spritz?'

Men's perfume. 'Oh, no, I'm sorry,' Lucas said, moving on. The woman looked after him.

Koop was moving, and Connell beeped. 'He's headed toward the north door. Still moving slow.'

'I've got him,' Lucas said.

Sloan said, 'I'm going through the skyway.'

'I'll move into Sloan's spot,' Del said. 'Meagan, you've been the most exposed, you either oughta go through way ahead or stay back.'

'It's too soon to go through ahead of him,' Connell said. 'I'll hang back.'

'I'll catch up to you,' Lucas said.

Lucas moved up to a glass case of Coach briefcases and looked down the store at Koop's back. Koop had stopped again, no more than thirty feet away, poking a finger through a rack of leather jackets. Lucas stepped back, focused on Koop, when a hand hooked his elbow. A youngish man in a suit was behind him, another to his left. The perfume woman was behind them.

'May I ask you what you're doing?' the man in the suit asked. Store security, a tough guy, with capped teeth. Lucas stepped hard behind the counter, out of sight of Koop, the two men lurching along with him. The security man's grip tightened.

'I'm a Minneapolis homicide cop on surveillance,' Lucas said, his voice low and mean, like a hatchet. He reached into his pocket, pulled his badge case, flipped it open. 'If you give me away, I'll pull your fucking testicles off and stuff them in your ears.'

'Jesus.' The security man looked at the bug in Lucas's ear, then at his face, at what looked like rage. He went pale. 'Sorry.'

'Get the fuck out of this end of the store, all of you,'

Lucas said. He pointed the other way. 'Go that way. Go separately. Don't walk in the aisles and don't look back.'

'I'm . . .' the man was stuttering. 'I'm sorry, I used to be a cop.'

'Yeah, right.' Lucas turned away and sidled out from behind the case. Koop was gone. 'Shit.'

Connell beeped. 'He's moving.'

Roux was scared to death. Connell's idea had scared her so badly that she thought about switching back to Gauloises.

But Jensen had come to see her the day before, wearing a power suit and carrying a power briefcase, and she'd laid it out: a sucker game might be the only way to take him.

Roux, stuck between a rock and a hard place, had gone for the hard place.

'Thanks,' Connell had said to Jensen when they were in the hall outside of Roux's office. 'Takes guts.'

'I want to get him so bad that my teeth hurt,' Jensen had said. 'When will he get out?'

'Tomorrow morning,' Connell had said. Her eyes defocused, as though she were looking into the future.

'And you,' Jensen said to Lucas. 'Did I tell you, you remind me of my older brother?'

'He must be a good-looking guy,' Lucas said.

'God, I'm sick, and he's trying to push me under,' Connell groaned. 'The nausea is overwhelming . . .'.

They'd tracked him from the moment Koop had left the jail. Took him home, put him to bed. Everything was visual: all the tracking devices had temporarily been taken off the truck. If he thought about his arrest, he might wonder how they'd picked him up at a liquor store.

The next day, he'd left the house a little earlier than usual. He'd gone to his gym, worked out. Then he drove to a park, and ran. That had been a nightmare. They weren't ready for it, they were all in street shoes. They'd lost him a half-dozen times, but never for more than a minute or two, when he was running hills.

'This guy,' Lucas said when they watched him run back to the truck, 'is not somebody to fuck with. He just did three miles at a dead run. There are pro fighters in worse shape than he is.'

'I'd take him on,' Connell said.

Lucas looked at her. 'Bullshit.'

The Ruger was in a mufflike opening of her handbag, and she slipped it out in one motion. Big hands. She spun the cylinder. 'I would,' she said.

After the park, Koop went home. Stayed for an hour. Started out again, and wound up pulling the team through the skyways, right up to Jensen.

'Where's he going?' Connell asked as Lucas caught up. She took his arm, made them into a couple, a different look. 'Is he going after her?'

'He's headed in her direction,' Lucas said. They were closing a bit, and Lucas turned her around, spoke into the radio. 'Sloan, Del, you got him. He's coming through.'

'It's ten minutes to five,' Connell said. 'She gets off about now.'

Sloan beeped. 'Where is he?'

Del: 'He's stopped halfway across, he's looking down at the street.'

Lucas pulled Connell to one side. 'Walk across the entrance sideways, glance down there. Don't come back if he's looking this way.'

She nodded, walked across the aisle that led to the skyway, glanced to her left, continued across, looked back, and said, 'He's just looking out.' She waited a moment, then crossed back to Lucas, again glancing down the skyway.

'He's moving,' she said to her radio.

'Got him,' said Del. 'He's out of the skyway.'

'Coming through,' Lucas said. 'Raider-Garrote's in the Exchange Building.'

Another department store separated them from the Exchange Building, but Koop didn't linger. He was moving quickly now, glancing at his watch. He went through the next skyway, Sloan out in front of him, Del breaking off to the side, then dashing down half a block and recrossing in a parallel skyway, turning back toward the surveillance team.

Lucas and Connell split up, single again, Connell now carrying her huge purse in one hand, like a briefcase. Lucas put the hat on.

'Sloan?'

'It's going down, man,' Sloan said, sounding like he might be out of breath. 'Something's gonna happen. I'm going past Raider-Garrote right now. I'm gonna stop here, in case he goes in, pulls some shit.'

'Christ, Del, move up . . .'

'I'm coming, I'm coming . . .'

Connell moved back to him. 'What're we doing?' she asked.

'Get close, but not too close. I'm gonna call Sara.' Connell strode away, her gun hand resting on top of her purse. Lucas fumbled in his breast pocket, pulled out the cellular phone, pushed the memory-dial and the number 7. A moment later, the phone rang and Jensen picked it up.

'It's happening,' Lucas said. 'He's right outside your door. Don't look directly at him if you can avoid it. He'll see the trap in your eyes.'

'Okay. I'm just leaving,' Jensen said. She sounded calm enough; he felt like there might be a small smile in her voice.

'You'll take the elevator up?'

'Like always,' she said.

*   *   *

Lucas called the other three, explained. Del came up and they started off together, Sloan interrupting: 'Here he comes. And Connell's right behind him.'

'We're coming in,' Lucas said. 'Del's coming first. You better move out of sight, Sloan. What's he doing?'

'He's looking through the windows . . . I see Connell.'

Del tottered on ahead, perfect as a skyway wanderer, a little drunk, nowhere to go, staying inside until the stores closed, and moving out on the streets for the night. People looked away from him – even through him – but not at him.

'I just went by him,' he called back to Lucas. 'He's looking through the window, like he's reading the numbers off their boards. Jensen's on the way out.'

'I just walked back past him,' Sloan said. 'Del, you better get out of sight for a minute.'

'I'm coming,' Lucas said.

There was a moment of silence. Lucas was conspicuous, loitering in the skyway, and he crossed to a newsstand cut as a notch into the skyway wall. Sloan came on. 'Jensen's out. He's walking away, same way I am, coming at you, Lucas.'

'I'm going into the newsstand,' Lucas said. 'I'll pick him up.'

A moment later Sloan said, 'Christ, Lucas, put your radio away. I think he's coming in there.'

Lucas turned it off, slipped it into his pocket, grabbed a copy of *The Economist* from the newsstand, opened it, turned his back to the entrance. A second later, Koop came in and looked around. Lucas glanced at him from the corner of his eye. The store was just big enough for the two of them plus the gum counter with a bored teenager behind it. Koop took down a magazine, opened it. Lucas felt him turn toward the skyway, glanced at him again. Koop's back was turned, and he was looking over the top of the magazine. Waiting for Jensen.

Sloan walked by, kept going. Koop was close enough that Lucas could smell him, a light scent of aging jock-sweat. People were streaming by the doorway as offices closed throughout the building, mostly women, a few of them still wearing the old eighties uniform of blue suit and after-work running shoes. Koop never looked at Lucas: he was completely focused on the skyway.

A man came in and said, 'Give me a pack of Marlboros and a box of Clorets.' The girl gave them to him, and he paid, opened the cigarettes, and threw all but two of them in a trash can and walked away.

'Doesn't want his wife to know,' the girl said to Lucas.

'I guess.' Shit. Koop would look at him.

Koop didn't. He tossed the magazine back on the rack and hurried out. Lucas looked after him. Just down the skyway, he saw Connell's blond hair and Jensen's black. He put the magazine back, and started after Koop, using the radio again.

'They're coming at you, Sloan. Del, where are you?'

'Coming up from behind. Sloan said you were pinned, and I stayed back in case he came that way. I'm coming up.'

'Elevators,' Connell grunted.

'I'm coming,' Lucas said. 'Del, Sloan, you better get your rides.'

Sloan and Del acknowledged and Lucas said, 'Greave, you guys ready?'

'We're ready.' They were in the van, on the street.

'Elevator,' Lucas said. He took the bug out of his ear, put it in his pocket.

Koop was facing the elevator door, waiting for it to return. He'd be the first on. Four other people waited, including Jensen and Connell. Jensen stood directly behind Koop's broad back, staring at the seam at his neck. Connell was beside her. Lucas edged in, just in front of Connell.

The elevator light went white, and the doors opened. Koop stepped in, pushed a button. Lucas stepped in beside him, turned the other way, pushed the button for Jensen's floor. Connell moved in on the other side of Lucas, in the corner, where Koop couldn't see her face. Lucas stood a half-step from the back of the elevator, quarter-turned toward Connell. Koop had never gotten a straight-on look at them, but they couldn't do this again, not for a couple of days. Jensen and another woman got on last, Jensen stepping immediately in front of Koop. The doors closed and they started up. Lucas couldn't see Koop, couldn't look at him. He said, 'Long day,' to Connell, who said, 'Aren't they all . . . I think Del's coming down with a cold.'

Elevator talk. The woman beside Jensen turned to look at Lucas, and Jensen stepped back a bit, her butt bumping the front of Koop's pants. 'Sorry,' she mumbled, flashing a glance back at him.

When they got off, Lucas and Connell got off behind her. The doors closed and Koop went on up. He was parked on seven.

'I saw that,' Connell said to Jensen, grinning. 'You're the bitch from hell.'

'Thank you,' Jensen said.

'Don't do it again,' Lucas said as they walked toward the cars. 'Right now, we're golden. A little too much, and we're screwed.'

Koop followed Jensen out to a small strip shopping center; waited outside while she bought groceries.

'He's gonna do it,' Connell said. She was watching him with the binoculars. She sounded elated and grim at the same time, like a burned survivor of a plane crash.

'He hasn't looked away from the door since she went in. He's totally focused. He's gonna do it.'

Koop tracked Jensen back to her apartment, the pod of cops all around him, running the parallel streets, ahead and behind, switching off. Jensen rolled into the parking ramp. Koop stopped, watched for a few minutes from his truck, then began wandering, out on the interstates. He did a complete loop of the Cities, driving I-494 and I-694.

'Go on back, you fucker,' Connell hissed at him. 'Get back there.'

At nine o'clock, they sat at a stoplight and watched two middle-aged men on a par-three golf course, one with white hair and the other with a crew cut, trying to play in the quickly closing darkness. The crew cut missed a two-foot putt, Lucas shook his head, and Koop moved on.

Ten minutes later, he was on I-35, heading north. Through the Minneapolis loop – and then, like a satellite in a degrading orbit, watched as he was slowly pulled back toward Jensen's apartment.

'He's headed in,' Lucas said. 'I'm breaking off, I'll beat him there. If he changes direction, let me know.'

He ran the backstreets, Connell calling Jensen on the cellular phone. A minute later they rolled into Jensen's parking garage, dumped the car.

'Where is he?' Lucas asked the radio.

'He's coming,' Greave answered. Greave was riding the van. 'I think he's looking for a parking place.'

'Let's get set up, gang,' Lucas said. Then the elevator came, and he and Connell rode up.

Jensen met them at the door. 'He's coming?'

'Maybe,' Lucas said, stepping past her. 'He's just outside.'

'He's coming,' Connell said. 'I can feel him. He's coming.'

33

From the moment he'd left the jail, Koop had been consumed by his hunger for the woman.

Couldn't think of anything else.

Worked out, muscles still sore from jail, until he was loose again. Took a shower, thought about Jensen.

Went for a run in Braemar Park, up and over the hills. Went to an Arby's, ordered a sandwich, wandered away without it. The counter girl had to catch him in the parking lot. Thinking about Sara Jensen.

Then, in the elevator, he was crowded against the back of some big dude in an expensive suit, and Sara stood just in front of him. Halfway up, she stepped back and gave him another butt-rub. Yes.

She knew about him, all right.

This was the second time.

No mistake.

Koop drove the Cities, barely aware of the road, and found himself, just after dark, coming up to Sara Jensen's apartment house. He walked across the street and looked up. Frowned. The light wasn't quite right. She'd pulled one of the drapes in the bedroom at least partway.

Koop felt a pulse of danger: had they figured out the roof? Were they waiting up there? But if they had, she'd never have pulled the drapes. They'd leave everything alone.

No matter.

He'd go up anyway . . .

'He's inside,' Greave called. 'He had a key.' Greave was still on the street, with the van. Del and Sloan had taken the elevators up as soon as it appeared that Koop was looking for parking. Sloan would wait at another apartment. Del was on his way to the roof.

'He did that couple, the woman across the street. To get the guy's keys,' Connell said. 'For sure.'

Lucas said, 'Yes.'

Connell was sitting on the kitchen floor, below the counter. Lucas was in the hallway between the living room and Jensen's bedroom. Jensen was sitting on her bed. She'd partially pulled the drapes in her bedroom, so there was a two-foot-wide slit in them. Lucas had objected: 'We should leave things the way they were.'

'Wrong,' she'd said. 'I know what I'm doing.'

She sounded so sure of herself that he let it go. Now he stood up and stepped toward her room. 'Cameras,' he said. 'Action.'

She stood up. She was wearing a white terry-cloth bathrobe, and showed bare legs and feet. 'I'm set,' she said. 'Tell me what he's doing when you get it from Del.'

'Sure. Don't look at me when I'm talking. Just keep reading.'

They'd decided that she'd be reading in bed. Koop would be able to see most of her through the slot in the drapes. She picked up copies of the *Wall Street Journal* and *Investor's Daily*, spread them around, and dropped on the bed. 'I'm a little jumpy.'

'Remember: when I say get out, you don't do a thing but get,' Lucas said.

They had an apartment down the hall, an older woman recommended by the manager. She'd agreed to let them use her apartment as long as she could be around for the action. Lucas had been unhappy, but she'd been firm, and he had finally given in. The woman was there now, opening the door for Sloan. Greave and the van waited on the street, with two more guys from intelligence.

When Koop entered Jensen's building – if he did –

Greave and his partners would turn off the elevators from the main-floor control box, and seal the stairs. At the same time, Jensen would go to the woman's apartment, with Sloan, for safekeeping. Del would come off the roof, down the stairs, step into a maintenance closet at the other end of the hall.

When Koop arrived at Jensen's, they'd wait until he'd made a move at the door – tried to unlock it, tried to break it. Lucas would give the word, and Sloan would take him from one end of the hall, Del from the other. Lucas and Connell would come out of the apartment. Four-on-one.

Connell had her pistol out, checking it. She'd fed it with safety slugs. They'd rip massive holes in a slab of meat, but would pretty much fall apart when they hit a wall. She held the gun with the barrel up, her finger alongside the trigger guard, her cheek against the cylinder.

'On the roof. He's on the roof,' Del called from Jensen's roof. He was breathing hard: he'd beaten Koop up to the top by thirty seconds. A moment later: 'He's on the air conditioner.'

Koop pulled himself up, crawled to his protective vent, looked across the street. Sara was there, on the bed, reading. He'd seen her doing this twenty times, prowling through her papers. He put the Kowa scope on her and saw that she was looking through long lists of tables. Her concentration was intense. She turned a page.

She was wearing a white terry-cloth robe, the first time he'd seen it. He approved. It set off her dark, dramatic looks like nothing else would. If her hair had only been wet, she'd have looked like a movie star, on stage . . .

'He's on the air conditioner,' Lucas said quietly to Jensen. She showed no sign that she'd heard, although she had.

'He's got a scope, and he's watching her,' Del said. 'Christ, he must feel like he's inside the room with her.'

'I'm sure he does,' Connell murmured into her headset. Lucas looked across at her: the gun was still against her cheek.

Jensen put down her newspaper and rolled off the bed, wandered toward the bathroom. This was not part of the script. 'What?' Lucas asked.

She didn't answer, just ran water in the bathroom for a moment, then walked back out. The bathrobe had fallen open. Lucas was looking at her back, but he had a feeling . . .

Jensen came out of the bathroom. The bathrobe had fallen open, and she was wearing only underpants beneath it. Her breasts looked wonderful against the terry cloth, alternately exposed and hidden. She was apparently upset by something. She spent a few minutes pacing, back and forth across the gap in the curtains, sometimes exposed, sometimes not. All told, it was the best strip show Koop had ever seen. His heart caught in his throat each time she passed the window.

Then she dropped on the bed again, on one elbow, facing him, one breast showing, and began going through the papers. Then she rolled onto her back, bare legs folded, feet flat on the bed, knees up, head up on a pillow, the robe open again, breasts flattening of their own weight . . .

Koop groaned with the heat of it. He nearly couldn't bear to watch it. *Absolutely* couldn't bear to take his eyes away.

Lucas swallowed, glanced back at Connell. She wasn't getting any of this. She simply sat, staring sightlessly at a cupboard. He looked back at Jensen, on the bed. Jensen's eyes had flicked toward him once, and he thought he saw the thinnest crease of a smile. Jesus. He began to feel what Koop did, the physical pull of the woman. She gave off some kind of weird Italianate hormone-cooking vibrations.

Where'd she'd get the name Jensen? Had to be a married name; whatever was bubbling out of the woman on the bed, it wasn't Scandinavian.

Lucas swallowed again.

If there was such a thing as a politically correct cop manual, this would be specifically outlawed. But Lucas had no objection: if this didn't do it to Koop, nothing would.

Sara got out of bed again, robe open, went into the bathroom, closed the door. When she did this, she usually stayed awhile.

Koop dropped back behind the ventilator duct, tried to light a cigarette. Found that the cigarette was damp, realized that he was soaked with sweat.

He couldn't do this. He had the hard-on of a lifetime. He found his knife, pushed the button. The blade sprang out like a serpent's tongue.

Time to go.

'He's down,' Del said. 'Holy shit, he's down. He's walking across the roof, he's through the door . . .'

'Greave, you hear that? It's on you, man,' Lucas said.

'We got it,' Greave said.

Lucas stepped into the bedroom. 'Sara. Time to go.'

Jensen came out of the bathroom, the robe tied tight. 'He's coming?'

'Maybe. He's off the roof, anyway,' Lucas said. She felt vulnerable, intimate; he'd seen the show too. 'Get your slippers.'

Jensen got her slippers, a bundle of clothes, and her purse, and then they waited, waited, Jensen standing next to Lucas. He felt protective, sort of big-brotherly. Sort of . . .

'He's out the door,' Greave called. 'He's crossing the street.'

'I'm coming down,' Del said.

Greave: 'He's got a key for that one, too, he's coming in, he's in the building . . .'

'He's coming,' Lucas said to Jensen. 'Go.'

Jensen left, running down the hall in her robe, with her purse and clothes, like a kid on her way to a slumber party. Connell, on her feet, moved back to the living room, still with the dreamy look in her eyes, the gun in her hand.

Lucas went with her, caught her arm. 'I don't want any dumb-shit stuff. You've got a weird look about you. If you pull the trigger on the guy, you're just as likely to hit Del or Sloan. They'll be coming in a hurry.'

She looked up at him and said, ''Kay.'

'Look, I fuckin' mean it,' he said harshly. 'This is no time . . .'

'I'm fine,' she said. 'It's just that I've been waiting a long time for this. Now we got him. I'm still alive for it.'

Worried, Lucas left her and moved into the kitchen.

As soon as Koop opened the door, Lucas would hit it with his body weight. The unexpected impact should blow Koop back into the hallway. Del and Sloan would be coming, and Lucas would jerk the door open, be right on top of the guy. Greave and the other two would be on the stairs, coming up . . .

They had him sewn up. They might already have enough for a trial, just with the entry across the street and the peeping.

But if he cracked Jensen's door, they had him for everything. If he just cracked it . . .

Koop went quickly through the building straight to the stairs, pulled open the door and into the stairwell. Before the door shut completely, he thought he heard a *flap-click*.

What? He froze, listening. Nothing. Nothing at all. He started up, silently, listening at each landing, then padding up another.

'He's taking the stairs,' Greave called. 'He's not in the elevators. He's on the stairs.'

'Got it,' said Lucas. 'Del?'

'I'm set.'

'Sloan?'

'Ready.'

Koop wound around the concrete stairs. What had that been, the *flap-click*? Like somebody running in the stairwell, a footfall and a door closing. Whatever it was, it had come from high in the building. Maybe even Jensen's floor. Koop got to the top, reached toward the door to the hall. And stopped. *Flap-click?*

There was one more flight of stairs above him, going to the roof of Jensen's building. Was he in a hurry? Not that much, he thought. Cat burglar: move slow . . .

He climbed the last flight, used his key – Sara's key – to let himself out on the roof. Nice night. Soft stars, high humidity, a little residual warmth from the day. He walked silently to the edge of the roof. Jensen's apartment would be the third balcony from the end.

At the edge of the roof, he looked over. Jensen's balcony was twelve feet below him. A four-foot drop, if he hung from the edge. Nothing at all. Unless he missed – then it was a forever and a day down to the street. But he couldn't miss. The balcony was six feet wide and fifteen feet long.

He looked across the street, at the apartment building where he'd spent some many good nights. There were lights, but only a few windows with the drapes undrawn, and nobody in those.

Twelve feet. *Flap-click.*

'Where'n the fuck is he?' Del asked from his closet. 'Greave? You see him?'

'Must be on the stairs,' Greave said. 'You want me to go up?'

'No-no, stay put,' Lucas said.

Connell was listening to the conversation through her earplug, and almost missed the light-footed *whop* fifteen feet away. With Lucas's 'No-no,' in her ear, she didn't even know where it came from, didn't think about it much, looked to her right . . .

Koop landed in front of the open balcony door, softly, both feet at once, absorbing the shock with his knees. The first thing he saw, there in the fishbowl, was the blonde with the pistol beside her face, one hand to her head, pressed against the wall, waiting for the hallway door to open.

Koop didn't need to think about it. *He knew.* And he had no way out. The rage was there, ready, and it blew out.

Koop screamed and charged the woman on the wall . . .

Connell saw him coming when he was ten feet away, had less than a half second to react. The scream froze her, the words in her ear scrambled her, and then Koop hit her, an open-handed blow to the side of her head. The blow knocked her down, stunned her, and then he was on top of her and there was blood in her mouth and the pistol was gone.

Lucas heard the scream and turned and saw Koop hurtle past the archway to the living room wall, and he screamed 'He's here he's here' into the headset and he ran toward the living room, where Koop and Connell were in a pile. Her pistol skittered across the rug and disappeared half under a couch. Koop's back was toward him, rolling over on Connell. Lucas couldn't use the pistol, not with Connell there; instead he raised it over his head and swung it at the back of Koop's head. Koop felt it coming: he cranked his body half around, one eye finding Lucas, the blow already on the way. Koop had time to bunch his shoulder and flinch, and the barrel hit him on the big muscle of his shoulder and Koop somehow found his feet and was coming at Lucas.

This was no boxing match. Koop launched himself straight up, came straight in, and Lucas hit him hard with a roundhouse left, but Koop blew through it as though he'd been hit with a marshmallow and his arms wrapped around Lucas's ribs.

Lucas and Koop staggered backward, together, wrapped up like drunken dancers, banging around inside the small kitchen, the pressure from Koop's arms like a machine-press around Lucas's chest, crushing him. Lucas slapped him on the side of the head with the pistol, but couldn't get a good swing. Feeling as though his spine might break, he finally pressed the pistol to Koop's ear and pulled the trigger, the slug going up through the ceiling.

The noise of the explosion an inch from his ear blew Koop's head back, stunned him like the blows hadn't. Lucas caught a breath, but a bad one: pain lanced through his chest, as though a bone were being pulled loose. Broken ribs. He caught the breath and hammered Koop once in the face, and then Koop stepped back and caught Lucas in the ribs with a short roundhouse. Lucas felt the ribs go, felt himself bounced by the blow, helplessly pulled his elbows in. He took one blow there, slapped the pistol weakly at Koop's face, cutting him, not breaking him, and Koop was crushing him again, Lucas wiggling, trying to hit, both of them crashing back and forth across the kitchen. Lucas could hear the beating on the outer door, people shouting, strained to look that way, Koop crushing him, crushing . . .

Connell landed on Koop's back. She had short square nails but big hands and powerful fingers, and she dug them into Koop's small eyes, not more than two inches from Lucas's face. He saw her fingers dig in, way in, pulling at Koop's eye sockets, and thought, deep at the back of his mind, *Christ, she's blinded him.* . . . And she sunk her teeth into Koop's neck, her face contorted with hate, like a rabid animal's.

Koop screamed and let go of Lucas, and Lucas hit him again in the face, cutting him more, still not putting him down. Connell's fingers went deeper in his eyes and Koop bucked, tried to throw her. Her feet came off the floor and wrapped around his waist, her middle fingers digging into his skull, Koop screaming, twisting, dancing, reeling, Lucas hitting him, closing on him.

Then Koop, with a wild, blind, backhanded spin and swing, caught Lucas on the side of the head, coming in. Lucas lost everything for a moment, like a blown switch knocking out the lights in a house. Everything went dim for a moment, and he lost his feet, rolled back against a cupboard, scrambled up, headed back toward the twisting pair of them, Koop trying to wrench the woman free.

Still she rode him, and she was screeching now, like a madwoman . . .

The door popped open and Sloan was there with his pistol, aiming at them, starting across, Lucas a stumbling step in front of him as Koop staggered backward, onto the balcony.

Connell felt him bump the railing just below his hips. She looked down. She was actually over. She unwrapped her legs, stood on the metal rail, saw Lucas coming . . .

And Lucas screamed at her: MEAGEN . . .

Connell, wrapped into Koop, pumped her powerful legs once, backward, and they both flipped together over the railing and out into the night.

Lucas, two steps away, dove then, actually touched Koop's foot, lost it, smashed into the railing, felt himself caught by Sloan. He leaned over the rail and saw them go.

Connell's eyes were open. She loosened her grip on Koop's head during the fall, and at the end, they were in a splayed-out star shape, like sky divers.

All the way to sidewalk.

And forever.

'Jesus Christ,' Sloan said. He looked from Lucas to the railing to Lucas again. Blood was pouring from Lucas's nose, down his shirt, and he was standing with one shoulder a foot lower than the other, crippled, hung over the balcony.

'Jesus H. Christ, Lucas . . .'

34

Lucas sat in his vinyl chair, staring at the television. A movie was playing, something about an average American family that was actually a bunch of giant bugs trying to blow up an atomic power plant and one of the kid-bugs smoked dope. He couldn't follow it, didn't care.

He couldn't think about Connell. He'd thought about her all he could, had considered all the different moves he might have made. He made himself believe, for a while, that she was ready to die. That she wanted it. That this was better than cancer.

Then he stopped believing it. She was dead. He didn't want her to be dead. He still had things to say to her. Too late.

Now he'd stopped thinking about her. She'd come back, in a few hours, and over the next days, and the next few weeks. And he'd never forget her eyes, looking back up at him . . .

Ghost eyes. He'd be seeing them for a while.

But not now.

A door opened in the back of the house. Weather wasn't due for three hours. Lucas stood, painfully, stepped toward the door.

'Lucas?' Weather's voice, worried, inquiring. Her high heels snapped on the kitchen's tile floor.

Lucas stepped into the hallway. 'Yeah?'

'Why are you standing up?' she asked. She was angry with him.

'I thought you were operating.'

'Put it off,' she said. She regarded him gravely from six

feet away, a small woman, tough. 'How do you feel?'

'I hurt when I breathe ... Is the TV truck still out there?'

'No. They've gone.' She was carrying a big box.

'Good. What's that?'

'One of those TV dinner trays,' she said. 'I'll set it up in the den so you don't have to move.'

'Thanks ...' He nodded and hobbled back to the vinyl chair, where he sat down very carefully.

Weather looked at the television. 'What in God's name are you watching?'

'I don't know,' he said.

The doctors in the emergency room had held him overnight, watching his blood pressure. Blunt trauma was a possibility, they'd said. He had four cracked ribs. One of the doctors, who looked like he was about seventeen, said Lucas wouldn't be able to sneeze without pain until the middle of the summer. He sounded pleased by his prognosis.

Weather tossed her purse onto another chair, waved her arms. 'I don't know what to do,' she said finally, looking down at him.

'What do you mean?'

'I'm afraid to touch you. With the ribs.' She had tears in her eyes. 'I need to touch you, and I don't know what to do.'

'Come over and sit on my lap,' he said. 'Just sit very carefully.'

'Lucas, I can't. I'd push on you,' she said. She stepped closer.

'It'll be okay, as long as I don't move quick. It's quick that hurts. If you sort of snuggle onto my lap ...'

'If you're sure it won't hurt,' she said.

The snuggling hurt only a little, and made everything

feel better. He closed his eyes after a while and went to sleep, with her head on his chest.

At six o'clock, they watched the news together.

Roux triumphant.

And generous, and sorrowful, all at once. She paraded the detectives who worked on the case, all except Del, who hated his face to be seen. She mentioned Lucas a half-dozen times as the mastermind of the investigation. She painted a mournful portrait of Connell struggling for women's rights, dedicating herself to the destruction of the monster.

The mayor spoke. The head of the Bureau of Criminal Apprehension took a large slice of the credit. The president of the AFSCME said she could never be replaced. Connell's mother flew in from Bimidji, and cried.

Wonderful television, much of it anchored by Jan Reed.

'I was so scared,' Weather said. 'When they called . . .'

'Poor Connell,' Lucas said. Reed had great eyes.

'Fuck Connell,' Weather said. 'And fuck you too. I was scared for myself. I didn't know what I'd do if you'd been killed.'

'You want me to quit the cops?'

She looked at him, smiled, and said, 'No.'

Another television report showed the front of Lucas's house. Why, he didn't know. Another was shot from the roof of the apartment across the street from Jensen's, looking right into Jensen's place. The word *fishbowl* was used.

'Makes my blood run cold,' Weather said. She shivered.

'Hard to believe,' Lucas said. 'A hot-blooded Finn.'

'Well, it does. It's absolutely chilling.'

Lucas looked at her, thought about her ass, that day in the bathroom. The aesthetic ass that led to all of this . . .

Lucas urged her off his lap, stood up, creaking, hurting. He stretched carefully, like an old arthritic tomcat, one piece at a time, and suddenly his smile flicked on and he looked happy.

The change was so sudden that Weather actually stepped away from him. 'What?' she asked. Maybe the pain had flipped him out. 'You better sit down.'

'You're a beautiful woman, with a good mind and a better-than-average ass,' he said.

'What?' Really perplexed.

'I gotta run into town,' he said.

'Lucas, you can't.' Angry now.

'I'm stoned on Advil,' he said. 'I'll be all right. Besides, the docs said I'm not that badly injured, I'm just gonna have a little pain.'

'Lucas, I've had a broken rib,' she said. 'I know what it feels like. What could be important enough . . . ?'

'It's important,' he said. 'And it won't take long. When I get back, you can kiss the hurt for me.'

He walked very carefully down toward the garage, feeling each and every bruise. Weather tagged behind. 'Maybe I should drive you.'

'No, I'm okay, really,' he said. In the kitchen, he picked up the phone, dialed, got homicide and asked for Greave. Greave picked up.

'Man, I thought you were incommunicado,' Greave said.

'You know that kid that does chores over at the Eisenhower Docks?' Lucas asked.

'Yeah?'

'Get him. Hold him there. I'll meet you in the lobby. And bring one of the cellulars, I'm gonna want to make a phone call.'

Greave was waiting in the lobby when Lucas arrived. He was wearing jeans and a T-shirt under a light wool sports jacket, with his pistol clipped over his left front pelvic point, like Lucas. The kid was sitting in a plastic chair, looking scared. 'What's going on, sir?' he asked.

'Let's go up on the roof,' Lucas said, leading them toward the elevator. Inside, he pushed the button for the top floor.

'What're we doing up there?' Greave asked. 'You've got something?'

'Well, Koop's gone, so we oughta solve this case,' Lucas said. 'Since the kid here won't talk, I thought we'd hold him off the roof by his ankles until he gave us something we could use.'

'Sir?' The kid squeezed back against the elevator wall.

'Just kidding,' Lucas said. He grinned, painfully, but the kid still pressed against the wall of the elevator. From the top floor, they walked up the short flight of stairs to the roof, wedged the door open, and Lucas asked, 'Did you bring the phone?'

'Yeah.' Greave fumbled in his pocket and pulled it out. 'Tell me, goddamnit.'

Lucas walked to the air-conditioner housing. The housing was new, no sign of rust on its freshly painted metal. 'When did they put this in?' he asked the kid.

'When they were remodeling the building. A year ago, maybe.'

High up on the edge of it was the manufacturer's tag with a service phone number, just like the tag he'd seen on the air conditioner across from Sara Jensen's building. Lucas opened the portable and dialed the number.

'Lucas Davenport, deputy chief, Minneapolis Police Department,' he told the woman who answered. 'I need to talk to the service manager. Yeah, it has to do with repair work on one of your installations.'

Greave and the kid watched him as he waited, then: 'Yes, Davenport, D-a-v-e-n-p-o-r-t. We're conducting a homicide investigation. We need to know if you repaired an air conditioner at the Eisenhower Docks apartment complex last month. You installed it about a year ago. Huh? Uh, well, you could call the department and ask. Then you could call me back . . . Okay.' Lucas looked at

346

Greave, his ear to the phone. To Greave he said, grinning, 'He's got to call up a listing on his computer, but he doesn't remember it.'

'What?' Greave was as perplexed as Weather. He looked at the air conditioner, then at the kid. The kid shrugged.

Lucas said into the phone, 'You didn't? Isn't it under warranty? Un-huh. And that would cover all repairs, right? Okay. Listen, a detective named Greave will be coming over to take a statement from you later today. We'll try to make it before five o'clock.'

Lucas rang off, folded the phone, handed it back to Greave, and looked at the kid. 'When I talked to you, you said you were helping Ray with the air-conditioning.'

'Yeah. It was broke.'

'But nobody came from the air-conditioner company?'

'Not that I saw.' The kid swallowed.

'What'd you do to it?' Lucas asked.

'Well, I don't know. I just handed him screwdrivers and helped him take shit apart. Sir.'

'The ducts.'

'Those big tubes,' the kid said. *Ducts* wasn't solid in his vocabulary.

'You didn't mess with the motor or anything.'

'No, sir, not me. Not anybody. Just the tubes.'

'What?' asked Greave. 'What? What?'

'They froze her,' Lucas said.

Greave half-smiled. 'You're fuckin' joking.'

'Well. Not exactly froze. They killed her with hypothermia,' Lucas said. 'She was an older woman, underweight because of her thyroid condition. She took sleeping pills every night with a beer, or maybe two. Cherry knew about the pills and the booze. She apparently joked about her medicine. So he watched her window until her lights went out, waited a half hour, and turned on the air-conditioning. They pumped cold air meant for the entire building into that one apartment. I bet it was colder in her apartment than the inside of a refrigerator.'

'Jesus,' Greave said, scratching his chin. 'Would that do it?'

Lucas nodded. 'Everybody says it was hot inside, because the air-conditioning was broken. The pictures of the body showed her curled up on a sheet, no blanket, because it *was* hot when she lay down. By age and body weight, she was the kind of person most susceptible to hypothermia,' Lucas said. 'The only thing that would make somebody *even more* susceptible is booze.'

Greave said, 'Huh.'

'The thing that cinches it,' Lucas said, 'is that the cheapest goddamn real estate hustlers in town never called for warranty service. The air conditioner is covered. The service guy just told me that they'll fix anything that goes wrong for five years. He said if a screw falls out of the housing, they'd come out and put it back in.'

'I don't see . . .' Greave said, still not believing.

'Think about the body shots again, the photographs,' Lucas said. 'She was on her side, curled, fetal position, as if she might have been cold, and unconsciously trying to protect herself. But the drugs knocked her down and out. She couldn't get back up. And it worked: they killed her. Not only did it work, there was no sign of what they did. No toxicology. The doors were bolted, the windows were locked, the motion sensors were armed. They killed her with cold.'

Greave looked at the kid. The kid said, 'Jeez. I helped Ray disconnect all them tubes and put them back together, but I didn't know what he was doing.'

'They ran the air conditioner after he pulled the tubes, I bet,' Lucas said.

'Yeah. They said they was testing it,' the kid said.

'Kiss my ass,' said Greave, a sudden light in his eye. 'They froze the old bat. A batsicle.'

'I think so,' Lucas said.

'Can I bust them?' Greave asked. 'Let me bust 'em, huh?'

'It's your case,' Lucas said. 'But if I were you, I'd think about playing them off against each other. Offer one of them a plea. They're all assholes, every one of them. Now that you know how they did it, one of them'll turn on the others.'

'Froze her,' Greave said, marveling.

'Yeah,' Lucas said, looking around off the roof at the city. He could see just a sliver of the Mississippi in the distance. 'It makes your blood run cold, doesn't it?'

Lucas stopped to talk to Roux, and told her about the batsicle. 'Is your butt saved?'

'For the time being,' she said. She sounded unhappy. 'But you know . . .'

'What?'

She had a half-inch-thick sheaf of paper in her hands. 'We've had seven bank robberies in the last two months, by the same people. There were two here in town, one in St Paul, four in various suburbs. I'm starting to get some heat from the banking community.'

'That's supposed to be the Feds,' Lucas said. 'The Feds do banks.'

'The Feds don't want to run for the Senate,' Roux said.

'Oh, my achin' ass . . .' Lucas groaned.

As he was leaving, he ran into Jan Reed, looking very good. 'Oh, my God, I was was worried,' she said, and she looked worried. She touched his chest with an open hand. 'I heard you got banged around pretty badly.'

'Not that bad,' he said. He tried to chuckle in a manly way, but winced.

'You *look* beat up,' she said. She glanced at her watch. 'I've got an hour before I've got to be back at the station

. . . Would you have time to finish that croissant and coffee we started last time?'

Jesus, she was pretty.

'God, I'd like to,' Lucas said. 'But, you know . . . I gotta go home.'

Lightning Source UK Ltd.
Milton Keynes UK
UKHW010752030620
364330UK00001B/80